Alex
"You've been matching me up?"

He didn't know why he was surprised. But it seemed pretty cold to him that his nurse was trying to marry him off to someone he didn't even know. Somehow, he had thought *Maryann* was interested in him. Well, it was nonsense, of course.

"I'm sure she won't do," Alex said with as much dignity as he could manage. "Now, if you'll excuse me, I need to go write some prescriptions."

He walked down to the exam room and closed the door.

He was finally interested in a woman, and she was trying to match him up with someone else. Of course, it was probably for the best. He was leaving in a few weeks anyway. And, just because he was interested in her, didn't mean he had anything to offer someone like that.

Alaskan Bride Rush:
Women are flocking to the Land of the Midnight Sun with marriage on their minds

Klondike Hero—Jillian Hart
July 2010

Treasure Creek Dad—Terri Reed
August 2010

Doctor Right—Janet Tronstad
September 2010

Yukon Cowboy—Debra Clopton
October 2010

Thanksgiving Groom—Brenda Minton
November 2010

The Lawman's Christmas Wish—Linda Goodnight
December 2010

JANET TRONSTAD

grew up on a farm in central Montana, spending many winter days reading books about the Old West and the gold rush days of Alaska. During college she got a chance to see the beauty of Alaska for herself when she worked a summer on Kodiak Island in a salmon factory, packing fish eggs for a Japanese firm. Because of those experiences, she is excited to be part of this series. Janet lives in Pasadena, California, where she writes full-time when not dreaming of other places.

Doctor Right
Janet Tronstad

Steeple
Hill®

Published by Steeple Hill Books™

Special thanks and acknowledgment to Janet Tronstad for her contribution to the Alaskan Bride Rush miniseries.

STEEPLE HILL BOOKS

Steeple
Hill®

Recycling programs
for this product may
not exist in your area.

ISBN-13: 978-0-373-87620-4

DOCTOR RIGHT

www.SteepleHill.com

Printed in U.S.A.

I will lift up mine eyes unto the hills, from whence cometh my help. My help cometh from the Lord, which made heaven and earth.

—*Psalms* 121:1–2

This book is dedicated to my friends in the
Love Inspired Historical discussion group on
Goodreads. We've taken many exotic trips together
in our minds and I hope they'll love this one
to Alaska, too.

Chapter One

If she opened the clinic door, Maryann Jenner knew a gust of cold wind would blow inside that would smell of wood smoke, mostly from the stovepipes jutting up from the row of flat and peaked roofs that lined the main road into Treasure Creek, Alaska. As much as she liked the scent, not all of the patients did, so she left the door closed and instead looked out the window at the rugged, green mountains that edged the backside of this small tourist town. She still couldn't believe she was working in this postcard-perfect place.

For the first time in her twenty-six years, she was beginning to feel like she had a chance at the peaceful life she wanted. She'd been an unwilling participant in other people's dramas—mostly her parent's—since she was born. Now she was far enough away that she could love her mother and father without being dragged into the soap operas that were their respective, disconnected lives. As though to celebrate her new life, she'd landed the perfect job, working with the ever so perfect Dr. Alex Havens in this perfect little clinic in paradise.

"Oh, no," she muttered to herself and took a quick

glance over her shoulder to be sure the doctor was still in the back room examining six-year-old Johnny Short's ear infection. She had a bad habit of actually believing what she conjured up in her day dreams when looking out that window. Treasure Creek was wonderful, of course, but the pediatrician could be, she had to admit, a bit demanding at times. And particular. And downright testy about some things. He'd even been dubbed The Ice Man by her predecessor. And, since Maryann was now his nurse, it was apparently her job to make his days run smoothly.

Ordinarily, that wasn't much of a problem. She was good at maintaining order. Besides, the doctor might be an ice man around adults, but children seemed to love him, and since they were his patients, everything moved along fine in their small clinic. She and Alex had figured out how to work together.

But if the line of women marching up the slight hill toward them were the ones she thought they were, she was going to earn her salary today. The final thing he'd asked before hiring her last month was if she knew how to keep the fancy women away. She'd assured him she did, even though she was new in town and hadn't known what—or who—he was talking about.

Today she knew. Several months ago, *Now Woman* magazine had run an article on the bachelor tour guides in Treasure Creek, and before Maryann arrived, women had started swarming up here in hot pursuit of husbands. The locals called them fancy women because they looked like exotic tropical birds when set against the sturdy, practical dress of the local people.

Maryann had never heard of the women attacking

their target all together, though. Not like this. Alex was only a part-time guide with Alaska's Treasures tour company, earning just one brief mention in the article.

Of course, he was completely single and unattached. But—oh, dear.

The door flew open before Maryann had time to retreat. The smell of perfume followed the women inside, along with a surprising number of the rather large mosquitoes Alaska is famous for. She wasn't sure if it was the heavy floral scents that attracted these insects so late in the season, or if it was the red shine on the women's lips and nails. Either way, the fact that the women didn't complain about the bites they must be getting only proved how determined they were to be here.

"This is a pe-dia-tric clinic," Maryann raised herself up to her full five-foot-seven-inches and announced in her strictest nurse voice. "Adult patients need to go down the street to Dr. Logan's clinic."

She'd worked on that voice in her nurse's training, until it could silence a group of rowdy boys. It didn't even stop the women from chattering long enough for them to really listen to her. Of course, part of that could be because they were reaching up to try and tame their windblown hair.

"I have full-coverage insurance, so any doctor will see me." A showy blonde, with a dandelion head of bleached hair and the plumpest purple lips Maryann had ever seen, sat down in one of the few adult chairs in the waiting room and crossed her nylon-encased legs in a theatrical gesture. Then she looked at Maryann. "It was part of my last divorce settlement. The doctor can do any test he wants on me. My ex will cover it if the insurance doesn't, so the doctor doesn't need to worry about the bill being paid."

"I just need a prescription refill," a young waif-like woman whispered as she slipped into one of the nearby children's chairs. She had long brown hair and a slight overbite. "Do you know if the doctor likes to walk on the beach in the moonlight? I adore the beach. Not the Alaskan beach, of course—it's too rocky and cold—but, you know, the regular beach."

The wind had ruffled the young woman and she nervously tried to pull her tangled hair into place.

"I can't—" Maryann said, her voice rising slightly. She looked around. Eight women were in the room. None of them looked sick, especially since the cold outside had given their cheeks higher than normal color. Besides, together they were wearing enough gold jewelry to open a pawn shop. They had marched up here in full battle armor. But why had they come, now of all times—on this cold, blustery day?

And then the realization hit her and she felt a twist in the pit of her stomach. It was her fault. She'd told her cousin last night how much his young patients would miss Alex after his contract expired at the end of the month. Her cousin remarked that if she wanted the man to stay in Treasure Creek, she needed to get him happily married to a local woman. Which led to the unfortunate remark by her that no woman with warm blood flowing through her veins would marry The Ice Man. Which led to her cousin saying that there was a match for everyone and Maryann could find someone for the doctor if she put her mind to it. After all, her cousin added, Maryann was good at managing other people's romances—hadn't her parents relied on her to help them find their next soul mates? And the ones after that?

Unfortunately, she and her newly-engaged cousin, Karenna, had been eating hamburgers in Lizbet's Diner when they'd had their conversation. Someone must have overheard. Gossip traveled fast in a small town like this, and it often got twisted. Maryann knew she shouldn't have said anything about Alex. And worst of all, she had taken a guess at a woman who might suit him, and, even though it wasn't one of the fancy women, the whole thing must have resulted in today's sudden invasion.

"I'm sorry, but you'll have to leave," Maryann said, as she tried to herd the women to the door. They weren't budging. She didn't suppose she could call 911 over something like this. "The doctor is in the exam room with a patient and—"

"He can be my doctor any time," a woman with bouncy, copper ringlets said, as she wiggled out of Maryann's herd, walked over to a chair and sat down looking pleased with herself.

The fancy women all giggled.

Why did people seeking romance all become silly as teenagers, Maryann wondered. She raised her voice. "What I'm trying to say is that there are no appointments left for today."

She hoped that would do it.

"Or tomorrow either," she added quickly just in case. "We're all booked."

She really liked this job; she didn't want to be fired. Alex had promised to give her a good recommendation to his replacement. Well, it would be his temporary replacement. The agency had already said they could only send someone to fill in for a few months while they kept looking for a new scholarship doctor to take over the clinic for another three years. If they couldn't find someone, they would close the clinic in six months.

Why did it all have to be so complicated? The children here needed a doctor. And Maryann didn't want to lose her job and return to the lower forty-eight. The obvious solution was to have Alex put down roots here in Treasure Creek. Of course, he'd have to want to stay. Her cousin was right about a wife being the answer, but—despite her earlier comments about him being The Ice Man—Maryann knew full well he could have his pick of brides. Some women would tell themselves he would thaw eventually; others might not care.

No, he would be the one who was hard to please when it came to marriage. The nurse before her claimed Alex hadn't dated anyone in the time she'd known him. All he cared about was that clinic he was going to build in Los Angeles.

"I'm Delilah Carrington. I'm sure he'll see me," the copper ringlet woman said as she gave a grand wave with an arm wrapped in thin gold bracelets. Then she looked around and slowly frowned. "I would think a doctor's office would be better equipped though. This place is a little old and scruffy, isn't it?"

She made it sound as though the patients regularly stuck their old chewing gum under the chairs bottoms, Maryann thought—which she was sure they did not, since she'd checked a time or two.

"He's a scholarship doctor," another of the women said, as though that explained any shabbiness. "You know, the government pays for him to go to medical school and he has to work in a place like this for a few years to pay them back. All the poor kids do it."

Maryann bristled at the implication that because Alex didn't have money, somehow that made him less of a success. He was a brilliant doctor. She'd known that after working the first day for him. Plus, he really cared about his little patients. He even treated the children from the Taiya Village, part of the Tlingit tribe, for free. If the town got another scholarship doctor, he probably wouldn't go out to the village at all. It was extra work, and not part of the agreement the doctors signed. That was another reason she wanted Alex to stay on here. The Tlingit kids needed him as much as the kids in Treasure Creek did, and probably more.

"The city owns this clinic," Maryann said firmly. "The place is charming and very neatly organized. It might be a little scratched up, but we keep it very clean. Besides, Dr. Havens knows all of the latest treatments."

The room was quiet as the women looked around. Apparently, they'd been surprised enough at that declaration to listen.

"What kind of treatments?" one of the women asked, looking around the office dubiously. "Those herbal things?"

"Medical treatments," Maryann snapped back. She saw no reason to admit that he studied the native remedies of the Tlingit people. She'd already said too much about the man last night. "They're the kind any good, well-trained doctor uses. Some from the Mayo Clinic."

Then she scowled at the women, daring any of them to make more remarks about this building or the doctor who ran it. The clinic was set in one of the restored log cabins that were left over from the original gold rush prospectors who had founded this town in 1897. She'd like to see how these fancy women would have stood up a hundred years from now. Besides, people should be proud to use this place, she told herself; it had solid history.

The town had taken ownership of the cabin decades ago, renting it out to a souvenir shop for years until someone decided they needed a children's clinic in town. They widened the doorway and added a side ramp off the porch for wheelchairs, and the cabin became a clinic. Except for the thickly lacquered logs, the only other holdover from its tourist days was Horace, the slightly droopy moose head hanging over the door.

"So this means our doctor is poor," Delilah finally said in the silence, that same frown on her face. "If he had to have a scholarship, I mean. That can't be good. Does he have any money at all?"

"Honey, a man with looks like Dr. Havens doesn't need money," another of the women—Joleen something—declared with a warm chuckle. The woman was wearing a spandex jumpsuit in a leopard print and spiked black heels. A long gold chain hung around her neck, and somehow she'd managed to get her blond hair rearranged after the wind. "Besides, he's not going to stay poor. He's a doctor. He'll be rich before you know it, especially since he's going back to Los Angeles. You should see the expensive cars men like him drive down there."

That started the rest of the women talking about the doctor again. And they weren't just talking about his money.

Maryann didn't need to hear the women to know what they were saying. Alex was tall, dark and handsome—she'd be the first to admit it. Any woman who sighed over Rhett Butler—and she had a feeling most of those women in the waiting room had—would be drawn to the good doctor. He had that same kind of jaw. Plus, he had strong biceps, a chin with a dimple—just like they said, and with all the glowing adjectives they used. It was amazing that the fancy women had taken this long to fill up the man's waiting room.

The more they talked, the gloomier Maryann got. Until last night, she'd found working with Alex companionable enough that she'd almost forgotten he was drop-dead gorgeous. Years ago, she'd vowed never to trust a handsome man. Assuming that vow still held, her cousin had made the criticism rather loudly last night over dinner that, because of it, Maryann might be a little bit unfair to her employer when she called him The Ice Man. Everyone deserved a chance to prove himself, her cousin said; maybe Maryann needed to get to know him better. Besides, no boss was perfect.

Which reminded Maryann, if she wanted to keep him as her boss, she needed to warn him about these women, and quickly.

"Let me go see how long the doctor will be," she announced casually as she started toward the back exam room. There was a good-size window on the side wall. It was a bit of a drop to the ground, but Alex was in excellent physical shape. At least the fancy women had gotten that much right.

If she hadn't been looking straight at the door, Maryann wouldn't have seen the knob turn. She formed her lips and called out, "Nooo."

But it was too late. Her voice came out thin and the door opened anyway. Johnny Short walked out with his mother. Both of them looked surprised at the crowded waiting room.

"Isn't he cute?" a brunette with diamond clips in her hair and gold chains on her ankles said, as she stood up and beamed at the wide-eyed little boy. She tugged on her V-neck sweater, which only made more skin show. "Aren't you a sweetie?"

The diamond woman took a step toward the boy before his mother put up a hand to stop her. "He's only six and his ear hurts. He's not used to women like—" Mrs. Short stopped and pursed her lips. "Well, let's just say, most of the women around here wear sweaters to keep their necks warm. This is Alaska, after all, not Las Vegas. It might be September on the calendar, but we're already feeling the nip of winter. Besides, we're a small, decent town."

Maryann half-expected the fancy women to be offended, but it was clear they weren't even listening to Mrs. Short. They had all stood by now and were arching their backs and puffing up their hair as they stared at *him.*

Alex stood in the open door of the exam room. The sunlight streamed through the window behind him and made him look bronzed. Maryann blinked. How had that happened? He was wearing the same white lab coat with a stethoscope hanging around his neck that he'd been wearing all day. But he looked different. Maybe because of the angle of the light behind him the lab coat suddenly showed that his shoulders were satisfyingly broad. His dark hair was ruffled and his blue eyes were fringed with black lashes. If it weren't for the look of dawning horror on his clean-shaven face, he could have graced the cover of *GQ* magazine. It would have all been comical if Maryann didn't feel called upon to do something to rescue him.

He cleared his throat and the women looked like they would swoon.

She looked at the salivating women staring at him. So, the man was good-looking. Well, okay, more than good-looking. That didn't mean he was a rock star or anything.

"What's wrong?" Alex finally asked. "Is someone hurt?"

He sounded so suspicious that she had to smile. Maybe he didn't realize how great he looked standing there.

"Careful. They're all —" Maryann started, but she was too late. The women had broken rank and were rushing toward Alex, waving their hands in the air. There was only one thing to do, she decided, as she put her fingers to her lips and gave a shrill referee whistle.

There was a moment of absolute silence. Even Alex looked stunned.

Maryann gave a decisive nod. She had taken a self-defense class in high school and the whistle was all she had mastered, but today it was enough. "First, Mrs. Short, you take Johnny out on the porch. I'll be out in a second to give him his lollipop—he likes lime, doesn't he? We'll set up a follow-up appointment. Everyone else sit back down, except for the doctor, of course."

She was almost surprised when everyone obeyed her.

"These women say they need to see you." Maryann waited for the Shorts to leave the room before raising her eyes to Alex. "For medical reasons."

The doctor nodded and turned to the seated women. He looked stern enough to make Maryann glad she wasn't one of the fancy women.

"I'm a pediatrician. You'll have to go down the street to Dr. Logan's office. He's the general doctor in town." And then, as though he wasn't sure they understood, Alex added. "I only take children as patients."

"I already told them that—" Maryann started, but she was ignored.

"My feet haven't grown much since I was a girl." Delilah stood up and moved a step closer to Alex, before taking his arm. "And it hurts to walk. Really, feet are feet. It doesn't matter if I'm a child or not. Men always tell me I have such nice-looking ankles."

Delilah stood on her toes so her ankles showed to their best advantage. "What do you think, Doctor?"

Maryann watched the thundercloud settle on Alex's face. He didn't say anything though.

The waif woman sitting in the corner looked up. "Dr. Logan's office is closed this morning." Her voice managed to sound pitiful and sultry at the same time. "There's no place else to go. I need something for all these mosquito bites."

Alex removed Delilah's hands from his arm as

he glanced over at the small pink dots on the other woman's arm.

"Baking soda," he said in a curt voice and then looked around. "Just to be sure, are any of you really injured? Or having a heart attack? Even an asthma attack? We'll take an emergency, but that's all. The rest of you will have to see Dr. Logan instead. If he's not there, call later and make an appointment."

The chatter started up. It was impossible to sort out what everyone was saying.

Alex turned and looked at Maryann. "Have them fill out medical forms just in case. And find out if that one woman is allergic to insect bites. Then come back to the exam room. We need to talk."

"Yes, sir." Maryann resisted the impulse to salute. She was in trouble enough as it was. He probably expected she should have locked the door when she saw the women coming.

Alex had no sooner turned to go back to the room when Maryann heard footsteps running up to the porch. She recognized a medical emergency when she heard one and wasn't surprised when Alex turned around to face the door.

"Everybody sit down. Clear some space. We have a patient coming in." Alex said as he headed toward the door. At times like this he blessed the workmen who had made the new doorway and the ramp outside both sturdy and wide.

He'd been through this drill often enough up here, he thought to himself. A siren never announced an emergency as it did back in Los Angeles; here it was the thump of the heavy boots the men wore. The faster the footsteps were coming up the steps to his porch, the worse the problem. The most serious injuries came by the steps and not the ramp; it was in recovery that the patient used a wheelchair. Alex had the door open before the men outside could touch it.

"It's Timmy Fields," the man standing in front said as he pushed his cap back on his forehead and looked behind him to where two other burly men in flannel shirts were carrying the boy. They were all breathing hard and the boy was moaning.

"Easy now," Alex said when he saw how they were carrying his patient. Every spring he gave a first aid emergency course and showed people how to transport injured hikers, but it never seemed like the right people came. Next time he was going to go down to one of the bars and give his demonstration there. Oh—he stopped. He'd be gone by then. He'd have to leave a note for the next doctor. Or maybe Dr. Logan would do it, although people didn't tend to bring him the emergency cases since he lived a mile from town and most problems seemed to happen after the clinics were closed.

"Lay him down here." Alex put his hand on the gurney Maryann had just wheeled over to him.

"Thanks," he said to her as she stepped back so the men would have enough room. Maryann always knew what to do without him telling her.

Together the men gently laid the boy down.

"What happened?" Alex asked the men as his hand reached out to take the boy's pulse. It had been several weeks since he'd seen eight-year-old Timmy for that cough of his. The boy's skin was clammy now, but

Alex doubted it was from fever. It was pain making him sweat.

"We found him up on Chilkoot Pass. Fool kid shouldn't have been up there alone. He said some tourists gave him a ride out of town to the base. They should be shot for leaving a kid like that there by himself. Don't know what he was doing. He must have slipped on some rocks or something. We wouldn't have found him if we hadn't been out looking for that Lawson fellow—the one who's been missing."

Alex nodded. He'd been on the search team that had come upon Tucker Lawson's crashed plane. They'd found some blood and his business card with a stake driven through it, but there was no one around. Searchers, under the direction of the sheriff, had been looking for the man, or his remains, since then. Surely the boy hadn't been up there looking for Lawson, though.

Timmy groaned.

"Easy now," Alex said as the boy started to move. "Let me check you out first."

"He's got a lump on his head," one of the men said.

"I see that," Alex said as he ran his fingers over the rest of the boy's scalp, then he turned to Maryann. "Flash—"

"Here."

"Thanks." She'd given him the flashlight before he'd even gotten the word out. Things like this were why he'd promised to write her a letter of recommendation and leave it for the next pediatrician that came here. She was an excellent nurse. She didn't insist on being personal with him, either. His last nurse had wanted him to—well, he wasn't sure what she had wanted. She'd resigned when he refused to have dinner with her one night after work.

Timmy opened one eye and stared.

"Don't worry about focusing," the doctor murmured to the boy before remembering to use simpler words. "Don't worry about what you see. It might be fuzzy."

"I see an angel choir," Timmy said in quiet awe.

Alex choked back his chuckle as he looked over his shoulder. Children were so honest about their feelings. He saw that Maryann was doing the impossible and getting the fancy women to exit the room. All those women with their dyed blonde hair and sparkling gold might look like a band of angels because of the sun shining on their jewelry as they tiptoed past the gurney, especially when Maryann wore her white uniform to usher them out. No wonder Timmy saw angels.

"Don't worry," he said. "It's Nurse Jenner and some friends of hers."

"They're not my friends," Maryann protested from the door as the men who'd carried Timmy down the mountain followed the last of the fancy women out of the clinic. Alex realized with a jolt that he was teasing Maryann. He'd never done that with any of his other nurses. He believed in professionalism in the clinic. But he liked the way her cheeks pinked up and her brown eyes sparked with indignation. She had dark, fringed bangs, and her hair shone as it floated around her head in the breeze from the open door.

"Is she an angel?" the boy asked.

"Some days," Alex said. Then he forgot himself enough to grin at Maryann. He decided it would be okay to relax with her; he'd be gone before long, so what could it hurt?

Maryann tried to give him a stern look, but the blush on her face spoiled the effect. She shut the open door, but her hair still floated around her face.

"Does that mean I'm dead?" Timmy asked with some anticipation.

Alex looked down at the boy and smiled. "Not today you're not."

"Oh," Timmy said, and with that, he closed his eyes.

Alex looked up at Maryann again, but she was one step ahead of him. She held out an ice pack she'd brought from the back room along with the gurney. He pressed that against Timmy's face. "The cold will wake him up."

"I'll call his parents," Maryann said.

"No." Timmy opened his eyes in alarm. "You can't call them."

"You know we have to," Alex said gently as he finished running his hands over the boy's legs. "You took quite a fall. Does your leg hurt?"

Timmy winced and nodded. "They'll kill me for sure."

"I'll tell them you're a brave soldier," Maryann said as she walked over to the phone.

Alex imagined she would say those very words to them, too. No one could accuse her of not caring about everyone who stumbled across her path. She was generous to a fault and that was the only reason he could think of for her to have sat in the diner last night talking with her cousin about matching him up with someone.

Not that either one of the women had shown an over-abundance of caring when Maryann had called him The Ice Man. Wait until that nickname made the rounds of Treasure Creek. He wasn't the kind of person who talked about himself to everyone he met, but he'd helped enough children in this town to have some friends among the parents. He'd been warned about last night's conversation by two sources already.

He watched Maryann as she held the phone to her ear and talked to Timmy's parents. He couldn't hear the words she was saying, but he could hear the soft tones of her voice.

He supposed the matchmaking had been inevitable. Maryann was the kind of woman who'd bring home stray cats. He knew that when he hired her, but he'd had no other choice. Women like her just couldn't accept that some men—like some animals—were better off alone. She must have sensed the sadness in him and decided marriage was the solution.

He'd meant to tell her today that he was fine with the single life, but he hadn't quite figured out the right words. Usually, he'd just blurt it out. He didn't know why he was hesitating. As near as he could figure, he didn't want to make her feel bad for caring that he was alone. Also, it bothered him that she thought of him as an ice man, and part of him wanted to prove her wrong.

He must be going soft from living in Treasure Creek. People around here wanted to be connected. They weren't content with just loving their neighbor, they wanted to know where the guy was going for Sunday dinner, and if he needed help defrosting anything. Maybe it was some primitive emotional throwback to the freezing winters of old when people relied on their tribes for a safe existence. People needed other people then. And at least in this small town, that feeling seemed to still hold true.

He hadn't thought much about that until one day when people came from miles around for a simple funeral. Even if people didn't know the old man who'd died, they knew someone who knew someone who knew him. So they mourned the loss of those connections. The tribe had been lessened.

And then every year there was a Christmas pageant at the church that attracted the whole community. Even though he hadn't been going to church, he'd always been drawn to the pageant.

He wasn't used to a place like this. He envied the people here their connections, but he didn't belong.

He should head south for Los Angeles as soon as he could. He'd been saving his money for years so he could open a clinic there. No one would be inviting him to any Christmas pageant down in L.A.

Not that he had time to think about that now, when it looked like Timmy had a fractured bone in his leg as well as the bump on his head. What had the boy been doing out on the pass, anyway?

Maryann hung up the phone and turned back to them. Alex could see why Timmy had been confused enough to think she was some celestial being. Her pink cheeks made her glow. She looked sweet. He had a hard time believing she had talked so openly about his personal life in front of everyone. If she knew anything about the tour guides of Treasure Creek, she'd know they would be making jokes at his expense from now until he left here. In fact, they'd be making jokes about it long after he was gone.

But seeing her in front of him, he couldn't convince himself she'd meant any harm. Maybe the gossips had it wrong and it had been her cousin who had said those things about him. That thought made him feel better, although he didn't dare ask himself why he cared which woman had spoken what.

Chapter Two

Maryann put another cool cloth on Timmy's head. His breathing was still ragged, and Alex had given him a shot to help with the pain in his leg. Alex planned to put a splint on the injured limb as soon as the boy's parents came, so he'd gone into the back room to pick out what he needed from the supply cabinet. Ordinarily, Maryann would have done that, but Timmy had asked her to stay with him and Alex had nodded his agreement.

"You've got to pray for me," Timmy whispered to Maryann as soon as Alex left the room. He was still lying on the gurney and she had pulled a sheet over his legs. "Times are dire."

"Dire?" She was surprised he even knew the word at his age.

But he nodded. "Bad. Real bad."

"You know I'm not really an angel, don't you?" She reached under the gurney to find another pillow. "I can pray for you, but I have no special powers."

Timmy nodded. "It's just for when my parents come in. Look like you're praying for me. And do you have a Bible? They never yell when there's a Bible around."

She stopped, the pillow still in her hands, to look at the boy. "Your parents don't hit you, do they?"

She'd only seen the Fields in passing. They must be Christians, if Timmy wanted a Bible. On the other hand, she knew some people took the Bible and twisted what it had to say. She had no idea why Timmy would be so intent on reminding his parents of their faith, unless he was afraid of them.

"They yell a lot," Timmy admitted. "And my mom cries some."

"But do they hit you?"

Timmy shook his head. "You're still going to pray though, aren't you?"

"I'll see what I can do." Maryann set the pillow on the end of the gurney where Timmy's legs didn't reach. Then she walked over to the drawer where she kept her belongings. She carried a small Bible with her. She'd been going to the church here with her cousin, and re-connecting with her childhood faith. It had been a long time since she had regularly read a Bible like she was doing nowadays. Her turbulent adolescence, as she played referee to her parents' arguments and subsequent new loves, had caused her to drift far away from God, like it was His fault in some way that she had to endure it. She was glad to be back. Her restored belief centered her; she should have never stopped going to church and praying. Even those bad years would have been better.

She held the white Bible up for Timmy to see. "You can borrow this if you want to read something."

"Put it in my hands like I'm dead." Timmy crossed his arms over his chest and closed his eyes.

"I most certainly will not." Maryann walked back to

the gurney with the book in her hand. "Your parents are worried enough as it is." Then she thought a moment. "Besides, it's a girl's Bible. You'd look too sweet in your casket if you were holding it. You could as well be holding a bouquet of lilies."

"Oh." Timmy opened his eyes and frowned at the Bible. "I don't want to hold no girl's Bible."

"I didn't think so," Maryann said as she laid the Bible beside him. "But it won't hurt to have it close, just in case. Like you're alive and reading it. You might try a psalm."

"Maybe you could put a ninja sticker on it." Timmy cautiously took hold of the Bible. "Then it'd be okay for boys."

Maryann smiled.

She heard more footsteps on the porch and turned to the door. "I bet that's your parents."

Maryann walked over to greet the Fields as they opened the door and stepped inside.

"Where is he?" Mrs. Fields asked breathlessly, even as her eyes came to rest on the gurney. She was a slight woman with a harried expression on her face, and she was wearing a stained sweatshirt. Maryann remembered that there were a couple of children younger than Timmy in the family. They were all due for shots and Alex had them on the list for her to call.

"What kind of a fool thing were you doing, boy?" Mr. Fields asked as he followed his wife into the room. He was overweight and puffing hard, but he zeroed in on Timmy right away. "You know better than taking off like that."

Maryann saw Timmy's face crumple in misery.

She stepped back to the gurney. "I was just going to say a prayer for Timmy. Would you both join me?"

"Oh." Mrs. Fields looked up in surprise.

"I—" Mr. Fields started to say something, then stopped.

Maryann walked closer to Timmy and winked at him. She had a moment's hesitation. It had been a long time since she'd prayed in public and she wasn't sure if it was the right thing for her to do now since it was all for show. Of course, it was for Timmy's benefit and God loved children, so it would likely be all right with Him. She bowed her head and started.

"God of all the beings on earth and in heaven," she began. She thought Timmy would like that since he seemed preoccupied with death and angels. "Timmy here is hurting, and we ask that you make him comfortable. He feels bad for what he did and he asks You to help him do better next time. Amen."

"Amen," the Fields both muttered.

When Maryann opened her eyes, she saw that Timmy had been right. His parents did look subdued. They moved over to their son and each gave him a pat on his head before moving back and looking at Maryann, as though waiting for further direction. She nodded approvingly at them, and smoothed the sheets on the gurney. She heard them walk away from the gurney and stop by the door.

They had started talking to each other, thinking she couldn't hear them. If everything else hadn't been so quiet, they would have been right, she admitted to herself.

"You were supposed to be watching him," Mr. Fields hissed at his wife.

"Me? You should have been watching him," Mrs. Fields said, her voice low and tense. "It's not like you're working anymore. You should at least help with the kids."

"It's not my fault I can't find work. These are hard times and you know it. Besides, you're his mother. Don't lay it all on me."

Maryann looked down at Timmy. He could hear his parents, too, and embarrassment covered his face. She remembered what it felt like when her parents were arguing. If someone outside her family heard them, she'd wanted to disappear.

"The doctor will be here in a minute," Maryann said in her most professional voice. Maybe the couple wouldn't know she had heard them. If she was calm enough, she might even fool Timmy. "In fact, I think I hear him now."

The voices all stopped. And then, as if on cue, Alex walked into the room.

Something inside her applauded. He might be an ice man, but she could count on him to show up when she needed him.

"Doctor," Mrs. Fields said, looking up and giving him a tight smile, "how is he?"

"Your son will be fine. He's running a slight fever. Keep him inside and warm. Let me know if he develops a cough or the fever goes higher. But the immediate thing is that he fractured a bone in his right leg. I'm setting up a splint for it now. I just want your signature before I treat him."

"Can it wait?" Mr. Fields asked with a forced smile on his face. "Don't bones sometimes heal by themselves?"

"Wait?" Alex looked taken aback. "I'm afraid not in this case."

Mrs. Fields stepped closer. "How much will it be, doctor?" She kept shifting the handle on her purse from one side to the other. "I get paid next week, but—"

"We'll pay our bill somehow," Mr. Fields finished for her. His face was red with embarrassment. "We might need to wait until our Permanent Fund checks come. I lost my job. It was the one that carried our health insurance, but we'll get you paid somehow—" He looked at Alex. "You've been here long enough to know about the Permanent Fund checks? They're the ones we get from the state for all the oil that's pumped out of Alaska? Those checks are good as gold."

"Ah." Alex cleared his throat. "Sure, I know about the checks. Don't worry, though. I don't have the figures added up, but I could use some new shelves in the waiting room. If you're interested, we could trade services." He looked at Mr. Fields. "I hear you're a good carpenter."

"I've nailed a few boards together in my time," Mr. Fields said proudly. "Your shelves are as good as done. I can come back later today to measure everything."

Alex nodded. "Good. I have some lumber in the back we can use."

"Thank you," Mrs. Fields muttered.

Maryann watched the whole scene with satisfaction. She knew she was right that the children of Treasure Creek needed this doctor. She only had to look at the sudden hero worship in Timmy's eyes to know that. Alex didn't make anyone look small, and that won him the respect of his young patients.

"We'll just take Timmy in the back and get him set up," Alex said as he motioned for Maryann to follow him. He looked at Mrs. Fields. "I'll need to cut the leg off his jeans, but I'll do it as carefully as I can, so you can sew them back together later."

The woman nodded. "Thanks. He doesn't have enough pairs as it is."

"Say, Doc," Mr. Fields said from beside the door. "If the shelves aren't enough, my wife here can introduce you to some of the local women. You know, it'd be like one of those matchmaking services they have in the big cities."

"What?" Alex turned to look at the man.

"I heard you were looking," Mr. Fields said as he reached for the doorknob. "We could help you out. Nothing fancy, but the wife here knows everyone. She'll fix you up."

Maryann felt the breath leave her body. She had a bad feeling about this.

"Hush about that." Mrs. Fields turned to her husband. "How can you be thinking about that when our son lies there in pain?"

Then the woman turned to the doctor. "Should we go back in the room with you when you work on Timmy's leg?"

Maryann risked glancing at Alex. His face looked frozen.

"I'm fine." Timmy spoke up from where he lay.

Maryann noticed the boy had a strong grip on that

small Bible of hers. She wished she was the one holding it, though.

"Maybe you and Dad could wait here," Timmy added. It looked as if there was a ragged piece of old paper peeking out from the pages of the Bible. Timmy must have put it there. "In this room."

"Well, I guess." Mrs. Fields muttered, as if she didn't know what to do.

"I could wait with you if you'd like," Maryann offered. The doctor didn't really need her for the splint. Besides, she'd give anything not to have to face him right now. She could tell he knew all about the conversation she and her cousin had had about him. "We have a few magazines on the table by the chairs."

She saw Timmy's parents sit down in two chairs and noted they left an empty one between them. She figured that was where Timmy usually sat. No wonder the boy was torn apart by their arguing; he'd grown up right in the middle of things. Just as she had.

"Nurse Jenner. You're with me," Alex said before she even moved.

"Yes," she said as she gave the chairs one last look and walked toward the gurney.

"Here, I can do that." Alex reached the gurney first and put his hands on it.

"But I usually push the patients. That's my job."

"We're a team," Alex said, wheeling the gurney back to the examining room.

Well, Maryann thought, *what was that supposed to mean?* If she didn't know better, she'd think The Ice Man was melting. But that was unlikely. Perhaps he was planning to fire her. Not that she could blame him if he did. She hadn't intended for the whole town to be talking about Alex's love life. When would she ever learn to keep her mouth shut?

"It was a mistake," Maryann muttered, as she followed Alex down the hall. "That conversation with my cousin."

Alex finished pushing the gurney into the room and Maryann turned on the lights.

"We can talk about that later, Nurse Jenner," he said.

Maryann nodded as she stepped closer to the gurney and bent slightly to adjust a corner of the sheet. At least Alex wouldn't fire her as long as there was a patient around to hear him do it.

Timmy gave a weak snicker.

"What?" She glanced over at the boy. His face was still pale, but his eyes were mischievous.

"You still look like an angel," he said, and chuckled a little louder.

Maryann straightened up and glanced at the mirror by the sink. Her hair was just as windblown as it had been after she'd stepped outside to give Johnny Short that lime lollipop. Why did her hair always have to look so wild? It was puffed up in a circle around her head. No wonder Alex hadn't shown any interest in the women up here. He probably liked women with their hair smoothly drawn back in elegant styles, like the models wore in those glossy magazines. Ever since last night, she'd wondered what kind of a woman he would marry. She hadn't meant to accept her cousin's challenge, but she'd been thinking about it ever since.

She eyed Alex as he stood beside the gurney. Whoever

he married would need to fit into the world of a prosperous doctor in Los Angeles. Those fancy women were probably right about the expensive cars he would drive. Cooperative hair would be important. He'd want a young trophy wife to ride in his red BMW convertible. Or maybe it would be a top of the line Lexus.

"You might want an angel by your side for the next few minutes," Alex muttered to the boy, as he removed the sheet that had covered his leg. "I'll have to cut off part of your jeans before we can set your leg."

Timmy nodded.

"It'll do my best to be careful, but it's bound to hurt some." Alex smoothed down the sheet beside the boy.

"Okay," Timmy said, as he gripped the Bible.

"I can take that for you," Alex said, as he held out his hand for the book.

Maryann noticed the boy was reluctant to give it up. "We can put it on the shelf by the doctor's desk," she said. "You'll be able to see it."

Timmy shook his head.

Alex looked over at her. "It's okay. He can keep it."

It was time for them to get to work.

Alex was focused on getting the plaster splint on Timmy's leg quickly. At times like these, he liked working with an efficient nurse like Maryann. Even though he could sense she was nervous, she anticipated what instruments he'd need and she had them ready for him. More importantly, she kept up a steady stream of soft conversation with the patient, so he didn't need to think of words to say to distract the patient. For some reason, she was talking about cars today.

He'd given a local anesthetic to Timmy to dull most of

the pain in his leg, and the boy was groggy, but Timmy still laughed at Maryann's chatter.

"There. We're done," Alex said, as he finished the splint.

"I think our patient will need a minute to recover," Maryann said.

He looked up at Timmy's face and saw he was almost asleep. The book had slipped from his hands and was lying on the gurney beside him.

Alex picked up the Bible. "I'll move this to the shelf so it won't fall off the gurney."

"Careful with it," Maryann said.

Alex nodded as he walked over to the bookcase. "Timmy sure is attached to it. Although I suppose that's true for lots of children."

"It's natural for children to believe in God," Maryann said, with a nod.

Alex grunted as he laid the Bible down on an empty shelf. "Maybe, but it passes soon enough."

Maryann looked over at him curiously. "Why do you say that?"

"The minute we're born people start having problems. Sooner or later, everyone comes up with a problem God can't solve for them. And it's usually sooner."

"Oh." Maryann looked at him and then blinked.

"I'm not the only one who has been disappointed in God," he added, softly. The sympathy in her brown eyes grew and he found the words escaping him. "And, at that, I'm better off than—" He broke off, but he didn't stop. "Well, I'm better off than my brother."

Alex held his breath. He never talked about God or his brother. He must be more bothered than he'd thought about Maryann calling him The Ice Man. Why did women judge a man by how easily he spilled his emotions, anyway? Or maybe it had nothing to do with her. Maybe it was the confidence Timmy had in his face when he held onto that Bible. It made Alex remember the way he used to feel a long time ago. Back then, he'd embraced God in the same way he loved his pet frog and the stack of comics under his bed. It was all part of a carefree childhood.

But then came the moment when everything that was good in his family shattered—the day Alex's life had been spared when his older brother shoved him out of the way of a runaway car. Even though they had carefully checked that the light in front of them said it was okay to walk, the car's brakes had failed and the driver couldn't stop for the two boys crossing the road. Within seconds, Alex had landed safely back on the sidewalk, while his brother, Frank Rocco Havens, was crumpled on the street, with his body so damaged he'd never walk again.

"You mean your brother that phones?" Maryann finally asked.

Alex nodded. "His first name is Frank, but we don't call him that anymore."

Now, why did he have to say that? He never even thought about Rocco's old name anymore. Their mother was the one who had renamed Frank after the accident. The first time she'd heard another kid draw the name Frank out into Frankenstein, she'd told the family they'd use Frank's middle name, Rocco, from now on. His mother had been kind back in those early days; she fought the whole system to get her son care. It wasn't until later, when the doctors said his brother would always be paralyzed, that she drew away from the rest of the family. Shortly after that his father started traveling more.

Alex had felt like it had been only him and Rocco that made up the family after that. Alex had to fight his guilt, wondering why he couldn't have stayed out of the crosswalk that day, instead of trailing behind his brother who'd already made it clear he wasn't to come with him. If Rocco had been alone when the car came, he could have jumped to safety. Instead, he'd turned and pushed Alex out of the way. Alex had idolized his older brother. Couldn't he have obeyed and stayed behind just that once?

"I'm sorry," he finally said. He looked over at Maryann. "I don't mean to stand here talking about someone you don't even know."

"But I feel like I do know Rocco a little," Maryann answered gently. "I didn't know his real name was Frank, but when he calls, I answer the phone. He always wants to know what the weather is like up here, so I look out the window and describe what I see. Once we saw a bald eagle fly by."

Alex was surprised. "I thought he just asked to speak to me and that you put him straight through. He doesn't usually talk to strangers."

"I'm not a stranger, I'm your nurse," Maryann said. "Besides, he seems nice. He likes what I say about the mountains. Why wouldn't he talk to people?"

Alex could hardly say it was because Rocco was bitter. His brother's mouth might still work, but he was so self-conscious about his legs he'd managed to become a recluse in the middle of the largest city on the west coast. Granted, Rocco hadn't sounded as grim the last few times Alex had talked to him, but something was wrong. Rocco kept saying he wanted to talk in person and Alex kept saying he needed to just speak on the phone for now. Alex would be in Los Angeles in three weeks anyway, so he couldn't make a special trip down there now, not when he had so much to do to wrap up his practice here.

"How long does he talk to you anyway?" Alex finally asked.

Maryann shrugged. "It's only a few minutes. He usually wants to know if we have snow on the mountain yet. And what the lunch special is at Lizbet's Diner. And if you've been out on any tours lately as the guide. He's very interested in Treasure Creek. You should invite him up to visit."

"Rocco? He never goes anywhere." Alex's voice sounded harsh to his own ears. He knew Rocco *could* go places, but he never even went to the grocery store anymore.

It was silent again, but finally Maryann said, "Maybe he likes to stay home."

Alex grunted. "He has a choice. I'm not saying it would be easy. He's in a wheelchair. My brother can only go out if someone is with him. I got him an attendant last year, to help him with this exercise program that could make him more independent, and if he wanted to go outside he could—"

Timmy moaned and Alex looked down at the boy.

After that, he and Maryann worked in silence.

By the time they had Timmy ready to go back to the

waiting room, the child was almost able to sit up. The boy was still disoriented, but his parents could take him home with crutches.

This time Maryann wheeled the gurney back into the waiting room. Alex swore he could hear her singing a lullaby to the boy as they went down the hall, but he had to get the prescription written, so he sat at his desk in the examination room while she took Timmy back to his parents.

Alex decided it was a good thing he was leaving in a few weeks. This whole thing about the ice man label and people worrying about him getting married had him feeling strange inside. He'd never told anyone about his brother. He didn't know why he was opening his mouth about it now. Fortunately, he'd stopped before he told Maryann everything. Knowing her, she'd just feel sorry for him. Then he'd need to do more than stop her matchmaking, he'd also have to stop her from poking around in his heart to see what his guilt and sadness was all about. And then she'd move on to worrying about Rocco. He knew her kind. And his older brother wasn't any more free with his emotions than Alex was. They'd never even talked about "that day" with each other. There were just no words for some things. Alex wasn't even able to say he was sorry, not until he could do something to make up for the part he'd played in the accident.

When he finished writing the prescription, Alex took it out to where the Fieldses were sitting. He reminded them to bring Timmy back if he developed a cough or high fever, and they agreed. Then they left.

The second the door closed behind the family,

Maryann turned to him. "I'm sorry. I had no business saying anything about you last night."

Alex felt himself relax. As long as she forgot about him and Rocco, he didn't care what she wanted to discuss.

"Just for the record," Alex said to keep her talking, "what exactly did you say, anyway?"

He wondered if what he'd heard was true. Maybe she'd said something completely different, and the gossip had turned it into something else.

Maryann hesitated. Her whole face looked pinched by nervousness. "I said that you needed to be poleaxed by love."

"What?" Alex was amazed. "I don't even know what 'poleaxed by love' means."

"It's a Jenner family expression," Maryann muttered. "You get sick. You want to die. All for the sake of love."

"Sounds awful." Alex noticed that his nurse was getting her color back. He felt they had averted some crisis.

Maryann smiled up at him. "I think it is actually. You should see my parents when they're in love. Not with each other, of course. They've been divorced for years. But each time one of them is poleaxed, they stare into the eyes of their latest and get all disoriented just talking about it. They're like children."

Alex was quiet for a bit. Maybe there had been no discontent in the words she'd spoken about him to her cousin after all. "And how about you? Did you ever fall in love like that?"

"Me?" Maryann squeaked. She looked alarmed. And

then much too pale. Finally, she shook her head. "I'm immune to that kind of stuff. I've seen it go wrong too many times."

Alex frowned. That didn't seem right. "But surely you plan to get married."

"If I do, I plan to pick my husband based on reason. And genetics. I think good genes are important, don't you?" Her cheeks were still pink, but he suspected it was indignation turning them rosy this time.

"Yes, but…" Alex was taken aback. He'd never met a woman who didn't long to feel some intense emotions, especially when it came to marriage. He knew he had a reputation for being a little detached, but it didn't seem right for someone like Maryann to feel that way, too.

Finally her face went back to its normal color, and she swallowed. "Look. There's no need to beat around the bush about what happened the other night. I want you to know I didn't mean anything by it. I was just talking with my cousin about how much I wanted you to stay on as the doctor here and, before you know it, she was talking about how you'd stay if you met someone to marry."

Alex was beginning to feel better already. "So she was the one who was supposed to match me up with someone?"

Maryann swallowed again. "No, that was me."

"You're the one who was supposed to help me get poleaxed? With some woman you picked out?" He wondered if Maryann knew how cute she was. Funny, he'd never noticed before how her nose turned up just enough to make her look mischievous. And her eyes—the gold flecks in the brown made them look like they were twinkling. "I suppose I should be grateful I have a strong constitution. That whole thing sounds a bit tough."

"Now see, that's why I told my cousin I shouldn't mention anything to you. I knew you'd just make fun of it and—"

Alex put up his hand. "I think it's kind of sweet that you're worried."

The sun was shining in the window and Maryann's face lit up in a smile. "You do?"

"You're not thinking of one of those fancy women, I hope." Alex said, wondering why he was going so easy on her.

Maryann shook her head. "I was thinking of Belinda Edwards."

"Who?" Alex's smile disappeared. He hadn't really thought she had someone specific in mind for him. That changed everything.

Maryann took a step back. "You know. She's the single mom who works in the office at the grade school. Long red hair and glasses. Midtwenties. She's taking some online college courses to improve herself. She likes camping and watching DVDs at home. I'm pretty sure she'd go out with you if you asked."

Alex was stunned. He still couldn't believe it. "You haven't just been talking? You've actually been matching me up?"

"Well, I haven't asked her if she's interested, but she does seem nice."

Suddenly Alex didn't feel like teasing her anymore. How could she call him an ice man, when she was trying to marry him off to someone he'd never even had a conversation with? That was more than a little cold. "Do you even know this woman?"

"Belinda gets her hair cut at the same place I do. She's got gorgeous hair, by the way. And I like her."

"You haven't been in Treasure Creek much more than a month. How often have you had your hair cut in that time?" he asked.

Alex couldn't believe Maryann was standing there smiling at him, like he should be grateful she was trying to find some woman to marry him. Like he was desperate. Like he didn't have things he needed to do before he settled down and got married.

"I don't have time to date anyone," Alex said with as much dignity as he could manage. "Now, if you'll excuse me, I need to do some paperwork."

He walked down to the exam room and closed the door. He didn't have anything to write, and she probably knew it.

But at least he'd gotten away with his self-respect intact. He'd been so sure the story had been reported to him with errors. He hadn't admitted it to himself until now, but he'd been confident she'd started that conversation with her cousin because Maryann was interested in dating him herself. *Her,* not some Belinda Edwards who liked to camp.

He had been planning to turn Maryann down gently, of course. They'd had a quiet friendship that was building during the time she'd been here, and he was afraid to disrupt that. He didn't want her to hand in her resignation as his previous nurse had done, either. But apparently he'd been mistaken. She wasn't interested in dating him at all.

It took him a moment or two, but he finally told himself it was for the best.

He already had his plane tickets to leave in three weeks. He'd get someone to fly him to Juneau, and then on to Anchorage. He'd take a flight south from there. A month from now, he'd be looking for property in Los Angeles where he'd build his clinic.

He had plans. He'd been awarded a large grant from a local foundation to cover the cost of the ground he needed. And he'd saved every extra penny he made moonlighting as a tour guide up here, to help with the construction. He'd have to take out a loan of course, but his savings would provide just enough for the needed downpayment. Until he did something to pay back his brother for saving his life, Alex didn't feel free to live a normal life. The small clinic would be named after his brother.

After all, Rocco couldn't get married, since he couldn't even meet a woman, as long as he confined himself to their parents' house. Worse yet, his brother couldn't realize his childhood hope of being a surgeon, not with his hands and his legs as crippled as they were by the accident. Alex knew he could never give his brother his dreams back, but the plaque for the clinic he planned to build would show his brother how much he appreciated the sacrifice he had made.

He needed to do *something* before he could even say he was sorry.

He'd tried to give his brother other things in the past. So far, the only thing Rocco had accepted was the money to pay for that attendant. His brother said no to anything else, saying money couldn't buy him what he really needed. There was nothing else Alex could give him, except a clinic built in his name. He knew Rocco liked the idea, because he smiled every time Alex mentioned it. Maybe, once the clinic was built, Rocco's bitterness would fade.

And if Rocco was happier, maybe Alex could ask him for forgiveness. Maybe his parents could also forgive the past and live in the present. Right now, no one was free of the accident. His parents avoided each other and Rocco. Maybe, when the clinic was completed and Alex was home, he'd have his family back again.

Chapter Three

Later that afternoon, Maryann was sitting at a small desk in the waiting room, staring at the wall when the bell over the door rang. She should have been going through the list of patients to call for tomorrow's appointments, but she'd become distracted thinking about what had happened that morning. Alex was in the examining room and it was good that he was. She felt closer to him because of what he'd told her about his brother, and farther apart at the same time, because of the gossip she'd caused. Mostly, she didn't want to think about it, even though she couldn't get it out of her head.

"Amy!" Maryann said as she looked up and saw the owner of the local tour company. The young red-haired widow always had a smile on her face, and she was one of Maryann's favorite people in Treasure Creek.

For the first time, it occurred to her that Amy James came to the office more than was necessary. There always seemed to be a good reason about the twins to stop by, but maybe she was interested in Alex in a romantic way. Maryann wondered if the answer to who the doctor should marry was right in front of her.

"Here to see the doctor?" Maryann asked, keeping her voice neutral. She should feel more excitement at the thought that she might be talking to Alex's future wife, especially because Amy had deep roots in this place and could convince Alex to stay.

Oh—Maryann just remembered that she hadn't combed her hair back into place after being out in the wind.

"Am I interrupting something?" Amy walked over to the desk. "I can come back."

Amy was always neatly dressed, and Maryann didn't want to look like a hooligan. Not that she was competing with Amy for anyone's attention. It was just that all women liked to look their best.

Maryann smiled. "No, I just—well, my hair." Then she reached up to smooth her hair back into its usual bobbed shape.

Amy laughed a little. "That happens up here, especially this time of year. I know it's happened to me. Of course, Ben always thought it was funny. I'd be there with my hair going every which way, and he'd be grinning like a kid at the circus."

The widow's laugh faded as she remembered her late husband. Then she seemed to shake off her memories. "Well, I just came around because I'm putting together a choir for the Christmas pageant, and I wondered if you'd come help us sing."

"Oh, I can't," Maryann said as she heard footsteps in the hall. "I'm not much of a singer."

Amy shrugged. "That's not important. Ben always said it was the spirit of the thing that counted. I'm hoping to do the best pageant ever, in his honor this year, but

I'm not sure I'm up to it. I figure if we can get started early by practicing the carols, we'll have a chance of pulling it off."

Alex entered the room. "The pageant is nice. Every year it gets a little better."

"Well, that's going to be hard to do this year," Amy said, as she sat down in one of the waiting room chairs. "I'm hoping that, if we can get going now, maybe we'll gain some enthusiasm."

"Well, I'm sure whatever you do will be great," Alex said, then he looked at the woman more closely. "Are you all right?"

Maryann watched Alex walk over to Amy. Now why did he have to stand there and look at the woman as if she was a delicate flower?

"I can give you a vitamin B shot if you need one," Alex offered as he reached out his hand to touch Amy's forehead. "You've been going through a tough time. If anything troubles you, let me know."

Maryann hoped none of the fancy women heard about Alex being willing to treat Amy, even though she wasn't a child.

Amy looked up at him and Maryann wondered if the two of them needed to be alone.

"I have been worried," the widow said softly before Maryann could think of an excuse to leave. "Something's been missing and I don't know where...well, it's the treasure map we talked about. You know the one?"

Then Amy dropped her voice even further, until Maryann couldn't hear her words. Maryann walked toward her desk and sat down to finish the filing she had to do. She told herself she should be happy. She wanted Alex to stay in Treasure Creek. If he fell in love with Amy, he'd have to stay. Maybe the treasure map that Amy's sons had found would bring them together. Some people thought the map showed where an ancestor of Amy's had hidden the gold.

Maryann saw Alex frown as he looked down at Amy. "That doesn't sound good. Have you reported that it's gone?"

Maryann couldn't help but notice that he didn't act anything like The Ice Man when talking to Amy. He leaned over her most solicitously. Maybe it was only nurses and fancy women Alex wanted to avoid. She supposed he figured one was work and the others were gold diggers.

"I don't want to report it to anyone official yet," Amy said in a louder voice and gave a glance at Maryann. Then she shook her head and turned back to Alex. "I just wanted to ask you to keep your eyes open."

Alex nodded.

"Anyway," Amy said with a bright smile that included Maryann, "I hope you can both sing in the pageant."

"I'll pass," Alex said as he turned to go into the exam room.

Maryann tried to remind herself of her goal to get Alex to stay in town.

"You should sing," Maryann said.

Alex frowned. "What's the point? I'm not going to be in town for the pageant."

"Well, coming to a few practices wouldn't hurt," Maryann said. "Maybe some other men will join if they see you're practicing."

Alex lifted an eyebrow in protest. "I'm not that influential."

"You are," Amy stepped in, fairly gushing. "And it's not just the men you'll inspire. I'm sure half of the single women in town will volunteer, too, if you do. That'll give me plenty of people for the choir."

Maryann figured Amy had underestimated the doctor's impact. If all of the single women were there, the single men wouldn't be far behind.

"You won't need to wear a costume or anything," Amy promised.

"But," Alex tried again, "You need to remember I won't be here at Christmas. I'll be down in Los Angeles, putting together my new clinic."

"Oh," Amy said. "That's right."

Maryann felt her enthusiasm fall to the floor right along with Amy's. He was still so set on leaving town.

"You could still practice with us," Amy finally said. "Even just one or two times might be enough to get the women there. You wouldn't even need to sing. Just stand around. I could put you in charge of lighting or something."

"I could do that," Alex said. "I'm sorry I won't be here for the pageant."

"Thanks," Amy said, and then straightened up as if she was bracing herself. "I was going to wait a few weeks to start rehearsals, but I better get them going now."

"Three weeks," Alex reminded her. "That's how long I'll be here." Then he grinned. "Maryann will be there, too. She can take over my place when I'm gone. Singing."

"But I—" she sputtered.

"That's perfect," Amy beamed at them both and stood. "I better get going so I can tell everyone. We have the tour team meeting tonight so we'll plan to meet Thursday night at the church for the carol rehearsal. Let's say five-thirty to nine."

"People can't sing for three and a half hours," Maryann managed to gasp. "Not amateurs anyway."

"You're right," Amy said. "We'll need snacks and something to drink. Maybe hot tea. We'll take a nice long break."

"They'll still strain their vocal chords," Maryann added.

"That's it." Amy snapped her fingers and looked at Alex. "You can be the choir doctor. You won't have to sing a note."

"I treat children," Alex protested.

"That's why you're perfect," Amy said as she headed for the door. "Children are screaming all the time."

Maryann and Alex both watched her walk toward the door. Just before she got there, Amy turned around. "Oh, and Maryann, why don't you come to our team meeting with Alex tonight? I've wanted to get your perspective on our tours, since you're new in the area. You know, specialty tours, that sort of thing."

"But I—" Maryann protested.

"It won't take long," Amy assured her as she turned the knob and half-opened the door. "We're meeting for hamburgers in the back room at Lizbet's Diner at seven." And then Amy turned to flash a smile at Maryann. "I hear you like eating there."

With that, the other woman turned to walk through the door.

"She knows," Maryann muttered glumly as the door was closed.

"The whole town knows," Alex replied.

They stood there for a minute.

Finally, he put his hands in his pockets. "I have those insurance forms to fill out, so I plan to stay late tonight. I'll just walk over to Lizbet's at seven, if you want to go with me."

Maryann nodded. "I have some paperwork, too." She paused. "You know, I'm really sorry I said anything last night."

"Well, what's done is done," he said briskly. "In the meantime, we have a clinic to run."

Alex walked back to the desk in his exam room and opened the bottom drawer. He'd sent away for the plaque a month ago, and it had only arrived last week. He liked rubbing his hands over the engraved brass plate. "The Frank Rocco Havens Clinic," it read.

Just holding the plaque made him feel good. His plans for the clinic were the reason he moonlighted with Amy's tour company. Every Saturday during tourist season, he'd taken a busload of people up along the Klondike Highway. He knew more about the gold rush that had ignited Alaska in the late 1800s than the men who had lived through it had probably known. He was certainly making more money off it than most of them had.

He wondered why Amy wanted him and Maryann at tonight's meeting. He didn't always attend the meetings, because he was part time, and, as far as he knew, Amy had never asked any outsider to come and give their feedback on the tours. Not that it was a bad idea, he told himself. She just hadn't done it before.

He looked at the clock on his desk. He had things to do, so he spent fifteen minutes writing up some notes from this morning.

"Doctor?"

Alex looked up to see Maryann standing in the open doorway.

"Sally Weston is here with her mother."

"Send them in," Alex said as he reached down to put the plaque back in the drawer.

His nurse gave him a completely impersonal smile and turned to leave the room. Which annoyed him, even though that is what he wanted her to do.

Maryann walked back to the waiting room.

"The doctor will see you now," Maryann said as she smiled at five-year-old Sally and her mother. "Just go on back."

Maryann waited for the two of them to leave the waiting room before she turned to address Belinda Edwards. By now she should have realized the conversation in the diner last night would have been relayed to Belinda. Maryann decided she would never talk about anyone's dating life ever again.

Belinda was sitting in one of the padded chairs that lined the right-hand wall of the office. Her red hair was piled on top of her head and anchored with a big clip. Maybe it was because of the red hair, but Maryann couldn't help but compare Belinda to Amy. The woman sitting in the doctor's office now was a lot more casual than the one who'd just left. And Alex didn't strike her as the informal kind.

"So, what'd he say?" Belinda actually snapped her gum.

"I can't ask him on a date for you," Maryann said. "I told you that. I mentioned your name last night, but I spoke too soon. He's not the easiest man to pin down. He says he's got things to do."

"Oh." Belinda stopped chewing and frowned a little. "Well, I'm not going to be around forever. If he wants to date me, he needs to make a move."

"I'm sure he's aware of that," Maryann said. "Maybe you could sign up to sing in the Christmas pageant. You could get to know him there. I hear he's going to be at the first few rehearsals."

"So will all the other women in town. Have you seen those fancy women?"

"Yes, but I'm sure none of them have a beautiful voice like yours," Maryann said soothingly.

Belinda looked up at her in astonishment. "I didn't know you'd heard me sing."

"And you have such beautiful eyes," Maryann finished. She'd heard Belinda humming one day at the beauty salon, and had been impressed. She figured anyone who could hum like that could sing. "Plus, your hair is so shiny. And with your kids and all, I think you'd make a good match for Alex."

"It would be good to be married to a doctor," Belinda finally said after a few moments. "At least, he wouldn't be like Arnie."

"Arnie?" Maryann asked.

"Yeah. My neighbor. He's always hanging around. Of course, he's good with the kids and all, but I figure, if I have a shot at a doctor, I should take it. My mother would be mad at me if I didn't. Arnie doesn't have much ambition."

"Do you mean he doesn't work?"

"Of course he works," Belinda said, looking offended. "He's a fine man. He works on one of the fishing boats. It's just that he's not a doctor or anything."

"He sounds like a good man to me."

"But I thought you wanted me to date the doctor," Belinda protested. "I can date Arnie any old time."

Maryann thought back to her mother's discontent in her various marriages. "Sometimes you just have to pick a good man and stay with him."

Belinda leaned back in her chair. "Are you sure you don't need me? You know I care about the children of this town as much as anyone. And this doctor is good to them. I've heard he tends to anyone who needs him, and he doesn't make them pay. At least not much. We want to keep him here if we can."

Maryann nodded. At least the gossips had adequately captured why she and her cousin were looking for someone for Alex. "He is a good doctor. But don't worry, I'll find someone else for him."

"Suzie Platter might be interested. I think she just broke up with Joe—you know? Joe Tribett?"

Maryann shook her head. "Maybe she'll join the choir Amy is getting together for the Christmas pageant."

"I don't think she sings."

"Neither does anyone else," Maryann said.

"Well, then maybe she will." With that bit of

optimistic news, Belinda stood up. "I better get home. Arnie is boiling eggs to make the kids some sandwiches for lunch tomorrow."

"Sounds like he's a keeper," Maryann said with a smile.

"I do kind of like him," Belinda admitted as she neared the door.

Maryann watched the other woman walk out of the office before she let her smile fade away. She shouldn't have been surprised when Belinda showed up at the clinic. When were people going to forget what she'd said last night at the diner? How could information travel so fast in this small town, when they didn't even have a newspaper? And—her heart sank—how badly had she messed things up with Alex? He might say it was okay, but had he really forgiven her? She'd gotten over being worried that he would fire her, but she was realizing she valued his good opinion above most anyone else's.

Chapter Four

Alex closed the door to the clinic. Dusk was quickly turning to dark, and Maryann was waiting for him on the porch. She'd walked back to her room at Lindy's Boarding House to change out of her uniform and into a pair of jeans. He flipped the sign on the door, so it showed the clinic was no longer open. The sign, like so many others in Treasure Creek, had the dark imprint of a moose on it.

It was growing colder by the second. Indoor lights had already been turned on in the nearby buildings, and the smell of wood fires drifted through the air.

"How's your brother?" Maryann asked as she pulled up the hood on her jacket and slipped her hands into her pockets. "He didn't have his usual questions when he called. I hope he's okay."

Alex hesitated and then told himself that, if he wanted to change Maryann's opinion about him being an ice man, he needed to open up more. Besides, he was a little worried about his brother. "Rocco has been saying he has something big to tell me for a while. He's getting agitated that I haven't gone to see him to talk in person. He won't say what it is, but today he added that he doesn't think I should leave Alaska. He says I should stay right here."

"Really?" Maryann looked up in surprise. "I thought he wanted you to come back to Los Angeles to live."

Alex nodded grimly as he held out his arm to Maryann. He didn't want her to stumble in the growing darkness. "He lives right in the middle of Duarte. That's the reason I'm going back there to build my clinic. I owe it to him. I'm not just dedicating the clinic in his name, I want him to feel like it's his. To have some place close enough for him to visit. Besides he's my brother. He needs me there."

"Well of course, your parents—"

Alex grunted. "My parents aren't even there most of the time. My mother's staying in Palm Springs right now, and my father is in Utah, going to some nutritional conferences. Since I got the attendant for Rocco, my parents are both traveling more. Which I thought would be good. Take the pressure off them. But it's like they've decided to divorce without taking the legal step. They didn't spend much time with Rocco before, anyway, but at least they were there in the house. Now he has been alone too much."

Maryann nodded and put her hand on his arm. Neither one of them started down the steps, though. Alex was noticing that a few strands of Maryann's hair had escaped when she pulled the rest of her glorious hair under her jacket hood. He felt like tucking the strays in, but he resisted the urge.

"Maybe he just meant you should stay here a few

weeks longer," Maryann finally said. "That would make sense."

"Nothing makes sense," Alex muttered and then stopped. He wasn't sure what he was talking about any longer. He suddenly wondered if Maryann had ever gone for a moonlight walk down the road to where the log jam usually occurred on the creek. It would only be a mile past the boarding house where she stayed. When there were no street lamps, the sky was deep black and the stars even brighter. Of course, she couldn't go on that kind of a walk by herself; even he took flares with him to scare away any wild animals.

He mentally shook himself. The two of them alone in the dark together was a bad idea. He needed to remember he was leaving here and that the Northern nights played with people's emotions.

"Actually, Rocco was very clear," Alex said, bringing himself back to the conversation. He had no business wondering how much Maryann's brown eyes would deepen in the moonlight. "He thought I was moving back to take care of him and—"

"Well, aren't you?" Maryann asked when he stopped.

"Of course I am. I owe him everything. He saved my life."

"What do you mean?" she asked.

He suddenly found himself speaking of the accident and how his brother had been injured saving his life. Maryann said nothing, perhaps realizing how painful the memory was for him. She merely squeezed his arm in support as they continued walking in silence.

"I wish we weren't going to Amy's meeting," Alex

finally said as they started walking on the edge of the asphalt. Light was spilling out from the businesses, many of them wood frame buildings with frontier facades, adding charm to their walk.

Maryann turned to face him and asked, "It's because we're going to Lizbet's Diner, isn't it? By now, everyone in there must know what I said last night. Again, I'm so sorry."

The both stopped. They were in front of the Treasure Creek General Store. Alex looked through the display window and saw Harry Peters, the owner of the store, scowling at a fishing rod he was trying to hang on a rack. If anyone had been inside to listen to him, the middle-aged man would be complaining. The man did a lot of that lately, Alex realized.

"They don't call Harry an ice man, do they?" Alex suddenly wanted to know. He didn't want people to think he suffered the same disgruntledness that seemed to be part of the other man's life.

"No, they call him a curmudgeon," Maryann admitted with a slight smile. "You're the only ice man around that I know of."

Alex nodded as he rapped on the store's window with his knuckles. "That's good."

Harry peered at him a minute before giving him an unsmiling thumbs-up.

Alex nodded back. He supposed a thumbs-up was a start to having a happier day.

"Everyone knows what I said last night," Maryann muttered. "Even Harry thinks you're on a date—with *me*."

So that's what the store owner was saying with his

gesture. Alex looked over and saw the miserable look on Maryann's face. "Would that be so bad? Lots of people go on dates."

"It just feels awkward."

"It's okay. We'll just walk into Lizbet's and pretend last night never happened."

"Just like that?" She looked up at him skeptically. Even though they had stopped, she still had her hand on his right arm and he put his left hand over it. Her fingers were cold so he left his hand there to warm them up.

"I don't see how—" she continued.

He interrupted. "We'll make it fun."

Since Alex still had his hand on her fingers, he could feel the shock go through her.

"It's not like I never have fun," he said, defending himself softly, hoping she wouldn't ask him to give specific details. It was longer ago than he cared to remember. Probably the last time he'd laughed very much was when he'd been down to visit Rocco in the spring. It was now well into September.

Maryann nodded, but she didn't look convinced.

"Here." He lifted his hand and smoothed the wayward strands of hair under the hood of her jacket. Her cheeks were as smooth as he'd imagined. And her eyes opened wide enough in surprise that he had a glimpse of how she'd look when staring at the stars.

If he didn't get her to the diner soon, he'd kiss her right here in front of Harry's window. He didn't even want to count all of the reasons that would be a bad idea, although he had to say, it would definitely be fun. And it might give Harry some ideas of his own.

Alex cleared his throat. "Amy reserves the back room when we meet for dinner." His voice sounded hoarse.

Fortunately, Maryann didn't seem to notice his voice. She just started walking with him to Lizbet's.

Maryann pushed the jacket hood off her head as she and Alex stood under the diner's porch light. By now the sun had set and it was totally dark. She lifted her hands to puff her hair up a little. The hood had a tendency to squash it down, and she didn't want to look flat headed. Like fur-trimmed parkas, hair that was pressed down was a common sight around Alaska. At least for those people who liked to stay warm.

"You look good," Alex said as he smiled down at her.

She felt a tiny little tremble in her knees. It was to be expected, she supposed. Alex was so focused that everything he did was magnified. Even a look that meant nothing to him could make a woman feel special. She needed to keep her feet on the ground and remember that. "We need to look more businesslike if you want to avoid any teasing when we walk in."

They could smell the hamburgers being grilled and hear muffled laughter from the people inside. There was a window beside the door, and Maryann could see people sitting at tables in the dim light of the main dining room.

Alex grinned as he opened the door. "I could go around passing out those pamphlets we got from the CDC, urging everyone to get their flu shot this year."

"That would be better," Maryann agreed with a quick smile as she straightened her jacket. "They shouldn't tease a doctor, anyway. You care for the sick. They might need you someday."

If Maryann didn't believe she had to give Alex support because she was the one who had started all of the gossip, she would have turned around and said she'd decided to go home after all. She couldn't imagine what Amy would want from her at this meeting. That question had gone through her head all afternoon. There were dozens of new people in town who could give input into the kind of tours Amy's company should give. Besides, the woman needed to have a focus group and not rely on one opinion. Maryann hadn't noticed that anyone was complaining about the tours the company currently offered, anyway. It sure seemed to her that there was something for everyone's taste.

The chatter inside the diner didn't cease as Maryann stepped into the main room. The place was packed. People at several of the tables shared pizzas on tin trays that were elevated in the middle of their tables. Others had regular plates topped with sandwiches and hamburgers. She thought she smelled chili cooking in the kitchen, too.

"You know the way to the back room?" Alex asked her quietly.

She nodded. "I should have reserved it last night for dinner with my cousin. At least then no one would have heard us."

Alex chuckled. "You need a minimum of ten people to use the room. Trust me, one of the ten would have sold you out for a slice of pizza before you got out of here, anyway."

Maryann carefully wound her way through the gaps

between the tables. Men with untrimmed beards and flannel shirts shared tables with tourists in khaki pants, with baseball caps perched on their heads. She saw several of the fancy women sitting with some of the local men. Joleen, the woman who'd been so friendly this afternoon, looked up at her as Maryann walked by, and nodded. The woman was sharing a plate of nachos with a man Maryann didn't know.

"Hi there." One of the fresh-faced waitresses waved to Maryann and Alex as they walked by. "Need a table?"

"No, thanks, we're going to the back room," Alex said as he guided them past another few tables.

"I wonder if she's the one who heard me and my cousin talking," Maryann muttered to Alex softly.

He smiled. "The way I hear it, all the waitresses took turns going over and listening. Then they pooled what they heard. They should work for the CIA."

The door to the back room was almost closed, and light was shining out from around its edges. Maryann was surprised she didn't hear any noise on the other side of the door. "I thought we would be a little late."

Alex pushed the door open.

"Surprise!" The call rang out and confetti flew through the air. A "Happy Birthday Alex." banner was strung across the far window, and colorful balloons were hanging from the ceiling. The walls of the room were paneled in oak, and tiny white lights outlined the windows. On a table underneath the banner was a double-tiered chocolate cake with unlit candles.

"Happy Birthday," one of the other tour guides, Nate McMann, said as he stepped closer to them and thumped

Alex on the back. "Why didn't you say something? I would have taken you out to breakfast."

"I forgot my birthday's tomorrow," Alex said with a grin. "You've still got time."

"Breakfast?" Gage Parker, a tall, dark-haired tour guide, came over to stand by Maryann. He looked down at her with a grin. "I gave him a better gift than that. I sent the fancy women over to visit."

Maryann gasped. "*You* sent them? I thought *I* was responsible."

Gage was her cousin's new fiancée, and as smitten with love as any man Maryann had ever seen.

He grinned. "Well, I did use the words you and Karenna threw around to get the women motivated. Good work, by the way. Ten people told me about it before I saw Karenna. Nothing makes a man more appealing than knowing some woman is out looking for a match for him. Everyone's afraid they'll lose out if they don't act right away. It's like a clearance sale. Women fight to buy something they're not sure they want, just to be sure no one else gets it before they can decide if they do want it or not."

"Thanks a lot," Alex muttered. "You've just compared me to sheets and towels."

Gage shrugged with another grin. "Hey, you've got to give women what they want."

Maryann elbowed Gage. "My cousin didn't find you in the bargain basement, you know."

Gage grew suddenly serious. "I wouldn't have cared where she found me. Just that she did."

Maryann nodded. Karenna was the one member of

the Jenner family who had managed to find true love without losing her mind completely.

By this time, Amy had walked up to Alex and given him a hug. After she greeted Alex, the other woman turned to Maryann. "I'm so glad you came. I knew Alex would want you here for his party, and I couldn't think of much of a reason to get you to come without spoiling the surprise." She paused. "Not that we don't want your input on the tours. We're always looking for more ideas."

"I didn't even know it was his birthday," Maryann confessed to the other woman. "And I'm his nurse."

"Don't worry about it," Amy said. "He never tells anyone something like that. I just know because he put it on his application for the tour guide job. I never ask the year, but I do ask the day. Besides, it's not until tomorrow."

Nate was slapping Alex on the back. "Maybe instead of breakfast, I should set you up with a date. I wouldn't want to be shown up by Gage. Just because he's found his happiness doesn't mean I can't come up with someone for you to date." Then Nate turned to Maryann. "Who was it you wanted him to date, anyway?"

"I don't really have anyone," Maryann stammered. "I mean, it's none of my business, anyway. And people need to find their own…" She spread her hands. "Anyway, I'm sorry I said anything."

Nate just laughed. "Don't worry about it. Alex here probably needed some encouragement." He turned to face his friend. "How old are you now?"

"Thirty-two, and I can find my own dates," Alex said

with a grin. "And since we're on the subject, how many women came to see you today?"

"Okay, point taken," Nate said. "But you have to admit I live out of town so it's harder to get to my place. I'd have to draw the women a map."

"Well, you're here now, and I don't see them gathering around," Alex said.

Both men started to laugh.

Just then one of the waitresses came in carrying a tray of grilled hamburgers. There were plates of sliced tomatoes and onions on the side of the tray. Then another waitress walked in, carrying a tray with tall glasses of ice tea and water.

"Let's pray before we sit down," Amy invited them as she walked to the table that was set with silverware and napkins for everyone. She bowed her head. Everyone followed her lead.

"Father, we thank you for our good friend, Alex, here. Bless not just his birthday, but the rest of his life. And strengthen us with the food You provide. In Jesus' name, amen."

Amy looked around at the tour guides. "Before we sit down, I have an announcement. I expect you all to keep it confidential, but—as most of you know already— someone has stolen the treasure map."

Maryann knew of the map that Amy's great-great-grandfather had drawn, back when Treasure Creek was founded. It supposedly led to a valuable treasure. Since Amy's two young boys had found the map a few months ago, it and its treasure had been the talk of the town.

She looked at Alex. "Do you think there is real treasure buried around here?"

Alex shrugged as he pulled out a chair for her. "I suspect whoever has that map hopes there is gold. And who knows? It does sound like there was treasure at some point, because Amy remembers her grandfather saying his father had said the treasure should only be sought if their family ever had 'dire times.' That sounds like gold to me."

Maryann stopped. "What did you say?"

"That sounds like gold to me."

"No, the dire times. Were those the exact words?"

Alex nodded. By now, everyone else had been seated at the table, and they were looking at them. "Why?"

Maryann looked over at Amy. "I think I know where your map is. When Timmy Fields was at the clinic this morning he said something about dire times and I noticed he'd slipped an old sheet of paper into the Bible I'd given him to hold."

Amy gasped. "He was over playing with my sons before the map disappeared. My boys know about the prediction for dire times. It's an old family story."

"Timmy must know then, too. He was found along the Chilkoot Pass."

"I was afraid something like this would happen. The poor boy could have died out there, looking for that treasure," Amy said.

"And he probably only wanted to help out his parents," Maryann said. "They're certainly hurting for money, now that his father is out of a job."

"Dire times." Amy nodded. "There's a lot of that around here these days. Treasure Creek has really struggled economically since Ben died and the tour business took a hit."

"I can walk back to the clinic and get the map for you right now." Alex started to rise from his chair.

"Certainly not," Amy said, as she motioned for him to sit. "It can wait. We're going to eat and have some of your cake. If that map's locked up in your clinic, it isn't going anywhere—tonight anyway."

An hour later, Alex looked around the room and decided he was a contented man. Even the few good-natured jibes about him and the fancy women didn't trouble him. In fact, he had started rather enjoying them, once Maryann began to turn pink every time someone mentioned the women.

"You're a good sport," he said to her quietly. They'd both finished their hamburgers and fries. "No one blames you for those women showing up today in the clinic. The guys were just having fun."

Maryann shrugged and smiled with her brown eyes. "I figure they'll stop joking when they get a piece of your birthday cake."

Alex chuckled and put an arm on the back of her chair so he could lean in and lower his voice even more. "I wouldn't count on it. I've seen these guys in action. They know how to out-wait a polar bear in spring thaw. They just don't let go when they have something on their mind."

Alex hadn't thought about it before he put his arm on her chair. But once it was there, he didn't want to move it away. The table was crowded and their chairs were close enough together that he hoped it didn't look like he was putting his arm around her. At least Maryann didn't seem to take it that way, although he did notice a slight frown forming on her face.

"You don't see polar bears on those tours you take, do you?" she asked him in alarm. "That doesn't seem very safe. You could be hurt."

"Eaten alive," he confirmed cheerfully. "Although it's usually the grizzlies that do that."

Her eyes grew wider still.

Alex couldn't remember the last time someone had worried about him. He shouldn't tease her about this. "Actually, I do the bus tours—basically following the White Pass Trail, with stops at every photo op we can find. Some of the guides are experienced enough to go after the wild animals, but not me. The scariest things I'm likely to see are mosquitoes. "

"Well, that's good," Maryann said as she settled back into her chair.

The instant she leaned back far enough for her neck to touch his arm, she stiffened. Alex didn't move; he didn't even breathe. The skin at the back of her neck was soft and felt vulnerable. Gradually, he felt Maryann relax against his arm. She accepted him. He wished he'd put his arm there sooner.

Just then, Amy stood up at the front of the table. When she had everyone's attention, she lifted her hands to lead everyone in singing "Happy Birthday" to him. Alex wished they would finish the song as quickly as possible. He wasn't used to this kind of attention, with everyone looking at him.

Of course, the other guides had to add some offbeat verses to the birthday song, so they could keep singing. On the second time around, Alex surprised himself by blinking. His eyes were moist; he was suddenly realizing that he was going to miss this little northern town when he went back to Los Angeles.

He blinked again. When he'd first come to Treasure Creek, he couldn't wait to leave. He had bristled at the high cost of everything that had to be shipped in or flown down from Anchorage. The summer days were too long, and he never thought he'd adjust to the brief episodes of gray light people here called daytime in the winter months.

But he had friends here. He'd been so busy with med school that he hadn't had a normal life for years. He didn't want to tell these friends, but this was the first party he'd had in years. Usually, he got a congratulatory call from Rocco, and that was it. His parents had given up marking his birthday when he'd left for college. Even before that, there had been so much isolation and sadness in his family, a celebration had never seemed quite appropriate for holidays or birthdays.

"Alex?" He heard Maryann quietly speaking his name, and he realized he'd been lost in thought.

"Huh?"

"Amy asked if you'd made your birthday wish yet?"

He saw the waitress use a match to light the candles on his cake. He'd forgotten about the tradition of a wish. It didn't take more than a second, though, for him to know what his was. It was a foolish desire, but then this was a childish game. So he nodded. He wished he could stay right here in Treasure Creek and get to know Maryann better.

Someone dimmed the lights and the waitress who

had lit the candles brought the cake to him so he could blow them out. Before he did, he took a moment to see how Maryann's eyes looked in candlelight. They were dazzling.

Maybe that was enough good to come from a birthday wish.

Something was happening to him, he realized. His hands felt clammy and his breathing was suddenly a little labored. He wondered if he was coming down with something.

"What's wrong?" Maryann asked. Her brown eyes deepened.

"Nothing," Alex said. And there wasn't really anything amiss except that he so enjoyed looking at her.

"Go ahead, blow out your candles," Maryann finally said. "People are starting to look at you funny."

Alex leaned forward so much that his arm left the back of Maryann's chair and slid up to her shoulder. Then, with what breath he had left, he blew out his candles.

When he finished, he looked around at the other tour guides. They were staring at him like he'd changed into an alien right before their eyes. And, of course, he had. He'd started to show his emotions. The blinking had fooled no one. And the arm he had around Maryann's shoulders revealed that this was almost a date in his mind. If he ever had been an ice man, he was thawing. Of course, it couldn't be happening at a worse time. His heart might tell him to stay in Treasure Creek, but his duty lay back in Los Angeles with his brother.

It was a comfort to know that the guides sitting around this table were not strangers to that kind of duty.

Gage had taken his brother's son into his home when his brother couldn't care for him. Another guide was supporting his invalid mother. They had all rallied around Amy when her husband died. A man didn't just think of himself in this life. Not if he lived in Treasure Creek. Each of them had put someone else's needs before their own, at some time since he'd known them.

Which didn't explain why all of them were quiet right now. He was an easy target, sitting there. Ordinarily, at least one of the guides would make a joke about his wandering arm. Or his birthday wish. But they were all as somber as he was. Which, when he realized it, only told him how bad off they thought he was.

The waitress had cut the birthday cake and she gave him the first piece. He passed it on to Maryann. If he was thawing, it was because of her. Something about her had gotten to him. Not that it was likely to last beyond the night. He nodded his thanks when the waitress silently gave him a second piece of cake. Tomorrow, in the clear light of day, he'd be back at his desk, going about his routine, knowing he'd leave for Los Angeles in three weeks and never look back. It's what he had to do.

Just thinking about it made the cake taste like straw.

He looked over at Amy. "I'll slip back to the clinic and get that map for you." He set his fork back on the plate. "It'll only take a few minutes."

He could use the walk, he told himself. The cold air would remind him that nights like this weren't made for him, at least not until he'd finished building that clinic. Maybe once the place was up and running, he could leave it with his staff long enough for him to come back here for a few months some summer.

As he stood he found Amy looking at him with a small, secret smile on her face, and he didn't know what it meant.

"It's your birthday." Amy said. "When you finish your cake, why don't you walk Maryann home? I'll come by the clinic tomorrow morning to get the map. The stars are beautiful tonight. It'd be a shame to waste them."

Now he knew what that look meant. Amy had been as close as a sister to him and he appreciated her approval. Maybe he should take a chance. He slid his plate of cake back further on the table. Maryann had finished hers.

"How about it?" he asked Maryann.

She nodded. "I wouldn't mind getting home early tonight."

He and Maryann said quick goodbyes and were out in the evening air before Alex had time to realize what he was doing.

Alex watched Maryann pull on her jacket hood again. "You don't have gloves with you, do you?"

She shook her head. "I forgot them back at my room."

"Well," Alex said, blessing the forgetfulness that was so unlike her, "I can fix that."

He took his right hand out of his pocket and offered it to her. "I don't have my gloves either."

She took his hand.

Alex felt the warmth of her hand as his covered Maryann's. Then she slipped her other hand into her pocket. She had her chin down and he wondered if it was possible she was shy. The night seemed a bit less chilly now as they stepped off the porch together.

The stars were plentiful tonight. In a month or two anyone walking in their steps would have a chance of seeing the northern lights. But, for now, the deep soft black of the night was enough. He wondered if Maryann felt any of the emotions he felt, stirring inside him.

"There's a moose," she whispered as she took her other hand out of her pocket and pointed. "By that old building."

Sure enough, the moose was there, standing perfectly still, outlined in the night. And then, as they stood and watched, the big bull majestically strolled down the road out of town.

"Wow," Maryann whispered in awe. "I'd never seen anything like that until I came up here."

"Me neither." Alex nodded. She had no reason to know, he told himself, that he was looking at her instead of the moose. Her whole face was filled with joy. As had his heart.

Maryann didn't know what she saw in his face, but her eyes widened as though she was surprised by it.

"Do you think he'll stay?" she asked, and it took Alex a few seconds to realize she meant the moose.

Maryann turned her face away from him slightly and the night shadows covered her eyes with darkness.

"I'm sure he wishes he could," Alex finally said.

He doubted she recognized the longing in his voice, but she looked at him fully this time. Her eyes held a hint of sympathy, and some emotion he could not identify. The combination of the two was his undoing.

He kept his eyes trained on hers, looking for any

sign that she was uncomfortable as he leaned down. Her lips were soft. He knew he should stop the kiss, but he couldn't. He was leaving; he didn't deserve a kiss like this. But he was helpless to end it. He wondered if the northern lights weren't coming out early after all. Something around him seemed to light up the night.

Chapter Five

Maryann snuggled deeper into the covers of her bed. Light frost was on the square-paned window and she could hear the sputter of the old radiator heater as it struggled to raise the temperature in her cold room. She felt a warm contentment inside and wondered vaguely if it was Sunday morning. Usually Lindy, the owner of the boarding house, would be up and brewing coffee to lure everyone down the hall to the dining room. But the sky was dark and Maryann closed her eyes again, luxuriating in the knowledge that she didn't have to put her feet on the chilly wooden floor just yet. She had time to lie here and anticipate another perfect day in paradise.

Then it hit her. Her eyes popped wide open. Alex had kissed her, and she'd wanted him to. It was a foolish mistake on her part. He was leaving. She would be as unlucky in love as her parents were.

Not that she had been in love last night, she assured herself quickly. Temporarily insane maybe, but not in love.

She closed her eyes and willed the sun to stop rising.

Nothing could black out her memory, though. She drew in her breath before she could even think the words.

Last night she'd kissed her boss.

It wasn't quite dawn yet, but it would be soon. In the dim light, Maryann looked around the small room. An old mirror hung over an oak dresser and there was a sitting chair by the window. Too many of her belongings were still in the boxes she'd had sent up from Spokane.

For the first time since she'd come racing up to Treasure Creek—following her cousin, who'd driven up here in her bridal gown after her wedding had failed to happen—Maryann questioned whether she should stay. No one in her family seemed able to have a calm, measured courtship. Maryann wanted to be the exception. This little town had seemed like such a peaceful oasis. She'd thought she would be free of chaos and drama here.

She forced herself to start breathing slower. She needed to calm down. It was a kiss; she hadn't murdered anyone or embezzled money or assaulted a policeman. Her embarrassment might be uncomfortable, but it would fade.

Maryann swung her feet around and set them down on the braided rug by her bed. If she could, she needed to get to the clinic before Alex did. It would feel less uncomfortable to see him if she was filing out a chart than if she was just sitting there when he came in. She stood on the rug and then quickly hopped along the cold floor to the closet, where she pulled out a clean white uniform. First the slacks and then a top.

She threw the clothes on the bed and raced back to the rug. Only a very small percentage of nurses still wore white uniforms. That's how traditional she was. There were no large flowers or laughing clowns on her clothes.

She didn't deserve to be overtaken by drama like this.

Maybe Alex wouldn't even mention the kiss.

Alex turned his key in the front door to the clinic. He'd decided to walk over from the house he rented on the far edge of town. Already, there had been a note stuck in his door this morning, from someone asking if he could put in a good word for them with his landlord. His was one of the few rentals in Treasure Creek, and everyone knew he would vacate it soon. Most people who moved here had to stay at the boarding house for a while, like Maryann was doing.

There he went again. He'd already noticed this morning that every thought that sprang to his mind somehow took him back to Maryann. Which was why he'd come over to the clinic early. He had a stack of medical journals to read. Usually, when he was reading them, nothing else mattered. They were his escape.

He'd barely put his feet up on his desk and leaned his chair back when he heard a knock on the clinic door. They weren't scheduled to open for another half hour, but he knew it might be an emergency, so he put his journal down and walked out of his office into the hall.

"Coming," he called out, as he made his way to the door. He wondered if Maryann had lost her key.

When he opened the door, it was Amy.

"Oh," he said as he stood to the side so she could come in. "Good morning."

"You thought I was someone else, didn't you?" she asked as she loosened the scarf she had wrapped around her neck. She stood in the open doorway with an unrepentant grin on her face.

"I did think you might be Maryann," he agreed calmly.

"I knew it," Amy said in triumph as she stepped inside and walked over to the chairs. "The two of you—"

"She works here. Of course, I thought it was her." He stood there, holding the door without moving. He wasn't going to give an inch. Not the way gossip spread around this town.

"Last night, I thought—"

"She and I have no future," Alex said, interrupting his well-meaning friend. "Remember, I'm leaving at the end of the month."

Just then he heard tentative footsteps on the porch. He looked over his shoulder. It was Maryann, and she'd clearly heard everything he just said.

"Good morning," Maryann said as she finished walking across the porch without making eye contact.

Oh, he was smooth all right, Alex told himself. He heard Maryann greet Amy with more warmth than she'd managed to do with him.

Finally, he remembered to close the door.

"You must be here about the map," Maryann said to Amy as she unsnapped her jacket and hung it on the hook behind the reception desk.

Amy nodded. "I thought Alex and you might have forgotten."

Please, dear Lord, Alex thought, *don't let Amy go into her explanation of why she thought he and Maryann would have forgotten.* He had the prayer finished before he realized it was the first time he'd prayed in decades. God probably wasn't very impressed with him. Amy stayed silent though, so God must still be merciful to fools and desperate men.

"I'll go get the map now," Alex said with as much dignity as he could muster. "It's on the shelf in our exam room."

"No, I can get it," Maryann insisted and turned. "You two sit down and figure out how you're going to handle telling Timmy we found the map.

"I didn't think of that," Alex said as he sat down. He shouldn't be surprised that Maryann saw through to the heart of the problem quicker than he had. He might know the names of more diseases, but she was an instinctive healer.

He didn't breathe easy until his nurse had gone down the hall and entered the office.

"We'll have to call the Fields," Alex said as he turned to look over at Amy. "Maybe Timmy will talk to us on the phone and we can explain that we have to put the map back where it belongs. He's old enough to understand that."

Amy nodded thoughtfully. "I know he didn't mean any harm, but I don't want him to think it is okay to take things that belong to other people."

"Yes, of course," Alex said, nodding.

Maryann came back with the white Bible, and, standing in front of them, opened it.

"That's it," Amy cried, relieved, as she reached for the old yellow paper that was folded between the pages.

"Poor Timmy. He wouldn't have started out looking for that treasure if he didn't think it would help his family," Maryann agreed quietly. "I bet he feels just terrible."

Maryann looked up at Alex, her eyes so full of concern for the boy that he knew she'd forgotten her earlier coldness to him. He smiled back. "It would be best if Timmy could give the map back. Like you said, I'm sure he must be feeling guilty that he took it. At least he should have a chance to make it right."

Alex knew more about guilt than most people, and he knew it was important for a man—or a boy—to face what he had done wrong and make amends. It was the only thing that brought healing. Alex looked forward to the day when he could say he'd made his own amends.

"You're absolutely right," Amy said, as she laid the map back down in the open Bible. "I'll wait for Timmy to return it to me."

"I could make a copy of it if you want," Maryann offered. "You wouldn't want to lose it. You might find the treasure."

Amy smiled. "There's no denying I could use some financial help, but the map is more than just some directions to a treasure. I like holding the piece of paper and thinking of my great-great-grandfather drawing it with his family in mind. It makes me feel so connected to the past. Like someone cared about me before I was even born. I wonder what he would have thought of me if he'd had a chance to know me?"

"He would have thought you are one gracious lady," Maryann said firmly before Alex had a chance to respond. Then she sat down beside Amy, the open Bible on her lap. "Not everyone would risk losing a treasure map to make a boy feel better."

They were all silent for a moment.

"Well, I should go to my office and call the Fields," Alex finally said. "With all those kids, I'm sure they're awake by now. Probably ready for a nap, in fact."

"I expect so," Maryann agreed.

He noticed she'd stopped looking at him again. They needed to sit down and talk. Maybe after Amy left there would be a chance. He didn't quite know what he would say, but they couldn't leave things the way they were.

Maryann watched Alex walk down the hall and open the door to his office. Once he was inside, she didn't even try to hide her misery.

"Trouble?" Amy reached out and put a hand on her on her leg.

Maryann shrugged as she looked over at her. "I get myself in some messes."

"Well, we all do," Amy said. "Want to talk about it?"

Maryann shook her head. "It's okay. It's just that things have been so peaceful here, you know, and then— well, I need to get myself grounded again. That's all."

Suddenly Alex came charging back to the waiting room and all thought of being grounded fled Maryann's mind. He had his black medical bag in his hand, the one with the double silver snaps that he kept for emergencies.

"I need to get out to the Fields's place," Alex announced as he reached for the coat he'd left on the rack by the door. He looked at Maryann, all traces of his earlier uncertainty gone. "Timmy's burning up with fever."

"Oh no," Maryann said, and stood up. "I thought they were supposed to let us know if he had a high temperature."

"It wasn't so bad yesterday afternoon, they said. So they decided not to come back," Alex said as he opened his bag and started checking the medications he had. "Timmy kept saying he needed to come back to the doctor's, but they said he wasn't sick enough. So the little fool went outside last night to get sicker. And now—" Alex turned to her. "I could only listen to his breathing on the phone, but it worries me. I didn't want to ask the parents to bring him in, because I wasn't sure they would. There was something about the pickup, and Mr. Fields doesn't want to take on more debt, he says. I told him there'd be no charge, but he still didn't seem convinced."

Maryann walked to the hook behind her desk and took down her coat. "You might need help."

Alex looked up at her. "Thanks."

"I'll put a sign on the door saying we've gone on an emergency." Maryann found a piece of white paper on her desk and picked up a black marker.

"We should be back in an hour," Alex said. "I'll check Timmy out and leave some antibiotics for him to take. If that's not enough, we'll need to decide what to do then."

Maryann made the sign for the door and picked up

her roll of tape, walking across the waiting room to the door.

"Here, let me get that," Amy said, as she met Maryann at the door and opened it.

"Thanks." Maryann pulled off a piece of tape and used it to attach the sheet of paper to the wood of the door. Then she turned around. Alex was at the door by now, too.

Alex looked at Amy. "Could you let Dr. Logan know I'm going to see the Fields? Just in case any of my patients go to him when they see I'm not here."

Amy nodded and then held out the Bible in her hand to both of them. "Timmy will want this."

Maryann noticed the yellowed paper peeking out from the pages, just as it had been when Timmy put it there.

"You don't really need to do that," Maryann said softly. "It's your map. We can keep it here if you want."

Amy smiled. "Timmy can give it back when he feels better. I think my great-great-grandfather would want me to do this."

Maryann nodded. "I'll see that he takes good care of it, then."

With that, she and Alex headed out.

"We'll take my Jeep," Alex said as they stepped off the porch.

Maryann nodded. She'd never ridden with Alex in his Jeep.

They walked quickly up the road until they reached the house where Alex lived. The house had once belonged to a single family, but it had been divided into apartments years ago. Maryann knew all about that house. Several people had already suggested she ask Alex to put in a good word for her with his landlord so she'd be in line to get his apartment when he left.

Maryann remembered to pay attention when they walked by the house. New white paint and green trim. It looked well maintained, and that was important in Alaska, as that meant things like the heating system were probably up-to-date, too. And the plumbing, which could be difficult when the ground was frozen.

"Nice curtains," Maryann said as Alex unlocked the passenger door of his Jeep.

He grunted in response as he opened the door, and stood there waiting for her.

Maryann climbed inside. The passenger seat was high because the whole vehicle set up off the road more than normal cars. She knew from what people said that the doctor's Jeep had a special four-wheel drive…something. He used it when he went to the Taiya village to preside over a health clinic.

"The road that goes to the Fields place is the one that follows the Dyea River through the valley," Alex said as he started the Jeep. "I hope you don't mind a few bumps. I'm worried about that boy. There's no way to get over that gravel road fast without bouncing a bit."

"Don't worry about me," Maryann said. "Drive as fast as you can."

Alex nodded as he backed his Jeep out onto the road.

"Do you mind if I pray?" Maryann asked.

He shrugged and she took that as permission, so she bowed her head right then. She could have prayed silently, but the Bible said that when two were gathered together in prayer everything was stronger.

"God," she began quietly, *"You have given Timmy every breath He has ever taken. We pray You will protect his body from the fever that is taking hold of him. Help us get to his home quickly, so we can help him. Be with us all today, Father. In Jesus' name. Amen."*

"Amen," Alex agreed softly as he kept his eyes on the road.

Maryann was surprised. "Amen? I thought you don't believe in prayer anymore."

"I don't really," Alex answered ruefully as he turned off the asphalt road onto one that was little more than a rutted path. Wild grass grew in clumps and threatened to overgrow the dirt tracks that led the way back to the base of the mountain. "It's just that the words sound so hopeful, I can't help but agree."

"Maybe you believe more than you think you do, then." She continued to look at him. This untamed country seemed to suit him. He had a half smile on his lips as he concentrated on the ruts in front of them.

"Well, for now, let's just say I don't mind other people praying."

They were both silent for a few minutes

"I meant to say happy birthday this morning," Maryann finally said, softly. "Since this is the day."

"Thank you," Alex said as he down-shifted gears to go up a small rise. "I appreciate it."

"I don't have a card," Maryann confessed. "I thought I'd go over to Harry's store during my lunch, and see if he has any."

"You don't need to get me one," Alex said. "Besides, neither one of us will get much time for lunch today."

Maryann decided not to press the point. She certainly didn't want him to think that he owed her any explanations about his life, just because he'd walked her home last night.

The Jeep went over a big bump, and she would have hit her head on the roof if she hadn't been wearing a seat belt.

"Is there homesteading out here?" Maryann asked, changing the subject. She knew that some of the more isolated areas in Alaska had been open to homesteaders until recently.

Alex shook his head. "Believe it or not, this isn't remote enough for that."

Maryann loved the wild nature of Alaska, but she had to admit, she wouldn't want to live out in the brush like this. Especially not when the bears woke from their winter hibernation and were hungry.

"The Fields place is just around this bend," Alex said. "I had to bring some medicine up here for Timmy one other time."

"Now, see? That's why you can't leave," Maryann said without thinking. "What other doctor would do that?"

Maryann wished she could call the words back the minute they left her mouth. "Not that I—I mean, I know you're leaving. It's your decision. Los Angeles must be a wonderful place to live."

"It's the pits," Alex said, sounding friendly enough. "At least the area around my parent's house is. It wasn't always that way, but they've lived there long enough for the stable homeowners to leave and landlords to buy the surrounding houses to rent out."

"Everything changes," Maryann murmured when he didn't say anything more. That was a comforting thought to her this morning. She needed to rein in her feelings about Alex; and she could, since even she could change.

"We're here," Alex announced as he pulled his Jeep to a stop.

A ramshackle house sprung up in front of her like a mirage. Different shades of siding covered the small square house in no discernible pattern. A mud-spattered white pickup of uncertain age was parked in front of the house. A bike with its front wheel off leaned against the corner of the house.

"They didn't hear us," Maryann said as she reached up to undo her seat belt buckle.

Alex rolled down his window. "Kids."

Maryann nodded. She could hear the screeching sounds. It didn't sound like anyone was injured, though—it was more like they were playing some game at the top of their lungs.

Alex opened his door and Maryann opened hers. He grabbed his medical bag and she took the Bible. The bite of the wind hit her in the face when she stepped out of the Jeep. She would have guessed that the vehicle kept very little of the wind away from its passengers, but she would have been mistaken. It was blowing fiercely out here.

They walked to the door of the house and knocked. Someone moved a curtain aside so they could look out the window. It was Timmy's father.

"I'm so glad it's you, Doctor," Mr. Fields said as he swung the door wide open.

The inside of the house was so hot it was suffocating. A couch covered with a pink Afghan was the main piece of furniture. The rest of the small room was filled with toys and children.

"I'm running out of ideas to try on Timmy, and he doesn't seem to be getting any better," the man said as he started heading down the hallway. "I tried to get the pickup going, but the battery is dead. He's having such a hard time breathing. I thought I'd take him to his mom, but she's at work. Then I was going to take him over to your place. I changed my mind after your call."

Mr. Fields opened the door to a small bedroom. A brown wool blanket was hanging over the only window and it blocked most of the sunshine from outside. Maryann could hear the labored breathing of Timmy, who was lying in the only bed in the room.

"Is he sensitive to light?" Alex asked as he stepped inside and walked toward the bed.

The room smelled of menthol and there was a blue jar of rubbing ointment on a metal nightstand, along with a couple of damp washcloths.

"He didn't complain about the light," Mr. Fields admitted. "I just thought it might be a problem. He was real sensitive to the light when he had measles a year ago."

"Take the blanket down then," Alex said as he set his medical bag on a straight-back chair near the bed. "Nurse Jenner and I will want to get a good look at Timmy."

"Do you have any ice?" Maryann turned to Mr. Fields

as he swept the blanket off the curtain rods. Light flooded the cluttered room.

Mr. Fields looked up at her and nodded. "I'll get you some."

Maryann stood by as Alex listened to Timmy's lungs through his stethoscope. The boy's eyes were closed and his face was flushed.

"You okay, Timmy?" Maryann whispered as she stepped closer. The boy didn't open his eyes to look at her. She didn't think he even heard her. He was such a lively boy ordinarily, that she knew he was very sick.

Alex turned to look up at her. "We need to get him to a hospital."

Maryann heard a gasp from the doorway, so she turned.

"We can't afford a hospital," Mr. Fields protested. He had a ragged dishtowel draped over one arm and a metal bowl filled with ice cubes in the other.

Maryann could tell by his eyes that he was frightened.

"Can't we just take him to your clinic?" Mr. Fields asked.

"I don't have the same equipment as the hospital," Alex replied calmly. "We don't have a choice."

Maryann was already gathering up some of the blankets on Timmy's bed. The first step to getting the boy to the hospital was to put him in the Jeep and drive him back to Treasure Creek. They'd need lots of blankets to keep him comfortable for that part of the ride. She was glad Alex was there to convince Mr. Fields his son would need to go to Juneau. That was the nearest hospital, and they had a good pulmonary department. She wasn't a doctor, but she could see how Timmy labored to breathe.

"He needs a hospital," Alex repeated. "It's important."

"Are you saying he might die?" Mr. Fields whispered hoarsely.

Alex snapped his medical bag shut and looked up at his patient's father. "I'm saying we can't take that chance."

Mr. Fields looked at Maryann imploringly. "I have to stay with my other children. Timmy said he liked you. He called you his angel. Don't let him die."

"We'll do all we can," Maryann assured him. "Dr. Havens is a very good doctor."

Mr. Fields nodded. "You still got that Bible?"

Maryann nodded as she put her hand on it. She had slipped it into her pocket earlier, so she could use her hands.

"Say a prayer over my Timmy," Mr. Fields said. "He likes the Twenty-third Psalm. Could you read it to him?"

Maryann nodded. "I will when he wakes up."

A slight moan came from the bed. The boy was starting to thrash around.

"And pray for that doctor of yours, too," Mr. Fields added quietly.

"I—" Maryann started to protest that he wasn't her doctor and then she stopped. Until the boy was doing better, she needed to put any of her personal feelings aside. She was a nurse. "Of course, I'll pray for everyone who takes care of Timmy."

She looked over at Alex. He was concentrating so

hard on listening to Timmy breathing, he hadn't even heard her conversation with Mr. Fields. She wondered how he would feel about her praying for him.

Chapter Six

Alex looked up from where he was crouched beside Timmy's bed. "Is there a phone?"

Maryann recognized the resolve in Alex's demeanor. He'd decided what needed to be done, and now he was just taking the steps. She could see why that kind of focus could be misinterpreted to be coldness. But that wasn't what it meant at all. He was merely determined to do everything in his power to help his patients.

"In the kitchen," Mr. Fields replied a little reluctantly. "By the refrigerator."

"Mind if I use it?" Alex stood and turned to the door.

"Feel free," Mr. Fields said, but Alex was already stepping out of the room.

Maryann watched him walk away.

"I hope it's not a long-distance call," Mr. Fields muttered when Alex was gone. Then he turned to Maryann. "I know how that sounds, but you've got to understand. A man like me—I don't have much. I want to take care of my family, but there's only so much I can do. I need help."

"I know, Mr. Fields," Maryann said as she stepped closer to pat his shoulder. She did feel sorry for the man. It's just that it was that kind of talk that had put them in this situation. "You might not want to worry the children, though. Timmy was trying to do just that—help you."

"Timmy?" the man stepped back in surprise. "How could he help? He's a kid."

"Maybe when this is all over, he'll tell you," Maryann said. "But for now, Timmy needs to be in the hospital. Dr. Havens wouldn't take him if it wasn't necessary."

Mr. Fields nodded. "I know. He's a good man."

Just then Alex came back into the room. "We're ready. Max O'Brian will fly us to Juneau." Alex looked at Mr. Fields. "He's not going to charge anything for the flight. He said he needs to fly there to pick up a passenger anyway, but we need to get back to Treasure Creek right away so we can go with him."

"Is there room for the missus?" Mr. Fields asked. "She'll want to go. And one of us has to stay with the other kids. But someone needs to be there with our Timmy."

Alex nodded. "Call her and tell her to meet us at Max's in twenty minutes. I'm afraid there's no time for her to drive out here and pack a suitcase."

"I'll call her," Mr. Fields said.

With that, Alex scooped Timmy up with half of his blankets. Maryann followed them out with the other half of the blankets in her arms. The wind hit her when she stepped out of the house. Surely, it was too early for winter weather, she thought to herself. It wasn't even October yet. She knew Fairbanks usually had snow this time of the year, but that wasn't true for Treasure Creek.

Maryann hurried to the Jeep so she could open the door for Alex. She shook out several blankets and laid them wide against the small backseat. Alex bent down and laid Timmy in the middle of the blankets and then wrapped the ends around him.

"Should I ride back there with him?" Maryann asked.

"If you don't mind," Alex said. "I think it's good if someone talks to him so he knows we're here."

Maryann lifted Timmy slightly and climbed into the seat so she could hold his head on her lap. She put her hand on his forehead. He was burning up with fever. She looked up at Alex, who was still standing in the open door. "I'm worried."

He nodded. "Me, too."

And then he shut the door.

When Alex started the Jeep, Maryann shifted herself so she would protect Timmy from the jarring movement caused by any of the bumps they might run into as they drove back to town. The Bible in her pocket pressed against the side of the Jeep. She'd squeezed into the back with Timmy, and there wasn't much room. She slipped a hand around and took the book out of her pocket. When she saw the yellowed edges of that old treasure map, she shook her head. No one was worried about that right now.

Holding the Bible reminded her of what she needed to do. She bowed her head and silently asked God to keep them in His hands. And then she began to quote one of the few sections of the Bible that she knew by heart. "Our Father, who are in Heaven, hallowed be thy name—"

Timmy moaned in her lap. She wasn't sure if he was trying to say that the prayer comforted him or distressed him. Maybe he thought it meant he was in danger of dying.

"It's all right," she murmured. "You're going to be just fine." Then she looked up and met Alex's eyes as he looked in the rearview mirror. "Dr. Havens is going to take really good care of you."

Alex stopped looking in the mirror and accelerated the Jeep slightly.

"We're almost to the asphalt road," he said.

Maryann nodded as she continued to rub Timmy's head.

Alex slowed down to take the turn by the creek. The water was still running, and anytime he drove by water, especially in the early morning hours, he knew to watch for animals. It would be a little late for them to be coming to drink today, but he didn't want to take any chances.

He knew Max would be ready to take off and that there was little time to spare. He was kicking himself for not calling Mr. Fields yesterday, after the clinic closed. If he had thought it through, he would have known something more than usual was wrong at the house because Mr. Fields had said he'd be back to start on the shelves, but then never appeared.

Alex figured that, if he had called, he could have talked to Timmy. Maybe if he'd talked to the boy, Timmy would have mentioned that map and he wouldn't have tried that fool stunt of trying to get sicker so his parents would bring him to the clinic.

Alex shook his head. He knew he wasn't responsible for missing things like that, but they always hit him hard anyway. Life seemed so out of control sometimes. He supposed he was still trying to find a way to make his peace with what he hadn't done when he was in that crosswalk with his brother so many years ago. He'd gone over that day so many times in his life, wondering what he could have done to change the events.

"We're almost there," Alex said as they neared Treasure Creek. In a mile or so, the road to the hangar where Max kept his floatplane would be off to his left. If the plane wasn't in the hangar, Max would have already brought it down to the dock where he loaded before takeoff. He hoped Mrs. Fields would already be around there somewhere. She worked at one of the hotels in town, so she'd be close enough to have arrived already if she got the message from her husband.

"I guess I haven't asked, but can you come with us?" Alex looked in the rearview mirror as he asked Maryann. "Max can probably fly you back when he meets his passenger for the return trip if you want, so you won't need to spend the night. I don't know how long Timmy will have to stay in the hospital."

Maryann nodded and swallowed. Then she met his eyes in the mirror.

"I've been wondering," she said hesitantly. "I know he needs to be in the hospital. But will they take him? Without insurance? I don't know how they do things up here, but in Spokane it would depend. It's not a heart attack or a gunshot wound."

"If you want to pray, that's what you need to pray for," Alex said, his mouth turning grim as his eyes met hers. "I don't know what they'll say. I just know he needs to be there."

Alex had thought Maryann would be pleased that he asked her to pray for something. He'd been sincere when he'd told her earlier that he had nothing against people praying. He had nothing against people howling at the moon either. He just didn't think either one of them changed the way things were. But he didn't see the smile he expected on Maryann's face. In fact her chin had gotten that slightly stubborn expression he'd noticed a time or two.

"Is there a problem?" he asked her.

"It's just that prayer works better if two people agree together on something," she said, her voice a little lofty. "I don't mind being one of the people, but I can't be both of them."

"Oh," he said. "Well, I can't help thinking someone else would do better at agreeing with you than I would."

The minute the words left his mouth, he realized they were wrong. "I mean, of course, I agree with you about many things. Especially getting Timmy into the hospital. But I don't need to pray to agree. Maybe Mrs. Fields will pray with you."

"That would work fine," Maryann said.

Now, why did he get the impression that she was trying to put him in his place?

"Some fine minds don't believe in prayer," he said in his defense.

"Yes, and those people are miserable fools," Maryann

snapped back. "I don't care how fine you think their minds are. They're missing out on peace. Eternal, everlasting peace—so there."

He could never tell her, but she was cute when she got worked up about something.

"There's Mrs. Fields now," Alex said as his attention was brought back to the gravel road heading to the hangar. A battered sedan had turned onto the lane ahead of him.

Alex drove up to the open door of the hangar. Max had already moved the small floatplane out of the hangar and down to the dock. He was standing on his small pier beside the pressurized metal ramp he had in place. Alex remembered when Max had first shown him that ramp. Because its small platform lowered automatically, he could carry heavier loads of freight on his plane. If they had been able to go back to the clinic, Max could have even gotten a gurney on his plane. That would make Timmy more comfortable, but they didn't have time.

Max had his hand outstretched by the time Alex stepped out of his Jeep.

"You made good time," the pilot said as they shook hands.

Alex nodded. "It'll just take me a minute to carry the boy on. His mother is coming down your road, and my nurse will be going with us."

Max smiled in delight. "Maryann?"

Alex glared at the man. A dark-haired Irishman with a wicked sense of humor, Max was one of Treasure Creek's most noted bachelors. "Yeah."

"Magnificent," Max said as he started to walk toward

the passenger side of the Jeep. "I'll just go give her a hand. Maryann's an Irish name, isn't it?"

"Not a chance," Alex said as he matched his steps to the pilot's. He wasn't sure whether he was referring to Maryann's name or the unspoken inference about the likelihood of her dating the Irishman. Alex knew the man's reputation, and it had only been confirmed when he stayed in Alex's house one time. "Besides, she's religious."

Alex figured that would give the man pause. From all he had heard, the Irishman liked women who were easy on the eye and had no opinions about right and wrong, especially none that would interfere with his plans.

Max stopped and looked at Alex. "My mom, bless her dear departed soul, always wanted me to marry a religious woman."

"You're not thinking of marriage!" Alex stopped in astonishment.

The Irishman shrugged and gave another grin.

"We've got a serious situation here," Alex said curtly. "Leave my nurse alone."

With that, he finished walking to the Jeep and opened the back door. Maryann had gathered the blankets around Timmy and had him ready to be carried. Alex lifted the boy up, not realizing until he was heading toward the plane that he had left Max to help Maryann.

He heard the man's laugh and Maryann's answering chuckle.

Alex turned to look over his shoulder. The man was holding Maryann's elbow like she was fine china and might slip on the perfectly dry dirt.

"Hey, Max," Alex called. "I'll need you to help with the ramp."

He waited until he saw the other man make a gallant bow over Maryann's hand and kiss it goodbye. That's all Alex needed—a Sir Galahad to pilot the plane. The look of pure delight on Maryann's face didn't sit too well with him either. She probably didn't realize that anyone could go around kissing women's hands. It took a real man to carry the blankets.

"I'm here," Max said as he ran up to Alex and gave him a pat on the back. "Let me be sure that ramp is lined up. Too bad we don't have the boy in a wheelchair. I could lift him right up to the plane door with this thing."

"Maybe we'll need it on the way home," Alex said. He looked down at Timmy. The boy's face was white and he was shivering.

Alex heard a car park behind him and the sounds of Maryann talking to Mrs. Fields. He didn't have time to turn and greet the other woman though. He needed to get Timmy on the plane and ready for takeoff.

Maryann had her arm around Mrs. Fields and was urging her toward the plane. The wind was continuing to blow, so they bent into it a little as they hurried. The other woman was scared so Maryann said the only thing she could. "Dr. Havens is a good doctor. Timmy will have the best care possible. And it's only forty-five— maybe fifty—minutes to Juneau. When we're in the air, we'll call the hospital and they'll have an ambulance waiting for us when we land. "

Mrs. Fields nodded. "We should have taken Timmy

back to the clinic yesterday, when he wanted us to. He must have known something was wrong inside."

Mrs. Fields stumbled slightly. The ground was rutted in one spot from the last rain.

"Careful." Maryann guided the other woman the rest of the way over the rough ground. Right then, there was no reason to bring up why Timmy wanted to go back to the clinic. There would be time enough to talk about the treasure map when Timmy was better.

Before anyone could say more, they were climbing inside the small plane. After being in the wind, the inside of the plane seemed very quiet. Alex had settled Timmy across two of the backseats and managed to use the seat belts to be sure he stayed safe.

"Someone will need to sit in the copilot seat," Max said as he boarded. He paused in the passenger area before turning to the small opening leading to the cockpit. "This Cessna only carries four back there—and the boy is taking two places already."

Maryann looked around. Alex clearly needed to stay with Timmy. And Mrs. Fields was looking at her son like she wouldn't easily let him out of her sight.

"I'll sit there," Maryann said, even though she wasn't sure she wanted the view out of the copilot's seat. Heights made her nervous and the windows allowed one to see so much more from the cockpit than from the back of the plane.

"Perfect," Max said from where he sat in the pilot seat. "Everyone get buckled in and we'll be out of here."

Maryann had heard about float planes, so she wasn't surprised when Max started the engines and then taxied across the water leading out to the ocean. She barely had time to grab the sides of her seat before she felt the small plane lifting up.

"You can relax now," Max said quietly from the pilot's seat.

Maryann forced herself to let go of the seat. "I'm just a little nervous."

"Maybe you should try praying," the pilot said.

Maryann looked at him to see if he was teasing her. She supposed the Bible in her pocket did stand out. "Maybe I should. Especially because…"

She craned her neck to look behind her. Timmy's face was white, but the boy managed to smile back at her.

She turned around and Max nodded. "My mother would be praying if she were here with us. She was a woman of deep faith." He paused. "I miss her."

"I'm sure you do," Maryann said, suddenly full of sympathy. She had misjudged the man, thinking he was trying to see how far he could get with her, when all the time he was only remembering his poor mother.

"Do you have any brothers or sisters?" Maryann asked. She had glimpsed out of the window and preferred to keep her eyes focused inside. The rush of the climb for altitude was behind them, but the ground still looked a long way down.

"I've a sister in Seattle," Max said. "She comes up to visit me now and again. Next time she does, I'll be sure and introduce the two of you. I think you'd hit it off."

"I'd like that," Maryann said as she turned to look behind her. The noise of the plane meant she couldn't hear Alex or Mrs. Fields in the back, but she could see them sitting there. Timmy had his eyes closed, but Mrs.

Fields managed to give a small wave to her, and Alex frowned at her for some reason. She smiled at them both.

When she straightened in her seat, Max had turned the plane slightly so they had a view of Mount McKinley in the distance. Wisps of clouds gathered around the snow-covered slopes of the mountain.

"It's beautiful," she breathed. The base of the mountain was covered with green pines, and the sun shining on the snow higher up made it look like the clouds and the mountain were merged into one. She had no idea there was so much verdant green in Alaska. From a distance, the trees looked like deep forest velvet, at least those at the lower regions of the mountains. Further up it was all shale and snow, with only slight traces of green here and there.

"Twenty thousand, three hundred and twenty feet above sea level," Max said, with pride in his voice. "They don't make them like Mount McKinley in the lower forty-eight. The natives call it The Big One."

Max turned the plane back to his original direction and continued, "I always like to pay my respects to The Big One when I set out on a flight. When you see her up in the sky like this, it's like she's there just for you. Someday I'm going to climb her. The north slope, I think."

"You'd remember it all your life if you did," Maryann said. Only now could she imagine the view from the top of the mountain. "It'd be something to tell your grandchildren."

Neither one of them spoke for a moment. The sound of the plane engine filled the air.

"So you're interested in having children, are you?" Max said with a sideways glance at her. "I mean, when the time comes and all?"

"Me?" Maryann hesitated. Not many men casually asked women that question. Then she realized he was probably asking because she was a nurse. "I love taking care of children. It's hard, of course, when they are as sick as Timmy."

She glanced back again. Mrs. Fields had her hand on Timmy's forehead, and Alex was leaning over him, too.

"Is he okay?" she asked loudly. The plane was noisy, but Alex managed to hear her anyway, and gave her a reassuring nod.

When she turned around they were no longer facing Mount McKinley. The view had changed to a series of smaller mountains and deep valleys. What wasn't covered with trees was gray shale.

"My sister says her kids scare years off her life," Max said with feeling. "But when a man gets as old as me— well, ask the doc back there, he's the same age—we start to think about getting married and raising a family."

"I wouldn't ask the doctor," Maryann said with a friendly smile. "He won't be marrying anytime soon. He's apparently got things to do before he even dates anyone."

"Really?" Max looked over at her in surprise. "He sure has me fooled, then."

"Well, it's true," Maryann said with more emphasis than was necessary. She needed to remember that herself. She more than anyone should know the pain that came from not facing reality in romance. Her parents had taught her that, if nothing else.

"Then he wouldn't mind if I ask you out sometime?" Max glanced over at her.

"Of course not," Maryann said just as firmly. It was none of Alex's business who she dated. Then she realized what she had said. "Not that—I mean, I haven't really had much time to go out since I've been in Treasure Creek."

"I see you going to church," Max said, his eyes straight ahead this time.

"Well, yes."

"A man like me doesn't always know what to do on a Sunday morning. Lately I've gone fishing early, and sometimes I sit in front of the General Store while the Olson twins dig worms for me out of their mother's rose garden. I've seen you walk out of Lizbet's in that pink dress you wear. It reminds me of—"

Maryann interrupted with a quick grin. "I know, it reminds you of your mother."

Max gave a rueful chuckle. "If I was to come to church some Sunday, would you let me sit with you? It's hard to sit down alone in a place like that."

Maryann nodded. "Everyone is welcome in church."

She thought for a moment and then added, "In fact, you can come Thursday night and sing carols with us. Amy is going to start us practicing for the Christmas pageant. You'll want to be part of that."

"Ah, the Christmas pageant. I might just do that. It's been a long time since I've used my fine Irish voice for singing. The ladies always comment on how they like that."

Max must have been content with that, she thought, because they spent the rest of the trip in silence. She gradually relaxed enough that she could lean forward so she could see more of the scenery as they passed over the mountainous area.

Maryann saw the airport at Juneau before she expected.

"I want to thank you for bringing us here," Maryann said. It seemed as though Timmy had done fine on the short flight. At least, no one had said anything, except to ask Max midflight to call for an ambulance to meet them.

"I was coming this way anyway." Max kept his attention on his instrument panel. "I have a passenger that needs to be picked up. The man said he's planning to surprise his brother."

"Oh," Maryann said, thinking maybe...and then dismissing her thought. "Did he say who?"

"The brother?" Max looked up briefly. "No, I didn't ask."

"What about the man who's coming? Did you get his name," Maryann persisted, but it was too late. Max had gotten his call back from the control tower and he was taking the plane down lower. The noise of the engines increased. She expected him to head for the runways by the low, flat terminal building, but instead he was aiming for the wooden structures along the edge of the ocean.

"It's the dock for floatplanes," Max said.

She gripped the edge of the seat again. This time

she remembered to pray at the same time, though. She glanced behind her to see that everyone was ready to land. Then she began to recite the Twenty-third Psalm. She was still reciting it, her lips moving almost silently, when Max shut the engines off. The sudden drop in noise made her look up.

"Smooth as rocking a baby to sleep," Max said proudly. "Bet you didn't even feel the landing. Not on water like this."

"It *was* smooth," Maryann agreed.

"Thank you," Max said with a grin. "They'll be out with some kind of a ramp for us any minute now. They know we have a special circumstance, so they'll bring the best they have."

The airport at Juneau was backed by green mountains, most of them with splotches of snow near their tops. Other than that, the buildings were wood frame and looked a lot like those in Treasure Creek, except for the fact that there were more onion roofs.

Suddenly, Maryann heard a siren approaching.

"That'll be the ambulance we called," Max said as he turned around to look into the back. "How's everyone doing back there?"

No one had a chance to answer him, because the airport crew was there with the ramp and so was the ambulance. It didn't seem possible that more people could fit in the plane, but a couple of the paramedics managed to squeeze inside so they could decide how to best carry Timmy out to the ambulance.

Maryann was permitted to ride in the back of the ambulance with Alex and one of the paramedics. Mrs. Fields rode in the front with the driver. The first thing the paramedics did was to wrap the blankets back around Timmy. Maryann couldn't get a good look at the boy, not with the paramedic, and then Alex, tending him so closely.

She knew he couldn't be in better hands, though. Alex might be The Ice Man in some ways, but he didn't give up on his patients. He'd pull Timmy through with the sheer force of his determination. He might be leaving Alaska in a few weeks, but he would do his duty by everyone until then. She had no doubt of that. Even as she watched Alex, he lifted his head and looked straight at her. She could see in his eyes that he was very worried. So she smiled at him.

In a moment, his whole face lightened and he nodded back. They really were a good team, Maryann told herself. She only wished that realization made her happy.

Chapter Seven

Once at the hospital, Maryann helped Mrs. Fields get Timmy registered, so he could be transferred to a regular room. Alex had been obviously reluctant for them to go, but he couldn't leave Timmy in the curtained-off cot where he was lying, and a nurse had just come over to explain that someone needed to fill out paperwork.

"So he's in emergency now?" the young woman behind the counter asked as she frowned at a computer screen. She didn't look more than twenty years old. "I don't see him listed here."

Maryann and Timmy's mother were standing side-by-side at the counter. Maryann had her nurse's uniform on, and she had been hoping it would help ease things along. So far the clerk had barely looked at it.

"We just brought him in," Maryann said in her most professional voice when Mrs. Fields didn't speak. "Timothy Fields. Pediatric. He came in by ambulance with Dr. Havens from Treasure Creek about twenty minutes ago. The boy doesn't have a room yet."

The clerk looked up. She wore gold-framed glasses and had her hair pulled back in a French braid of some sort. Her eyelashes sparkled. "Do you know which of our doctors here in the hospital is handling him?"

"I could go back and ask. The boy's got pneumonia and some complications—"

"That would be Doctor Stuart, then," the clerk said as she looked back at the computer screen and punched in some letters. "Ah, here I see it. Now, your question is?"

"We want to see about getting my son set up with a room in the hospital," Mrs. Fields said softly. She had her clasped hands resting on top of the counter. Maryann figured she was the only one who noticed how white the woman's knuckles were when she spoke. "He's in the emergency room, but—"

"It says here he's stabilizing," the clerk said as she read the computer screen. "Dr. Stuart indicated it's not required that he stay past the time in the emergency room."

"But that's not right," Maryann gasped. "Alex—I mean, Dr. Havens—said Timmy needs to be monitored closely. He's sick and—"

The clerk looked up from her computer. "Is Dr. Havens on staff here?"

"No, I don't think so," Maryann said. "But—"

"Of course, you can choose to admit the boy," the woman said with a smile. "Perhaps your insurance company will agree with your doctor and authorize him to stay."

Maryann's heart sank as she exchanged a glance with Timmy's mother.

"I'm afraid we don't have any insurance right now,"

Mrs. Fields admitted quietly. Maryann watched as she pressed her hands together more tightly.

"We can make payments, though." She took a deep breath and continued. "I have some pay stubs with me. You can deduct the payments if you want from my checks. And then we have our Permanent Fund checks coming. My husband and I are good for the money. We just need some time."

The clerk let Timmy's mother finish before answering. "I'm truly sorry. If you don't have insurance, we need prepayment of at least fifty percent of the expected total. In cash or credit card. That's hospital policy for optional admissions."

No one spoke for a moment.

"How much would that be?" Maryann finally asked the young woman. "The amount you would need for the prepayment? For this kind of illness?"

The clerk studied her computer screen before she looked up and spoke. "I'd guess we'd need eight to ten thousand. That covers part of the room, the tests, some of the doctor charges. If you don't have the cash, we do take a credit card."

Maryann put her hand on the middle of Mrs. Fields's back. She was worried the woman might faint. The young clerk hadn't sounded unkind, but there was no way Mrs. Fields had that kind of money. Not even tucked away in a bank account someplace. With her husband out of work and four little children, the household probably couldn't even pay all its regular bills.

Mrs. Fields shook her head, biting her lower lip at the same time. She was on the verge of tears. "What do we do? Is there someone we can talk to? Something we can sign? I suppose we could sign over the title to our car, but it's ten years old, so I don't know that it would do any good. And the pickup is practically worthless. We'll give you whatever you want, though. He's just a little boy."

The clerk concentrated on the computer screen, even though Maryann doubted there was anything new to be seen. Finally she said, "I'll get my supervisor. I don't think there's anything she can do, but, perhaps she can speak with Dr. Stuart. If he says it's necessary for Timmy to stay we have to admit him."

"Yes," Maryann said, nodding. Surely there had to be some provision for people without money. "We'll talk to her."

The young woman dialed a number on her telephone and spoke quietly into the mouthpiece. When she hung up the phone, she looked up and said. "It'll be a couple of minutes. Mrs. Haynes is in a meeting, but it's almost finished. You can wait over there."

The clerk gestured to a row of padded chairs on the far wall. Each chair was connected to the other by a black metal bar, but the chairs themselves looked comfortable. Maryann guided Mrs. Fields to where they could sit down.

"I'm sure they have many situations like this," Maryann said firmly when they had both seated themselves on the gray vinyl chairs. A framed print of Mount McKinley hung on the wall behind their chairs, a bald eagle flying across the corner of the picture. "This Mrs. Haynes will know what to do."

Mrs. Fields nodded. "You're right. Other people must be in our situation. I don't even know this Dr. Stuart.

It shouldn't be his opinion that prevents Timmy from staying. What if he's wrong?"

Maryann put her hand over the other woman's and leaned closer. "The important thing is that Timmy is here now. Maybe Dr. Stuart hadn't had a chance to examine him yet."

It was the only hope Maryann could offer, although she wondered how the hospital could let the man make that kind of decision without looking at the patient. If the doctor had gone to see Timmy, though, Alex would have convinced him the boy needed to be admitted. She had seen him stand up for his patients before, and he was fearless. If he thought Timmy needed to be in a room in this hospital, he would make it happen if he had to take it up with the hospital board of directors.

She wished Alex was here with her now; he'd know what to do.

"I'm going to get Dr. Havens," Maryann said suddenly to Mrs. Fields as she stood. "I'll be right back."

Maryann quickly followed the blue line back to the emergency room and spoke briefly with the nurse at the admitting desk there. They each remembered the other from when Timmy had been brought in, so Maryann was on her way in no time.

She checked the room numbers until she found the one the nurse had given her. There were several curtained-off areas in the room, but Timmy at least had a proper hospital bed. She hesitated at the door. Timmy was in the middle bed. Alex was standing at the foot of the boy's bed and he was talking in a low voice with another doctor. Alex had a chart in his hand that could only belong to Timmy.

"Excuse me," Maryann said as she walked to where she could see Timmy. The boy was lying so still in his bed that she glanced over at the monitor to reassure herself that he was breathing. She knew the little red lights would be flashing and a beep would be sounding if anything was wrong.

Alex turned and she felt a shiver of awareness go down her body. He was rumpled; his shirt collar was crooked and he'd been running his fingers through his hair. The lines in his face were more pronounced than she'd ever noticed before. His eye sockets were deeper and his jaw less relaxed. But the intensity on his face took her breath away. He might not be the most handsome man in the world right now, but he was her hero. He was already fighting for Timmy, she could see it in the steel of his eyes.

Alex said something to the other doctor before he walked back to the doorway with her.

"How's his mother doing?" Alex asked when he got close. He leaned against the doorjamb slightly and his back gave them some privacy from the doctor in the room. He hunched a little forward, as though he were creating a space for just the two of them. She had to mentally pull herself away. She couldn't take gestures like that personally, not when he was going away so soon.

"We're having a bit of trouble admitting Timmy," Maryann said, her voice low. She wasn't looking up at Alex. "Dr. Stuart says he doesn't need to stay—that he's stabilized. I don't even know this Dr. Stuart. What are we going to do?"

Then she felt Alex's fingers on her chin, tilting her head up.

"I know you're worried," he said softly, looking into her eyes. "I'm sorry I wasn't out there with you. We'll find a way. Trust me. I'm talking to Dr. Stuart now."

Maryann could only stare at him. She knew he was treating her like a patient, using that calm, steady "trust me" voice. But at this point, she almost didn't care.

"I was hoping you were," she finally said, not bothering to hide her relief. "I figure he just hasn't examined Timmy yet."

"He's seeing him," Alex said with a tight smile. "We just have a difference of opinion."

Maryann smiled. "Well, you'll just change his mind then."

Alex watched the stress drain out of Maryann's face. He was amazed and humbled that she had so much confidence in him, especially when he didn't know how he was going to get Timmy admitted as a regular patient here. Dr. Stuart had just been saying that the hospital was taking a hard line these days on noninsurance admissions that were discretionary. They had too many old, outstanding bills that would never be paid. It would be a fight to get Timmy admitted if Dr. Stuart didn't say it was absolutely necessary.

"I'll come talk to you when I get a chance," Alex said, giving Maryann his best shot at a smile. She really was a trouper. She hadn't even berated him for his poor behavior last night, and he wasn't sure when he'd get a chance to explain himself to her—or to sit down and figure out his reaction for himself. "I'll be right out."

"Just follow the blue line," Maryann said as she turned to leave. "Mrs. Fields and I will be waiting in admissions."

He watched her as she walked away.

"Friend of the family?" Dr. Stuart asked when Alex walked back.

"My nurse," he answered, wondering if he should add something more. That certainly wasn't an adequate description, but he doubted Dr. Stuart wanted to know the confusion he felt around Maryann these days. "Now, where were we."

"You were showing me that X-ray."

Fifteen minutes later, Dr. Stuart was paged and said he had to leave to see another patient. Alex suspected Dr. Stuart knew he was walking a thin line, but he was unwilling to authorize hospital admittance for Timmy. His parting shot to Alex had been, "If you're so sure the boy needs to stay, you find the money to make it happen."

Alex walked back to Timmy's bed. A nurse had just taken the boy's vital signs and he did seem better. Alex knew the improvement gave false hope, though. He'd treated Timmy through enough illnesses to know how the boy handled sickness. He'd fight it off and look as if he was winning, but then he'd crash.

"How's it going?" Alex asked, bending down.

The boy looked up at him and made the effort to smile. "When can I go home?"

If they took Timmy to Treasure Creek, they might not have enough time to get him back to the hospital when he became worse. Alex refused to risk it.

"Not until you're well," Alex promised him.

With that, Alex left and started walking down the hallway to the office, his eyes on that blue line as he thought about what he'd say to the woman who handled the admissions.

"Excuse me," a man's voice said.

Alex looked up from his thoughts. An orderly was standing there with an empty gurney.

"Oh, I'm sorry," Alex said as he stepped to the side of the hallway. He'd blocked the man's way. He should know better. The corridors of a hospital were busier than some major freeways at rush hour. He'd forgotten how fast-paced things were. Down in Los Angeles, it would be even more frantic. He hadn't realized how accustomed he'd become to the pace in Treasure Creek, where he had time to stop and think about something that wasn't related to his patients. He even regularly took a short lunch break. Of course, there had been more fast-paced moments his first year there, but now he was able to do so much to prevent problems with his patients that his days usually went like clockwork.

He looked around. The astringent smell was all too familiar. As was the flash of the nurse-call buttons over the patients doors. Then there was the sound of the metal cart rolling down the hall, signaling lunch for the patients. Adrenaline used to course through him when he was in a hospital as an intern. He had charged into medicine like he could bend the outcomes for the sick to his will. He knew better now, although he still, all too often, felt like he was the only advocate some of his smallest patients had.

Alex straightened his shoulders. Ironically, if

Timmy was a gunshot or stabbing victim, he stood a better chance of getting a room without qualifying financially.

He followed the blue line to admissions, taking long strides. He was going to justify Maryann's faith in him. He'd find a way to pull this off.

He turned the corner into the admissions area and saw a trim, dark-haired woman in a tailored suit walking toward Maryann and Mrs. Fields. She must be the admissions supervisor. She looked professional, right down to the high heels on her feet.

Alex took a moment to smooth back his hair and straighten his shirt collar. He wished he'd worn his oxfords instead of his sports shoes, but he'd hardly taken his dress shoes out of the closet since he'd been in Alaska.

"Dr. Havens," Maryann greeted him formally as he approached them. "Come meet Mrs. Haynes."

"Pleased to meet you," Alex said as he held his hand out to the woman. "You have a fine hospital. Worked here long?"

He guessed she'd come to Alaska recently, because of her heels, but he hoped not. Someone who had heard enough of the hardship stories around here might have more compassion.

She took his hand and inclined her head to him. "Not long. I used to work in Los Angeles. The Huntington Hospital."

Alex's heart sank, but he didn't stop to examine why. An expensive hospital in a well-to-do area had nothing in common with these small towns in Alaska that struggled to survive.

"I've heard good things about the place," Alex said. And he had.

"Thank you, Doctor. I was very proud to work there. Now, I understand you have a patient you want to admit." She paused and raised an eyebrow. "Without insurance."

Alex wondered if his clothes were more rumpled than he thought.

"I was hoping we could talk about that, yes," he said and forced himself to give a smile as close as possible to the one Max would be dishing out.

Mrs. Haynes did seem to relax more. "You must understand, we only accept true emergencies without insurance or a cash deposit. Perhaps the family could qualify for a loan from a local bank?"

Alex glanced down and saw the color drain from Mrs. Fields's face. He doubted there was much hope of a bank loan in the family's future.

"Mrs. Fields?" he asked gently.

She shook her head.

"I don't suppose the boy has any Native American heritage?" Mrs. Haynes asked. "We do have funds to accommodate those with enough Native American blood to qualify for them. I don't know the exact tribes off the top of my head, but I know it's generally one-sixteenth that they're looking for."

He saw Mrs. Fields start to wring her hands. She shook her head when he glanced over at her.

"I'm afraid not. But certainly, there has to be some grant money or something," Alex said. This was a hospital. They were supposed to heal people.

"I'm sorry," Mrs. Haynes said. She gave one of those

business smiles. "He does have the eight hours in the emergency room. Our Dr. Stuart feels the boy will be well enough to go home after that."

Alex started to protest that eight hours wasn't enough, when he looked down at Timmy's mother. She was practically in tears.

He turned to Maryann. "Maybe you could take Mrs. Fields to the cafeteria and get her some soup of something. It's been a long time since any of us had breakfast."

Maryann nodded and stood. She looked tired, too.

"I'll stay and figure this out," Alex said once both women were standing. He'd already realized that there was only one way to end this standoff with the hospital, and he didn't want either of the women to be around to witness his actions.

"Perhaps we can go to your office," Alex said when he was alone with Mrs. Haynes.

They walked down a tiled hallway and stopped at an office with a window overlooking the front lawn of the building. Her office was, of course, depressingly neat. Maybe she hadn't been there long enough to have a full in-box. She did have a rather large fern on her filing cabinet though, which encouraged him since they were hard to grow and that meant she must be giving it good care.

"Please, be seated." Mrs. Haynes gestured to the office chair sitting in front of her desk as she sat. "I find that these discussions about money always make me wish I'd taken time to eat a better breakfast before leaving for work."

Alex chuckled politely.

"You're sure the parents don't have some stock certificates their great-grandfather left them?" she asked when they were both seated. "Maybe a fishing boat they can sell?"

Alex shook his head. "I've been to their place several times over the past few years. They are who they appear to be. Hardworking for the most part, but down on their luck. Four kids, a couple of vehicles that barely run. Mrs. Fields works at one of the hotels in town, cleaning rooms. Even with tips, she doesn't make enough to keep the family in food and clothes. At least not all year round. She probably made enough to feed them this summer, but now that tourist season is coming to a close, she won't be seeing the same tips and will probably have her hours cut."

Alex felt discouraged listing the family's problems.

Mrs. Haynes was thoughtful for a moment. Then she asked, "You're sure they don't have any Native American blood? Maybe a great-grandfather or something?"

Alex shook his head. "The couple said once that all four of their parents were from Europe. They met in Seattle and moved up here ten years ago."

"Well, then…"

Neither one of them moved.

"If Timmy can only stay the eight-hour max—and we take him out of the emergency room after that—can we readmit him for another eight?" Alex asked finally.

Mrs. Haynes smiled but shook her head. "Afraid not. Rules."

Alex took a deep breath. There was no other way. Not that he could see. "Could you give me a total of what is needed for the deposit?"

She nodded and turned to the computer that was at the side of her desk.

Alex closed his eyes. He told himself he wasn't praying, he was thinking. If God happened to listen in, Alex had no problem with that. He could use some good advice.

He didn't know how to stretch what he had, not with all he needed to do. He'd saved every penny he'd made giving those tours for Alaska's Treasures over the three years he'd been up here. That included every tip he'd been given, even the small ones. He received enough in his monthly salary to pay for his needs and his brother's attendant. The total in his savings account was $20,456.22. He needed twenty thousand for the down payment on the construction costs. In order for the bank to give him a loan for the rest. The bank wouldn't go any lower than that. He'd asked the last time he was down in Los Angeles.

Alex couldn't stand by and do nothing. He hadn't been able to act to save his brother all those years ago, but he could do something now. He didn't know when he'd be able to replace the money from his savings, but he'd be alive to do it. Which was more than Timmy might be.

Mrs. Haynes cleared her throat. Alex opened his eyes and looked up.

"We'd need eight thousand six hundred dollars up front," the woman said, and lifted a hand to stall any protests. "That's already giving him every discount I can and some I shouldn't."

Alex nodded. "Do you take American Express?"

He pulled his card out, grateful that his occupation qualified him for their gold.

Mrs. Haynes nodded uncertainly as she eyed the card. "Is that from your clinic? Or The City of Treasure Creek?"

He shook his head. "No, it's my personal card." He held it up. "Alex Havens."

The woman leaned across her desk and took the card. "I see. I assume they'll pay you back then."

Alex grunted. The woman could make any assumptions she wanted. He was under no such expectations, however. The Fields family would never be able to pay him back. They just didn't make enough. He'd just have to find a way to replace the money himself.

He smiled. Maybe he'd find another treasure map like the one Amy had. More than one of those old prospectors must have hid their gold. None of them trusted the banks and few of them had much faith in their friends, so a hole in the ground probably looked pretty good to them when they pondered where to put their treasure.

"I'll take this up to the front desk and have them run it for you," Mrs. Haynes said as she stood and pointed. "Help yourself to some chocolates in the bookcase over there."

Alex turned his head to look where she indicated. Sure enough, there was a cut-glass dish filled with foil-wrapped candy. He stood up and walked over to them. He recognized the brand name on the foil; these were quality sweets.

He put two in his pocket. Maybe later he could share one with Maryann. That is—he thought for a moment—he assumed she wasn't just talking to him as Dr. Havens. He hoped she was still talking to him when he was only Alex.

He paused for a second and then put another candy in his pocket. It never hurt to have some extra persuasion.

Chapter Eight

Looking through the hospital window, Maryann could see that the sky outside had started to turn dark. She was sitting quietly in a chair next to the window in Timmy's room. The boy was sleeping and breathing more evenly than he had been since he arrived. The nurses and doctors had been hovering over him for the past hour and had just left a while ago. She did not know how Dr. Havens had performed the miracle of getting the hospital to admit Timmy as a regular patient, but she was grateful that he had.

She no sooner thought of the man than he silently walked into the room. He'd been working with the other doctors and nurses earlier, while she'd been sitting with Mrs. Fields. Ordinarily, she'd want to be closer to the action, but she knew how lonely it could get for someone in those big hospital waiting rooms, and Mrs. Fields did not look strong.

"Did Max pick her up?" Maryann whispered softly so she wouldn't disturb Timmy. Alex had taken Mrs. Fields down to the hospital entrance so she could join Max in the cab when he came by. She was flying back to Treasure Creek with him tonight, and then coming back tomorrow morning, when the pilot made another trip down to Juneau.

Alex nodded as he pulled a metal folding chair closer to where she sat. Quietly, he said, "I was afraid she wouldn't sleep if she stayed here. And she already looked ready to collapse."

Maryann nodded and kept her voice low. "She was probably worried about what to tell the other children, too. Not to mention her husband."

She scooted her chair closer to the window so Alex's would fit in better.

When he put his chair down, she said, "That was nice of Max to have his cab come by and get Mrs. Fields. I don't think she's ever taken a cab."

"He's a prince, all right," Alex muttered as he sat down in the chair. He reached into his pocket and pulled out a foil-wrapped piece of candy. "Want one?"

"Sure." Maryann took the candy from his open hand. "This didn't come from the vending machine, did it? I didn't see it there."

Alex shook his head in disgust. "There's nothing in that machine that even resembles chocolate. Which is shortsighted, if you ask me. No one wants vitamin drinks when they're waiting around here."

Maryann unwrapped the candy and put it in her mouth.

"Humm," she said as she closed her eyes. "That's delicious."

"Does that make me a prince, too, then?" Alex whispered, his voice low and teasing.

Maryann opened her eyes and shook her head. She

was glad to see he was smiling, instead of looking as grim as he'd been.

"You're not a prince," she informed him quietly. "You're the king."

Alex raised his eyebrow. "You mean the grand pooh-bah?"

She nodded her head and licked the last of the chocolate off her lips. "That's exactly who I mean. Anyone who gives out chocolate like that deserves a good title."

Alex felt his whole body go on alert. His heart was tottering on some brink, and he couldn't afford for it to go tumbling over, no matter how pink her cheeks got when she struggled not to laugh. He'd just postponed the date at which he would have that clinic in Los Angeles up and operating. He wouldn't be a free man until he'd put the money back into his savings account and managed to build that clinic. It could take years, and he couldn't ask someone to wait for him that long— certainly not someone as full of life as Maryann.

"Ever been to Southern California?" he heard his voice ask, even though his head was wondering what he was doing. "You know—Hollywood, surfers, the beach?"

"Do you like the beach?" she asked with a new light in her eyes.

"I can handle the beach," he answered, thinking he'd have to get that old umbrella out of his parents' garage. It was probably falling apart by now, but it might look charming. He hoped she didn't expect him to surf. "Malibu or Santa Monica are both great."

She nodded. "One of the fancy women wanted to

know if you liked the beach. I think she might be the best one of the bunch. Maybe I should introduce you."

"Maybe you should," he said, just to show that her words didn't sting. "At least she might not prefer Irish men to me."

Maryann looked up at him in surprise and asked, "What do you mean?"

Then she suddenly sat up straighter. "Max said you were ready to start dating someone. I told him he was wrong and that you weren't, because you sure hadn't seemed—"

Maryann stopped and closed her mouth tight. Then she crossed her arms.

Alex couldn't tell whether to give her a hug or some space, so he reached into his pocket again. "Another chocolate?"

At least that made her look at him.

"I didn't quite realize you were asking me if *I* liked the beach," she finally admitted. "I don't really know, I've never been in a beach community. I know we're close to the ocean here, but no one can really claim it's part of a beach area. People seem to refer to it mostly as 'the coast.' And with the water being so cold, no one goes swimming, even in the summer. And no one ever suns themselves. I mean it's hard to think of it as the beach and—"

Her voice was starting to break up, so he lifted the chocolate higher in his hand.

"I think the green wrapper means it's mint," he whispered. Her face flushed and he wasn't sure quite what that meant. He reached over and brushed her cheek with the back of his hand. He still held the chocolate. "Warm enough in here?"

The light was dim and the shadows hid her eyes. She was silent for a moment and then she nodded. "It's fine. I was just a little confused," she said, and he held his breath. Maybe she was feeling some of the stirring he felt. "The other candy was mint, too, and it was a blue wrapper."

"Well, I guess it's not a perfect system, then," he said. Which had to be the understatement of the year. He was down two pieces of chocolate, and he still hadn't figured out whether it would be okay to ask her out.

"I could do some per diem work when I get back to L.A.," he said, thinking it couldn't take that long to earn another seventeen thousand. Maybe he was only putting himself behind six months or so.

"Any hospital would be fortunate to have you," she said. But he noticed her shoulders had stiffened as she sat there. And she wasn't looking at him now. He wasn't talking work with her—he was talking their future. But he could see where she wouldn't understand that.

He felt a catch in his throat. The moment was going to pass him by.

"So, do you want to go to the beach with me sometime?" he asked, his voice coming out a little hoarse and raspy. He resisted the urge to clear his throat.

"Around here?" she asked, her eyebrow rising in astonishment.

He realized he couldn't very well invite her to Los Angeles; he wasn't even there himself. "Sure. It'd be fun."

"Okay," she said, and then swallowed. "But we'd have to go to church first."

"Why?"

"That way, we'd be friends."

"But we're friends now, I hope. I—" And then it hit him. "Max already invited you to go to the beach with him, didn't he?"

Alex felt his jaw tense. That would be just like his pilot friend. He'd lure a woman down to that dock of his and put a candle on a blanket and spin her some yarn about it being the beach. Then he'd snuggle with her until she didn't care if they were sitting on some sand or an iceberg.

Maryann shook her head. "No, he asked if he could come to church with me."

Of course, Alex thought to himself, the man was more devious than even he had given him credit for. The beach was nothing compared to sitting in a pew with a woman like Maryann. "*I'm* free this Sunday."

"Don't forget Thursday, when we rehearse for the pageant," Maryann said with a tiny smile on her lips.

"I'll be there on Thursday, and on Sunday as well," Alex said decisively.

"Really?" She seemed surprised.

"And Sunday dinner afterwards," he said firmly.

Maryann nodded. "That would be nice."

There was a slight moan from the hospital bed and Alex went over and put his hand on Timmy's forehead. The boy was hooked up to the best machines in the hospital, Alex thought to himself, and it still seemed natural to read his temperature by touching his forehead. He hadn't always been that kind of a doctor. He'd learned a lot by tending to the children of Treasure Creek. It wasn't always about the exact number of the temperature. Sometimes people just wanted to feel someone's hand on their head when they were sick.

Alex turned to look at Maryann. "He's fine. I'd like to eat dinner together, but I think one of us should be here in case he wakes up. We'll be here all night. So if you want to take the first meal shift, I'll go eat when you come back."

Maryann stood and reached in her pocket. She pulled out that Bible she'd been carrying around. "If he wakes up, could you read him the Twenty-third Psalm. I told his father I would and—"

Alex swallowed. "Sure. I could do that."

"I've marked the place with the blue candy wrapper," she said as she handed him the white Bible. "The print's kind of small, so you'll have to sit in the light when you read it."

Alex smiled. He'd already promised to go to church with her and to the rehearsal for the Christmas pageant. He should have known she'd have him reading a psalm or two next.

"Have a nice dinner," he said as she left the room.

Maryann decided she needed to do something before she went to the hospital cafeteria. She needed to call her cousin, so she went down to the hospital entrance and walked outside to use her cell phone. The night was early, but the temperature had dropped significantly when the sun went down. She huddled between the glass doors to the hospital and a side column.

"Karenna?" she asked when someone answered on the other end of the phone.

"How are you? Amy dropped by to tell me you had flown to Juneau with Timmy Fields. That poor kid. Is he okay?" Karenna asked in a rush.

"Thankfully, yes," Maryann said. "Dr. Havens moved heaven and earth to get him admitted, so he has a room and his breathing is better. Everyone is encouraged. They think another day or two will get him well enough that he can go home."

"Oh, good," her cousin said.

"I'm staying with him tonight though," Maryann added. "Dr. Havens is here, too, and..."

She was suddenly conscious of the heavy silence on the other end of the phone. By now, her cousin should be trying to talk over her.

"Karenna?"

"You're staying there with The Ice Man?" her cousin asked. She didn't sound very pleased. "He should have let you come home. Most employers don't require their workers to stay all night, especially when he's there to handle it."

"I thought you wanted me to get to know him?" Maryann countered. "Didn't you sit there the other night in the diner and say I needed to get to know The Ice Man before I judged him?"

"Well, yes," Karenna admitted. "But I didn't mean you should spend the night with him."

"We're in the hospital with hundreds of other people," Maryann protested.

"Oh, I didn't mean I was worried in that way. I know you. Besides, your doctor would never—"

"He asked me out," Maryann interrupted. She might be stretching that a little, but it felt good to say it to her cousin, because—well, just because her cousin shouldn't be making assumptions.

The phone was silent for several seconds.

"Really?" Karenna finally asked. "He asked you out? Like on a date?"

"Yes, he did," Maryann said a little smugly. "He's coming to church with me and then he invited me to dinner. And then sometime, we're going to the beach."

"That's very nice," Karenna said, her voice sounding cautious. "But did he say it was a date?"

"It was implied."

"Because I'm wondering why he'd ask you out now, when he's leaving in a few weeks. Of course, it's still good. Don't get me wrong, but—"

"You think he's just being nice, don't you?" Maryann said. That thought had occurred to her, too. She hadn't really believed it, but maybe that's the way it was.

"No, not that—" Karenna was quiet for so long Maryann wondered if they'd been disconnected. And then she spoke. "It's just that Gage told me the guys had given your doctor a hard time at Lizbet's during his birthday dinner. I mean, at first, because of the fancy women. And then they noticed he seemed to be, well, putting his arm around you and everything, and they thought— well, they hoped it wasn't just—you know how guys are when they're being teased. Like their manhood is called into question. Gage thought they might have given him too hard a time and he was trying to prove something to them."

"Oh," Maryann said. Gage did have a point. The doctor had certainly acted different after that dinner than he had before it. Usually, she picked up on those kinds of things. And she was sure she would have figured it out eventually, if anything like that was happening. "Well, it probably won't come to anything anyway. He'll probably call to say he's sick on Sunday morning. Or tired. He could certainly claim to be exhausted. I would understand that, after the last few days."

"I could have Gage talk to him if you want," Karenna offered.

"Please, no," Maryann said. "That would be awkward. Remember, I have to work with the man for another…" She thought a moment. "Two and a half more weeks."

"But if you want to date someone," Karenna said, "I'm sure Gage can find someone for you. There are lots of single men around here."

"No, no. I wanted to get settled here before I started to date," Maryann said. "I still haven't unpacked all my boxes."

"That's smart," Karenna said. "You make sure the doctor doesn't work you too hard, either."

"I'm not working at all right now," Maryann said. "I'm on my way to the cafeteria to get something to eat."

"Be sure and stay away from the mashed potatoes," her cousin advised. "They're always instant. And the vegetables are usually overcooked."

"I'm sure I'll find something worth eating," Maryann said. Now that her cousin had ruined her fantasy of having a date, she didn't want her to ruin her dinner, too. However, Karenna did mean well, she told herself. "I'll call you when I get back home."

"Love you," Karenna said softly.

"Me, too," Maryann answered and meant it. Then they hung up.

Maryann realized she was shivering and she slipped her cell phone into her purse so she could hug herself for warmth as she walked back to the glass doors that opened into the hospital. The doors opened automatically and she was thankful for small favors. Until a person had put their cold hands on a freezing metal bar to open a door, they didn't truly appreciate the automatic ones.

Inside the hospital, she made her way to the cafeteria. She'd been there earlier with Mrs. Fields, and the vegetable soup had been tolerable and hot. She hadn't noticed what the posted menu listed as entrees for tonight, but she thought she smelled spaghetti as she walked down the hall to the dining area.

It didn't take her long to eat her plate of spaghetti and string beans. Then she poured herself a cup of decaf coffee and sat back down to sip it. She felt right at home in her nurse's uniform here, although she noticed there were more blue-and-green uniforms than white. She supposed she was just a traditional kind of a person.

When she finished her coffee, she stood up. She wondered if Timmy had woken up at all while she'd been gone. She stopped in the gift shop to buy a magazine on the way back through the lobby area, and saw that they had a few birthday cards. Most of them were for little kids, but there was one with a sailboat that simply said

"Happy Birthday" inside. She bought it for Alex. She'd sign it "Your Nurse," but at least he'd have a card.

She walked down the hallway toward Timmy's room and wondered if she should have bought some of those red silk roses in the gift shop for the boy. They would have certainly brightened up the room.

Alex put a thumb on the page to keep his place. He was reading to Timmy, and the boy was altogether too alert.

"You ever been to The Valley of the Shadow of Death?" the boy asked. His voice wasn't firm, but it was clear. "Makes me think of Darth Vader—some creature that breathes like that." Timmy's eyes brightened. "Did I sound like that when I was breathing with this machine on? I think I could."

"Don't even try it," Alex said as he noticed his young charge trying to hold his breath so he could make the machine distort his breathing. "And I think the reference is an actual place."

"Like a valley of death? Like what? Like the north slope?" Timmy asked, puzzled.

"Well, I suppose in a way," Alex agreed. "It's a real place where people went back then."

"Humph. Like 'Hey there! Though I go through the north slope, I shall fear no evil'." The boy said, weighing his words. "Naw, that just doesn't sound right. No one goes through the north slope."

"Well, then think of a valley," Alex said, trying to curb his impatience. "Anyway, as I was saying, 'Yea, though I go through the Valley of Death, I shall—'"

"What's the name of the valley by Treasure Creek?" Timmy asked.

"I don't think it has a name," Alex said as he lay the Bible down on the bed. "Maybe it's time for you to take another nap."

"I am a little tired," Timmy admitted. "Can you tuck me in?"

"What?" Alex was already starting to stand up so he could turn the light off.

"My mom always tucks me in when it's time to go to sleep," Timmy admitted a little sheepishly.

"Oh, well," Alex stammered and then reached out and pulled on the covers so that they rested just under Timmy's chin. "There. Is that it?"

Timmy looked at him, clearly uncertain about whether to proceed.

"You can tell me," Alex said gently.

"She sometimes kisses my head," Timmy said. "Just for good sleeping."

Alex smiled. "Of course. I should have known."

He leaned over and kissed his patient on the forehead. "Sweet dreams."

Timmy nodded and closed his eyes. Alex figured he would be sound asleep within seconds, given the amount of medication he was taking.

He reached up and turned off the light near the bed. The overhead lights were off as well, so the only light was coming from a couple of plug-in lights along the wall. Of course, the door was open, and—he turned around and saw Maryann leaning on the doorjamb with a look of pure mischief on her face.

"What?" he said.

"I didn't know good-night kisses were something doctors were giving out now," she said softly as she stood there. "That was cute."

Alex leaned back in his chair. It was a rare treat to be sitting in a dark room and seeing Maryann backlit from the lights in the hallway. It gave golden tones to her brown hair and added shadows to her face that seemed to shift with her expression.

"Did you read to Timmy?" she asked as she walked into the room.

"Tried to," he said as he glanced over to where the Bible still sat on the bedcovers. "But not hard enough, I guess. We didn't make it through the whole psalm. He had questions about The Valley of the Shadow of Death."

Maryann nodded. "It was good to see him talking again."

"It would be better if he wasn't talking about death."

"I doubt it's because he's thinking he might die."

Alex nodded. He supposed that was true.

Maryann walked over to the bed and picked up the Bible. "Want to keep it for awhile?"

Alex shook his head. Reading that Bible had been hard for more reasons than that Timmy had been distracting. It was difficult for Alex to even pick it up, because he felt like he didn't deserve to read it. He'd been a Christian once, or at least he had gone to church as a child. And he'd given everything up, with no more thought than if he'd given up an old pair of sneakers. Something like that wouldn't be easy for God to forgive.

Maryann lifted the Bible into the light and looked at it closely. "The map's still here."

Alex shrugged. "Timmy hasn't mentioned it and neither have I."

"I wonder if he's forgotten," she said thoughtfully.

"I'm sure it will come back to him," Alex said. The promise of treasure seemed to take hold of people and not let go. Although, from all he could tell, Timmy hadn't wanted the fortune for himself, so maybe that made it less consuming.

Maryann sat down in the chair she'd used earlier, and Alex pulled his folding chair closer to her so he wouldn't disturb the boy.

"They have spaghetti for dinner," she said after a few moments. "It's not bad. It's even got some fresh mushrooms in it. And they serve it with garlic toast. Nice and crispy."

Alex nodded. He could sit here all night doing nothing, but he was hungry. And if this cafeteria was like all the other hospital cafeterias he'd eaten in, the food didn't improve as the night wore on. In fact, it often didn't even last that long. He'd best get down there.

"Timmy is going to be all right, isn't he?" Maryann asked quietly from the chair.

Alex nodded. The treatments had been working. By now even Dr. Stuart acknowledged how sick the boy had been. "He's over the worst of it."

Alex looked at Maryann. Her face was not turned toward him, but he could sense she was tired, so he added, "You don't need to worry."

Getting Timmy admitted to the hospital had saved

the boy's life, but Alex didn't want Maryann to know how close it had been.

"That's good," she said. "I think I should go back to Treasure Creek tomorrow morning, when Max flies back. I could at least call and reschedule the clinic appointments, rather than ask someone else to do it."

Alex put his hand on her shoulder.

She looked up at him. "Timmy won't need someone sitting with him after tonight, will he?"

"Probably not," Alex said as he squeezed her shoulder. "He's responding very well."

Alex would miss her, but he couldn't ask her to stay for that reason.

"Enjoy your dinner, then," Maryann said as if everything was settled.

Alex stopped himself before he answered. He'd grown accustomed to having her by his side and almost said as much. She was right, though. There was no real reason for her to stay with him.

So he nodded. "I don't think Timmy will be ready to go back until late in the day on Thursday. Max said he'll make a trip whenever the hospital releases the boy."

"Well, that's good then," Maryann said. He looked over and saw she had opened her Bible.

"You'll need better light," he said as he walked over and unclipped the lamp from the top of Timmy's bed. He brought it closer to her. He hooked the lamp on the metal chain hanging from the window blinds. The cord still stretched to the plug-in, so he clicked it on. "There, that'll do."

It wouldn't pass the hospital safety check, but the

cord was well out of the way of anyone walking around Timmy's bed.

"Thank you," Maryann said, looking up.

She was perfectly polite to him and his heart sank. Something was wrong. Alex thought they had gotten past his earlier awkwardness, but apparently not.

"If you'd rather go someplace other than the beach, that's okay," Alex said softly. "I'll take you any place you want."

He should have known. People always said they were giving someone else a new start, but it rarely happened in his experience. It had become a politically correct pretense in these past few years that all should be forgiven. But in reality, it was never that simple. Forgiveness needed to be earned; no one knew that better than him.

"You don't need to take me anywhere," Maryann said.

"But I want to."

Maryann turned her face slightly and the light from the lamp showed her eyes clearly. She was serious. "We'll talk about it later."

"I'm not suggesting we take off for the beach when Timmy's in the shape he's in, but we don't have much time," Alex said.

"I know," Maryann said as she looked back down at the Bible she still held. "But for now—enjoy your dinner."

Alex figured they would sound like strangers to anyone close enough to listen. The thought made him lose his appetite. He wondered if this is the way it would be for the next few weeks, until he left. If that was so, maybe he should stop at the pharmacy and get some antacids, because the prospect made him feel sour inside.

"I'll see you later," Alex said as he walked toward the door.

Chapter Nine

By the time Maryann stepped out of Max's floatplane and onto his dock the next morning, the sky had cleared. Everyone at the Juneau airport had commented that it was such a sunny day, saying they didn't get that many nice ones this far into the month of September. Maryann wouldn't have cared if they'd announced a hailstorm was under way; she'd smiled politely and agreed with whatever anyone said about the weather.

Then she'd hitched the strap of her purse higher on her shoulder and continued walking to the plane. She'd wanted to get home. That was the place she was at peace—Treasure Creek.

The flight had taken fifty-nine minutes.

She was so happy to be back in the small town, she almost skipped off the dock and kissed the earth at her feet. The only problem was that it was Max's dirt, and he already thought she was more thrilled with him than she was. Not that he wasn't a perfectly fine man and a conscientious pilot. It's just that he smiled too much. She took a moment to ponder how that could be. Surely she wasn't against smiles. But every time he broke forth with one, it seemed he expected her to smile right back at him. By the time they landed, her jaw was tired.

"You're welcome to fly to Juneau with me anytime you want," Max said as he stood on his dock with his legs braced against any possible movement, looking as if he was the captain of the sea. "No charge. I'll let you ride in the copilot seat. I don't usually have a passenger sit there anyway, so it's no loss to me."

"Thank you. That's most kind." She stopped. Then she smiled at him because that seemed the only polite thing to do after such a magnificent offer. It was worth hundreds of dollars, and she wished she could get more enthusiastic about it.

She started to turn to leave, but Max wasn't done yet.

"Some weekend we could fly down, just the two of us, and catch a movie in that new theater on Front Street." He continued with such confidence, she knew he didn't expect to be refused. "Maybe have some dinner at this Thai place one of the other pilots told me about—you know, have a good time."

Unfortunately, she did know.

"I'm afraid I'll be busy most weekends until the doctor leaves." She didn't bother to attempt a smile. "I'll be going through patient files, making sure everything is ready for the next doctor."

Max frowned. "Alex shouldn't make you work like that. Everyone needs some time off."

"Yes, well… "Maryann murmured as she turned. This time she kept walking as she spoke. "Maybe it'll be better next spring."

And maybe there would be a heat wave at Christmas,

she thought. *And diamonds in everyone's stockings. And*—she stopped herself. In all fairness, she needed to ease up on Max. He wasn't the one who had upset her, anyway.

It was the other arrogant man of the day. *Him.*

This morning she had woken, sitting upright in that hospital chair, with a red silk rose and the keys to the Jeep in her lap. The nurse, who had been making up the bed in the room, said Alex had gone with Doctor Stuart and Timmy, to run some more tests on the boy. He'd left word Maryann was to use his Jeep to get back to town from the dock where Max would land his floatplane.

Without thinking, she had brushed the silk rose across her cheek, just to feel its softness. That's when she was hit by the wave of anger. Why would Alex give her a rose, when he was leaving? He probably already had his boxes packed and his reservations made. In two weeks, he'd start forwarding his mail. It was too late for silk flowers. Sure he'd invited her to dinner, but the man was leaving. He should have done something weeks ago if he had any feelings for her. Which he obviously didn't.

The very thought made her turn half of that anger on herself. She was the one who had dived into this confused mess of emotions all by herself. If she wanted to have a peaceful, smooth relationship with someone, she needed to keep her emotions in check.

Just two days ago, she had everything under control. He was The Ice Man and she was the nurse. The only reason she had cared if Alex left Treasure Creek was because of the children.

All of those thoughts raced to a stop when Max—the

handsome, generous pilot—appeared in the doorway of the hospital room. He had flown Mrs. Fields back to be with her son. He informed Maryann that he was in a hurry to make the return flight, and if she wanted a ride, she'd have to hurry. He was impatient, confident—a man all too sure of himself. Just like someone else she knew.

So she had picked up the Jeep keys, tossed the rose into the trash and said she was ready to go. She told Mrs. Fields to explain to Timmy that she was flying back to Treasure Creek. Within fifteen minutes, she and Max were in a cab going to the airport. She'd been annoyed with Max the whole flight. It was unfair, and she didn't think he'd noticed, but it was the truth.

And now she was on the outskirts of her small town, walking toward Alex's Jeep. The keys opened the driver's door and she was inside in seconds. She drove slowly—the last thing she wanted was to hit something while driving a borrowed vehicle—but she still made it past the welcome-to-town sign in less than ten minutes.

She pulled into the large space behind Lindy's Boarding House. Her seldom-used car was where she had left it, over by the trees. The area in the back of the boarding house was graveled to keep down the mud, and there were no clear parking spaces. At this time of day there were only a few other vehicles around, so no one paid much attention to who parked where.

As she walked toward the house, she faced the one unit with an entrance off the back. It was a ground-level apartment that had been the maids' quarters a hundred years ago. Maryann noticed there were now curtains in the windows. She wondered if Lindy had finally been persuaded to rent the double room plus bath to one of the tenants who had been begging for it. She had been keeping it vacant in the hope that she would find someone willing to rent it in exchange for giving her help with the cooking, and, as Lindy delicately referred to it, the guest management part of her job. That was the rent collection, noise control and complaint departments.

Maryann told herself she'd go up to her room to change clothes and then she'd ask Lindy if there were any leftovers she could have for a late breakfast. Within a half hour, she'd be down to the clinic, rescheduling tomorrow's appointments. She'd leave the ones for Friday in place, as Alex would probably be back in time for them.

She walked around the side of the building and climbed the steps to the wide porch. The wicker rocking chairs were still there. In a few weeks, they would be put in storage for the winter. She opened the main door to the boarding house and, as always, triggered the ringing of the tiny bell that hung over the door. Something smelled good, and bursts of laughter were coming from the rooms in back.

Maryann closed the door and Lindy herself appeared in the hallway, coming out of the kitchen.

"You're home," Lindy said with a great deal of warmth she walked toward her. "And I hear Timmy Fields is doing much better."

Lindy had her blond hair pulled back into a ponytail, a blue-checked full apron tied over her jeans and a white T-shirt. She had flour on her hands and a streak of it on her cheek. She looked cream puff sweet, but she made no secret of the fact that she'd come from a rough background. She never knew her father, and her mother had spent most of Lindy's childhood in jail for one thing or another.

"I'd hug you, but I'm all full of dough," Lindy said, her eyes shining.

"I see that, and, yes, Timmy is doing much, much better," Maryann said as she leaned in and gave Lindy a loose hug anyway. "I hope all that flour means you're making biscuits. I'm starving."

Lindy laughed. "I owe you more than biscuits. Name it and I'll make it for dinner—if I have the ingredients. Chicken cordon bleu, ostrich burgers, crab chowder. I forget…what are your favorites?"

With that, Lindy started back to the kitchen.

"Is this about Timmy?" Maryann asked, trying to figure out why her landlady was making her a special dinner. Granted, Maryann had gone with the boy to the hospital, but she could hardly claim a hero's reward. The doctors and nurses in Juneau, with Alex's help, had pulled the boy through.

Lindy stopped in midstep and turned around. "I guess you don't know? Oh, I assumed he'd told you."

Maryann looked at her blankly.

"You got me a new tenant," Lindy explained, her face glowing. "He said you spoke highly of my place. He called when he was on the plane coming into town, and asked if he could rent something for a few weeks."

Maryann's heart sank. Surely she hadn't mentioned anything to Max. She knew he was looking for an apartment, but she hadn't thought he'd be content with a room.

"I'm renting him the maids' quarters," Lindy continued, looking pleased with herself. "I've decided no one's going to peel potatoes and dust for me anyway. At least, not right now. And he needed the door back there."

The private entrance in the rear of the house had been built extra wide for the laundry that used to pass through, so it could be hung on the clothesline just feet from the door.

"I'm sure he'll be very happy here," Maryann said. It was now official; Max was the most charming man in the whole state of Alaska. No one else could have talked Lindy out of her dream of a maid.

"I hope he is happy," Lindy said, her voice low so it didn't carry far. "I am, too. He's in the kitchen right now, folding napkins for dinner. He knows a million things about cooking. I felt bad letting him help out like this, but he said he wanted to put all those cooking shows he's watched on television to good use. He's going to show me how to braise things. Just as soon as we finish making these orange cranberry rolls for tomorrow."

"Max?" Maryann asked. She couldn't picture the pilot working in Lindy's kitchen. And how would he have gotten here that fast from his plane, anyway. Then she realized. "It's not Max, is it?"

"No. He said you know him though. Rocco Frank is his name." Lindy's face lit up with pride. "Isn't that the most handsome-sounding name ever?"

Maryann was stunned. She stood and stared at Lindy.

"Somebody must be playing a practical joke," she finally said. "Rocco wouldn't just show up here. How could he get here without us knowing? Alex said he never traveled. And that's not his real name anyway."

All of the light drained from Lindy's face. "Not his real name? He's not hiding from the law, is he? I never thought to ask that. When he said he knew you, I just assumed—I should have known better. I'm a magnet for trouble."

"No, no. It's nothing like that," Maryann assured her as she reached out to put a hand on the other woman's shoulder. "He's a model citizen as far as I know. He's just—well, he's in a wheelchair and—"

"There's nothing wrong with being in a wheelchair— nothing," Lindy said, her color coming back. "I have a stepsister in a wheelchair. Besides, President Roosevelt was in a wheelchair. And what's his name—the man who's a genius?"

"Stephen Hawking."

"Yeah, that's him."

"Of course there's nothing wrong with people being in wheelchairs. Unless they let it stop them from doing things. And Alex said his brother didn't even go to the grocery store." Maryann wanted to lie down in a dark room and put a cold washcloth on her forehead. "Can I see the man?"

Lindy looked at her, measuring her.

"If you're sure you won't make him feel uncomfortable," Lindy finally said. "I've never had anyone offer to help in the kitchen before. Well, at least not with something like folding napkins. He's making swans."

"I'll be warm and welcoming to him," Maryann said, with a smile. "No matter who he is."

Lindy nodded. "Good. And since you're hungry, I

can make you a meatloaf sandwich while we're back there."

"I missed meatloaf night?" Maryann asked as she followed Lindy through the wide hallway and back to the kitchen. "Why do I always miss my favorite?"

"So that's it. Your favorite," Lindy said as she stopped in the doorway to the kitchen.

Maryann looked over the other woman's shoulder. There was indeed a man in a wheelchair leaning over a short table someone had set up in the corner. He had a couple of dozen cloth napkins stacked on the table, and he was folding them into all kinds of shapes. He had some white ones that looked like chef hats.

The man turned to look at them.

Maryann didn't need more than a glance to know he was Alex's older brother. The two of them shared the same shape to their nose and jawline. Of course, a few old scars marred the skin on Rocco's face, and it was obvious he hadn't spent much time in the sun in the past years. His hair had some gray in it, but it had the same fullness that Alex's had. And there was an almost identical tilt to the head when they were listening for something.

"Rocco?" Maryann finally asked. She swallowed. How had he managed to end up in Lindy's kitchen?

He looked at her and squinted. "Nurse Jenner? You sound like Nurse Jenner."

"I need to sit down." Maryann stared at him for another minute. Then she walked over and pulled a chair out to sit down at the table with him.

"How did you get here?" she finally asked. "I mean,

Alex has told me you never left the house." She stopped to swallow. "This is a pretty major trip."

"It's amazing what a few calls can get you."

"I see you figured it all out," Maryann said, starting to be proud of him.

Rocco nodded. "Direct flight. You leave Los Angeles, take a short nap, and before you know it, you're in Alaska. At least Anchorage. That's what gave me the idea of coming up here. I could hardly get lost when, from start to finish, I'd be on the same plane."

Maryann looked around. She'd forgotten he was a young teen when he'd been hit by the car. "And you managed to get here from Anchorage."

"It was simple." He seemed pleased. "I flew down to Juneau and arranged for a private plane to pick me up. The pilot, Max, delivered me right to Lindy's place."

Bless Max's heart for thinking of Lindy's empty maids' quarters, a place that could easily accommodate Rocco's wheelchair. But still…"I heard you had an attendant. Didn't he come with you?"

Rocco shook his head. "I sent him on vacation for a few days. He' been teaching me how to do things for myself, but it's not a real test if he's there to rescue me."

"I suppose," Maryann said.

Rocco bent his head down and folded a napkin. This one appeared to be in the shape of a star. Maryann started to stand.

Then he looked at her again. "My brother's going to be mad, isn't he?"

"You didn't tell him you were coming, did you?" she asked, even though she knew the answer.

Rocco shook his head. "He kind of—what do you think he'll say?"

"Well, I don't know. I expect he'll be surprised. Very surprised."

"It wasn't as hard as I always thought it would be." Rocco gave a small, satisfied smile. "The people on the airplane were really nice."

"I'm glad—and I'm sure your brother will be grateful, too, when you tell him."

Rocco looked back down at the napkins he was folding, and it made Maryann uneasy. "You have left a message for your brother that you're in town, haven't you? I know he picks up messages from his home phone when he's away."

Rocco shook his head without looking up. "I thought I should rest up first."

"Oh," Maryann said.

"Don't worry," Rocco continued. "I'll tell him—soon." He thought for a moment. "Maybe Friday."

"Friday!" Maryann protested. "Today's Wednesday. You can't possibly plan to hide out all day tomorrow and wait to see him Friday."

Rocco shrugged. "I just want to see if I can be on my own for a couple of days. Lindy will let me help in the kitchen in exchange for meals, and I can roll my wheelchair out my door and see the mountains. Lindy says there's a moose that's been coming to town around dusk each night. What I wouldn't give to see a moose."

"Yes, but—" Maryann started, and then remembered the first time she'd seen a live moose.

"If Alex knows I'm here," Rocco interrupted, "He'll make me move into his place and try to do everything for me. It's time for me to take care of myself for a change. Please don't tell him I'm here. Not yet."

Maryann shook her head. She knew just how he felt. "I won't lie to him, but I won't call him in Juneau and tell him either. He's bound to find out when he gets back to town, though.

Rocco nodded with a grin. "That's why I haven't been using my last name. You're the only one who knows Alex is my brother."

"Wonderful," Maryann muttered. She really did need to lie down for a few minutes before she went to the clinic.

"I'll be grateful to you forever," Rocco said.

She sighed. "I don't think he'll be back here before Thursday, late afternoon."

Since it was Wednesday morning and Alex couldn't do anything until Friday anyway, that gave Rocco two days.

"I sure hope that moose comes around tonight." Rocco said. "And maybe a bear would come to town, too. I've never seen a bear either."

"Bears don't usually—" she started, and then stopped. "If I see one, I'll come down and knock on your door."

A day really wasn't too much to ask of life, she thought, as she started to push her chair out so she could stand. Alex would just have to cope with it. She had no doubt he'd find out eventually that she had known and not called him.

"Not so fast," Lindy said, as she walked over to the table. "I just made you the best meatloaf sandwich of your life. I used my imported mustard and some of that home-canned relish I got at the farmer's market at Harry's last summer."

"It looks wonderful," Maryann said as she sat back down and looked at the thick sandwich. She just wished it didn't have the feel of being her last meal. Alex might be more angry with her than with his brother. In fact, he might think she encouraged his brother to come up here, with all of her talk about how the mountains were so beautiful and the air so fresh.

For someone seeking a peaceful life, she was sure managing to stir up trouble. She cut the sandwich in half and gestured for Rocco to have some. When he took it, she knew she'd at least made a friend today.

Chapter Ten

Alex was in the copilot seat of Max's floatplane, headed down to Treasure Creek from Juneau. It was late afternoon on Wednesday and the sun was beginning to set. Alex hadn't felt much like talking since they left the hospital.

"I bet you'll be glad to be home," Max said as he began to turn his plane so he could approach his dock for landing. "I know I will be."

Alex grunted. He needed clean clothes and a shave. Timmy and his mother were wrapped in blankets in the backseat and sound asleep—which reminded him that he needed a nap, too. The last two days had been a roller coaster of despair and jubilation. But it was worth it. Timmy was going to be all right.

"I hope you don't mind that I called ahead to let Amy know we're bringing Timmy home today instead of tomorrow," Max said as he shifted something on his control panel. "She'd called earlier and left a message. I have a feeling she wants to organize something."

"Of course I don't mind," Alex said a little surprised it was even a question. Maybe he'd been a little too silent on this trip. "The boy deserves a hero's welcome after what he's been through. He won't be able to stay for the celebration, though. He needs to be home in bed."

The boy had not only survived pneumonia, he'd pulled through with his faith intact, Alex marveled. The boy really thought God was there for him.

It was the Twenty-third Psalm that had made that clear. Earlier today, after they did the last of the tests, Timmy had asked Alex for that Bible again.

Alex knew where the book was, because this morning Maryann had left it on the shelf by Timmy's bed. Unlike the rose she'd left in the trash, which had obviously been discarded, he was sure the Bible had been merely forgotten. By the time he opened it to where the blue candy wrapper had been placed earlier, he realized Timmy didn't even need the written words. The boy already had his eyes closed tight and was repeating the psalm from memory.

"The Lord is my shepherd," Timmy mumbled. Then he opened his eyes and looked directly into Alex's eyes. "It's better if two people say it together." Then he held out his hand and took Alex's in his own.

Alex was surprised he remembered the words, but together they managed to haltingly make their way through the psalm. It was just as well he wasn't reading it, Alex told himself halfway through, since he wouldn't be able to see the words anyway due to the tears in his eyes anyway. Saying these words with Timmy affected him. At first he thought it was because he was remembering how he'd shared the boy's feelings at one time and was feeling nostalgic.

But, by the middle of the psalm, Alex realized his

big problem wasn't even with God. It was with himself. The day Rocco had saved his life was the day Alex no longer felt like he deserved to be in contact with God. He felt like he should be banished, not welcomed. Maybe he would have gotten over that feeling, but everything in his family also changed that day.

They stopped going to church. They no longer prayed before meals. To Alex, it was as though he had led his whole family out into the wilderness. He believed his family was sharing his apartness from God, giving rise to the suspicion that maybe they knew something he didn't about his lack of closeness to God after all that had happened. Not that he had blamed God for any of it; it was just the way things were.

They had finished the psalm before Alex even realized it.

"Don't cry," Timmy whispered. "Everything's going to be okay."

Alex opened his eyes and nodded, even though he didn't believe Timmy's words. Not anymore. Too many years separated the man he was today from the faith he had as a boy. Besides, a man was called to be more accountable than a child, even if it would be nice to feel there were no hard feelings between him and God. Maybe he should try to resolve things. There should be something he could do that would make God's heart soften toward him.

Amy said that the church needed a new organ. Maybe once he earned enough to build that clinic, he'd send a check to the Treasure Creek church so they could get a new organ. That should get God's attention and make Alex feel like he could talk to Him again.

* * *

Max dropped the plane down and landed next to that special dock of his.

"If you give me a minute, I can get my ramp elevated so we can carry the boy down. I had a man in a wheelchair use it yesterday. The ramp worked like a charm," Max said as he turned off all the knobs on his panel. "We had the guy out of here and down to the dock in minutes."

"Good for him," Alex said, thinking of his brother. Now why couldn't Rocco try something like that? He needn't make such a big trip, of course, but he could at least get out of the house. Rocco had his attendant; the man was supposed to help him learn to get around better. Rocco should at least be wheeling himself out to the curb.

Alex had checked his messages a couple of times yesterday. He had expected Rocco to leave a few words acknowledging it was his birthday. But if Rocco called he didn't leave a message.

Mr. Fields was there with the car, to give everyone a ride into Treasure Creek. Alex squeezed into the backseat with Timmy on his lap.

"You'll want to give this back to Maryann," Mrs. Fields said as she turned from the front seat and held out the white Bible to him. "I know she sets great store by it."

"That she does," Alex agreed as he took it back. The sky had darkened, but Alex could still see the edges of that old map in the middle of the Bible.

He noticed Timmy eyeing the Bible, too.

"I figure maybe you can come to the clinic tomorrow

for a checkup," Alex said to the boy. "That'll give us a chance to discuss things."

Timmy nodded, his eyes wide.

"I didn't mean any harm," he whispered, with a glance at his parents sitting in the front seat.

"I know. We'll talk about it tomorrow," Alex said.

When Mr. Fields turned onto the main thoroughfare of Treasure Creek, Alex looked down the street. There was a light on at the clinic. The stress of the day eased out of him. Maryann must be there still.

"You can let me off at the clinic," Alex said to Mr. Fields.

"I was hoping you'd want to stop by Lizbet's with us," the other man answered. "We've been invited over to celebrate Timmy's homecoming. We won't stay, of course. But Timmy can hear the cheers through the car window."

"I'll be over later," Alex said.

The man nodded. "I want you to know I'm much obliged for what you did for us. My wife told me you talked the hospital into giving us credit. I plan to call them tomorrow and make arrangements. The missus didn't have time to stop in and ask them about payments."

Alex froze. "I didn't really—well, about the payments—the hospital doesn't really…"

Mr. Fields stopped his car in front of the clinic. "We're here now."

"When you bring Timmy in tomorrow for his appointment," Alex said to Mr. Fields, "we'll talk about everything then. It's just—well, don't worry. The finances will be all right."

The other man nodded and Alex opened the car door. Then he said a quick goodbye to everyone and, Bible in hand, stepped out of the car and walked toward the clinic. He was glad he had the book with him, since he knew Maryann would be happy to have that returned to her, even if she might have problems with him showing up sooner than she expected. He wished he could convince himself there was some benign reason for that rose to have been in the waste basket in Timmy's room. It sure didn't build a man's confidence.

Alex opened the door and took a moment to enjoy the astonishment on his nurse's face when she saw he was there. She was sitting at the receptionist desk, the lamp behind her putting out a yellow light that gave her brown hair a shine. She didn't have her usual white uniform on. In fact, she was wearing a rose-colored sweater and some silver earrings. All in all, she looked very nice—too nice for work.

"You're back?" Maryann finally seemed to find her voice.

"Timmy was okay to come home earlier than we thought," Alex said, as he walked over to her desk and set the Bible down. "Brought this back to you. The map's still there. Timmy's coming in tomorrow and we'll have our talk. Amy will want to be here, too."

Maryann nodded and swallowed. "I'm sure the boy didn't mean any harm."

Alex frowned. Unless he was mistaken, Maryann was nervous around him. There was no reason she would be, unless...

"You're worried I'll get the boy in trouble with

his father, aren't you?" he asked. "I can assure you I won't."

Maryann shook her head. "I can't imagine his parents will be too upset with him after what he's been through. He's only eight years old."

Something still wasn't right, Alex told himself. He knew she cared about the boy. He wondered who else she cared about.

"Max called, didn't he?" Alex finally asked. "And said…what?"

Maryann shook her head.

There could only be one other thing, Alex thought. "Don't tell me you set me up with one of the fancy women?"

"No, it's not that," she said.

He was completely out of theories, Alex admitted to himself. "Well, whatever it is, it can't be that bad. Just tell me. Come over to the diner with me and we can talk while we have some pizza."

Maryann smiled and finally looked him in the eyes. "I'll come for pizza, but I still can't tell you anything. I promised I wouldn't. Not until tomorrow—if you don't know by tomorrow evening, I can probably say something."

"Probably?" He lifted an eyebrow.

"I'd have to ask the other person first."

Alex felt a sudden stab of jealousy. "It's not Max, is it?"

Maryann shook her head emphatically. "And no more guessing. Not that you'd guess right anyway, but…"

As long as she wasn't going to announce that she was running off to be Max's full-time copilot, he figured he could wait to know what she was talking about. Women sometimes liked to have their secrets, and he consoled himself with that certainty.

"Nice hair," he said as she stood up and reached behind the desk for her coat. "You've done something different, haven't you? Added those—what do you call them—'lights'?"

"Highlights?" Maryann said as she turned around, her coat in hand. "No, I don't have highlights."

Alex stepped over to help her with her coat. As he did so, he said, "Well, highlights would be wasted on you. Your hair is beautiful just the way it is."

"Thank you," Maryann said as she slipped her arms into her coat. Then she looked up at him with mischief on her face. "I'm still not going to tell you what you want to know, though. Not until the end of work tomorrow. And then only if I get permission."

Her face was so alive that he almost kissed her. Then he remembered the last time they'd almost kissed and how conversation had stopped for the rest of the evening. And tonight he wanted to talk to her and hear her laugh. He did put his arm around her shoulders as they walked through the door though.

"It's dark out here," Alex said, as she looked up at him. "Wouldn't want you to trip."

She seemed to accept that explanation, because she didn't pull away. They walked down the stairs in harmony.

"I wonder if that old moose will show up tonight?" Alex said as they started to walk down the street.

He felt Maryann's shoulders tense beneath his arm. He supposed the reason he had thought of that animal was because they saw it on their previous walk together. He didn't want her to feel uncomfortable about that, though.

"It's not very likely," Alex said. "They don't come out as much as they used to."

"He could be there," Maryann declared. "I hope he is."

Alex was now thoroughly confused. Not that he minded the feeling, since he was walking down the street with Maryann on his arm.

"The stars should be out tonight, too," he ventured to add. "A little later, that is."

Maryann worried as they walked down the street. What if Rocco was out taking a tour of the town? In the little bit of time she'd spent with him earlier, she had decided he had become fearless. Of course, if she only had one day to look around paradise, she supposed she would be curious to see what it was all like, too.

They made it all the way to the General Store before Alex said anything. "I suppose you like things that are alive instead of, well, not?" he asked with such a studied casualness that she knew it was anything but that.

"What?" She stopped to look up at him in confusion. "I'm a nurse. Of course I like things to be alive. What kind of a question is that? Are you saying I don't take my job seriously?"

Enough light streamed through the large glass pane window of the store that she could see Alex's face. He had dark stubble on his face from not shaving for a couple of days. And his hair was tousled, as though he hadn't been combing it that much. He had the faint air of someone who was haunted by something. He looked more like a biker than a doctor. And the whole combination was way too appealing for her.

"I *do*—take my job seriously," she repeated, when she found her voice again—even though, from the look on his face, she had already figured out that that wasn't what he was talking about at all.

"It's the rose," he finally muttered, just as she was afraid he would.

"I thought maybe you only liked fresh ones," he added. "If they had any real flowers in the gift shop, I would have gotten you one of those instead."

Maryann's mouth went dry. She hadn't meant for him to see the rose. She thought the orderly who was making the bed would empty the trash as well.

"I—ah—I," she stammered, "I do like the fresh ones better. That's true."

She took a breath to tell him the real reason she hadn't liked the silk flower, but when she opened her mouth nothing came out. He was looking at her so intently. His eyes darkened until they looked warm and caring. She forgot for a moment what she was supposed to say.

"I—ah—I…" She took another run at it, but only produced a breathless squeak. Finally she settled for, "I'm sorry. Truly sorry."

He smiled and his whole face turned boyish. "Just as long as it's only the rose you don't like."

And then he turned to begin walking again. This time he cuddled her more closely under his arm, and she didn't say anything. Alex's brother wasn't the only one who was exploring new territory tonight, she told herself. She knew full well that the fantasy she was living while walking down this street would expire in a couple of weeks. She figured her emotions would be in upheaval until Alex left, and then she'd know bleakness for days or weeks. It would be worth it though, she knew.

Chapter Eleven

The light on the porch outside of Lizbet's Diner had burned out, so the steps were hidden by the growing shadows of nearby buildings. The night was getting darker and colder. Even with her jacket on, Maryann was grateful for Alex's arm around her shoulder as they made their way to the top of the wide porch. Besides, she liked being this close to him.

"So, when do you leave again?" she asked, just to remind herself of reality.

He didn't answer for a bit, then he said, "The twenty-seventh. That's a Saturday. I take the red eye flight out of Anchorage, down to Los Angeles."

She nodded. Sixteen more days. The answer helped numb her feelings. She needed some perspective; he was still leaving. Maybe he would say something about keeping in touch or coming back to visit. But maybe he'd say nothing. People tended to leave acquaintances more easily than they used to in earlier days. Her parents had taught her that. "Out with the old and in with the new"—that was their motto.

"I keep meaning to stop by Harry's store and post a

sign on his bulletin board to sell my Jeep," Alex added quietly. "I bought it used when I first got here, and I don't know what I would do with it if I drove it down to Los Angeles. The roads are so different down there. Faster, more congested. And the freeways..."

Maryann nodded. Everything would be new for him when he moved. "Someone's sure to buy your Jeep when you're gone. And they'll treasure it like it deserves."

She shouldn't have added the last. It revealed too much about her heart, but he didn't seem to notice. He was leaving her behind, too, though. That much was growing clear.

The light shifted inside the diner, like maybe someone had turned on a couple more bulbs, and the light streaming out was mellow and golden. Maryann felt like she was in one of those old forties movies, where everyone wore hats and there was always some man saying goodbye to the woman he loved, because he had to make good on some promise, instead of standing by her side.

Maryann took a deep breath. She had never understood why those women wept over their men. If the men didn't want to stay, who needed them? A true man found a way to take his woman with him. Or he stayed behind. She could understand wartime, but for Alex it was a clinic.

She stopped herself. She was not going to be sad or angry tonight. She looked up at Alex and smiled. Rocco had already taught her something at the kitchen table this morning. She was going to live today to the full.

Just then Linda, one of the uniformed waitresses,

opened the door and came outside with a light bulb in her hand and a slight frown on her face.

"Oh, it is dark out here," she said, fretting as she stood beneath the light fixture. "Nobody's paying me for this. Someone said we needed a new light, and I just got elected to change it." The waitress turned to look at Maryann and Alex. "Do I look like an electrician to either of you?"

"No," Alex said and held out his hand for the bulb.

"I'm no electrician either," he said when Linda opened her mouth to protest. "But I am taller, and I can reach the fixture without you needing to get a ladder."

"Thank you, then," the woman said as she gave him the bulb. "You're all right, you know? For a doctor, that is. You're not stuck-up or anything."

"Thank you." Alex screwed in the new bulb.

Light flooded the porch. Maryann blinked.

Then Alex opened the door for them and they walked inside. The diner was overflowing with people, half of them standing and half of them seated at tables. People were laughing and having a good time.

Linda nodded at the two of them and went back to work.

Someone gave a shrill whistle and Maryann looked over to see Max, sitting at a small round table, and waving toward them.

"Guess we should go over," Alex said.

The smell of pizza and grilled hamburgers filled the air as Maryann and Alex side-stepped their way to the table where Max was. It wasn't easy to move through the crowd, since almost everyone wanted to slap Alex on the back and tell him he'd done a good job for their little Timmy. He smiled and nodded to them all.

"Hey, there," Max said when they got close enough to hear. "Sorry there aren't many empty seats."

At that moment Max and Alex both looked at the one empty chair.

Max started to stand, then sat back down, a grin covering his face. "Maryann can sit on my knee. She doesn't weigh but a bit."

"She can take the chair. I'll stand," Alex retorted as he guided Maryann to the empty chair.

Max gave a low chuckle. Alex knew, without looking at the man's face, that he'd been hoping Maryann would perch herself on his leg while she ate. But that would never happen.

Alex nodded in satisfaction to no one in particular. He was glad Maryann was safely sitting in her own place. He leaned down and put a hand on the back of her neck.

"What would you like me to order for you?" he whispered in her ear. He could smell her floral shampoo and feel wisps of hair along her neckline where his thumb rested. He'd never noticed before how delicate her earlobes were. "Maybe some hot green tea?"

She turned her face to look up at him, and suddenly it felt as if the fifty or sixty people in the room had disappeared and there were only the two of them. She met his eyes in surprise. "How'd you know that's what I'd like?"

"You drink a cup every day at your desk."

"I didn't know you paid any attention," she said.

Alex hadn't known he'd noticed as much as he had

about Maryann, either. His previous nurse had worked with him for much longer, and he couldn't remember what *she* liked to drink at her desk. But he could fill a notebook with things about Maryann. The way she liked to stop in front of the window and tilt her head up at the mountains. The way she lifted her eyebrows when she disagreed with him. And the way her lips curled just so when he said something that amused her.

"I've noticed more than I realized," he finally said, bending close enough to her ear so only she would hear him.

A woman cleared her throat and Alex looked up to see the waitress, Linda, standing beside him with her order pad in her hand. He looked across the table and saw Max with a stunned look on his face.

"Decided to come back to earth and join us?" Max asked, but here was no rancor in his voice.

"It's been a long day," Alex said as he straightened to his full height.

"You know what you want?" Linda asked. "I've got a full house here."

Alex nodded and ordered tea for Maryann and sodas for him and Max. Then he looked around. The place was filled with plates of nachos dripping with processed cheese, and hamburgers with double sides of mayonnaise. People were eating as if they were bears ready to hibernate for the winter.

"What do you put on your vegetable pizza?" he asked.

"Onions, red peppers, mushrooms and olives."

"Any tomatoes?"

"We haven't gotten our fresh delivery yet," Linda said. "It comes on the early-morning plane."

Alex nodded. "We'll take your biggest size, and bring a salad with it."

"There's nothing but lettuce. But we do have some coleslaw."

"That'll do," Alex said.

Just then a loud bell rang out. Everyone knew that meant someone wanted to say something. Sure enough, Amy climbed up on a chair so the whole diner could see her, then she started to talk.

Alex wasn't really listening. He was paying more attention to Maryann's hair. Several strands of her hair curled around her ear—strands that had escaped the discipline of her brush.

Then Alex heard his name and his attention was caught by Amy's speech.

"...our very own Dr. Havens got Timmy to the hospital in time to save his life." There was a smattering of applause at this, and Alex waved at people to stop. Instead, they got louder. Finally someone rang the bell again.

Amy continued. "As you know, hospitals are not cheap, and the Fields family will have a big bill soon." There was a wave of murmurs at this. It gave Alex a bad feeling, since he was the only one there who knew there was nothing due on Timmy's bill.

The bell rang again, and Amy continued. "Everyone's invited to the fellowship hall of the Treasure Creek Christian Church this Saturday for a pancake and caribou sausage breakfast. The proceeds will go to The Timmy Fields Fund, to help pay off that bill. Mr. Fields will let us know on Saturday just how much we need to collect, so bring your wallets and don't be shy about opening them up for our own Timmy Fields." People cheered.

Alex didn't feel any better than Timmy probably did about now. It hadn't occurred to him that the town would start raising money for the bill he'd already paid. He hadn't planned to tell anyone what he had done. He hadn't really thought about what the Fields family would think. If anything, he figured they'd think the hospital had forgotten them somehow. And since they had a hard enough time paying the bills that came to their door, he thought they'd just forget the one that didn't.

Alex had had no idea all the people in town would be involved. They knew about the clinic he was building for his brother in Los Angeles, and he didn't want them to worry that he wouldn't be able to do it now. It would be different if they could earn enough money at their breakfast to cover the bill, but they'd do well to raise a few hundred dollars. And if they went to the hospital with the money in hand to make a payment, they would know the bill was paid.

The cheering died down.

"Your order's here," the waitress said as she slapped a wire holder on the table with one hand and then lowered the big tray of pizza with the other. "I'll be back with your drinks."

"Smells good," Max said from where he'd moved his chair. The other man hadn't pushed his chair as close to Maryann as he could, and Alex felt as if they'd turned some corner. He couldn't thank Max right now, though.

So instead Alex took a deep whiff of the pizza smell. It had been a long time since he'd had a slice of pizza. Then he looked around at the children watching him. Some of them were from Treasure Creek and some from the Tlingit village. He glanced down at Maryann and saw she was watching him being scrutinized by the children, too. She looked up with a smile for him and whispered. "Little eyes. They want to see what the doctor eats."

Alex nodded. Then he held out a hand to Max and one to Maryann.

"Let's pray," he said. Somewhere in the time he'd spent with Timmy, he'd grown convinced that the children in his medical care needed spiritual health as well. He planned to talk to Reverend Michaels about that when he got a chance. In the meantime, he needed some help. "Maryann, will you lead us in prayer?"

She was surprised. He could see that plainly. But she looked around at the gawking children and bowed her head anyway.

"Dear God," she began. "Thank You so much for making Timmy well again. We ask that You help us all to keep healthy. Help us to not cry when we get our shots and to brush our teeth after every meal. We thank You now for this food, especially the coleslaw the doctor is eating. Vegetables are important, and we thank You for them. Amen."

"Amen," Alex said with a smile. He leaned down and whispered to Maryann, "Thanks for the public-service announcements."

"Well, they should brush their teeth," Maryann said. Then she grinned at the children who had nudged closer, and added more loudly, "Just like I'm going to brush my teeth after I eat some of this pizza."

"Is it the vegetable?" a little voice asked. A Tlingit boy walked closer to the table, his brown eyes as big as the pizza he was starting at. "I've never had mushrooms before."

A couple of other Tlingit children edged closer, too. Alex noted that Max was getting a worried look on his face. The rules of village hospitality were very clear. Food was shared. Another child lined up at the table and the adults were outnumbered.

Alex motioned for Linda to come back.

"Yes?" she asked when she got there.

She frowned at the children. "Do your parents know you're over here begging pizza?"

They didn't answer, and she sighed and said, "Yeah, I suppose not."

"I'd like to order another pizza," Alex finally said. "Make it a big one just like this, only double the mushrooms."

"Gotcha," Linda said with a smile.

The pizza was gone all too soon. The children left, and half of the other diners had gone as well. Alex finally had a chair, so he could sit at the table with Max and Maryann. He did it, but he wasn't sure he wouldn't have preferred to stay crouched by her chair like her protector.

It didn't occur to Alex until they started to walk out that he'd meant to ask a question. He quickly excused himself and went in search of the waitress. She was back in the kitchen, filling a bowl of chili.

"That shipment you get in," he said to her. "Can you call tonight and add something to the order?"

"Sure we could," she said. "What do you need?"

"I was wondering if you could order me a dozen red roses to come in with your shipment. Real roses—nothing plastic or silk or chocolate. And make them the long stem kind. Deep red."

Linda set the bowl of chili down on the metal counter and a grin spread across her face. "A dozen long stem red roses? That sounds like you're trying to impress someone. I don't suppose you'd like to tell me who? I've got money riding on which of the fancy women you've got your eye on."

"I don't have my eye on any of them," he said, trying to be patient, because it would only make any gossip worse if he wasn't. "I just want some roses. What do I owe you?"

"I don't have a price," she said. "They'll be expensive, though. Maybe seventy or eighty dollars. Ninety even."

"Fine," he said. "Let me know when you want the money."

The waitress nodded. "Sure will. I'll call when the shipment comes in tomorrow. You can pay me when you pick them up."

Alex walked through the diner, looking for Maryann. She wasn't there, so he assumed Max had walked her home. But when he stepped out the door he saw her waiting on the porch.

She held up a white paper bag that held the leftover pizza. So that's why she'd waited. Still, a man took his chances when he could.

He grinned. "Want to take a walk?"

"I'm sure you're tired," she answered hesitantly. "I just wanted to give you your pizza. And to say thank you. I liked that you bought the other pizza so the kids could have some, too."

Alex basked in her approval. "I'm not tired."

"Well then, I wouldn't say no to a short walk," she said with a smile as they both turned to walk off of the porch and down to the main road through town.

A few vehicles were parked alongside the asphalt road, and most of the businesses had dim lights showing through their windows, even though they were closed.

He took a moment before he moved in a little closer and put his arm around Maryann as they walked.

"Don't want you to get cold," he said, as though that was the reason. He hadn't noticed before how she was just the right height. She fit under his arm perfectly.

"You'll never see temperatures like these when you get back to Los Angeles," she said, sounding wistful.

"I'll miss it," he said, feeling pretty forlorn. He didn't want the evening to end like this, though, so he added, "Let's go see if we can find that moose anywhere around."

"Oh," Maryann stiffened. "I'm sure he's not here. We really shouldn't even be out on the streets tonight."

"What?" Alex said, figuring he had missed a step, but he didn't know where. "I thought you liked that moose! It could be related to our Horace—you know, in the office?"

"I know Horace," she said, and then seemed at a loss. "I just realized that I'm a little tired after all. I really better get home."

"Well, I can at least walk you there," Alex said.

"Oh, no." She sounded truly alarmed. "I mean, there's no need. I'll see you tomorrow. Bright and early."

And with that she hurried away from him. There was nothing for him to do but to watch her dark shape as she walked down the street to the boarding house where she lived.

He stood in the middle of the almost empty street and shook his head. Maybe he did need to get some sleep. Nothing much made the kind of sense that it should. He watched until Maryann went into the door of the boarding house, and then he turned to walk back to his place. She was right, he would miss the cold bite of the air around here. He'd even miss Horace. But most of all he'd miss seeing Maryann's eyes light up when she saw an old moose walking around, or when—he stopped. He hadn't realized until now that he wouldn't be here the first time Maryann saw an Alaskan snowstorm. Her whole face would radiate delight at that.

The price of doing his duty had finally climbed so high that he wasn't sure he could pay it.

Chapter Twelve

Maryann wore gloves the next morning, and it was still difficult to get the clinic's front door to open with her key. The lock was partially frozen. That sometimes happened when there was heavy dew the night before, and the temperatures fell. Last night had been cold, and according to Rocco, the moose had not shown up on the street in Treasure Creek.

Alex's brother had wheeled himself down the ramp of the boarding house many times during the early evening to look out at the street. Only Lindy's outspoken concern had kept him from rolling his wheelchair out onto the main road to go searching for the animal. She reminded him that moose might not be as interested in seeing Rocco as Rocco was in seeing the moose.

Maryann finally opened the door, and the air inside was no warmer than outside. The cost of fuel oil was going up all the time, and at this time of year, no one kept their heater on overnight. When it got colder there would be concern for the pipes, so the heater would be left on, but just barely. That's why she kept her jacket on while she started her day.

The first thing she did was start the coffee brewing.

This morning, she looked through the list of appointments she'd rescheduled yesterday, to see if any of them would be ones she could rebook for their original time. She had ticked off four appointments when the phone rang.

"Hello," she answered. It was only ten minutes after eight. The clinic wasn't open for another twenty minutes. "Dr. Haven's office."

"Is he in?" a woman's voice asked. "It's Linda from the diner."

"Oh, hi Linda." Maryann relaxed when she knew who it was. "No, but he should be here before too long. Can I take a message?"

"Yeah, you can tell him that his flowers came in," Linda said. "They're ready for pick-up."

Maryann tried to keep the pleasure from warming her. She knew he made that remark about replacing the silk rose with a real one, but she hadn't expected this. Then she told herself she couldn't assume anything was for her.

"What kind of flower?" she asked.

"Long stem red roses that would make you sit up and weep," Linda said, her voice dropping down in awe. "I keep wishing they were just a bouquet and not a dozen. There's no chance of stealing one on the sly. Twelve is twelve, and whoever gets these is going to count. At least, I would. Do you know which fancy woman they're for?"

Maryann stammered, "I—don't think—"

"I have twenty bucks on Delilah," the waitress said.

"She might be a little overblown, but I think she's got a heart of gold."

"I'm sure she does, but—" Maryann started, but the waitress was already talking to someone on the side.

"Oops, gotta go," Linda said. "Someone didn't get their eggs sunny side up enough. Whatever enough means. Sunny side up or over easy—there's only two sides to an egg that's been fried."

"Well, I'll tell Dr. Havens about the flowers," Maryann managed to say.

"Thanks. I'll expect him later. Bye now," Linda said, and hung up.

Maryann just sat there for a little bit after she put the phone back on its cradle. Finally, she looked up at Horace, the moose head, and asked him, "Well, what do you think of that? A dozen long stem red roses."

Of course, Horace never answered—and another phone call came in right away, so she tried to put the flowers out of her mind, too. After all, it was going to be a busy day, especially if she got the appointments back. She'd need to leave space for the meeting with Timmy, and then they'd want to close early tonight because of the choir rehearsal for the Christmas pageant. And at some time today—most likely after it was too late in the day to get anyone to fly them to Juneau—Rocco would tell his brother that he was in town.

Alex stopped at Lizbet's on his way to the office, just on the chance his flowers had come in. The diner didn't look as cozy in the daytime as it did at night. The outside paint was scuffed in places, and the porch tilted a little, maybe because it needed some work on the support beams.

The smell of coffee and fried bacon greeted him when he opened the door, though, and he rubbed his hands together, grateful for the warmth. He stood just inside and looked for Linda. She was in the corner, her order pad in her hand as she talked to the people at the far table. Since she was the one who handled the shipment coming in, he figured he needed to wait for her. He sat down at a side table.

"Coffee?" one of the other waitresses came up and asked.

"Please," he said, and she filled the cup in front of him.

He cradled the cup in his hand, wondering for the hundredth time since he'd woken up what was going on with his brother. When Rocco didn't answer the phone call last night, Alex had assumed his brother was already sleeping. But when he didn't answer this morning either, he began to worry. If his brother was sleeping that much, it must mean he was depressed. Maybe that's what Rocco had been trying to tell him— that he needed his brother to come and be with him. Alex would go, of course, regardless of how reluctant he was feeling.

"Here you are, Romeo," Linda said, as she came up to him carrying a large crystal vase filled with roses. "Whoever she is, she's one fortunate woman."

Linda handed him the roses and he took a deep breath of their scent. They were fragrant and full, their deep red sure to please. He set them on the table so he could pull out his wallet to pay for them.

"What do I owe you?" He took a sip of his coffee.

"Ninety-seven dollars even," Linda said. "I'll knock off the seven dollars if you tell me who they're going to."

Alex chuckled. "Are you gals betting again?"

Linda shrugged. "The days are long. Our feet hurt, so we put them up and talk about what we see. So what if we sometimes have a little competition to see who's right?"

Alex grunted in disbelief. "A *little* competition? That's like saying you serve a *little* cheddar on your double-double cheeseburger."

Alex pulled his wallet out of his pocket and began to count out bills. When he finished, he added another ten-dollar bill for a tip and said, "Thanks for the roses. Maybe someday I'll tell you who I gave them to—she's kind of private and shy though. I don't think she'd want everyone to know."

Linda scrutinized him as though he might have a name tattooed on his forehead. "I understand Delilah can seem shy to those who know her best."

"Delilah?" he asked. "The fancy woman? No, she's not the one."

Linda peered down at him. "Don't worry. I'll find out who she is. I already asked your nurse. She'll eventually tell me."

"Maryann?" Alex croaked out, as he half-rose from his chair. "What did you say to her?"

Linda's smile faded as realization struck her.

"Oh, I had no idea." She was silent for a moment and

then she added, "You could tell a person, you know, before she steps in it."

"It's hopeless anyway," Alex muttered, as he sat back down. "I just wanted to go out in style, you know? Leave her some reason to think kindly of me in the future when I'm gone."

"She isn't going to think that kindly of you," Linda said, bracingly. "Not from just a bouquet of flowers, no matter how lovely they are. You need to romance her. With more than flowers. Maybe some music. And jewelry—nothing says 'remember me' better than a diamond bracelet."

"Diamonds?" Alex protested. "How much of a cut are you getting off those flowers anyway?

"I make a modest living," Linda said with dignity. "People give me tips all day long. Why not when I deliver something like this?"

"I'm not complaining," Alex said as he took a long sip of coffee. "I just mean, who has the money for diamonds?"

"You will, someday," Linda said. "You're a doctor. When you go down to Los Angeles, you'll make the big money."

Alex shrugged. "Medicine has never been about the money for me."

"Well, no one will blame you if that's what it becomes," Linda said. "We could use some of it around here."

With that, Alex drained his cup and stood up. "Thanks for getting the flowers." He picked up the vase.

"I hope they work for you," Linda said, with a smile.

"I figure she'll probably remember you kindly no matter what."

He walked fast from the diner to his clinic. He had forgotten how cold it was out. The roses he was carrying weren't used to temperatures like these. He was relieved when he got to the door of the clinic without losing any leaves or petals. He put his hand on the cold metal of the doorknob and turned it. Maryann was standing facing the file cases where they kept their patient files. It had only been recently that he noticed how she always looked so fresh and calm. He supposed it was that she almost always wore the white nurse's uniform.

"I have Timmy scheduled for eleven o'clock," Maryann said, without turning around to look at him. "His father will bring him in."

"Good, I'll have to let Amy know."

"I already did," she said as she pulled out a file and closed the drawer. "In the meantime, you have an appointment coming at nine and one at nine-thirty. I'm still working on ten and ten-thirty."

Alex nodded.

That's when Maryann turned around. He saw the soft expression transform her face.

"For you," he said as he held out the vase to her.

She walked toward him. "Those are even more gorgeous than Linda said."

"I wanted you to like them," Alex said as she got close enough to take the flowers.

Maryann held the vase and buried her face in the roses. "They are wonderful."

"Good," Alex said in relief. He had wanted her to

be pleased. "I hope you know how special I think you are. Not only as a nurse but also as a woman. If there was any way I could stay here with you—" He stopped before he started to tear up. "My brother needs me."

Maryann seemed to stiffen at his mention of Rocco.

"I know it might be old-fashioned to have that kind of a commitment to a brother," Alex said. "But Rocco saved my life. I owe him everything."

She seemed to soften at his words. "Maybe Rocco doesn't want you to owe him everything."

Alex shook his head. "I wish I could believe that. But right now he's sitting in our parent's house down there, so overcome with depression that he's sleeping his life away. I doubt he knows what he wants. I've tried calling him and no one ever answers."

"Oh," Maryann said as she looked up at him. "Maybe he's gone out or something?"

"Not Rocco."

"Have you ever asked him what he wants?" Maryann said as she turned to go back to her desk. "Maybe you should talk to him. He might surprise you."

Alex grunted. "I have to reach him on the phone first. He hasn't called here, has he?"

"Here?" Maryann repeated the word as she set the vase of roses on her desk. "No, he hasn't called here."

"It's not like him to miss my birthday," Alex said with a frown. "I wonder if I should have the police check the house and see that he's okay. I'd hate to think of him taking a fall in his wheelchair and lying there not being able to get to the phone or anything."

"I don't think you need to call the police yet," Mary-ann said.

Alex nodded. "Yeah, I suppose. After all, he does have that attendant. Maybe Rocco decided to try and go to the grocery store and I've just missed him. Why knows, maybe he even decided to wheel himself around the block and get some sunshine."

"I'm sure it's something like that," Maryann said as she walked around her desk and sat in her chair. She reached across her desk and adjusted the placement of the vase. "If you don't hear from him by tomorrow, then you can call."

"I guess," Alex said as he started walking back to his office. "Who's my first appointment?"

"The Hazzel baby. An earache. The poor thing," Maryann said. "The file's on your desk already."

Maryann held her feelings in check until she heard the door close on the back exam room where Alex had his office. Her heart had jumped when she saw the roses; she'd never expected a dozen such beautiful flowers. And just when she thought maybe he had feelings for her, too, he said he was leaving anyway. She would cry, but she couldn't even do that, because she was too upset.

Just then Mrs. Hazzel came in the door with her baby wrapped in a blanket, and Maryann tried to put her emotions on hold. The day had begun for the clinic. She was a professional and she couldn't lay her head down and cry. It wasn't easy, but Maryann alternated between calling patients to reschedule their appointments and assisting Alex in the exam room. It was ten forty-five before she knew it.

Maryann sat down at her desk to rest. She was staring at the vase of roses when Amy came into the clinic.

"I'm early," the red-haired woman said breezily as she stepped through the door. Then she looked at the flowers. "What gorgeous roses."

Amy walked over and took a deep breath of their fragrance. "Oh, that smells so good. How do you get any work done? I'd sit and look at them all day."

"I do admire them here and there," Maryann said, trying to match the other woman's enthusiasm. She should have stopped there, but something in Amy's face promised understanding. "I only wish they were real."

Amy frowned and leaned closer. "They look real to me."

Maryann tried to smile. "The roses are. The sentiment isn't."

"Ah," Amy said as she stepped back and then got a chair to pull over so she could sit down beside Maryann's desk. "It's Alex, isn't it?"

Maryann glanced back to be sure that the exam door was shut. Their ten-thirty appointment had called to reschedule for this afternoon, so Alex was using the time to finish some of his notes.

"I don't know if it's him or me," Maryann admitted. "I'm all churned up inside, and I don't like it. He gives me the flowers and I'm all happy inside. Then he tells me he's leaving anyway, so I'm down. I think maybe we can work it out long-distance, and all he can talk about is his duty. I hate feeling this way. I moved to Alaska to have peace of mind."

"Really?" Amy leaned back and looked bemused.

"Yes," Maryann said emphatically. "And I've done everything right. I went back to church. I feel God so solid with me. I've been praying. I clear my mind every night before I go to bed so I can sleep peacefully. If I do what I know to do, I figure God should do the rest."

There was silence for a moment.

"So God is supposed to keep everything serene?" Amy asked.

"Well, yes," Maryann answered, relieved to finally say the words aloud to someone who would understand. Then she added, "You have to understand, in my family everyone seems to be so dramatic every time they fall in love. Drama in, hysteria out. And then it starts all over again. I thought here in Alaska—away from them—I could be my own person and have a relationship that is calm and orderly." She paused and then realized all she had said. "Not that Alex and I have a relationship. I mean he's leaving, it's just that…"

Her voice trailed off and she sat there, a ball of misery if there ever was one. Amy was so quiet Maryann started to worry she wasn't going to answer.

Then she did. "You remind me of myself when I first met Ben. Years ago. I was so scared, and I wanted everything to be perfect. It wasn't, of course. I suppose I could have blamed God for it, too, but…" Amy gave a wide grin to Maryann. "Forgive me for saying so, but God doesn't promise any of us a lack of pain and anguish. I think His peace is supposed to come in the bearing of our problems, not in the lack of them. We can't have a full life if we can't accept some drama in our emotions."

"Oh," Maryann said, as she looked at the other woman. "You're sure about this? Because I had my heart set on things being easier."

Amy smiled. "I'm sorry."

"You don't think Alex is going to stay here, do you?" she asked the other woman, not bothering to hide all of the yearning she'd recently discovered in her heart. "I didn't even know I cared until a couple of days ago."

"Caring is always a precious thing," Amy said softly. "And no, I don't know how it will turn out for you and him." The widow hesitated for a moment. "And even if you do marry, there are no guarantees you won't be parted."

"Oh, dear," Maryann realized who she was talking to about this. "I'm so sorry. I wasn't thinking."

"You don't need to apologize." Amy had a tear in her eye. "God and I are working on my peace just like He is working with you on yours. We all travel our own path with Him. I have noticed, though, that peace doesn't mean things are smooth."

Amy took Maryann's hand and pressed it. "I'll be praying for you."

"Thank you." Maryann nodded. "I'll do the same for you."

The two women sat together for a few moments in silence. Maryann wondered how she had missed seeing the difference between the kind of chaos that surrounded her parents and the kind of problems that were part of an authentic, deep life. She still wished someone could tell her whether to withdraw and shield herself from disappointment with Alex, or whether she should go forward and care about him more deeply, whether he could return her feelings or not.

Chapter Thirteen

Alex sat at his desk, his hands holding a medical journal and his mind not bothering to read any of the words in front of him. He'd caught Maryann looking at those roses when she didn't know he could see her, and he knew they made her sad.

Just then, there was a knock on the door and he put his journal down and straightened his lab coat. "Yes?"

Maryann opened the door. "The Fields family is here. Amy's out here, too."

"Why don't you give me a minute alone with the parents and then we'll talk to Timmy," he suggested.

Maryann nodded. "I'll tell them to come in."

Alex resisted the urge to tap his fingers against his desk. He hadn't quite figured out how to tell Mr. and Mrs. Fields he had paid the hospital bill. He hadn't considered their pride when he'd done it. Although he had no choice, not if Timmy had been going to get the care he needed.

"Ah, come in," Alex said as he stood up. Timmy's parents were standing in the open doorway, looking hesitant, so he added, "Please have a seat."

Alex decided he'd do better if he didn't sit behind his desk, so he moved his chair to the side of the desk and arranged the two office chairs across from him.

"Did you have a good drive into town this morning?" Alex asked the couple, as they were getting seated. He was babbling and he knew it.

Mr. Fields nodded politely. "The roads haven't been bad lately, and I got my pickup fixed."

"Good," Alex said as he sat down.

"I'm looking to get some work at the General Store with Harry," Mr. Fields said proudly. "He's changing out some of his stock, and he said he could use help two days a week."

"We're going to put every one of his checks towards that hospital bill, too," Mrs. Fields said, satisfaction marking her voice. "I don't want you to think we're not going to pay it off as fast as we can."

"'Course, I only have work through October," Mr. Fields admitted. "But it'll pay down a few hundred. That'll get us started."

Alex cleared his throat.

"About the hospital bill," he said and then paused. "The thing is—I paid it."

There was absolute silence in the room.

Mrs. Fields shook her head. "You mean you arranged for us to pay it?"

Alex shook his head. "No, I paid it. They wouldn't admit Timmy any other way."

"You saved our boy's life," Mrs. Fields said, and a tear rolled down her cheek.

"But we can't let him pay the bill," Mr. Fields protested, as he turned to his wife. His face was red, either with embarrassment or shock, Alex didn't know which. "What will people say when they know he paid it?"

"A doctor has a duty to his patients," Alex said, trying to explain.

"But the whole community is raising money to pay this bill," Mr. Fields said. "It's one thing to have everyone chip in a dollar or two. We do the same when someone else needs it. But to have you pay the whole thing—that's nothing but charity."

"I don't think I'd call it charity," Alex protested.

"It's not the way we do things up here," Mr. Fields said adamantly. "You wouldn't understand that, being an outsider, but we have our ways. And taking charity isn't one of them."

"I treated Timmy for you earlier," Alex said, confused now.

"But I'm building you those shelves," Mr. Fields said. "That's fair. But the hospital bill—I can't build anything to equal that. I'd have to put you up a skyscraper."

Everyone was silent for a moment.

"How much was the bill?" Mrs. Fields finally asked.

Alex told him.

"I thought they were giving us a discount," Mrs. Fields protested.

"That was with the discount," Alex said.

"We're going to have to tell people," Mr. Fields said. "At that pancake breakfast on Saturday, we'll have to get up in front and tell everyone Dr. Havens paid off the bill, so they can keep their money for another cause."

"I'd really rather you didn't mention my name," Alex said. "People don't need to know who paid it."

"Well, they would figure that out real fast without us saying your name anyway," Mr. Fields said. "Who else was up in Juneau to do something like that? They know your nurse doesn't have that kind of money."

"It could have been Max," Alex said. Maybe his friend would enjoy the attention.

Mr. Fields shook his head morosely. "No, he wouldn't do something like this. He keeps all his money for those airplanes of his. Nobody would believe he'd pay for Timmy."

"You can say it was an anonymous donor," Alex pleaded. "People give money all the time, and don't want their names mentioned."

"They're going to think I robbed a bank or something," Mr. Fields said, fretting as he turned to his wife. "Or maybe they'll think I found that treasure that Amy's great-great-something buried all those years ago."

"I don't know—" Mrs. Fields began.

"Mark my words," her husband said, interrupting her. "People are going to be out at our place, digging holes all over, trying to find some of the treasure they think I have, if we don't tell everyone what happened."

"Well..." Alex said. He could see the other man wasn't going to wind down anytime soon. "Please just think about it. We have some time between now and Saturday."

"Thank you," Mrs. Fields said quietly as she stood up. "Maryann said you didn't need us when you talk to Timmy, so we'll wait outside. I have a few things to get at the general store, so we'll be back in a bit to pick up Timmy."

Alex nodded as he stood up. "That works very well."

He shook hands with the couple, and then they left the room.

He sat down. It was worse than he'd thought. He hadn't even begun to consider all of the complications if his role in paying Timmy's bill became known. It did mark him as an outsider. Not many people in this town had enough in savings that they could have paid the bill off completely.

It wasn't long before Amy and Timmy were standing in the open doorway. Amy was carrying the Bible that had the map inside of it.

"Maryann's not coming?" he asked.

Amy shook her head, but didn't offer any explanation.

Alex let Timmy sit in the chair for a bit before he began.

"How are you feeling?" he asked the boy. "Are you doing okay?"

Timmy nodded. He kept looking at that Bible. "I'm a little tired."

Alex didn't have the heart to chastise the boy, but it had to be done. Boys didn't grow to responsible men if they didn't face the consequences of their actions. If there was one lesson that had been seared on his heart, that was the one.

"We need to talk about the map," Alex said. There was no reason to delay. "Do you know who the map belongs to?"

Timmy nodded his head and gave a sideways glance at Amy. "It's hers."

"Okay then," Alex said. "What do you think you could do to make things right with Amy?"

Timmy looked up and scrunched up his face in thought. "I could give the map back."

Alex nodded, "That's the first step. What else?"

"I could find the treasure for her," Timmy said. His face lit up at this prospect. "I think I saw something when I was out there. Maybe we could go back and find it. I know just where to look."

"You're never to go back there alone." Alex kept his voice soft and tried not to show the panic he felt when he saw the excitement on the boy's face. "You need someone older to go with you. And not just another kid. An adult. Besides, I was thinking of something you could do to show Amy how sorry you are that you took something that belonged to her—nothing to do with the treasure."

Timmy thought some more, his face twisted in the effort. "I could give her my bike, but it lost a wheel, so it doesn't work too good."

"I think maybe a simple 'I'm sorry' will do," Amy said as she smiled down at the boy. "With a promise not to steal anything again."

Timmy's face brightened. "I *am* sorry, and I promise never ever to take anything that's not mine. Not ever again."

"Well, that settles it then," Amy said.

"No, I think he needs to do something to earn his forgiveness," Alex said. "Maybe he can help you in your garden for a couple of days. That's good hard work."

"It's September," Amy protested. "There's not much that's still growing."

"He could help you get the ground ready for next year," Alex said. He didn't want Amy to go to soft on the boy. Timmy's actions had serious consequences, and he needed to understand that.

"You don't mean digging up the dirt!" Amy looked shocked. "He's too young."

"He could help with the digging," Alex said. "Maybe move some of those rocks around to make a new border for your flower beds."

Alex looked over at Timmy. The boy was looking worried. "Of course, you'll need to wait until he's completely well."

"Can my friends help me?" Timmy asked.

"We'll talk about it later," Alex said. He was convinced the boy understood the gravity of his poor choices.

Timmy swallowed. "You're not going to tell my parents, are you?"

Alex wondered if everyone hadn't had enough emotion-packed confessions for the time being. "Not today. But you'll need to tell them yourself in a day or two."

"I'm sure they'll understand," Amy added. "If you want, you can have them call me and I'll tell them it's all right."

Alex frowned. "You mean, it will be all right when he helps you get the garden ready for next year?"

Amy frowned back at Alex before she turned to Timmy and smiled. "Just have them call me if they have any questions—"

Then Amy stood up and reached out for Timmy's hand. "I'm sure your parents want to get you home again. The day is nice right now, but it could turn cold again as the afternoon goes on."

Timmy stood up and took her hand.

"I'll talk to you later," Amy said to Alex and he figured she meant to tell him why he was wrong in suggesting Timmy help her with her garden to make amends for what he did. She didn't know, though, what guilt did to a man when he couldn't do anything to fix the things he'd done wrong in this life.

He knew Timmy was a young boy, but Alex hadn't been much older when the accident happened. It would have been helpful if someone older and wiser had been there to tell him it was good to do something hard and physical to show how sorry he was. Maybe then he could have found a way to actually say the words.

He listened until he heard the door outside close a few times. Then he went back to his journal.

Chapter Fourteen

Maryann knew from the darkness outside the clinic windows that it was past closing time, but she had postponed walking to the door and flipping the sign because she kept thinking Rocco would show up. She knew he wasn't accustomed to wheeling himself down rough asphalt roads, so she figured he might need extra time. She kept walking to the window to look outside toward the boarding house, but no one was coming down the road.

Her heart sank. The longer she had to hide what she knew from Alex, the worse she felt. She knew she hadn't lied to him about Rocco, but surely he deserved to know.

She had closed her eyes a few minutes ago, and prayed that Rocco would come; but the clock kept ticking, and he hadn't arrived. Technically, she supposed, he had until midnight to tell Alex he was here, but it didn't seem likely Rocco could wheel himself down to his brother's place that late at night.

She glanced over at the vase of roses that stood on her desk. She couldn't even solve the problems *she* had;

she shouldn't fret about other those of other people. She had run Amy's words round and round in her mind since they'd had their talk. Was she really trying to run away from all of the emotions of life? She wondered how to strike a balance in her feelings. Maybe she could feel the full range of emotions without exaggerating them, as her parents did.

She looked up when she heard Alex walking through the hall, coming toward the waiting room.

"Ready to go?" he said, when he got to her desk. "Amy's going to be calling the choir to order any minute now."

Maryann nodded as she stood up from her desk and reached for her jacket. "Are you taking your medical bag—since you're the doctor?"

"I've got it covered," he said with a grin as he pulled a packet of cough drops out of the pocket of his jacket.

Maryann smiled. "You might want to grab another bag. I think you might have lots of singers coming to you for voice strain."

Alex lifted his eyebrow in a question.

"The fancy women," Maryann said. "They'll want to talk to you, and what better way than to say they have a sore throat from singing so much."

"You're probably right," he said as he turned to walk back to the exam room where they kept the supplies.

While he was doing that, Maryann decided to make a sign saying Dr. Havens was at the church. That way, if Rocco did want to see him tonight, he'd know where to look. She wrote the letters of her note in bold, black marker, and got out a piece of adhesive tape so she could be sure it stayed on the door.

"Expecting someone?" Alex asked as he came back and saw her taping the note to the door.

"You never know," she said.

Alex shrugged. "It's probably a good idea all right. There could be an emergency."

Once she had the sign posted, they turned off the inside light and closed the door. The faint light coming in from the nearest street lamp would be enough for someone to read the note without a flashlight.

They made their way down the porch steps. Except for the circles of light from the street lamps, the night was dark. The sky had been overcast earlier, and the clouds must still be up there, because there were no stars showing. The air had a raw coldness to it that promised snow before too many more days.

Alex put his arm around her shoulders with a naturalness that indicated he thought it had become the way they walked together. She supposed that was true by now. She was determined not to try to avoid any feelings, so she didn't back away when Alex pulled her a little closer. She did not have many more night walks with him, and she'd want to remember them later.

Warm, yellow light streamed out of the windows of the Treasure Creek Christian Church. There were a dozen or so steps leading to the porch of this plain, white clapboard church, and a steep wheelchair ramp ran up the side. The most impressive thing about the church was its high steeple. Maryann had heard it said that the founders of Treasure Creek put up the tallest steeple they could find so miners could find their way to town when they were coming down from the mountains. Over the years, the church had expanded on its reputation for being a beacon to guide people home.

When they got to the top of the stairs, Alex reached for the door handle, but then drew his hand back and turned to her until both of his arms were on her shoulders. He was standing so close that his open jacket formed a cocoon of warmth and comfort with her in the center.

"Do we have to go inside?" he whispered.

"I—I don't know," she said, her heart thumping. She could see his face in the darkness—the line of his jaw, the half smile on his lips. "Amy is counting on us."

He nodded, but did not move. A minute passed.

Then he murmured, "Sometimes I get so tired of doing my duty. Even when I have to—even when people are counting on me."

Maryann nodded, but she didn't answer. She didn't know what to say to the yearning in his voice. His eyes were intent.

"I just want you to know I want to stay here with you. Even if I go, I want you to know I wish it were different."

Maryann felt hope rise up inside of her and then crash to the ground.

"Don't say that," she said, as she took a step back. "Not yet. Not until you talk to your brother."

It wasn't fair, she reminded herself, to let him make any kind of declaration when he didn't know that his brother wasn't lying in bed in Los Angeles, barely able to move because of some great depression. It was easy for Alex to declare he wanted to stay when he knew he had to leave. But how would he feel if Rocco said he didn't need him, that Alex was free to live where he wanted?

"I just think you should wait a bit," she said when he didn't say anything more.

Finally, he nodded and reached for the door handle again. This time he opened it and waited for Maryann to enter first.

The sounds of talk and laughter drifted back to where they stood, in the shadows of the entryway.

Alex had never felt so alone. Not even after the accident. It didn't matter if Maryann stood by him or not. He needed to wait for a minute or two before he was ready to face the group of people who were getting ready to sing together. He had misread Maryann's feelings for him, that much was clear. He supposed in time he would feel mortified at how open he'd been with his own feelings when she did not share them. For now though, he was too numb to care.

"You go ahead," he finally had breath enough to say to Maryann.

"I—" she started.

But he shook his head. "We'll talk later."

He still couldn't turn and look at her, but he heard her take a first hesitant step away from him, so he added, "Please."

She would need to talk to him later, he knew. Nothing would be easy about this. She couldn't bear to hurt anyone. She'd want to bandage his wounds, and he would have to let her, listening to her say how sorry she was, and how he would find someone else and that he'd be happy in time. He knew she would have to say the words and he would have to listen, but he just couldn't do it yet.

He watched her walk down the aisle to the front of the church and stop to whisper something in Amy's ears. Then he saw the other woman look back to where he stood. Fortunately, Amy turned back to Maryann and nodded. Then Maryann kept walking—and slipped out the door at the side of the church.

Alex needed to sit down, so he walked to the last pew. He sat down and leaned forward until his head rested on the top of the pew in front of him. For the first time since he was a boy, he started to pray. He had no fine words to say, he just knew he needed mercy. The chasms between him and the people he loved were too deep for him to cross alone.

He sat there for a long time, the people in the front of the church managing to sing through the whole song of "Amazing Grace." He'd never known it to be a song used in a Christmas pageant, so he figured Amy was trying to comfort him as best she could.

And then he felt a firm hand on his shoulder. He looked up to see Reverend Michaels, middle-aged and kind, sit down next to him on the pew.

"Can I help?" the man asked softly.

Alex looked up and tried to smile. "Not unless you have a 'Get Out of Jail Free' card."

Reverend Michaels grinned. "Actually, I have something that works even better."

Alex expected the reverend to start preaching at him with that, but the man just sat and let his presence be comforting. They were quiet together for a few minutes.

"I guess I have a problem," Alex finally said. "At least Amy thinks I do. I've always thought a man should make amends for what he's done to hurt others. Even a boy like Timmy Fields needs to learn to make amends. How else do you show someone you're sorry?"

The reverend nodded. "And that's what you're trying to do, too, I'm guessing."

Alex nodded. "It's killing me."

"God knows a man's heart," Reverend Michaels said. "He knows who is repentant. I noticed you were praying."

Alex nodded. "Praying, but not believing He'd answer. And why should He? I've let Him down, too."

The reverend was quiet for so long Alex thought he had discouraged the man. Then he spoke again.

"How would you like that 'Get Out of Jail Free' card?" he asked. "To have a new start, where someone else paid your amends for every failure in your life? Where you were forgiven for every bad thing you did and every good thing you failed to do?"

"I don't think it's that easy," Alex said.

The reverend smiled. "God says it is."

Alex closed his eyes. No one needed to connect any more of the dots. But did he dare risk believing God would do that for him? He felt the ice inside him start to melt. He had to believe.

When he opened his eyes, he faced the reverend squarely and nodded.

Just then, he noticed the church had become very quiet. He looked up toward the front and saw that Amy had walked closer to him. The others were up there, standing still and watching as if they were expecting something to happen.

The double door to the church opened and a man walked in.

"Nate? Nate McMann?" Amy said as she hurried down the aisle. "You're just the man I wanted to see. I thought you were still out on that fishing boat."

Nate grinned at her. "I had to come back to see what people were up to here. Why?"

"I just thought you might want to help lead a tour for me," Amy said.

Alex recognized the matchmaking look on Amy's face, but he didn't think the other man did. He wondered who the tour boss had in mind for the man.

"Sounds great," Nate said, then he looked around. "I saw the lights on here, so I came on over. It's a good thing, too. I needed to help someone outside."

"Oh, we forgot about the ramp," Amy exclaimed as she continued toward the door. "I should have sent someone with her."

Nate reached the door ahead of her. "I was just giving them a minute to get ready for their entrance."

Alex had the strangest sensation that they were talking about Maryann and someone. But he couldn't figure out what all the secrecy was about. Then he remembered she'd had something she couldn't tell him.

Nate opened one side of the double door while Amy opened the other and Alex felt his world spin. The entryway to the church wasn't well lit, and the man in the wheelchair was still on the porch outside in the dark, so Alex couldn't see his face yet. But he recognized the heft of the shoulders and the tilt of the head.

"Rocco?" he whispered.

Maryann stood to the side of where Rocco sat in his wheelchair, getting ready to go inside the church. He had come so far, he deserved to make the final few yards of the journey alone. She had prayed with him before he'd maneuvered himself squarely in front of the door. Then she stepped aside.

She looked at the astonishment on Alex's face. She could almost see him putting all of the pieces together and trying to find answers to his question as Rocco slowly wheeled himself inside the entryway of the church and faced him.

"Where's that attendant of yours?" Alex finally managed to say. "He should know better than to bring you this far. I can't believe—"

Alex stood up and started to walk to the door, like he was going to search outside for the man.

"He's in Denver," Rocco said calmly. "Visiting a niece."

If Alex could look more shocked, he did. "Then who? Surely our parents didn't—"

Rocco laughed as he wheeled himself further inside. "Not likely."

Alex stopped and stared at his brother. Finally, he demanded to know, "Then who?"

Rocco sat up straighter in his wheelchair. "Me. I brought myself here."

"But you won't even go to the grocery store," Alex protested weakly. "How?"

Maryann hugged herself when she saw the look on Alex's face. He did not like to be unprepared. Every square needed to be placed just so for a plan to work in his mind. Maybe he truly had meant what he'd said earlier about wanting to be with her, but not knowing how the squares would all fall into place had meant he couldn't commit to more than the feeling.

"I've been practicing and working out," Rocco said proudly. "The attendant you hired showed me how. I do pretty good now."

Alex finally sat down again, this time in a straight back chair that had been set beside the coat rack for when people needed to take off their boots. "But why didn't you tell me you were coming?"

Maryann watched the brothers.

Rocco rolled closer and sat eye-to-eye with his brother. "You would have told me not to come. You would have said you have a duty to give me this or build me that. I wanted to come and see a live moose. And see the mountains I've heard about. And eat the apple pie at the diner. "

Alex looked at his brother for a long time before he smiled. "And have you eaten some apple pie? And seen a moose?"

Rocco shook his head and grinned. "Not yet. That moose hasn't been in town since I've been here, and I wanted to take you with me to get the apple pie."

"Well, we've got time," Alex said as he reached over and hugged his brother. When he pulled away, he asked. "How long are you staying, anyway?"

Rocco looked away at that one. For the first time, Maryann sensed that Rocco needed some help. She walked in and squatted by his wheelchair. He nodded gratefully to her and then turned to Alex. "I thought I might—well, you see Lindy offered me a job and—the maid's quarters are pretty comfortable. It might take some time to actually see a moose."

Maryann noticed that Alex was now looking at her.

"You knew all of this," Alex said, his voice flat. "This is what you couldn't tell me."

Maryann nodded. She was miserable, but she'd not lie.

"You didn't—" Alex started and then stopped.

She knew what he meant, and she shook her head. "I didn't even know he was here until I saw him at Lindy's when I got back from Juneau."

"She worried the whole time about how you would take it," Rocco added softly. "I'm the one who asked her not to tell you. I was afraid you'd make me leave before I got a chance to look around."

Alex stood then, and walked toward her. She couldn't read his expression, but she thought he looked nervous. She'd never seen that look on his face before. He appeared very uncertain,

"Is that why you didn't want me to continue earlier?" he asked softly.

Maryann looked around her and saw the church was empty, except for the three of them. Amy must have ushered the others out the side door.

She nodded. "I thought you shouldn't say anything until you knew."

She heard Rocco wheeling his chair to the front of the church.

Alex grinned. "Then let me tell you again. I want to stay with you. Here in Treasure Creek. I want us to walk with each other and God here, in this place. I know it's too soon to talk of marriage, but I figure, in a week or so I'll have earned the right to ask you to marry me."

"Yes," Maryann said.

Alex drew in a quick breath. "When you say 'yes,' is that 'yes, I'll have earned the right to ask'? Or 'yes that'—"

She stood there in the entryway to the church and watched the hope build in his eyes. His hand reached out to smooth back her hair, and she reached up to touch his cheek just for the pleasure of it.

"We should probably go on a few dates before I say yes," she finally said. She took a deep breath. "Just so we know for sure."

"I forgot," Alex said, with a smile. "You want to make your decision based on logic, wasn't it? Genes and common sense and—"

Alex's voice trailed off, and he looked at her for a long moment before bending down to kiss her.

Maryann's head swirled.

"We can go on a hundred dates," he whispered, after that. "I love you and already know for sure you're the one for me. I want you to feel the same. What is it you Jenners need? To be poleaxed by love?"

"I'm immune to that," she murmured, as he kissed her again.

Epilogue

A few months later, when winter had firmly taken hold of Treasure Creek, Maryann and Alex were married in the old Russian church. The city had decided to sell the building, and Alex had purchased it for his new clinic, with the understanding that he would preserve the historic building and let tourists gawk at it as often as they wanted. There would be enough room for all the new equipment he wanted for his practice, and Alex liked the image of healing the sick in a house of worship.

Maryann now stood at the end of the aisle, waiting for the processional to begin. The fragrance of the fresh red roses in her bouquet mingled with that of wax. Mr. Fields had worked for days, buffing and polishing the old wood floor until it shone. The light coming through the windows on the sides of the church showed it off beautifully.

There had not been enough chairs for all of the people who wanted to come, so Lizbet's Diner closed for the day, and Max had hauled all of their chairs over in his pickup.

Maryann marveled at the community of friends she

had here. The Reverend Michaels had happily agreed to conduct the service, and people had came from all around to see their doctor marry his nurse. The Fields family was proudly sitting in the front row.

The music finally began and her maid of honor, Karenna, started down the strip of carpet that been laid down the aisle. Then it was time for Maryann to walk toward Alex. It wasn't until she was halfway down, looking into his eyes the whole way, that she started to feel a little faint and couldn't quite catch her next breath. Then the butterflies in her stomach increased their flutter and she gripped her bouquet tighter before swaying a little. And then her knees felt funny, as if they were made of Jell-O.

The next thing Maryann knew she was lying on the carpet with Alex kneeling beside her, taking her pulse and smoothing back her hair.

"What's wrong?" The reverend was standing there, staring down with a worried look on his face.

Karenna started to chuckle as she bent over and winked at Maryann, and then Alex joined in.

"She's been poleaxed by love," Karenna said as she straightened up. "It's a family trait, and it's about time, if you ask me."

"I wasn't—" Maryann started to protest, but then she looked up at Alex and grinned. The man did have a powerful effect on her. Maybe it wasn't so bad to feel all of her emotions after all. "You know, I think Karenna's right."

Alex's grin turned triumphant.

Then he leaned down and kissed her.

* * * * *

Dear Reader,

I still remember my first view of the mountains in Alaska. I was sitting in the copilot seat of a small plane, and the view was absolutely breathtaking. Those mountains are majestic. And it isn't just the scenery that makes it a great state. My impression of the people of Alaska is that they are rugged individuals—just the kind of people, like Alex, who would put everything on the line to save a small boy's life.

As you can tell, I was ready to revisit the state through my imagination, so I was delighted to join the other authors in this series as we figured out how to tell the story of a small tourist town and the treasure map they sought.

Of course, each book is different in the series and I was fortunate enough to be assigned the story of Alex and Maryann—a doctor and a nurse, both committed to taking care of others, even when they don't always take the best care of themselves. Alex had made a mistake as a child and is planning to make amends by building a medical clinic in his brother's name. Together Alex and Maryann discover that God is bigger than all their mistakes and plans. I hope you enjoy their story.

If you have a minute, I would love to hear from you. Just go to my Web site at www.janettronstad.com and e-mail me from there. In the meantime, God bless you and keep you.

Sincerely,

Janet Tronstad

QUESTIONS FOR DISCUSSION

1. Dr. Alex Havens had his life all planned—he was going to build a clinic—and then he found out that God had something else in mind for him. Do you believe Christians should even bother making plans? Do you make them?

2. Maryann Jenner raced up to Alaska because she was worried about her cousin. She obviously acted quickly and didn't make much of a plan. Are you more like her or Alex? How so? Do you think God has a preference for planners or impulsive people?

3. Can you name a character in the Bible who planned and one who didn't?

4. The fancy women had a plan, as well. They came up to Alaska in response to a magazine article that spoke of the bachelor tour guides. The desire of their hearts was to get married. We know God cares about the desires of our heart, but He does not always answer these prayers the way we want Him to. What do you say to people who are disappointed that their prayers are not answered the way they want?

5. Even little Timmy had a plan. He was going to find the treasure so his parents would be happy. His

parents were stressed because of finances. What stresses do you have in your life? How do you think these stresses affect the people around you? What would you say to parents like Timmy's whose stress affects their children?

6. Alex made his plans because of the guilt he felt for what had happened many years ago when his brother was crippled saving his life (when Alex wasn't being obedient). Have your actions ever caused someone to be hurt? Did you feel guilty for this? How did you respond?

7. Alex had told his brother he was sorry, but Alex didn't feel words were enough. That's why he wanted to build the clinic in his brother's name. Do you think there are times when "I'm sorry" isn't enough? Under what circumstances?

8. Did Alex go overboard in deciding to build the clinic? Why or why not?

9. Have you ever been hurt by someone's actions and they then tried to do something big to make it all better? Do you think a big gesture does make it better? When does it and when does it not?

10. Maryann moved to Alaska partly because she was tired of the chaos of her parents' lives. Different people are able to handle more chaos than others. Where do you fall on the spectrum?

11. The town Treasure Creek plays a big part in this series. Would you like to live in a place like Treasure Creek? Why or why not?

12. Is the town different from what you imagined Alaska to be like? If so, how?

13. One of the delightful things in this series is the treasure map. The prospect of finding unexpected treasure cheers up most people. Have you had a time in your life when you thought you might get an unexpected treasure? What happened?

14. If you (like the author of the treasure map) were going to leave something to your descendants, what would it be?

15. At this point in the series, do you have any guesses as to what the treasure is?

Love Inspired

TITLES AVAILABLE NEXT MONTH

Available September 28, 2010

HIS HOLIDAY BRIDE
The Granger Family Ranch
Jillian Hart

YUKON COWBOY
Alaskan Bride Rush
Debra Clopton

MISTLETOE PRAYERS
Marta Perry and Betsy St. Amant

THE MARINE'S BABY
Deb Kastner

SEEKING HIS LOVE
Carrie Turansky

FRESH-START FAMILY
Lisa Mondello

LICNM0910

LARGER-PRINT BOOKS!

GET 2 FREE
LARGER-PRINT NOVELS
PLUS 2 FREE
MYSTERY GIFTS

LoveInspired

Larger-print novels are now available...

YES! Please send me 2 FREE LARGER-PRINT Love Inspired® novels and my 2 FREE mystery gifts (gifts are worth about $10). After receiving them, if I don't wish to receive any more books, I can return the shipping statement marked "cancel". If I don't cancel, I will receive 6 brand-new novels every month and be billed just $4.74 per book in the U.S. or $5.24 per book in Canada. That's a saving of over 20% off the cover price. It's quite a bargain! Shipping and handling is just 50¢ per book.* I understand that accepting the 2 free books and gifts places me under no obligation to buy anything. I can always return a shipment and cancel at any time. Even if I never buy another book, the two free books and gifts are mine to keep forever.

122/322 IDN E7QP

Name _____ (PLEASE PRINT) _____

Address _____ Apt. # _____

City _____ State/Prov. _____ Zip/Postal Code _____

Signature (if under 18, a parent or guardian must sign) _____

Mail to **Steeple Hill Reader Service:**
IN U.S.A.: P.O. Box 1867, Buffalo, NY 14240-1867
IN CANADA: P.O. Box 609, Fort Erie, Ontario L2A 5X3

Not valid to current subscribers to Love Inspired Larger-Print books.

**Are you a current subscriber to Love Inspired books
and want to receive the larger-print edition?
Call 1-800-873-8635 or visit www.morefreebooks.com.**

* Terms and prices subject to change without notice. Prices do not include applicable taxes. Sales tax applicable in N.Y. Canadian residents will be charged applicable provincial taxes and GST. Offer not valid in Quebec. This offer is limited to one order per household. All orders subject to approval. Credit or debit balances in a customer's account(s) may be offset by any other outstanding balance owed by or to the customer. Please allow 4 to 6 weeks for delivery. Offer available while quantities last.

Your Privacy: Steeple Hill Books is committed to protecting your privacy. Our Privacy Policy is available online at www.SteepleHill.com or upon request from the Reader Service. From time to time we make our lists of customers available to reputable third parties who may have a product or service of interest to you. If you would prefer we not share your name and address, please check here. ☐

Help us get it right—We strive for accurate, respectful and relevant communications. To clarify or modify your communication preferences, visit us at www.ReaderService.com/consumerschoice.

LILP10R

mercial for an ABC show called *Before They Were Stars*. Suddenly there I was on-screen, in 1985, doing stand-up on amateur night in Eufaulla, Alabama. My shirt was pretty cool but never in my wildest dreams did I imagine that that old videotape would ever air on national television. It really stopped me in midscrub. I said to my wife, "Honey, if I'm on a before-they-were-stars show, does this mean I'm a star now?"

She handed me the crusty roast pan; a reality check if ever there was one. We both knew that even after more than ten years of entertaining everyone from coeds on spring break to the chief executive at the Ford Theater, that I still didn't think of myself as any more than just a regular guy. Of course, once I could run out for milk and diapers without a second thought, but now, people I didn't even know—including some fifth and sixth cousins who, I should point out, have *just recently* declared themselves family relations—think of me as some sort of celebrity.

I still don't believe it. The company that books my concerts always tells me I have the smallest backstage catering bill in the history of entertainment. At one of my biggest shows last year, we had three six-packs of Sprites and 7-Ups—in case somebody came up—a pot of coffee, some candy bars, and a container of Tic-Tacs. The tab came to almost $25.

As you can tell, none of this has gone to my head.

A person's idea of celebrity constantly changes. When I was twelve years old, just seeing the sportscaster from WSB, Channel Two in Atlanta, in a restaurant, prevented me from eating because I was so excited. All I could do was whisper, "Art Eckman's right over there!" I never talked to him, of course, because you didn't approach Art Eckman in *public*. Nooo.

Now I see Art Eckman on ESPN doing "Motor World" and I still get excited. I just don't understand why my wife thinks it's strange when I point at the TV and whisper at the top of my lungs, "Art Eckman's right over there!"

Any entertainer can perform for years without crossing the line where one day he notices that people notice him more than he notices them. Then it happens. At first, the lingering stares can feel awkward. You're not sure why people gawk at you so intently. Suddenly you're wondering if your shirt is on inside out. If your socks match. Are your pants pulled up all the way? Are you even wearing pants? The thought of dandruff is scary because the flakes would have to be the size of tadpoles for someone to see them at that distance. If it's none of the above, that's when the thought that maybe someone recognizes you might creep into your head.

Just hope it's not your parole officer.

I have performed across this country more times than most of my childhood friends have learned to count, and even I have suffered from the delusion that everyone knows who I am. Fortunately, that's just when I am forced to confront my own foolishness. Just because I say, "Hi, I'm Jeff Foxworthy," not everyone will go, "Ohhh!" Lots of times, no one does. They have no idea who I am. This is toughest when I've stepped outside the concert hall for some air before the show and the stage door locks behind me. When the guy taking tickets at the front door doesn't know me from Spike, it has a way of planting one's feet back on the ground. Suddenly you're scrubbing the roast pan.

Being or not being recognized is both better than *kind of* not being recognized. It cracks me up when someone asks, "Are you somebody?"

"I hope so," I usually reply.

"Who are you?"

"Well, if you don't know it doesn't matter, right?"

Well, not always. Not everyone who stares at a celebrity is a fan. Once, while walking through the Detroit airport, a group of men suddenly locked their eyes on me. "Okay," I thought, "I can take a compliment. I just hope they don't ask for autographs in awkward places." I smiled politely and kept walking. They didn't smile back. Suddenly one of the men yelled, "Hey! Who are you? What's your name?" I walked faster.

It was freezing cold, I wanted to get to my hotel, and I was in no mood for meeting people who didn't even seem to know me. As I walked, I asked myself if I'd made any jokes onstage the night before that I might regret today. Had I said *anything* at all that would cause ten men in dull business suits to follow me from one city to another?

That's when they surrounded me. One guy said, "Let's see some ID." I said, "Who wants to know?" I figured out they were cops when the guy flashed his badge. I'm sharp that way.

My wallet and airline ticket were in my coat pocket. I reached in to get them. They pulled their guns on me. I'm not lying. I've seen this happen so many times in the movies you'd think I'd know better.

I eased my hand back.

Later, they apologized for the inconvenience and told me they were searching for a guy on the Ten Most Wanted List who looked an awful lot like me. Same height, weight, and coloring. Only, it seemed, not nearly as nice. Mr. Most Wanted would not have wiped his feet before getting into the squad car.

"The guy kidnaped and murdered five people," one cop said. Then they let me go and gave me some advice: "Be careful. This might happen again."

It didn't, but a couple of weeks later, a buddy of mine in Baltimore sent me something he'd discovered in his local post office: a Wanted Poster.

"Fox, you're not gonna believe this," he wrote. "Look how much this guy looks like you!" He was right. Same mustache, same haircut . . . we could have been twins. I don't know if the Detroit police ever caught up with this man. I hope so. But the memory of being drawn down on still lingers. That's why now, when strangers approach, my smile usually says,

"Howdy," but my eyes say, "I swear I didn't do it."

I wonder if my wife would ever buy this explanation?

✻

There are many degrees of celebrity. For instance, there's fame and then there's *fame*. When I was a teenager playing air-guitar in front of the mirror, I imagined that being famous involved many women and a lot more leisure time. Now I think fame is like money. Any time you get to where you think you've got it, you don't have to look very far to see somebody who's got a lot more than you.

One type of fame is called "Only *You* Think You're a Celebrity." This is not the real thing, but a delusional state that is often incurable. Even with years of therapy it's hard to convince some people that others don't know who the hell they are. In clinical terms this is known as the "Rumor in your own time, legend in your own room" syndrome.

There is also "Fifteen-Minute" fame. If you ever get that far, the trick is to make it stick. Good examples are any panelists on a daytime talk show, or Kato Kaelin. He's already had about seventeen minutes. His time is really up.

He'd better check the buzzer. Now if I could only get him to vacate the guest house.

More types include notorious phenomenons, personalities, stars, superstars, legends, and the kind of ultimate celebrity that both you and I don't really ever want to be. The last is easy to spot: You know you've reached that pinnacle when *someone else* can make a living being your celebrity double.

Once you become like Elvis or Michael Jackson, that's not celebrity. That's prison. Too bad neither one has helped his own cause much. Elvis used to bitch he couldn't go to the movie theater, but maybe if he didn't take twelve cars and wear the cape, he could've snuck in and seen the show.

I finally understood the enormity of Elvis—and I'm just talking about his fame—once I toured Graceland. I'll never forget the moment I stood in the Jungle Room and surveyed the green shag carpet and the leopard skin throne. I had one all-consuming thought: "You cannot give Rednecks money. You can't! We don't know what to do with it." Somebody should have had the guts to go, "E, man, this is really tacky stuff here. Perhaps a nice Ethan Allen sectional would be better."

Elvis also had a whole hallway—more like a runway—lined with gold and platinum records.

That's a problem I *do* understand. Now, all of a sudden, *I've* got gold and platinum records. What I need is a sensible outdoor storage shed to put them in. I've also got pictures of myself with guys like Johnny Carson, David Letterman, Bob Hope. Gregg likes the new double-platinum albums because they've got mahogany frames, and she wants to put them up in the living room. I can't. They'd detract from the antlers and my collection of cologne bottles shaped like automobiles.

My big question is: At what point does my ego allow me to put up this stuff in my own home? I'm uncomfortable. It's like a salute to myself. I think I should just put these mementos in my office where people can walk in and see them if they move a couple of packing crates and look around really hard.

There is one picture, though, that I *did* want to put up. I once worked at a comedy club in Daytona Beach during spring break. They took my publicity photo, which was really nice, blew it up, and made a sign that read, "Back by popular demand! Jeff Foxworthy." Right. I'm *sure* those college kids demanded that I come back. They probably thought I was the Budweiser delivery man. But the photo was cool and my wife framed it. Now it's in my office, and I can honestly say it looks really stupid next to me with Johnny Carson, me with Milton Berle, and me with Travis Tritt. "Oh, and there's Jeff, back by popular demand at the CocoHut in Daytona Beach."

*

Some celebrities don't know how to act when a fan wants an autograph. I think "gracious" is a good word to keep in mind. Signing anything from slightly used table napkins to sweaty chests is easy and just being polite. I'm happy to oblige. I remember when no one wanted my signature except on speeding tickets. If I could, I'd also give away twenty-dollar bills with each autograph, just to show my appreciation for your support. (If you believe that, please place this book next to your copy of *UFO's Are Real!* Not a bad read, by the way.)

*

What if a fan wants more than an autograph? That can be confusing. I've sat in a hotel lobby, and all of a sudden somebody just slaps the hell out of my back and goes, "Hey, next time yer in town, come out to the house and have dinner with us. You come in a day early, by God, and

we'll go huntin'. I'll put you on some squirrels." Honestly, I'd like to. Maybe next year.

Otherwise, I have no problem with being recognized: on the street, in the supermarket, or
even at the Victoria's Secret store over in the
mall. Hey, it's tough, waiting thirty days between catalogs. A man's got to keep up with
fashion.

✻

Here's something I learned: When you meet a
celebrity you admire you should say, "Hello"
and "It's a thrill to meet you." Then shake their
hand and leave. The longer you stay the less
you're welcome—unless they *want* to keep
talking. Just don't mistake the smile and automatic head nod as a signal that you should run
down your life story. Celebrities appreciate
your good wishes. They like to know that
something they do is all that makes your life
worth living. They're probably even thrilled to
hear about how their sitcom/movie/album, etc.
made the week you spent in the hospital, for
double hernia surgery, bearable. But please
don't feel obligated to describe the recuperation
process, especially if it involves drainage, rot,
or highly infectious liquids.

Am I rude to say all this? It's just good fan

manners. I'll give you another great tip: Don't bug famous people while they're eating. Whenever my mother is in L.A., she wants to go to Dan Tana's restaurant. She thinks it's the best Italian place in the world, which means she likes it better than the Shakey's Pizza in Stockbridge, Georgia. Last time we were at Dan Tana's Bob Newhart came in with Dick Martin and sat two tables away. My mother squeezed my leg, and said, "That's Bob. That's Bob Newhart. Go over there and introduce yourself to Bob."

I said, "Mother, they're eating. I will *never* go interrupt somebody's meal just to say hello."

Well, the whole meal she wouldn't let up. "*He's* a comedian, *you're* a comedian. Go and say hello." Made sense to her.

We finally finished our meal and paid the bill. I looked over at Newhart. He'd also paid the check and was having coffee. My mother squeezed me again. "Go on!"

Against my better judgment, I said, "Okay!" I walked over to the table, head down, tail between my legs, and said, "First of all, I want to apologize so much for coming over to your table and . . ." That's when Bob Newhart looked up and said, "Jeff Foxworthy!"

"Right. And this is my mother, Carole."

He was as generous and as nice as he could be. My mother, well, you could have struck her dead with lightning. She could finally go out the door.

*

Some people try to meet performers after a show. Don't. If you can get a backstage pass, meet them *before* the show. I do a two-hour set and I'm pretty sweaty at the end. That's why I always feel bad when people come back for meet-and-greets and I have to put my arm around them for the picture. I smell like a buck in rut. I just stand there the whole time going, "I'm so sorry. I'm so sorry. I hope the stains come out."

*

I also have my heroes. When I was growing up, my heroes tended to be ballplayers. To this day one of the highlights of my life was meeting Dale Murphy. He played center field for the Braves until he ended up going to right. Won the MVP back-to-back years. He was a great player on a bunch of really bad ball clubs. But he always treated people nicely. He always signed autographs. Had a ton of class. He felt and lived up to the obligations of being a role model. I never heard anybody say anything bad about Dale Murphy, and this was a guy making $2 million a year.

One day I picked up a newspaper in the Atlanta airport. On the airplane I opened to the sports page. The headline read: "Dale Murphy Traded." I'm not ashamed to tell you that, even as a grown man of 32, on a crowded flight, tears were streaming down my face.

When you're famous, you *always* meet people who think you're their best friend. But occasionally you run into someone who actually knows you. Only you've forgotten his name. This can be a problem, unless you're from the South.

"Jeff! How the hell are ya?"

All you have to say is, "Hey, Buddy." Then you try to get some information to help you place them. "You still workin' at the same place?"

"Uh-huh."

"So where you living now?"

"Same house."

"Still married."

"Hell . . . yes."

Meanwhile, you still don't know who you're talking to.

"Well, good seein' ya'll."

"Back at ya."

Things could be worse. Once, a guy who spent three minutes with me in a comedy club bathroom ran into me eight years later and expected me to recall the whole experience as if it had happened the day before.

"You remember when we were together at the Chuckle Hut?"

I wouldn't exactly call it "together" either.

Then there was the good ole gal who cornered me at a baseball game. She couldn't stop venting about her "Yankee husband" and his side of the family. "They're such complete idiots that I'd like to choke them and drop them in the swimming pool."

Now, *that* made me want to grab the first guy who passed by and say, "Hey, Buddy? About that time we spent together at the Chuckle Hut . . ."

My fans don't send normal gifts. I already told you about the Redneck china cabinet. Rod Stewart gets a gift basket with a bottle of Dom Perignon and caviar. I get baskets with six-packs of Red Dog, some chewing tobacco, and some grits. I bet people laugh when they send this stuff. I've now got cabinets full of grits and chewing tobacco. Look, if you must send a gift, a six-pack of Sprite, a couple of candy bars, and a cheap lease on a storehouse for all the grits and tobacco would be just fine.

Flowers can also be troublesome. Sometimes fans bring me bouquets, which is nice, but please, not in the middle of a show. Women get really upset if I don't come down to the front of the stage, pick up the flowers, and acknowledge them. (Not that they aren't appreciated by my wife when I act like I bought them for her.) Also, unlike panties, flowers are not easy to pick up with the microphone. And when I'm setting up for a punch line, it's not time to be putting anything in a vase.

*

I confess: I have occasionally used my celebrity to get things I wanted. I'm not talking about being able to get a table at a high-class restaurant—without a reservation. More like getting my car repaired. You see, I own a lemon. This car breaks down more than little Ricky Schroeder in the movie *The Champ*. I have even had dreams of it being stolen. I'm not a yelling guy or a throwing-things guy, but I was so pissed off at the damn thing never working that all of a sudden I found myself saying to the service manager, "You know, this car's been in here eight times, and if we don't get it fixed now I think I'm just gonna have to write a bit about it and go on the *Tonight Show* and tell everybody in America and the free world what a piece-of-crap car you guys make." Meanwhile, I could hear myself thinking, "What kind of threat is this? Listen to yourself, you dumbass."

It got fixed, though. Thank God. I didn't want to write the bit.

By far the best use of celebrity status is on airplanes. You can get that first-class seat on the upgrade, no matter who is waiting in line. They'll do it for you in a second. You walk up to the counter, lay down your boarding pass, and go, "Are there any more seats available in first class."

The person behind the counter will say, "Well, there's a long waiting list and . . ."

Then they take a look at you.

"Ohhh, yeah, I believe we *do* have one more seat up front."

I've always been proud to be one of the common people, but when I started flying in first class . . . well, anybody who thinks that all men are created equal has never flown in the front of the plane. It only took me about 2 million miles to realize that I *did* want to escape from coach class. Now when sitting in that big, comfortable, leather seat, wondering if it's okay to take home my personal salt and pepper shakers from dinner, I have the overwhelming urge to jump out of my seat, rip open the curtain, poke my head into the netherworld of coach seating, and laugh and shout, "They're puttin on the steaks now! And we're having ice cream sundaes for dessert. Ha. Ha. Ha!"

The best part of flying first class is that it's all free. "Sir, would you like another complimentary cocktail? Free headsets, anyone?" Well, some of it is free. Actually, it *should* be free considering that the difference in price between a coach ticket and a first-class fare is greater than the gross national product of most Third World nations. We get the leg room and the butt room, and it only costs $1,200 more. Bet you thought celebrities didn't pay a price for being able to afford the ultimate in luxury. Of course we do. I just can't figure out if we pay because we're famous or we're famous because we can pay.

If you're famous, people laugh louder at your jokes. Travis Tritt once told me, "It's funny: You get your own tour bus and people laugh a little harder at everything you say."

It's not necessarily fair. People also tend to think you're smarter. Somehow your IQ goes up. They figure that if you were smart enough to figure out how to get a job entertaining them, then you must have something on the ball. Some do, but let me tell you: A lot of idiots get famous. But only an idiot would name names.

*

One thing I don't do is spend any time thinking that I want to be *more* famous. In fact, being famous *every other day* would be just fine. I could show *Entertainment Tonight* my home on one day, and the next I could go out without washing my hair.

Of course, when I run out unwashed and wearing my crappy clothes, I'm sure to run into somebody with whom I went to high school. Suddenly there's the girl I had a crush on in tenth grade, who would never speak to me. She recognizes me. I can see it in the way her eyes light up that she has lived *every day* of the past fifteen years believing that she made a big mistake ignoring me and dating the varsity quarterback instead. Since graduation he's fathered her children, consumed a minibrewery's worth of bad beer, and never made it out of the shoe department at Wal-Mart. Meanwhile, she's followed my career and kept scrapbooks. I open my mouth to speak. Then she takes a good look at my raggedy sweatpants and the Braves T-shirt that's three sizes too small, and she thinks, "Maybe I did the right thing marrying Kyle."

I don't think this alternate-day celebrity plan is such a good idea after all.

*

My sister, Jennifer, doesn't think of me as a celebrity. But she likes the fact that other people do because through me she can meet famous people. She went to the Country Music Awards and she thought it was bizarre that her big brother Jeff would be there. That is, until Alan Jackson walked up. Then it was okay because I could say, "Alan, this is my sister."

*

One of the weirdest things about being famous is that I now have relatives I didn't have just a couple of years ago. But amazingly, they never call my brother or my sister or my mom. They just call me. I don't want to embarrass them here by telling you their names. (Though you'd think that after having the nerve to call me they could stand a little shame.) Let's just say they're cousins so far removed that they might as well live on the other side of the international date line. They've read that I'm now making money, so they call and say, "We jus' wan' keep the family together." I nodded in agreement and said, "What's your name again?"

I remember one conversation with a lovely woman:

"Well, it's so nice to see you're doing so well, Jeff. Things hadden been quite so good for us since Harlan hurt his back. Mama's been in and out of the hospital and what-have-you. You know, God, it looks like we're gonna lose the farm. Sure would be nice if somebody in the family could buy it—you know, for sentimental reasons."

When these "relatives" call they also feel obliged to give my number to somebody else. So when I've finally got that rare two hours at home with my kids, I end up spending thirty fascinating minutes on the phone with Wayne Hutton.

"Hey! I'm a distant cousin of your Uncle Mike. We's wunderin', if we come out to California, we talkin' about stoppin' by and see y'all a little bit. You know, just throw the kids out in the yard, shoot the shit for a while."

"Who are you?"

"Well, we love ya whole family. We've always been crazy about yer mama."

"But who are you?"

"Wayne Hutton, boy! Didn' I tell you?"

Afterward I called my mother. She said, "Seems to me like there *was* a cousin Wayne . . ."

These people show up at my concerts, too. They call my manager's office and say, "Hey, when Jeff comes to Missouri, tell him he's got some kinfolks out here and we'd like for him to come to dinner, if that'd be aright. He can just come out. Hell, you can come too if you want. By the way, we's wondering if we might get a few tickets fer the show."

"Well, how many do you need?"

"Oh, 'bout forty-five'll do it."

Afterward, they get mad if I won't come to the house. Frankly, I'm kind of scared to leave with them. Scared I may not come back.

Atlanta, being my hometown, is the most fun place for me to play. It's also the most aggravating. Every time I swear I will never do it again. Everybody with whom I went to elementary school, high school, and college wants to come to the show. Everybody I hung out with while I was single, worked with at IBM, ever dated (and now their husbands and kids), and every schoolteacher I had—all want to come to the show, God bless them. I get twenty complimentary tickets a night, I end up buying another hundred and fifty, and there are *still* always fifty people pissed off at me. Maybe what I'll do is this: JEFF FOXWORTHY, ONE NIGHT ONLY. THE PEOPLE-I-KNOW SHOW. Then they can feed me material from their seats. "Hey, tell 'em about the time . . ."

When my first book, *You Might Be a Redneck If . . .* , came out, I finally had an inkling that my fortunes were improving. My family stopped telling me that I might eventually have to go back to my job at IBM. The lines at the malls were often as long for my book-signings as they were for the House of Venison "young buck" specials. I remember my mother telling me that she had the book at the family Christmas party. She said she stood in the middle of the room, reading the one-liners out loud, and everyone laughed. But on every third joke, all of a sudden, somebody wouldn't laugh—because they'd realized that the joke was about them.

"I started to read that one about 'if your junior-senior prom had a day care center . . .' " my mother said, "and all I could think about was your cousin Tracy sitting over there in the corner, and how she and Bob got married cause she got pregnant in the tenth grade."

I finally had to tell her, "Where do you think I come up with this stuff, Mom?"

✳

Fans have heard me talk about my wife forever. Sometimes when we're out together, they'd rather talk to Gregg than to me.

Often when I play someplace and we know people in town, they'll invite Gregg to sit with them in the audience. She won't do that anymore. She says people end up not laughing every time I say something about her. That's because they turn to see how she's going to react.

You know, folks, it's not like she hasn't heard these jokes before. Almost every one of them began with me asking for her reaction. Our entire life is me coming out of the shower going, "Is this funny?"

It just hurts when she says yes before I've even told the joke. (Don't you make believe you don't know exactly what I mean.)

✽

Being well known hasn't really affected my kids yet. They don't give a damn that I'm famous. I could have dinner at the White House, and that's not going to stop them from getting up seven times during the middle of the night. I'm just Dad.

I've never really tried to explain my job to my daughters. One reason is that they're only two and four. But I think my oldest understands. The last time we went to see my wife's folks, we were walking through the New Orleans airport and she was riding on my shoulders. Somebody came up and wanted an autograph. I stopped—she's still on my shoulders—and I signed this thing. The guy said, "Thank you," and shook my hand, and walked off. She said, "Daddy, why do people like you so much?" I said, "I don't know, Peanut Butter, why do you think?" She said, "Cause you make them laugh." I turned to Gregg and said, "Wow."

✽

makeup. This is im-
e a man. For the first
...t something on your
...dumbass grin. But
... the ...et or stage and
...you and your
...all of a
...'m still

to ...
of my car. ...up
...shville ... ot *makeup*
... I had to drive up ... Georgia
...show, and then I had to drive over."
...me night to catch a plane in the morning ...
a gig somewhere else. Back then they put on
heavy makeup. I'm talking the pancake stuff
and the thick eyeliner.

I left right after the show and drove back to
Atlanta through the north Georgia mountains.
Suddenly red lights flashed and I saw a UFO—
no, I got pulled over by the cops. I didn't think
anything about it because I was only going
about five miles an hour over the speed limit.
Then the state trooper came up to the driver's
window and he shined the light in my face. I
could see right away that he felt *mean*. He
looked like he'd been cast in *Smokey and the
Bandit* and had been pissed ever since the pro-
duction left town. I just sat there thinking,
"Now, what have I done?"

When he finally spok
ized. He said, "You gonr
car, boy?" I did as he
wouldn't take the flash
smiled and said, "Well,
I realize I was doing like
get back to Atlanta and c
early, and . . . God, I'm

PROBLEM!

real-

"Git yer ass back here
walking toward the rear
and then it hit me: "Shit, I've
in the middle of the night, in the north
mountains, and a cop just pulled me ov
There was only one thing I could do. I stared
him straight in the eye and said, "You're looking at the makeup, aren't cha?"

His lip curled and he said, "Ye-ah."

I said, "Lemme explain. I *can* explain."

"Ye-ah?"

"I was just on *Nashville Now,* and I left right
from the set and got in the car and started driving. I forgot to take off the makeup."

He didn't say anything.

"It's the God's honest truth."

Then he said, "You on *Nashville Now*? All
right, who's on there tonight?"

"Porter Waggoner."

"You *met* Porter Waggoner!"

"Yessir, I sure did."

"What was he like?"

"Oh, he was as good as gold. Sir."

"Aright, you kin go."

This was a rare example of how *knowing* a celebrity can save your butt. That and telling the truth. Otherwise, I might have ended up as some skeleton that hunters find in the middle of deer season; a collection of bones after the squirrels have already taken the skull away.

You really know you're a celebrity when manufacturers send you free stuff. You only get this after you reach the point where you can finally afford it on your own. Travis Tritt and I were talking about this on the set of my TV show one day.

He said, "Tony Lama just gave me these boots."

I said, "Justin gave me *these* boots. Hell, you should see what I've got piled up in my trailer."

Then we both smiled and looked at each other. We knew what the other guy was thinking: "Where were these people all those years when we couldn't afford anything?"

What really astounds me about being well known is how my life compares to my circumstances when I was growing up. In October 1995 I was able to charter a Learjet to take me to Atlanta to see the Braves play in the World Series. As we landed the Learjet, which cost a load of money, and taxied down the runway, we passed by the place where I lived, in Hapeville, at the end of the old airport runway. I looked out the window and thought, "That's where my house was. That house had one bathroom. It had a dirt yard. We burned trash in a barrel. Now I'm roaring past it in a Learjet I just rented to go see one stupid-ass ball game." So I asked myself, "How did I get from *there* to *here*?"

That's a good question.

I hope in some ways I've answered it.

No Shirt. No Shoes....NO PROBLEM!

JEFF FOXWORTHY

No Shirt.
No Shoes....
NO PROBLEM!

HYPERION
New York

ISBN 0-7868-8916-0

ORIGINAL BOOK DESIGN BY KATHY KIKKERT

FIRST MASS MARKET EDITION

1   3   5   7   9   10   8   6   4   2

For my uncle Jack—
a great guy who owns
a mountain of comedy records
and let me listen
to every one of them

To Gregg and the girls
for this and everything else

CONTENTS

SPECIAL THANKS

I don't possess adequate words to thank David Rensin for the talent and effort he brought to this project. Without him, you would be reading a pamphlet, not a book.

When Hyperion approached me, I had just come off tour and had started a television series. I said I simply didn't have the time to write a book and I wasn't sure I had anything to say. Then, I was introduced to David. Because of him, I probably said too much. I knew he was a good writer. I had read his books and Playboy interviews (occasionally even glancing at the pictures). I just didn't know the depth of his skills.

He would meet me at my trailer (work, not home) every day at lunch. He made me talk, he made me think, and we shared a lot of laughs. With his help, I found myself remembering things long forgotten—some of which probably should have stayed that way.

So what you read is my book and his.

Thank you, David.

Jeff Foxworthy

ACKNOWLEDGMENTS

My deepest gratitude to J.P. Williams, Debbie Shaler,
Maggie Houlehan, Nina Weinman, Malaika Vereen,
Matt Labov, Paul Baker, Amber Gereghty, Mike Smardak,
John McDonald, Anne Sibbald, Laurie Abkemeier, Bob Miller,
Cynthia Lee Price, CAA, Jay Foxworthy,
Mike Higginbotham, and Richard Gudzan.

AUTHOR'S NOTE

Some names have been changed to protect marriages.
I'm still not sure it will help.

No Shirt. No Shoes....NO PROBLEM!

Welcome

I'm not ready to die just yet.

I have my reasons. Can you imagine the floral arrangements? When NASCAR driver Davey Allison was buried in Alabama, *People* magazine ran photos of the flowers at his funeral. There were black carnations in the shape of a race car, a big wheel, and who knows what else. It wouldn't surprise me if someone had made a set of points and plugs out of rose petals.

My wife, Gregg (I call her by her *middle* name), and I were reading in bed at the time. So I showed her the funeral pictures and said, "Since people know me mostly as that *Redneck* guy, I don't even want to *think* about the flowers you'd get if I died now. Rebel flags. Brown carnations shaped like a spit of chewing tobacco juice midflight. Huge bouquets set in tractor tires. And don't forget the wreath that spells out *You might be dead if* . . . You know I'm proud of my Southern roots, but don't you think I should get a little bit past this Redneck thing before I buy the farm?"

"Does this mean you'll finally stop making jokes about my butt being cold?" she asked. (Because I say onstage that women's rear ends are always cold in bed—and use Gregg's as an example—people stop us on the street and say to her, "So you're the one with the cold butt." She's tired of it.)

"But honey," I said. "That material is *funny*."

Gregg thought for a moment, then said, "Well, I think the worst thing about something bad happening to you—besides the kids and me being alone in this big house with all your stuff, then me having to date again and fall in love . . ."

"Hold on," I interrupted. "I haven't dropped dead *yet*."

". . . would be figuring out what to *do* with all the wonderfully tacky floral arrangements after the funeral," she added, with a reassuring smile.

"Oh, don't worry about that," I said. "You know my family. They'll *beat down* the door to get at those."

Gregg closed her eyes and quickly fell asleep. I didn't. The conversation made me wonder: What was going on in my life that I should have this weird fantasy? Why was I worried about floral arrangements when I should be concerned about more important things such as who would inherit my Ford pickup with the AstroTurf-lined truck bed. What about the pink plastic flamingos in our front yard? And my collection of stolen road signs?

It took a while before I understood what was bothering me. I felt a kinship with Davey Allison, a regular guy from the South who became a celebrity just doing what he did best. He pursued excellence at his craft and never forgot that he was no different from the people who cheered him on. Flowers in the shape of a race car were just his fans' way of showing their appreciation. Even so, if he'd been standing in the crowd at his own funeral he probably would have felt just like I did at that moment: You never totally adjust to the peculiar things that happen to you when you're famous. Or even semifamous, like me. Of course, I'm not complaining. Success *is* great. But one of my greatest gifts in life is being able to sit with a bunch of guys in a deer-hunting camp just as easily as with Johnny Carson—I'm comfortable in either place. I've always been able to fit in.

That started me thinking about where I'd come from and wondering what had happened to the little boy who grew up three doors down from the end of the old Atlanta airport runway. Believe me, I know I've come a long way. At least now I don't have to pause midsentence every thirty-five seconds to let a plane go overhead. But otherwise, how much is that little boy still a part of me today?

I needed to ponder the changes I'd been through. I ponder on paper; that's how I do my best thinking. The result is this road trip through my life. We'll stop along the way to admire the scenery, answer nature's call, steal a couple of road signs, and tell stories about growing up blue collar, about hunting, fishing, tobacco chewing, girlfriends, love, roommates, sex, work, crazy families, Rednecks, relationships, marriage, kids, comedy, celebrity, holidays, mooning, and a little something I like to call fishball.

I also asked some of my family and friends to add their memories, just to keep me honest. They graciously agreed. Then I changed my mind. It wasn't such a bright idea. They remembered lots of stuff about me that I had *mysteriously* forgotten, and when they reminded me of certain incidents, I suddenly remembered why. But so what if I once rode a pig bareback. And a goat. Just don't ask to see the pictures.

Since you're reading this, I'm assuming that you want to come on in, kick back, and stay awhile. That's fine with me. We're casual here. No shirt? No shoes? No problem! There are no rules to remember, no obligations, no salesman will come to your door. You don't have to kill or skin or gut anything. (The possum hunt comes later and is optional.) The idea is simply to have a good time. If that's not possible, then the idea is to at least get really drunk and think you did.

Either way, I'm hoping that by the time you turn the last page, you'll agree that however strange my life sometimes seems, it's really not so strange after all. Whether you're from North

Dallas or North Dakota, I guarantee you'll recognize many funny (okay, unsettling) similarities to your own life, family, and friends. Except for one thing. I'll bet that you've never gotten a gift as weird as the fine home furnishing that Mr. and Mrs. Orville Storch of Sioux City, Iowa, recently sent me. Being who I am and hailing from where I do, I knew with absolute certainty that I was the proud receiver of a wonderful and heartfelt tribute. Imagine: a piece of wood that holds paper plates with the phrase "Redneck China Cabinet" carved crudely across the front.

See, I told you it was too early to die.

Deep Blue
Collar

I grew up so deep blue collar that my mother had to wash my shirts separately, in cold water.

I was born in Atlanta in 1958 and lived in the small suburb of Decatur until I was about six. One of my earliest memories is of getting my head stuck between the porch railing posts. I tried putting my head between the posts to see what would happen—story of my life—and realized pretty quickly that God meant for my ears to bend only in one direction.

My father, Jim Foxworthy, worked for IBM. He's a big man, so we call him Big Jim. Before climbing the management ladder, he just fixed machines. That meant we lived all over the place. From Decatur they transferred him first to Knoxville, Tennessee, and then to Greenville, South Carolina. Along the way, Big Jim and my mom, Carole, had two more kids: my sister, Jennifer, eighteen months younger than me; and my brother Jay, five years younger. We were happy, or so I thought, until I was ten and my parents got divorced.

By the way, their separation didn't scar me for life. I'm not a comedian because I'm still trying to compensate for a bad childhood, being picked on in school, or having a prehensile tail (since removed). My childhood was okay, probably better than many. Divorce just happens, especially in my family. Between my mom and my dad they've been married nine times. As of this writing, they've got Elizabeth Taylor beat by one.

Anyway, we moved in with my mom's folks, James and Mary Camp. They lived on Union

Avenue in Hapeville, a small lower-middle-class town eleven miles south of Atlanta.

In Hapeville everybody knew your name. In other words, it was like hanging out at the *Cheers* bar. Such familiarity was mostly comforting, unless, of course, you were a kid who had done something you didn't want your family to find out about. My parents called these informers "good neighbors." We kids just called them snitches.

Hapeville was a great place. It was so small that our morning traffic report depended on a guy looking out his window and saying, "The light is green." Our fire department didn't have a truck, just a long hose. If an emergency happened, you just cupped your hand and yelled "9-1-1!" It was also a safe place. You could ride your bike or walk anywhere with no worries. Our home-security system meant latching the screen door. If our screen was ripped, that was still no cause for alarm. For extra protection we had a No-Pest Strip in the living room.

Our backyard was mostly dirt, but we filled it with interesting stuff like a beat-up basketball backboard and rim through which I could never sink a shot. My mother's family is so tall that nobody ever bothered measuring how high to set the hoop. Standard is ten feet. Ours was more like eleven and a half feet. No wonder in school I was only good at football and baseball.

The backyard also had a pile of concrete blocks, a barrel to burn trash in, and a double kitchen sink turned upside down. My grandfather kept crickets underneath to use as fish bait. My uncles had turned the shack behind the garden into a clubhouse. Inside, they'd hung hardware store posters of women in bikinis holding tools. At the back end of the yard stood a concrete block storage shed. My granddaddy never allowed us inside and never told us why. He guarded that thing. But kids being kids, we eventually picked the lock, snuck in, and poked around. What a disappointment. No beer, no racy magazines, no old hunting dog skeletons. All we found was a garden tiller, fishing gear, a refrigerator stocked with bait, and two huge plastic bags full of rabbits' tails. I think someone should have told Granddaddy that rabbits' *feet* were good luck.

*

The Hapeville postal service must have figured my family for the stupidest people on the block. Why? My uncle Jimmy one day decided to paint M-A-L-E on our mailbox in big block letters. It was just a joke. We're not idiots. Sometimes I think that living so close to the jet fuel fumes from the planes passing overhead might have had something to do with our odd ways. Every two years the fumes would strip the paint from our cars, so I suppose inhaling the stuff might have affected our brain cells. It certainly would explain the sixth toe on my right foot.

James Camp was Hapeville's assistant fire chief. He didn't have much work, though. Honestly, I don't believe he ever answered a fire alarm. (Once, the high school roof was ablaze, but the firemen couldn't find the school, even though it was just two blocks away. Kind of embarrassing.) Mostly, the firemen played Ping-Pong and cards, watched the *Beverly Hillbillies*, and made lewd comments about Ellie Mae.

Granddaddy was fun at home. As little kids, we'd bug him to death, but he never complained. I loved it most when he'd call the Wizard. He wouldn't do it often, but when he did we'd all gather around. First, Granddaddy would get a deck of cards from the gun rack by the front door (we kept a pellet gun there, just in case). Then he'd say, "Pick a card." We would. Then we'd show it to him. Next, he would dial the phone and say, "May I speak to the Wizard?" After a bit, he'd go, "Okay, hold on," and he would hand the phone to one of us. The voice on the other end would say, "Your card is the six of clubs," and then the line would go dead.

The Wizard was always right. It took me fifteen years to figure out the trick. Turns out . . . well, I promised my granddaddy I'd never tell. A promise is a promise. All I can say is that when I was a kid, the trick would blow my mind.

*

Childhood is full of mysteries. For me, one of them concerned the house next door, the one I could see from my bedroom window. No one ever lived there for very long. One great thing about transient neighbors is that they don't sink much money into drapes. If they have curtains at all, they're flimsy, thin, and always hanging open. This fortunate circumstance is how my brother and I got to see bras and panties on people other than those in our family.

First, we learned that the people next door couldn't see into our room if we kept the light off. Peering across the side yard night after night we caught many a good bra-and-panty shot. Well, to tell you the truth, we weren't really sure *what* we saw a lot of times, but as long as we spotted white cotton and flesh we counted it. For all we knew we could have been ogling a truck driver parading around in his

Fruit of the Looms and a CAT hat. For us, it didn't really matter.

On the other side of our house was a duplex. The McGuires lived closest to us. Mr. and Mrs. McGuire would sit in the living room and look out their window all day long. They knew everything that happened on our street, and even in our house. My uncle Jimmy used to say that he once called up the McGuires and invited them over to dinner, and they said, "Thank you, but we don't like green beans."

Mr. Cunningham lived in the other half of the duplex. He was a grumpy old man who kept any balls we hit over his fence. We'd have asked for them back if we weren't so afraid of him. Cunningham also had a little white poodle named Susie. Nobody liked her either. Susie was one of only two possible old-people-type dogs. The first is the ugly little white poodle with the very pink belly and the lactating eye problem. The other is the Chihuahua with the gray nose and cataracts that is so obese its nipples stick out sideways. Tell me there's *not* an old-people pet store somewhere where you can actually buy only these two animals.

I finally got brave enough to crawl into Mr. Cunningham's yard one night with my trusty penlight. I was eleven and I wanted revenge for all the missing baseballs he'd kept. So I tore thumb-size pieces from all the leaves in his vegetable garden. My plan was to make it look like some rabbit, psychotically depressed at the loss of its tail, had gone on a rampage. Or maybe Susie would be blamed. Unfortunately, old man Cunningham never said anything. If he noticed at all, then, as with our baseballs, he just kept it to himself.

⚓

My family has always been funny. My dad has the classic Redneck sense of humor. I remember one weekend when I was ten years old. We were at his farm on the opening day of dove-hunting season. By the time the shoot ended, thirty guys had gathered around the truck, and every one had a beer. (If you can't mix liquor and firearms, what's the sense of being outdoors?) As usual, my dad was up to something. He turned to one of the guys and said, "Hey, let's have a contest. Let's shoot each other's hats."

The guy put down his beer and said, "Aright."

My dad took off his hat and said, "You can shoot mine first." He threw it high into the air. The other guy wheeled his shotgun around and blasted it. The hat jumped a few feet higher, then floated down with fifteen pellet holes.

Then the other guy tossed his hat into the air. But my dad didn't even raise his gun. He just waited until the hat hit the ground. Then he walked over, put the shotgun to the canvas, pulled the trigger, and *obliterated* it.

Everyone broke up laughing. But all I could think of was how my dad was pretty cool and smart and funny. I wished I could also be that way. I guess you have to be careful what you wish for.

My mother's side of the family also had a few tricks to play. When I was seven or eight, Mom's oldest brother, Uncle Jimmy, and I would do improv gigs at the family's covered-dish Christmas parties at the Hapeville Recreation Center. Our act was simple. I'd sit in Jimmy's lap and play the dummy while he played the ventriloquist. Today they'd probably arrest us both for doing that.

Grandma Camp was also a little loopy in a wonderful sort of way. She'd pile up the sofa with pillows, put blankets on top of you, and bring out a TV tray with a huge bowl of sweet coffee—which was just coffee with tons of sugar and milk. We'd take toast cut in strips and dunk it while we watched cartoons. Talk about hyperactive kids.

Grandma Camp also introduced me to TV trays, and I will always love her for that. They were aluminum, with a clay-pot-and-flower design. Soon after we moved into the Hapeville house, my mother decided her parents needed *fiberglass* TV trays decorated with expressions from *Laugh-In*. Things like "Sock It to Me, Baby" in weird block letters. My grandparents still have them. There are few things you can count on in life, but those trays are one.

My mother's cousins, Dolores and Buddy, were also two of the funniest human beings alive. Sometimes Dolores would imitate someone she'd seen on TV. Or she would tell wild stories. Dolores always loved the one about the son of the lady who cleaned her house getting arrested again.

Dolores acted the housekeeper's part: She said, "They framed him. It was not his fault. He had loaned his jacket to a friend. The next day the friend had given him his jacket back, and he was just walking down the street, minding his business. But the police grabbed him and arrested him. The problem was that he had not checked his jacket pockets, and he did not realize that he was carrying somebody else's pistol and $3,000 in cash."

Or maybe it was only $150 and a penknife. My family remembers stuff and then elaborates. As the years pass we back up each other on our embellishments. It's like the "guy thing" that happens when two men are deer hunting. If one year you shoot a spike deer that weighs ninety-eight pounds, then every year the deer gains a couple of points and another twenty-five or thirty pounds. While you tell the story, your buddy, who was there with you, just sits and nods.

"Remember when we shot that twelve-pointer? That deer musta weighed three-hundred-and-sixty . . ."

No matter what, the story will never outweigh the accumulated BS.

✻

This story needs no elaboration. It's one of my earliest comic moments. Perhaps my finest.

When I was ten and my brother, Jay, was five, he had a . . . problem. Not a serious problem. Today he might say it was more of a personal choice. What I mean to say is that he would go days and days without going to the bathroom. My mother worried constantly, when she wasn't annoyed.

We had just moved to Union Avenue when the city decided to expand the airport and build a runway that started at the end of our street.

One day after a light rain, Jay and I were play-ing in the construction site and discovered some particularly nice mud. Not too wet, not too dry, sublimely textured. It was destiny. Rather than wallow in the mud like normal kids, I had a great idea: Build a turd.

We used a two-by-four as our platform. The finished product was close to three feet long. It was probably as big around as two fists put together. This thing would have done Man o' War proud. We picked out all the rocks and ta-pered one end. We really did a nice job.

After we let it dry in the sun we took it home. I carried one end of the two-by-four and Jay carried the other. We snuck it into the house— maybe the McGuires saw us, but they never said anything—and then into our only bath-room, where we installed it.

We put the blunt end down and stuffed it into the toilet as far as it could go. Then we wrapped it around the bowl once, and brought the ta-pered end out of the water, almost to the lip of the seat. It looked very much like somebody had forced an anaconda into a fishbowl.

After my brother and I discussed our plan, he nodded and set off to do what I said.

I went into our bedroom, lay on the floor, and laughed for fifteen minutes while he quietly sat in the bathroom, not making a sound. Pretty soon I heard his little voice going, "Mo-om!! Mo-om!!"

By this time I had moved to the closet, where I rocked back and forth with my hand over my mouth. I could hear my mother's footsteps in the hall. I heard the bathroom door open; she took three more steps. I moved from the closet to the bedroom door and cracked it an inch so I could hear. But I could only imagine the innocent look on my brother's face, gazing up at my mother as he slid off the commode. Then I heard her: "My God! Jay, when was the last time you *went?*"

"I think I went last week," he whispered, almost on the verge of tears. He was great. He was perfection. The next thing I heard was my mother rushing out of the bathroom, heading for the hall phone.

"I'm calling Dr. Seevrit. This is not normal."

I staggered into the hall, still laughing, and hit the phone switch hook. Then I told her. "No! Mom! It's not real! We made that out of mud!"

She should have killed us both. But I think she was too relieved to put up much of a fuss.

To this day my brother and I still love to bring up that story, particularly when there's company. "Hey, Mom, remember when we made the fake turd and fooled you?"

She just turns a bright shade of red.

I didn't realize it, of course, but somewhere in my little ten-year-old Redneck brain my future was sealed.

❦

To kids, hygiene is pretty much just a greeting. We brushed our teeth and considered ourselves clean. When I played Little League, I'd rub dirt on my arms and hands between innings. Later when I got out of the tub, the water looked like mud. Dirty water was a badge of honor. The dirtier the better. I'd actually call people in to verify it.

"You think I didn't play hard? Take a look at that tub. Bathed yesterday. Got that dirty today." I had to clean the ring afterward, but it was worth it if I could make a witness say, "Oh my God." I suppose I could have taken a shower, but back then, Rednecks didn't have showers. Well, yes we did, but we called them garden hoses.

❦

When she met my father, my mother was a keypunch operator for the state of Georgia. While repairing a machine in Carole's office, Big Jim, in totally Big Jim fashion, flirted with the girls. He asked Carole out, and three months later they were married. Within two years I was born.

Big Jim has a magic way with women, and he is a legendary figure among my friends. Big Jim could romance women in a convent. You'd drop him off out front, and dollars to doughnuts, an hour later he'd leave with his arm around a nun. Recently, he got married for the sixth time. Each wife has been ten years younger than the one before. My brother, sister, and I are scared that if he gets hitched one more time that we'll be walking his wife to school in the morning.

"Look both ways, Mom."

She'll probably be a good cook, though, with that Easy-Bake oven. I love those cakes the size of quarters.

When Big Jim and Carole were still married, he was a Sunday school teacher and a deacon in the First Baptist Church. When we were old enough to understand, Mom informed us of his other interests. We were living in Greenville, South Carolina, when my mother figured out that Big Jim was fooling around with his secretary. Carole has always seen what she wants to see. Her attitude is "Fool me once, shame on you." By the time she and Big Jim separated, her attitude was "Fool me forty-seven times . . ." Big Jim was just a charmer. If Carole could have put up with Big Jim's ways, I think she might have stayed. In fact, I believe Big Jim could pick up the phone and call any woman he's ever been with, and I guarantee you they would start throwing things in a suitcase and come back.

✻

When the marriage ended, Big Jim moved to Washington, D.C., for a few years, then back to the north side of Atlanta. We moved to Hapeville. Grandma and Granddaddy Camp stayed with us in their house for about six months, and then moved a couple of blocks away. We didn't drive them away. My grandparents just kept moving for the heck of it. They'd buy a house and as soon as they'd get the couch positioned properly in the den, they'd start house-hunting again. They moved six times within a three square mile area before I got out of high school. Apparently, no one had ever explained to them the meaning of equity.

✻

When my grandparents moved out, my uncle Jack, the kindest, nicest human being I've ever known, moved in. A couple of years later my mom remarried. My stepdad's name was Paul. He worked at the same place my mother worked—a distribution center for small, off-brand grocery stores.

We all lived in the Union Avenue house for a while, then moved to College Park. I didn't like living there because none of my friends were around, and soon I started riding the city bus back to Hapeville High. However, I did manage to make a few friends in College Park. One, Buddy Hammond, lived two doors away. To this day, he remains one of my best pals.

With Buddy, you could take the "might be" out of "you might be a Redneck . . ." Buddy still eats sardines at 5 A.M. with a cup of coffee. He once made his mother a change purse out of deer testicles, as a present. Buddy took the scrotum sack, tanned it, and laced in a draw-string at the top. What mother wouldn't be proud to carry that? (I don't know what he did with the actual balls, but they probably wound up in someone's secret recipe, with butter and salt.)

Today, despite an obsessive interest in taxidermy that sometimes costs him more than his annual income, Buddy is a software specialist with IBM. And he's still a Redneck. Buddy trained himself to wear the wingtips and the jacket and the tie, but he has not been able to give up the chewing tobacco. The boss still yells at him for using a spit cup on his desk in front of other people.

"[spit] You know what you need to do with this here computer? [spit] You need to . . ."

When I was in college, I shared an apartment with Buddy. Our place looked like a salute to stuffed animals. Buddy had actually apprenticed at a taxidermist's one summer and took home everything that nobody came back to claim, including a goat. (Tell me, when is it *goat* season?) But I couldn't blame Buddy for his fascination with dead animals and parts thereof. Taxidermy is a male preoccupation. You never hear a woman say, "You know what would look nice over the sofa? A big dead fish. Wouldn't that look great?"

I've learned that women don't like *anything* from a taxidermist. In fact, if there weren't any women, men would have apartments full of dead, mounted animals. They'd spend the whole day showing them off to each other.

"C'mon in here, George. Take a look at this. That there is a white-tailed deer, a mallard duck, and a Siamese cat. Had to run off the road to hit the cat. They're quick!"

Don't write letters. It's a joke. I have two cats—one on either side of the fireplace.

Pawpaw is Big Jim's mom. She grew up on a farm in Denmark, South Carolina, about an hour south of Columbia. Now she's in her eighties. When I was little, we'd spend about a month with her each summer. The farm was in the middle of nowhere. We learned to milk cows and ride horses, and to otherwise amuse ourselves. (When I got older, amusing myself meant looking for girls. Girls in farm country get bored easily, too.) Pawpaw's brother, Bob, used to say, "When we were kids, we had no toys. We had to learn to walk a barrel." So one summer I mastered walking a trash barrel. Unlike some subjects I had to learn in school, barrel-walking *has* come in handy. You do it all day long in show business.

Another advantage of having relatives who lived on a farm was that we learned to drive early. I started when I was ten years old. By the time I got my learner's permit I'd been driving so many years that it was no big deal. Other kids were proud to do cartwheels in the living room. I could parallel park before my first kiss. I had the parking down. All I needed was the girl.

Bob taught me to drive. He put phone books under me and I had to stand up on the seat.

My first car was a truck with three-on-the-tree, meaning the stick shift was on the steering column. But Bob figured it was no big deal because the tractors had twenty gears. The adults thought nothing of letting kids drive because then you could do stuff for them on the farm. They didn't have time to bullshit around, they needed the help.

It was always, "Take this trash to the dump." Or "Go take the truck down there to Bobby's house, put those shingles on it, and bring them back up here."

My dad taught my brother, Jay, to drive. He took the truck out in the middle of the hayfield and said, "This is how you stop it, this is how you start it. Practice." It was a 200-acre field. You couldn't hit anything. My brother did. He hit a tree.

Jay said, "Daddy, I scratched the truck."

"Right," said Big Jim. "Scratched the rear quarter panel right off of it."

*

I should tell you right now that I am not the most famous product of my hometown.

Hapeville is where they invented the Chik-Fil-A. It's like a piece of breaded chicken on a buttered bun that, if you put one on top of your head, your tongue would beat your brains out to get to it. It's hard not to touch yourself when you're eating a Chik-Fil-A. We don't have Chik-Fil-A in California, but on the East Coast the mere mention of a Chik-Fil-A guarantees a gasp.

The first Chik-Fil-A was served at a restaurant named the Dwarf House, in Hapeville. I'm not making this up. The outside decor featured the Seven Dwarfs carved out of wood; they were painted and mounted on a movable track. Doug Davis, a Hapeville artist famous enough to have a street—Doug Davis Drive—named after him, had painted the Seven Dwarfs. I'm not sure where Snow White was. But the contraption never seemed to work and a couple of the dwarfs fell over out of sheer boredom. The restaurant also had a little bitty door that we, as kids, were obligated to go in and out of.

Everyone from high school hung out at the Dwarf House parking lot. I had my first sexual experience there, and my first bloody nose. Same night, same person. Also, my first Chik-Fil-A. I wanted no more out of life, except maybe to have a street named after me. And wouldn't you know it, recently Hapeville asked my mother if they could put my name on every city-limits sign.

*

Like I said at the beginning, I'm a blue-collar guy at heart. Now you know it's true. One reason I make Redneck jokes is, well . . . I have to. Otherwise, having to endure an attitude from the rest of the country that Southerners are stupid and backward would be too depressing.

Apparently we get our reputation because of how we speak. People think they need an interpreter to understand us. I've never met anyone who thinks Southern is the world's most intelligent-sounding accent. When people hear me talk they automatically want to deduct a hundred IQ points. (This may be at the root of many of President Clinton's troubles.) To be honest, I sort of feel the same way. None of us would want to hear our brain surgeon say, "Aright . . . now what we gon' do is saw the top of yer head off, root aroun' in 'er with a stick and see if we cain't maybe find that dad-burned clot."

You'd say, "No thanks. I'll just die, okay?"

This is also why Southern financial advisers have such a tough time. Nobody wants to give their money to somebody who talks this way. "[snort] Well, the key is you got to di-ver-si-fy wi' yer money. What we'll do is we'll take half of it, put it in a big mayonnaise jar, bury it out in yer backyard. The other half we'll take down to the dog track and bet on the one that does his business right before the race starts."

I'm still proud of where I come from. We may have words nobody's heard of, but we also have strong values. Most everybody goes to church and is pretty family-oriented. Boy Scouts, Little League, and scoring points for roadkill are a way of life.

And believe it or not, sometimes we're also guilty of being snobs. We rarely trust someone who isn't like us. We worry about people who would rather go to work than go fishing. But I'll tell you a secret rarely whispered north of the Mason-Dixon line: What we're *really* doing is keeping a good thing going. Our whole image of overalls, no shirt, no shoes, eating grits, chewing tobacco, butt cracks, and acting stupid is intentional and a total farce.

We just do that to keep the rest of the country from coming down here.

Y'all
watch
This!

hat are a Redneck's
famous last words?

Simple.

"Y'all watch this!"

Whatever the foolhardy act, his friends always oblige. In fact, they probably put the poor

guy up to no good in the first place, just for a laugh. Not that he minds. Men know that their friends are going to get them in trouble. They expect it. That's why they're called friends. Have you ever heard a guy describe friendship? There's *always* trouble involved.

"Ole George, boy, he's a great friend. He'll come get you out of jail at 3:00 in the morning."

That doesn't sound like friendship to me. If George was a great friend his ass would also be in jail, sitting on a cot, smoking a cigarette, going, "She didn't look like no cop, did she?"

The things we do for friends.

I once jumped onto a hay bale, off the back of a pickup truck moving at forty miles an hour. I was seventeen and my best friend, Larry Burns, talked me into doing it. It was easy. All Burns had to say was "You know, there's not *anybody* in the world got the guts to do that." We were at my dad's farm, and already a few underage beers into the twilight. "But I guess if *anybody* had those guts, Foxworthy," he continued, "you'd come closest. But *nobody's* got that many guts."

Five minutes later we were racing through

the 200-acre pasture. I tried to keep my balance in the truck bed. We passed the hay bale and I leapt. It *looked* soft—made of hay, right—but it was packed as solid as a rock. I hit the bale, broke my nose, and passed out. I woke up to the sound of Larry laughing. Later, the doctor asked, "How did this happen, son?"

I told the truth. "My friend dared me."

❀

I met Larry Burns in fifth grade, on the first day of school. We instantly became best friends. He can still verify what I was wearing that day: orange plaid pants and an orange shirt with a zipper. I went all out. I figured it would be hard to forget a kid so stylishly dressed. My Southern sense of cool also explained the blue plaid pants and the blue zip-up shirt in my closet—I wore them in the school pictures—and possibly why I was so hot with the fifth grade girls. Because of my fashion sense, Tracey Young and I went together for two or three months. We never touched or, I think, spoke. But that had nothing to do with Tracey and everything to do with where my real affections lay. I was really "going with" Burns and the guys. We were inseparable.

❀

Once Burns convinced me to run through an apartment complex buck naked.

"Jump out of the car," he said, "and Chastain [Danny, the third member of our group, and a year older] and I will pick you up on the other side of the building."

I was such a dumbass. I took off my clothes and got out of the car. No sooner had the door slammed than Burns locked me out, turned on the bright lights, and started honking the horn. I streaked, all right, right into a stand of nearby trees. Then Burns and Chastain drove off and left me. You don't have many options when you're naked in the woods at night. A discarded McDonald's bag starts looking like possible clothing, even a bag for a *small* order of fries.

Was I pissed? Yes, but only for a moment. After all, I could just as easily have put Burns up to bolting through the building wearing nothing but his horn-rim glasses while I pulled the double-cross.

This incident hardly dimmed my enthusiasm for being naked in public. (Only winter weather can do that because what man wants to look like he's carrying around a thirty-cent stack of dimes?) Later that year, Burns, Chastain, and I put on stocking masks and our football helmets and streaked through a high school assembly. We figured we were really clever and mysterious. But two minutes into the next class the PA system crackled to life: "Would Jeff Foxworthy, Larry Burns, and Danny Chastain come to Mr. Givens' office IMMEDIATELY!" Okay, so we were caught, but the worst part was that somewhere on the smirk-filled walk to the principal's office we figured out how. Our team numbers were on the backs of our helmets. The saddest thing was that we were some of the smartest kids in the school.

*

I first heard the term "Redneck" when I played baseball and football for Hapeville High. When we'd compete against teams from Atlanta's north side—the money side—they'd always call us "a bunch of Rednecks." Then, the term was still something of an insult. Now it just means a glorious absence of sophistication. Naturally, wc found ways to make the high-society boys pay—with compounded interest.

For instance, every year we'd play Pace Academy, a private school for rich kids, located right by the governor's mansion. Even in the ninth grade, Burns and I were already on the varsity baseball team. We just weren't good enough to start, so we mostly warmed the bench. During the Pace game we watched as their first baseman kept elbowing one of our guys, Danny Beck. Finally, Beck said, "If he does it again, I'm gonna hit the guy." Burns turned to me and said, "If Beck hits the first baseman, I'm gonna beat the crap outta the kid at second base."

Sure enough, an inning or two later, Beck singled. Pace's first baseman used his elbow, and Beck turned around and popped him. The benches emptied and so did the field, as everyone ran toward first base. Except Burns. He made a beeline for the second baseman and blindsided the poor guy.

From then on, and for the next four years, Burns beat this hapless kid, Chad Redman, into dogshit every time we played Pace in sports. During basketball Burns would say, "If I get in, I'm gonna deck Redman." Somebody would shoot the ball, everybody would look for the rebound, and Burns would . . . boom! hit Redman in the stomach. Then we'd have nine guys running down the court and one guy lying in the foul lane.

The weird thing was that Redman always knew it was coming.

We didn't discover why Burns had it in for Redman until our senior year, when someone just happened to ask him. We could never have guessed the reason, but the answer also didn't surprise us. It was pure Burns. "He's got orange hair," he said. "I *hate* orange hair."

Just my luck, I suppose, that he didn't mind orange *clothes*.

*

Knowing a kid's parents often explains the sometimes irrational acts of the friend you hang out with every day. Even if his ways still make no sense, you at least know what to expect. Later in life, this is why it's a good idea to meet your prospective in-laws long before the word "marriage" is ever mentioned. Just in case there's insanity or a severe case of midlife ugliness in your intended's family, it's not too late to get out and join the witness protection program.

Larry Burns's dad drove a truck that carried cars for the Ford Motor Company. I don't think I ever saw Mr. Burns with a shirt on. He had a gut like the front end of a '55 Buick, only without the headlights. Well, one big light in the middle. His navel was the size of a hubcap. He was a big, big man. Every kid in the neighborhood was scared to death of him, even though Mr. Burns's bark was far worse than his bite.

I remember once I called their house looking for Larry, and his dad answered.

"Hello?"

"Mr. Burns, this is Jeff Foxworthy. Is Larry there?"

"Ah, for cryin' out loud!"

"Something wrong?"

"Eeyeah."

"What?"

"Well, I been watching this movie for the past hour and a half. Guy finally gets the girl. Invites her back to his apartment, they have a few cocktails. They're on the sofa, they start kissing around a little bit. He talks her into the bedroom. Gets her in there, gets her blouse off, pulls her skirt off, gets her naked. He takes his pants off, pulls his shirt off. He's climbing into his bed, he's about to get on top of her . . . and the damn phone rings and it's YOU wantin' to know where LARRY is!"

Another time I went to visit Larry, and Mr. Burns was all smiles and glad to see me. He said, "Hey Fox! You want some homemade peach ice cream? Just made it."

"Yessir." He handed me this bowl of stuff. I took a spoonful and I can *still* remember that it was some of the worst-tasting glop I'd ever eaten in my life. But Lord knows, I didn't want to offend Mr. Burns. I managed to get the whole thing down and I carried my bowl into the kitchen.

He said, "Hey, you want some more!"

I said, "No sir, I'm full."

"You didn't like it?"

"No, it was really good. I'm just full."

He started laughing: "You dumb shit! That wasn't peach ice cream! That's a thing of apricot yogurt. Been in the refrigerator for a couple of months."

I knew that meant Mr. Burns liked me. Otherwise he wouldn't have wasted his time. He was not a cruel man. In fact, his attitude pretty much explained Larry's way of confronting life. He always had this look in his eyes like he knew something you didn't. It was usually true. I miss him.

❧

I loved hanging out at my friends' houses, especially Deke Cole's. Although Deke's dad had died, his mother was great because she allowed us to drop by at all hours.

At Deke's house we perfected our technique of dropping M-80s down street gutters, just to hear the explosions. Also, because we could hide behind the shrubs near the driveway, we could take a stuffed animal, tie it to some fishing line, and drag it across Jonesboro Road at night, right in front of an oncoming car. You could get some pretty nice-looking skids going. Until you've seen a family of four doing a "three-sixty" in a Ford wagon, you really haven't lived.

✱

By the time we were in the tenth grade, Danny Chastain had become legendary for his gas. On more than one occasion, anyone driving in a car with Chastain as a passenger had to pull over and get out on the roadside, just to prevent asphyxiation. Chastain could clear out an ROTC platoon, even though they knew that if they moved an inch they would have to do fifty push-ups. You *had* to move.

Because of Chastain's prowess Burns and I decided it was only right that we make our friend a World Heavyweight Championship belt in metal shop. We engraved it with those words, and a big cloud. Burns's dad, who made money on the side reupholstering furniture, supplied us with black vinyl. We added metal studs as a final touch.

Chastain was pretty proud of that belt, but one of the cooks at the Dwarf House complained that to give Chastain a trophy without a title bout just wasn't fair. He wanted to challenge Chastain for the crown.

We needed a place to hold the contest. Pete Riggins lived across the street from the Coles. Pete was Hapeville High's ninety-eight-pound weight class wrestling champ three years in a row. He wasn't big, but he was quick and nimble. Also funny. His dad was the pharmacist at the local drugstore.

We held the fifteen-round championship showdown in Pete's living room. (You learn to entertain yourself a lot in a small town.) Burns and I were Chastain's trainers. The afternoon of the fight we made Danny drink three beers, and his mother, who was also in on it, made hard-boiled eggs and a pot of broccoli. We loaded him up.

Pete Riggins, Steve Raymond, and Doc Riggins were our judges. They even had official clipboards. Now remember, with an event like this we had to *create* the rules because we had no previous competitions to go by. We decided that each guy had two minutes per round to work up his best effort. We judged by sound and stench.

To our complete amazement, Doc Riggins took his responsibilities very seriously. I will never forget him getting up, walking across the room, wafting the odor up with his hand, saying, "Oh my God!" and marking the score on his clipboard. He did this with each attempt.

What a great dad. Even if I thought he was totally nuts, I had to respect the man.

I think he was totally nuts.

✺

Burns and I also liked to hold contests at school. One was the King Slob competition. The idea was to determine who could dress the grungiest for a whole week. From Monday through Thursday we were both pretty equally matched: torn shirts, dirty tennis shoes, muddy pants. On Friday I decided to go all out to beat him. I didn't shower, wash my hair, or brush my teeth. I wore my three-day-old football practice undershirt and hunting pants, and added whatever extra dirt I could think of. When I got to school I looked around for Burns, confident I had him beat. Suddenly he walked up wearing the prettiest three-piece suit I'd ever seen.

"You win, Fox," was all he said. That was enough. I heard those words in my head the entire day, while I sat in class looking like the world's biggest dirt pile, and Burns beamed like a million bucks in his new threads.

✺

A major rite of passage in Hapeville was the trip to Shit Creek. Sorry, but that's what we called the two-mile stretch of woods through which ran the drain-off from the sewage treatment plant between Hapeville and Forest Park. The creek wasn't scary in the daylight, but when the sun went down no one was safe.

See, the rumor was that Goat People—half person, half goat—lived in the woods. And Waterhead families: people with *really big* heads. Supposedly entire clans of these freaks existed nowhere else in Georgia but in the woods surrounding Shit Creek. As far as we know today, that's still true.

The older high school kids would take the younger kids to Shit Creek at night. My initiation trip was in Ricky River's Volkswagen. I was in the eighth grade. Pete Riggins, Steve Raymond, and Tom Flood were there as well. We'd driven about a mile into the woods when several guys *thought* they saw a Goat Man on the edge of the woods. Then suddenly Ricky's car broke down in the middle of the road. The timing couldn't have been worse. Goat People and Waterheads were everywhere.

But Ricky said, "Stay calm. It's done this before. All we have to do is push-start it and the engine will kick in."

Warily, we all got out on the dirt road. I

swore I could hear the Waterhead families doing whatever Waterhead families did in their houses, back in the dark woods. I stood behind the Volkswagen, ready to push, when suddenly Ricky fired the engine. Flood, Riggins, and Raymond jumped in, Ricky put it in gear and took off, leaving me in the middle of Shit Creek.

I yelled and screamed for what must have been two or three seconds. Then I clammed up. No sense letting the Goat People and Waterheads know *exactly* where I was. Instead, I took off the way we came in. Had someone been standing by with a stopwatch, I would have set a new school speed record.

Everything that could possibly happen to me flashed into my head as I raced through the dark. I knew that calling my parents to come and get me was the least of my concerns. I feared that by the time the Goat People and Waterheads got through with me, there would be nothing left to take home. I imagined the kids at school talking about me the next day:

"Poor Jeff. So young, so funny. So dead."

"And brave. He knew it was coming."

"What do you mean?"

"Don't you know? Before he died he wrote his name and 'I died at Shit Creek' in blood on a big rock."

"The Goat Men and Waterheads have him now."

Of course, my friends were waiting for me in the clearing at the end of the road. I saw the car when I was a good hundred yards away. They sat around drinking Miller beer from pony bottles and laughing like hyenas. When I realized I would make it out alive I did what every victim of this ritual has ever done. I slowed, wiped the snot off my face and the tears from my eyes, and gathered my composure. Then I sauntered up acting all pissed off.

"You bastards! Leave me in Shit Creek! The Goat Man was *right behind me!* He was this close to catching me!"

I don't think they believed me.

Shit Creek was a scary place and it smelled bad. Being left alone there prepared me perfectly for one day getting my own sitcom on television. Stepping out onto the soundstage for the very first time is like being dropped off on that dirt road in the middle of nowhere. Right from the get-go they ask you to push, to help jump-start the show. Then they take off without you. Soon you're crying, you're scared, and you're pretty sure you're surrounded by Waterheads.

"Bomber One to Mother Hen. Come in Mother Hen."

"This is Mother Hen, Bomber One."

"Yeah, Mother Hen. Bomber One requests permission to fire on '77 Ford Galaxy."

"Affirmative, Bomber One. Do you prefer to press or hang?"

"Prefer to hang, Mother Hen."

"Roger, opening hatch. Lock, load, fire when ready."

"Hatch opening . . . Firing . . . Omigod! Direct hit. They're in the ditch! Repeat, they are in the ditch! Granny is out of the car and clutching her heart!"

No, this is not an excerpt from the long-suppressed *Mother Goose Meets Mad Max.* This is the game of "Search and Destroy" as played by three crazed teenagers speeding down the interstate in my father's Chrysler (with the electric bomb bay doors—I mean windows), *mooning* innocent motorists. What's even better, it's a true story.

Mooning was a great sport. Nobody ever got hurt. You didn't have to be in shape to play. The fatter you were the more you brought to the window. I'm still not sure why it was such a thrill to make somebody look at our naked butts; I just know we did it compulsively. Unfortunately, any time you mooned someone, you were also open to retaliation. Yes, it's funny to moon, but it's not so funny if it happens when you're with your mother. Once, when I was in the tenth grade, I remember riding to church with my mom, when I looked over to see my best friends drive past with a pressed ham against the passenger's window. Thank God my mom hadn't worn her glasses.

"Oh look," she said. "Uncle Buddy got a haircut. Looks good, don't it?"

We mooned whenever the opportunity occurred. One night, while we hung out in the Dwarf House parking lot, somebody told us they had discovered where Danny Chastain had parked with his girlfriend. They'd spotted his car under a magnolia tree by the mortuary. We immediately gathered ten guys, found the car, took our pants off, and crept closer while Chastain made out in the front seat. Someone counted very quietly to three and BOOM! Every ass was on all available window space. Chastain's date screamed his tongue right out of her mouth. We knew it would take a great deal of sweet talk and Windex to rectify the situation.

Almost nothing was sacred, except that Burns would never moon a car with kids inside. More than once he almost killed himself yanking his ass back through the window because, just as we pulled alongside our intended victims, he'd see a child or even a child's car seat.

"No! No! I can't! There are kids in the car."

If only Chad Redman had been smart enough to wear a diaper whenever he thought Burns might be around.

Church buses were the most tempting targets, but also off-limits. We were God-fearing and figured that if we gave in to temptation that one day we'd have to account for everything. We didn't want the Lord booming, "YOU MOONED THE CHURCH BUS."

"But, sir . . ."

"THOU SHALT NOT MOON. COMMANDMENT FIFTEEN. LOOK IT UP. NOW GET OUT OF HERE."

It was safer to be mooners with morals. But morality had nothing to do with why we didn't moon the girls we knew. Call us practical. Mooning a high school coed wouldn't get *anyone* on the have-to-date chart.

"Oh, everybody's seen his ass. I *must* go out with him!"

Mooning had many derivatives. We called them "BAs" for bare asses, and when we played high school football we cared less about our won-lost record than scoring BAs.

You could do BAs two ways. Drop your pants and bend over and wait for your victim to turn around. Or do the "red eye." A tasteful way of putting this is "a BA with a spreader." Either way, a guy had to admit when he saw it. It was a point of honor. You *had* to concede when you'd been scored upon.

We got bored with that pretty quickly, possibly because we *did it all the time!* So we created more elaborate variations. For instance, every guy knows that there is a complete lack of privacy in most men's restrooms. There are stand-up urinals and sit-down commodes, none of which have doors. This is especially true in athletic locker rooms. Before football practice, two or three guys would always be dropping a couple of "friends" off at the lake, so we'd creep in and do a little number that we liked to call a "train BA." Picture many teenage boys locking arms and bending over, while flashing past an unsuspecting halfback relieving himself in the set position. A common defense against the train BA was to immediately look skyward. That way you only saw one bare ass whiz by, and it didn't count. We defended against that move by silently positioning another man on top of the stall, doing the red eye. The victim looked up and he was had.

The worst BA was the *flying BA,* developed by Harry Hass. His was an ass you just didn't want to look at. Put it this way: Harry was a hairy guy. You've all been to the zoo. You've seen baboons with the same sort of problem. If a nine-year-old had ever seen Hass he'd have thought, "God, if that ever happens to me, somebody please shoot me."

Hass made the most of his gifts. He watched for someone to walk out of the locker room. Then he grabbed the equipment cage wire mesh, swung up, and wrapped his legs around the quarry's neck. We didn't invite Harry to many parties after that.

Did we have too much time on our hands? Yes. In fact, we had so much spare time that we extended the BA wars into the classroom.

Once Burns came into my history class with a note. "They want to see Jeff in the office," he told the teacher. When I walked into the hall two guys were bent over and *I* was history. We finally quit when we realized we had influenced the sub-freshmen. Morals, remember? One afternoon in math class I got bored and stared out the door. There in the hallway was an eighth grader with his pants around his ankles. He was doubled over, and looking between his legs, going, "Fox! Fox!"

I realized I had set a bad example. If he got caught, my conscience would have forced me to visit this kid at the juvenile home. I couldn't do that. They might have invited me to stay.

Another Larry Burns story that cannot go untold.

When Atlanta began building its new airport, Burns got in trouble for shooting doves under the landing lights at the end of the runway. Apparently the airport authorities frowned upon firearms being discharged into the air anywhere near the flight path. Go figure. A sergeant named P. D. Bosket ran him off.

The next weekend Danny Chastain and I listened as Burns told the story. According to Larry, Bosket had said, "If I ever see your ass down here again, even just standing around watching the planes land, I'm going to take you to jail."

Burns was unfazed. "You've never seen this many doves in your life," he explained. "We *have* to go down there and shoot some. The sky is *black* with doves."

For some reason we shared his enthusiasm and agreed to an immediate target practice. At the airport we climbed the fence, shotguns in hand, and sat under the landing lights picking off doves. There were doves everywhere. When we'd drop one, another took its place. (Note to the Olympic Committee. Need doves? Help yourself. They're free and there are still plenty left.)

Suddenly we heard a voice booming through a bullhorn: "Come out with your hands up."

I turned to see two cop cruisers parked alongside our car. We walked out, three geeky sixteen-year-olds, with our hands in the air, holding our shotguns over our heads. We looked like captured soldiers in a *Hee Haw* skit. As we walked, Burns whispered, "Let me do the talking."

No problem. Besides, it's not as if we could have actually hit a plane, I thought. Our guns could only shoot about thirty-five yards and the planes were at least fifty yards above us. That's at least a fifteen-yard margin of error, which is plenty, right?

The first officer said, "Let us see your hunting licenses." This should immediately tell you something about growing up in Georgia. Then the other added, "What in the world were you kids thinking?"

Burns had already prepared his answer.

"We would have never thought to do this on our own," he said somewhat contritely, "but I have a friend who's a police officer—name of P. D. Bosket—and P. D. said that we oughta come down here and shoot some of these doves at the airport."

The first officer said, "God, I've known P. D. all my life. I can't *imagine* him saying something like that."

Burns said, "Do you think we're *that* stupid to just come down here and shoot doves at the airport? On our own?" Now Larry was indignant. "No! P. D. said it was okay. Think about it. You always hear about doves flying into jet engines and costing the airlines millions of dollars, not to mention endangering passenger safety. I thought—I guess P. D. thought—we were doing a public service."

We had a name. We had the attitude. They let us go.

We didn't always get away with everything.

I'm not especially proud of this story. But I'd rather you hear it from me than read some inaccurate tabloid version that makes me sound like a hick and that will make my mother even madder because *I've never told her any of this before.* (Sorry, Mom.) Anyway, I believe the statute of limitations is up.

Long ago, when I was nineteen, Larry Burns once goaded me in to peeing into the Cincinnati Reds' dugout during a game with the Atlanta Braves. I know what you're wondering: Yes, there *were* players in the dugout at the time. Two, or maybe just one, laughed at the unexpectedly warm drizzle. I feel badly now, but I still like to think that my bravado, stupid as it was, turned out to be a good thing for the team because the Reds awoke that night from a midseason slump and went on to win the Series. They should have sent me a World Series ring.

I learned something, too: Ballpark bouncers *will* ask you to leave. At that point it's actually more of a demand. We were just lucky they didn't take us to jail.

Burns and I should have quit while we were ahead and gone home to sleep it off. Instead, we hauled down I-85 and I somehow confused the interstate sign with the speed limit sign. When I saw the flashing red lights in the rearview mirror, I said, "There's a cop trying to get around me. I'm going to pull over one lane, let him around."

To my big dumbass surprise, he pulled in behind us. As we slowed to a stop, Burns, always the optimist, kept saying, "Just be cool. Be cool."

I knew cool didn't matter.

When I was a kid I had once ridden in my dad's car when he'd been drinking beer all day. We got pulled over by the highway patrol. The officer walked up to my dad's window and said, "Excuse me there, sir. Can I see your license please?"

My dad mumbled something I couldn't quite hear.

"No sir, I don't need a cold beer and I don't think you do either," said the officer. "Mr. Foxworthy, do you know why I pulled you over, sir?

"Nope."

"Well it concerns that vehicle you're pulling behind you."

"That's not illegal," my Dad said.

"No sir, it's not against the law to tow a boat, but we do require that you put it on a trailer. Now, could you ask your friends to get out of the boat, please, sir?"

My dad protested.

"I don't give a damn if the fish *are* biting. Now, could you ask your friends to get out of the boat?" said the patrolman.

Okay, that's not a true story. (If you believed it, put this book next to your copy of *The One That Got Away*, by the One-Armed Fisherman.) But it still makes my point.

When the patrolman walked up to me, I tried to be casual. I said, "Good evening, Officer. What seems to be the problem?" His answer was to yank the door open and say, "You going to jail, boys. That's what the problem is."

Okay, just let me tell my friends to get out of the boat.

He took me around the back of my car, slammed me down, and frisked me. I had a pocket knife about three inches long. He took that away and later charged me with concealing a deadly weapon. You couldn't open a letter with that thing, but apparently the officers felt threatened. Then he took me to the drunk tank at Grady Hospital.

When the drunk tank door locked behind me I suddenly realized that I was scared to death and rooming with people sleeping in their own urine. I thought about Ned Beatty in *Deliverance*. I'm not egotistical about my looks, but I *was* the cutest drunk in the tank that night.

I was also alone. Burns wasn't behind the wheel so he got to call home and go free. I settled down on a bench. Then a guy came over and said, "This your first time in the joint?"

"Yeah." I said it slow, watching for any sudden moves. I thought we were about to dance.

He said, "This is bull. I was in the state pen for twenty years."

"Yeah?" Now I *knew* we were gonna dance.

Then he said, "I'm gonna take care of us."

Time to tango. I started a quick move to the left, but he got up before me, walked to the door, knocked, and told the jailer that he had to use the bathroom. They let him go down the hall. When he returned he said, "Shhh . . . Hold out your hands."

He had collected every cigarette butt out of every ashtray between the drunk tank and the bathroom. Menthol, regular, it didn't matter. I cupped my hands and he emptied the tobacco from each butt. Then he reached into his boot and pulled out rolling papers. He had enough to roll two cigarettes, one for him and one for me. Best cigarette I ever had in my whole life.

Four hours later, the cell door swung open and Larry Burns stumbled inside. It seems he had tried to get me out and he'd raised such a ruckus that they'd detained him for attempting to incite a riot. Before long we were transported, handcuffed, and in the paddy wagon, to a real jail. I was scared but Burns saw an opportunity to have some fun. At the processing center he looked at me and said, "What are you in for?"

I played along. "Going eighty-five in a fifty-five, DUI, attempting to elude arrest, and concealing a deadly weapon. What are you in for?"

He stood right next to a cop. Burns spit on the floor and, as casually as if he'd been arrested for jaywalking, said, "Murder one."

The next morning, Burns' father-in-law-to-be came and bailed us out. It was a proud moment that obviously had zero effect on Burns' engagement, except that his bride's family required him to post bond before the wedding.

Later the police dropped the charges against Burns. I had to get an attorney. I shaved my beard, and we went to court. They offered me a chance to plead *nolo contendere*, but I declined because if you plead it's on your record. Instead, I said "not guilty" and asked for a trial by jury. When the date arrived, no witnesses for the prosecution were present, including the arresting officer. So the judge said, "All right, if you don't get another ticket for nine months, we'll drop every charge against you." That was my plea bargain deal. I signed it, and nine months to the day I drank about 145 beers with Marty Sumpter to celebrate the end of my probation.

I did learn my lesson, though. Afterward I made Marty drive. I know I was a complete idiot for operating a motor vehicle under the influence. I've never done anything like that again, and I'd suggest to anyone out there IF YOU'RE DRINKING, DON'T DRIVE. I got lucky. You might not be.

But that's not the end of the story. I had to go to the weapons bureau and reclaim my pocket knife. They have big wire bins full of bazookas and machetes and submachine guns.

I gave a very pretty young woman clerk my claim check and she brought out my knife. She looked at me, then at the knife, and said, "You got to be kidding."

That was the most embarrassing moment of the whole incident.

✦

Larry and Danny were great friends. The only person closer to me is my little brother, Jay. At six feet three and 235 pounds, he is now my larger brother. Jay played linebacker for Duke University, and today he can pick me up with one hand. But he still can't beat me at Sega football. (The preceding sentence will cost me a choke hold.) Can you tell I'm extremely competitive? We often play long distance, over the phone, he at his TV and I at mine. No cheating allowed. And we still have a wonderful relationship. Next to my wife, Jay is probably my best friend.

When we were kids, my mother and sister used to think Jay and I were crazy. (This doesn't seem such a surprise to you *now*, I guess.) One reason was our strong sense of honor. That's not a bad thing. We just had an odd way of demonstrating it. This started very early. We both played sports, and we had a standing agreement that when one guy asked another to smell his socks or his shirt, or whatever, he *had* to do it. If my brother came in from football practice and said to me, "All right, smell this T-shirt," I couldn't fake it. I had to hold up the T-shirt to my nose and inhale. Then I could run around the house going, "Oh God! Oh God, that's horrible!" Then Jay owed me one. The next night I'd go, "Smell these socks."

My mother used to say, "You are outta your minds." I think she knew what she was talking about.

Jay and I constantly invented games. My mother used to say that you could lock the two of us in a room with a thread, a marble, and a pencil, and not only would we come up with a game, we would keep statistics. We played everything: underwear baseball, tube sock basketball. Once, in a highly creative moment in our garage, we decided to throw darts at a wiffle ball bat and see if the darts would stick. I was eleven and my brother was six. I swung the bat as hard as I could at the first dart he threw. The dart hit the bat, turned around, went right back at Jay—and all the way through his ear. Not the lobe, the hard cartilage part. It stuck out the back.

Jay stood there, stunned.

I said, "Does it hurt?"

"No, it dudden hurt."

"What should we do?"

"I think we have to go tell Mom."

I led him upstairs. She was cooking in the kitchen and still had her back to us when I said, "Uh . . . Mom, we made up this game and . . ." I guess she heard something in my voice. She turned around, took one look at the yellow plastic dart in Jay's ear, and said, "I KNEW YOU WERE OUTTA YOUR MINDS!"

She pulled out the dart. There wasn't much blood. I tried to joke about it. I peered at the hole and said, "Look! You can see the dining room!"

"That's not funny," she said.

Oh yes it was.

❀

When I think of everything my friends and I used to pull, I realize that most of it was completely crazy. Yet it bound us together for a lifetime. Boys will be boys, even long after they've become grown men. We were lucky that almost no harm came from our adventures, just lots of good stories. I loved my friends. I remember once looking at the gang and thinking that someday I'd get married, have kids, and a job I busted my ass at and hated, but as long as I got to hang out with my friends (and family) and laugh, that would be my salvation.

*

Burns and I may have been rascals, but we were also very popular throughout high school, even with the teachers. We may have rushed in where angels feared to tread, but we were always polite little devils when we got there. Somehow we managed to get out of trouble that a lot of other kids didn't even have the guts to get into. I think Burns and I were just full of the youthful arrogance that makes kids believe they can overcome just about any situation. Burns and I were also the funniest guys in school, which made it that much easier to get away with murder.

We were also very strong academically. (Shocking?) He was the valedictorian and I was fourth or fifth in the class. He won the Journal Cup and I won the Outstanding Senior Award. I became president of the student council, and Burns and I were co-captains of the football and baseball teams. My nickname in football was the Flint River Flash. I was very fast, until I hurt my knee. Yeah, yeah, wasn't everybody.

When graduation rolled around, they asked

me to make the class speech. I wrote my notes on index cards, then I practiced and practiced. I got so I could flip the cards in order and recite the speech without looking. I just had them for reference.

During the ceremony, I asked Burns to hold my cards for a minute while I went up to receive some award. That was a mistake. During the speech I began to lose my place. I knew I was on the fourth card, so I looked at my notes to see what came next. But instead of seeing card number four, I saw card twenty-three. I flipped it over and the next one was card number two. Then eighteen. Burns had shuffled the deck and he made me look like a total idiot. All I could hear while I fumbled and stammered was someone behind me laughing and, finally, falling off his chair.

I didn't have to wonder who it was. I knew in my heart that as I'd stepped to the podium, Burns had probably whispered to everyone within earshot, "Y'all watch this."

I would have done the same thing.

After all, what are friends for?

Say It with Krylon

What's the sexiest four-word sentence in the English language. I'll give you a clue. It's when a Southern woman says, "Hey, y'all, I'm drunk." Any woman from anywhere *could* say it, of course, but it's highly unlikely that she also fantasizes about some guy in a baseball cap laying on top of her, cooing, "Who's yer daddy, sweetie? A'right, sweet thang."

Southern women *are* different.

Where else can you find a woman who can chug a Miller pony beer, chuck the bottle out the window, and hit a road sign—without having to sit up?

Where else, when a woman gets mad, is the full impact of her fiery temper expressed as "I am so mad at yew"? True, it doesn't have the same impact as a housewife from New Jersey screaming, "Get your ass in the car!" but it means far more. The image of Southern women may be all fluttery and delicate, but it's just that steel magnolias get pissed with style. Instead of telling you to get into the car, she'll wait until your back is turned and drive the car into *you*. The really tough ones do it when you're looking.

By far the biggest difference between Southern women and all others is their Southern daddies. These men know why you're at their house. You can't bullshit them a bit, which might seem strange since these are the same men who will swear they were once abducted by aliens and forced to undergo a thorough body-cavity probe. (And wished they could have taken a probe home as a souvenir to use on the cat, or the wife, or on the next hunting trip.) But when it comes to their daughters, you can pet the dog, know every football stat for three decades, and actually *be* from another planet, and good old dad will still be ticked at you for sniffing around his baby girl. He knows you're there for the same reason he was somewhere himself, twenty-five years ago. He knows your mission is to get his daughter into the same state in which she came into the world . . . naked.

(Word of warning: I'm now a Southern dad and you better not be coming 'round my house in about fifteen years.)

It's easy to fool Southern moms, though. (We fooled them when they were daughters and nothing's changed, right?) Sweet talk about how wonderful the mashed potatoes, gravy, and rabbit stew taste works every time. Unfortunately, unlike Eddie Haskell on *Leave It to Beaver,* Southern men have to prove they mean what they say by actually eating the stuff.

However, here's the good news. Whatever you must endure to date a Southern woman, she will compensate you for your hardship and make it worthwhile. Southern women are truly the hottest creatures on earth, even with the windows open in midwinter. Their butts don't get cold until *after* marriage. Here's the good deal: You don't have to woo them much. Southern romance does *not* necessarily mean you have to buy presents or take your date somewhere nice. Saying, "You're prettier than a blue tick hound," will do just fine. Or, for that special occasion, "Your feet don't stink near as badly as my brother's." When you fall in love with a Northern girl, you have to send her flowers and candy and cards. When you fall in love with a Southern woman you just spraypaint her name on a water tower, an overpass, or a big rock—it all depends on your town's tradition. But this much is universal: Whether it's having sex or catching a fish, it doesn't mean anything until you tell someone. True love means "Say It with Krylon."

I once was so in love that I spray-painted a girl's name on the outside wall of the high school gymnasium. Unfortunately, it was only four feet off the ground. Not too impressive. Eye level does not equal everlasting passion. To have real impact you must stand a damn good chance of dying in the trying, or at least of walking with a limp for the rest of your life. In Hapeville the water tower was the true-love proving ground. If someone climbed to the top in the dead of night—during daylight the cops got upset—to declare his ardor, everyone knew it was serious.

By the way, the key word in the preceding sentence is "everyone." Less than an hour after the sun rose on a new name on the water tower, *everyone* in town knew the young folks involved. Once, after a midnight spray-painting run, I walked down the street and a complete stranger said, "Hey, nice job on the water tower last night."

I grinned and never heard the words "water tower" at all.

*

I liked girls early. Just about every young lady in the fifth and sixth grades wore my ID bracelet. Well, every cute one. It meant we were going together. It didn't mean we ever spoke on the phone or appeared in public together. Maybe we'd indulge in some intense cross-classroom staring during homeroom, but that was about as steamy as it got.

My only problem was that I was too shy to approach a potential steady myself. So I'd get Larry Burns to do it for me. Larry, as you know, would do anything.

I'd say, "Larry, will you ask Ellen Harrison if she'll go with me?" A while later he'd come back and say, "Yes, she'll go with you."

"Okay, give her my ID bracelet."

Two weeks later Larry would hand back the bracelet and say, "Now she's gonna go with [insert boy's name here]."

Thank goodness Larry took his job seriously or I'd have had to spend *all* my allowance on cheap jewelry.

✱

This is the only advice that my father, Big Jim, ever gave me.

"Son, the day will come when women won't sleep with you on a $1,000 bet. I don't care if it costs you your job or your health or your life: When you get on a hot streak, ride . . . it . . . out."

It was a *Father Knows Best* moment. I swear.

Otherwise, Big Jim didn't tell me much about women or, on a more basic level, sex. We never had the conversation parents should have with their children even if the children know more than their folks. Of course, I would never know as much as Big Jim. His mother once swore to me that when he was six years old, she'd caught him in a cornfield doing "something" with a local girl. Can you imagine that? When I was playing with GI Joes, Big Jim was playing with . . . no. It's not a picture I want to think about. No wonder he never told me about sex. He probably just assumed everyone did it at six.

My mother never told me about sex, either. I guess she was easily embarrassed. It makes sense. She went to church five days a week and is still the most conservative woman I know. Instead of a frank discussion about procreation (a strange word since we all begin as amateurs), my mom decided to bring home a pamphlet for me from the pediatrician. It was about boys turning into wolves. I didn't get it. I checked the mirror for facial hair. Seeing none, I decided not to worry about it.

*

Fortunately for everyone, I learned about sex on my own, and in the same way most boys do: in the street. Late one afternoon, during the summer before the fourth grade, my next-door neighbor, Brad, sat next to me on a curb and discussed the facts of life. Brad and I were the same age, but he'd already gotten the facts. We *knew* they were the facts because they came straight from his older brother, Rick. Rick was in the *sixth* grade. Then Brad said that Rick had a telescope. Now I knew for sure that he knew.

According to Rick, sex went like this: You got married. Then you got in your car, drove to a place where there weren't a lot of other cars, and parked. Then you unzipped your pants, you got on top of your wife, you put yourself inside her (he didn't elaborate about exactly where), you peed, and you drove back home.

I was perfectly fine with all of this.

My only question was why it had to be in a car. Why couldn't you do it in a house? But Brad said that's the way it had come down from his brother, and we knew that it had to be right.

Later that night I lay in bed and thought about the glories of sex. I also knew I'd forever miss them because there was no way I could ever pee inside anybody.

*

I knew you put "it" in "something," but I didn't know exactly where or what that something was. I finally learned when one guy in our group—yes, it *was* Larry Burns—reported on an actual close encounter with that particular animal.

He stunned us with its location.

Larry said, "It's much lower than you think it is."

We had previously imagined that the girl's "it" was almost like a second navel, but Larry set us straight. Then we couldn't get it out of our minds. (I've also never gotten over how he'd actually encountered the real thing in the eighth grade.)

Until then I'd been satisfied just watching cheerleaders jump high at football games and wishing that I owned a bike so I could date. Now it was even worse. I had to have that bike!

✶

As a kid, I often wondered how you could ever sleep with somebody and then, without giggling, actually speak to them *in front of other people*. Wouldn't you only think about what you had just done, whether it was five minutes or five days earlier?

Boy, life teaches you how wrong you can be. It's *entirely* possible. Not only can you do it with somebody and look at them without giggling, you can also change your phone number and move just to get away from them when they start making plans for the rest of your lives together.

"I'm sorry. The number you dialed is no longer a working number. Please check the number and try again. This is a recording."

✶

I kissed my first girl in the first quarter of the ninth grade. I also shot my first squirrel then. Cross your fingers that I don't get these stories confused.

Carrie Ann Campbell (the girl) was a real cutie at College Park High School. She lived three blocks from me, and one day I asked if I could walk her home. She said yes. Standing on her front steps, I kissed her—*smack*—quickly. She didn't seem to mind, so I did it three days in a row. On the fourth day, before I could kiss her, she invited me in. I'd have felt like Casanova had I'd known who Casanova was. Instead I felt like Barney Fife getting lucky. Inside, I was about to kiss Carrie Ann in the hallway when she stopped me and said, "Wait. You don't know how to kiss."

Suddenly I felt like Barney Fife in a swirl of skunk vapor at point-blank range. Then Carrie Ann surprised me and said she'd show me how to do it right.

I am *so* grateful.

French kissing was amazing. Back then I could kiss Carrie Ann for four hours and do nothing else. Or possibly I was just rationalizing because I figured that there was no chance in all of Greater Atlanta that Carrie Ann would ever let me do much of *anything* else. No, I really didn't mind. I've always been a pragmatic guy, interested in investing for the long term. If I could kiss Carrie Ann for four hours, perhaps one day she'd let me rub the outside of her sweater. So what if my faith in the future was remarkably similar to that of a contestant on *Let's Make a Deal*?

"Do you want to risk everything for what's behind door number three, or do you want to keep what you've got?"

I wanted to keep what I had. I didn't want to go too far and have a girl say, "You know what? You're an animal. You're not getting *any* of this. I'm taking away the kissing *and* the outside of the sweater because you tried to go *inside* the sweater."

Now, of course, everything has changed. I read in the newspaper that the rule at some colleges today is that people who want to make out must ask permission to move ahead *each step* of the way. I don't think this would work in the South.

HE: *Can I kiss yer neck?*

SHE: *Oh, baby.*

HE: *I'm gonna stick my tongue in yer mouth.*

SHE: *Only a little . . . Oh God . . .*

HE: *Where does this damn bra unsnap?*

SHE: *Here, let me.*

And later . . .

HE: *Why the hell cain't you wear jeans with buttons?*

SHE: *It's not my fault that the zipper's stuck. Now get off me you . . . you . . . fat . . .*

HE: *But baby, you know I luv yew.*

SHE: *Hold on. What's that smell? Did you spill Buck Lure in this car?*

HE: *Worked, didn't it?*

✳

Let me catch my breath.

Carrie Ann and I were as seriously involved as ninth graders could be, but being from Georgia I know that there are also kids who, at that age, are actually having baby showers. Pregnancy and parents with shotguns can really make the ninth grade hard. I was lucky with Carrie Ann because her parents never interfered. To be honest, I never actually *knew* how her parents felt about me because I'd never met them. I've since realized that Carrie Ann had no parents and lived in her big house all alone.

My routine with Carrie Ann Campbell was pretty much: get up, go to school, get out of school, kiss—we'd sit on the couch for hours after class, just making out—go home, eat dinner, go to bed. Sometimes I'd call her at night.

We even exchanged ninth grade photos. I didn't write "I love you" or anything on the back. I just signed my name.

One day, after a couple hours of swapping spit in her basement, I finally put my hand under Carrie Ann's sweater. I'm lying. *She* put my hand under her sweater. It's the truth and an important lesson: Long-term investment pays off. Guess what? She was wearing another sweater. But hey, if door number three opens, you stroll on in. At that moment life really, really changed. I walked home from her house and passed a woman watering her lawn. I looked at her and thought, "You know, I *know* what I'm doing now. You'd better be careful. I could wreck your home."

Carrie Ann and I went together until I decided I missed the guys at Hapeville High and started riding the city bus back there. Long distance relationships don't work, and Hapeville and College Park were four miles apart. Four miles is too far to ride a bicycle, especially when you can't spend the night. So we had to break up. It was tragic and it took Carrie Ann at least a couple of hours to get over me.

Carrie Ann ended up with Buddy Hammond. There was even talk of getting married someday. His wedding gift to her was going to be a set of handmade, all-leather luggage with fur handles. Buddy's grandfather died still wondering what had become of his prize milk cows and his squirrel tail collection.

✻

Even if I hadn't switched schools, my romance with Carrie Ann would have ended. I was ready to say, "I think we should see other people." You realize, of course, that nobody ever says that without actually *having* another person in mind.

I had my eye on Kellie Joyce, who lived in Hapeville. She was a year older than I was. Kellie and I had talked while sitting on the grass outside the public tennis courts, and I had a pretty good feeling that she would kiss me had I not been involved with Carrie Ann. So "I think we should see other people" meant for me to go home that night and call Kellie Joyce.

Kellie agreed to go out with me. I went to her house and met her parents. She actually *had* parents, which was a new thing for me. After I'd settled into their living room couch, her dad said, "Now, who is your mother?"

Having a conversation with a dad is uncomfortable. (A dad hanging around is unusual. Usually, the Southern father unloads a couple of mean, knowing glares and then sulks quietly away to the garage.)

"Carole Foxworthy."

"What was her name before she was married?"

"Camp."

Her dad jumped up and said, "Your mother is *who?*"

I repeated myself. "Carole Camp."

"What's her phone number?!" he said. I gave him the number and he started dialing. I thought, "Oh my God, what have I done?! Mom's got a prison record I don't know about!" Turns out both Mr. and Mrs. Joyce had gone to high school with my mom.

"God, isn't that ironic," Mrs. Joyce said. "Twenty years later and now our kids are going out."

I later found out that Kellie was my half-sister, which made her even more appealing.

I'm kidding.

❦

If any of you still wonder whether I'm a true Redneck, this long-repressed secret should convince you. Believe me, I never thought it could happen to me. A long time ago, *I was attracted to my cousin.*

We were only fourteen and we had spent the day at a family reunion. You know the routine: swim and hang out all day, and then eat lunch off concrete picnic tables. Afterward, she and I took a walk and pretty soon we were kissing. I don't know how it happened, but I do know my brain was screaming in my ear, "You idiot. You're kissing your cousin!"

Of course another part of me was also screaming: "*Second cousin.* C'mon, she's almost a stranger! Haven't seen her in six years!"

We cooled down short of sin and went back to our families. We didn't talk about what happened and have never discussed it since.

I later found out she was *also* my half-sister. Apparently Big Jim had had the same problem a generation earlier.

Again, just kidding.

🍒

When I was in the eleventh grade I finally went out with Betty Calloway. Every guy talked about Betty Calloway. She was stunningly beautiful. Lucky for me she was also Chastain's cousin. I have never been more nervous with a woman than before that date. I might as well have been dating Elle MacPherson *and* Cindy Crawford and their twin sisters.

We went to see the movie *Where the Red Fern Grows*. Short synopsis: dirt poor Appalachian family. The kid wants coon-hunting dogs. They have no money. The kid cuts fields for a penny. Takes him five years to save enough money. One night he runs away, takes a train, goes to this town, and buys two bloodhounds: Old Dan and Little Anne. Carves their names on a tree. Comes back and raises these dogs. They end up winning the state coon-hunting championship.

One night not long after that, they're hunting and a cougar attacks Old Dan. They take him back home, try to nurse him. He dies. They bury Old Dan in the yard. Then Little Anne will not eat. She just lies out on Old Dan's grave and moans. Pretty soon Little Anne dies from a broken heart. They bury her next to Old Dan.

Soon the family decides to move on. They're loading up the wagon and the boy says, "Let me go say good-bye to my dogs one last time." At the beginning of the movie, the kid's mother had told him a story: "And the place where the greatest love on earth is," she said, "a red fern will grow." So he runs over the hill and there, between the two mounds of dirt, grows a red fern.

Now, I am dating the most beautiful girl in

Hapeville High and I am sobbing uncontrollably. This movie made *Old Yeller* look like a comedy. I cannot quit crying on our first date. This is the saddest story I have ever seen. We're driving home and I'm *still* crying. I'm so broken up I didn't even care about what Betty thought of my blubbering.

Finally, I parked in front of Betty's house and started kissing her. By the way, parking in front of your date's house is, contrary to conventional wisdom, a very smart move. You can get away with almost anything. Even if her parents look out the window and see someone's heels pressed against the left rear passenger window, they don't *really* see them because they can't imagine you'd have the nerve to try and climb on top of their daughter *right* in their own driveway.

As for Betty, she kissed me enthusiastically. Apparently, not being ashamed to let her see me get in touch with my female side made her happy to let me get in touch with her female side. In fact, the kissing was so hot and heavy that she got light-headed and had to take a moment and stand outside to catch her breath. That was it for the kissing. In fact, we never went out again. Turned out she had the flu and I'd turned the car heater up too high, but it was a running joke that I kissed her so well that she almost fainted.

*

Technique is everything.

First you kiss for three hours. Then you move your arm up on her arm. The goal is to have the inside of your arm accidentally brush the outside of her breast. If she doesn't shift away, you may move on. "Okay, wait a couple of minutes and bring the arm back . . : Oops, bumped it again. Still okay. Okay, now let's see if we can put our hand on her side, between her waist and her chest. Still doing okay . . ."

The whole procedure is like monitoring a space launch.

"Okay, let's gently ease the hand up. T-minus-8, 7, 6, 5, 4, move, grab." Many times that's when a young woman will launch a pre-programed counterattack and stop your hand, or move it back to its original position. With any luck her primary systems will fail and her secondary systems will be forced to take over, and your hand will be cleared for takeoff.

Often, I would proceed to T-minus-four seconds and reverse course and start again, with ever-so-slight variations. It was confusing and satisfying. The idea was to wear a girl down. Eventually, she got damn tired of stopping you.

Too bad it never dawned on us that perhaps

our objects of desire might have *wanted* what we wanted as well.

As I matured sexually and socially and began dating regularly, I made some important discoveries. For example, girls in the country were easier targets than girls in the city. Girls in the city had other stuff to do. They could go to a movie, they could go to the mall. Girls in the country didn't have a whole lot to look forward to. So whenever I went on vacation or down to the farm, I immediately began looking for prospects.

I figured that out the summer between the ninth and tenth grades, when I went to Pawpaw's farm in South Carolina. I met a girl who was the friend of a friend and we were all going to ride horses. She was cute, with blunt-cut blond hair. After a morning on horseback, she and I tied our mounts outside my uncle's trailer. No one was home. We went inside to get something to drink, settled down into the sofa, and she shifted right toward me.

I liked to think I was just too charming. On the other hand maybe she figured that making out with me was better than cleaning up after the horses, or the usual country pastime of staring all afternoon at a tree. Like I said, there wasn't much to do. Anyway, she pretty quickly let me put my hand inside her shirt. Not only did I feel it, I saw it. It was so cute. You know how you open up a blanket and you see a puppy for the first time? So innocent, and it's looking right up at you. That's all we did, but it was enough.

Later Uncle Bob and I milked the cows and talked. Uncle Bob said, "Hey, you guys were gone for quite a while," he said, with a devious chuckle. My mind churned. Suddenly I had my first shot at actually getting a man's approval.

"Oh, yeah. Yeah." Remember, this is my *uncle Bob*. And we're *milking* a cow.

"So, how was it?"

"Good. Good," I lied. "Really good."

"Did you . . . ?"

"Oh, sure. Sure."

"You dawg."

His reaction taught me an important lesson: Lying works. I'm just glad Bob wasn't so impressed that he wanted to demonstrate any advanced techniques on the cow.

�֍

We always hear how men like to swap tales of a graphic sexual nature in the locker room. This is completely true. However, we can be more subtle. Occasionally we simply like to brag about our hot moves.

Whining is always at the top of the list.

HE: *Please, sugar dumpling, please.*

SHE: *No. Uh-uh. No way.*

HE: *But my girlfriend just don't understand me like you do.*

SHE: *Then break up with her.*

HE: *Cain't. She's also my maw.*

SHE: *You're sick!*

HE: *Me? Sick? You did it with your cousin!*

SHE: *I know. But he's nice.*

HE: *But sweetie . . .*

Even though this example is assumed to be true only in select regions of the country, guys everywhere are *still* pathetic. They prove it every year at spring break. My most vivid memory is of five guys crammed into a Camaro, going to Fort Lauderdale or Daytona Beach, saying, "We're gonna get some. We're gonna get some." Then six days later, "Next year. *Next year* we're gonna get some."

Nobody ever got lucky. It took me two or three spring breaks to finally figure out what I'd been doing wrong. Like everyone else, I'd been too overeager. Hollering things at women didn't work. And for most women projectile vomiting has never been a turn-on. Finally, I tried a different tactic. When we all went into some place selling quarter drinks, I let the guys roam the bar while I sat by myself at a table and acted uninterested. Within five minutes I had eight coeds saying, "Why are you just sitting here? What's wrong with you?"

Anything that works.

Travis Tritt's road manager showed me the all-time best way to pick up a woman. We did a show at the Omni for the Super Bowl when it was last in Atlanta. I noticed that he had on two different cowboy boots: one was red lizard, the other tan buckskin. I said, "Why do you have on two different boots?"

He said, "I've gotten more women doing this than I can handle. All I have to do is go out dressed like this to a bar. I don't have to say a word. Women just come up to me and go, 'Why do you have on two different boots?' *They* start the conversation."

Like I said, anything that works.

*

Men are hounds. We think nothing of dating someone who just broke up with our best friend. I once asked a friend if I could date his ex. He said, "Don't you recall me telling you about her chasing me through the parking lot with a butcher knife?"

"Yeah," I said, "but she's *really* good-looking."

DeWayne Twilley, another good friend of mine, once brought a girl to my house for me to meet. He said he just wanted to show her off because she was so damn pretty. He was right. But a sophisticate like Twilley should have known better. (In the land of guys with no shame, Twilley was the king.) The minute he went to pee I wrote down my phone number and told her to call me later. It was just one of those things. I knew she liked me and I liked her as soon as she walked in the door. After Twilley took her home, she called me and we talked from 1:00 in the morning until 5:15 in the morning. Then I went to meet her. I didn't even care that she lived across the street from Twilley. (Sorry, DeWayne.)

Some of the best advice I got about dating and women came from a little guy named Morris, who worked in the Kroger deli. "There's nothing free," he'd always tell me. "Nothing free, buddy. Always got to pay the price. Nothing free."

I always tried to remember Morris's advice at the end of dates where I knew I wouldn't be calling again. I had to because otherwise I'd give in to the devil himself and think that although I had no intention of asking the girl out a second time, well, hell, I'm here and I got nothing else to do, so I'll make my play. Maybe I could get something for free. I had to force myself to remember that if I was successful, there'd be a price to pay. It might be tearful telephone calls or the girl showing up at work unexpectedly. Carrying my baby. With her dad. Who had a shotgun. I had to learn to let it go.

Although my testosterone level overflowed, I never wanted to be like all the other guys, who I figured were pawing their dates and not taking no for an answer. That it worked for them didn't seem to matter to me. I somehow believed that after the heavy breathing was over and the girls were back in their frilly bedrooms clutching a battered Barbie and scribbling the evening's events in their diaries, that they somehow resented these overly-aggressive boys who had once again overwhelmed them with whining persistence and taken advantage of their virtue.

Boy, was I full of it.

In fact, my desire to be sensitive just made me lose girls to the bad boys. I don't know why I persisted in believing that by being the nice guy I'd win. I guess I thought that finally one day a grateful woman would lie on my bed and say, "You know, you're such a nice guy, I should just take off my clothes and let you lay on top of me." Unfortunately, no woman ever had that realization.

✻

DeWayne Twilley had been there, and done *that*—the whole thing!—by the ninth grade. His first woman was a junior at Hapeville High. They did it on her couch. We were pretty awestruck, and we all wanted to date her, but she wouldn't give us the time of day.

DeWayne was our idol. DeWayne was always bold. Once, in college, we were out at a club. I sat at the bar making nice small talk and trying to score with a pretty young woman. DeWayne said almost nothing. Suddenly he spoke up, but not to me. "You know what? I really don't want to kill the whole evening. Would you like to screw?" She said, "Yeah," and they got up and left. DeWayne got his face slapped a few times, but more often he left with a woman on his arm, and he didn't come back.

I don't know how DeWayne did it. No, that's not true, I know how he did it, I just never understood what the women saw in him that made them go along. I mean no insult to DeWayne. He was one of my best friends. He wasn't bad looking, but he was also nothing to write home about. I guess he just had the Big Jim touch, which very few guys are blessed with. It's almost a curse, because then you have to end up telling stories while the rest of your buddies go, "And then what'd she do?" DeWayne was in the middle of our circle for many years, and the rest of us were on the outside going, "And then what'd she do? Oh my God. Wait, back up, back up."

❦

Eventually I caught up. Patty West was the girl of my dreams. She'd dated a "bad boy" and it didn't work out. So our Spanish teacher set us up. I can still remember what Patty wore on our first date: a pair of double-knit peach-colored pants, and a brown sweater with some tan deer on the front. She had just gotten her hair cut that day in a little blunt swoop. She looked like a million bucks and she smelled great.

We went to see *Rocky* at the Varsity, the world's largest drive-in. We parked on the upper deck. Pretty soon we started kissing, and we were really, *really* kissing. I had misjudged how much Patty had wanted to kiss me, and thought, "This is easy city here." So I put my left hand on her right breast and she instantly got upset. She yanked my hand away and said, "You're an animal. I thought you weren't that kind of guy, and here you are, first date, and you're groping me."

I said, "No, I'm not that kind of guy! You know I'm not that kind of guy. I don't know what happened."

Maybe the heater was on too high again.

She forgave me. Patty and I continued to date, and I swear I would not have touched her breast had you balanced a million dollars on it and said "Take the money." I might just brush up against it accidentally, though.

We went out, on and off, for three years. Eventually, I got to touch her *there*. The Friday before homecoming we parked off the driveway to the community swimming pool in Hapeville. She took my hand and put it on her breast. (Why fix a method that's not broken?) It was nice.

That Saturday we made out on my dad's couch. I got bold and started to unbutton her pants. To my surprise, she lifted her rear end off the couch to help me slide off her jeans.

She had on another pair of jeans underneath.

Or she might as well have, because instead of focusing on what was about to happen, Larry Burns's voice popped into my mind, explaining his theory that the moment a guy always remembers is not when he has sex with someone for the first time, but "when a woman lifts her rear end to help you take off her pants." When Patty West raised her hips I knew I was going to do it. My brain overloaded. "I'm going to do it. I'm going to do it." Then a couple of seconds later, "Oh damn, I just did it."

Afterwards I knew it wouldn't count if I didn't tell someone. Naturally, I called Burns, even though it was three o'clock in the morning.

"Guess what? You're not going to believe what went on tonight."

"No, you didn't."

"Damn right I did."

"How long did you last?"

"Almost six seconds."

I was like an antiaircraft flare. They don't burn long, but boy, they are brighter than hell and it takes no time at all to reload.

Patty West was also the first girl to whom I'd ever said "I love you" and meant it. I may have said it to Carrie Ann Campbell, but that's just because she let me put my hand between her sweaters. Otherwise, I've always tried to avoid trading terms of endearment for sexual favors. I never wanted to be known as a guy who would say *anything* just to get what he wanted.

I wanted to get it without having to say anything at all. So I took that bullet out of the love gun, and that weapon out of the arsenal. I've always played fair. I have never been a game-law violator.

I like to hunt within the rules.

Hunting, Fishing Chewing, and Other Turn-Ons

All men delight in pursuits that disgust women. Hunting is near the top of the list.

No woman, not even my mother nor my wife, can understand the pleasures of rising before daylight, in subfreezing temperatures, to sit in a tree for four hours, waiting for the chance to shoot an unsuspecting deer. I can spend an entire vacation doing that. I have.

Hunting makes a man more male. If he kills a deer, a man will cover himself with as much blood as possible while gutting it. Then he'll bring home the carcass and let it sit out in the open. Men know that blood and carcasses drive women crazy. After a week, a dead squirrel or possum on the coffee table is guaranteed to cause marital problems. A dead deer can be grounds for divorce.

Men who don't hunt can also upset that special someone and be included in this virile brotherhood. Simply slice your finger on a beer can pop-top, and smear the blood everywhere. Then use the half-empty can for an ashtray, and let the carcass stand out overnight to allow the three odors to mix and create a sweet perfume that will render an entire room uninhabitable to women for at least forty-eight hours.

Men hunt deer from deer stands. For the uninitiated, "stand" means a platform in a tree, maybe fifteen feet above ground. You drive spikes into the tree trunk, climb up to your private perch, and then wait for a deer to wander by. The stand is a sacred place, the sportsman's holy ground. No blasphemy intended, but I still have one question: How come it's called a stand when all we do is sit?

A really good stand depends on its location. A really *great* stand has its own mailing address. Being close to those places deer frequent helps immensely. Also important is the platform's condition. Wood rotted so badly that every time you sit on it you take your life into your hands rates high. It means the stand is productive.

Since we hunters spend so much time in trees, it's fortunate that the stand is also a good place to think. Thinking for me usually means writing jokes. Another favorite place to write jokes is on a long car trip. It drives my wife crazy because I have to write longhand, which is pretty tough when you're going seventy miles an hour and you've got a notebook on the steering wheel. I'm careful about doing this now because my wife will inevitably scream, "Just let me out of the car!" So I wait until we're driving at night and she's asleep.

There are very good reasons to be in the tree. First, you don't have to employ camouflage, as you do when you're waiting in a duck blind. Second, sitting up high reduces your chance of getting shot by other hunters who've mistaken your Day-Glo orange parka and red hat for a deer. Third, deer don't often look up. Even deer can't understand why somebody would spend his vacation sitting in a tree.

At its most basic, waiting in the deer stand is a rite of passage to manhood, very much like chewing tobacco and sex, though not as messy. We'd sit in our stands from about half an hour before daylight until ten or eleven in the morning. Then we'd climb down, go back to the house, and eat breakfast. We'd lollygag around the den for a bit, swap sightings and "almost" stories, and then head out for a couple of more hours. The rule was that you had to sit in the tree until it got too dark to see your hand in front of your face. This, in turn, led to another adventure: shooting at noises.

❧

I first hunted with my dad. We'd set out in the pitch-black dark woods and I'd never admit to him how scared I was. At first we shared a deer stand. However, the only father-to-son knowledge that passed between us in those memorable and sentimental moments was when I'd say, "Dad, Dad . . . ," and he'd whisper hard, "Be quiet." You had to learn to settle in and be still.

One day my dad let me sit in a stand on my

own. He picked one near his and I felt safe just because he was close. As I got older, he'd park the truck and go, "All right, you go into the stand over there at the bottom of the creek, and I'm going to be over there on the one by the cornfield." Then I'd have to take the flashlight and walk by myself through the woods. I'd always do something like step into the middle of a covey of quail, which would then explode. Only my laundry man knew for sure how scared I really was.

When men hunt together, the first thing they do is jockey for stand position. My dad had about thirty stands on his property. Some were in good shape. Some were comfortable but in a bad location. Some had no redeeming qualities except that they were actually up in a tree. Who got which stand was a seniority thing. It started with my dad and his guests and worked its way down to the youngsters. Usually, I sat around drinking coffee in the dark, cursing while guys picked among the better stands.

"Tom, where do you want to go?"

"Ah, I think I'm gonna go down there to that stand right there behind the pond."

ME: "Damn."

"Bub, where do you wanna go?"

"I'm gonna go down there to the other end of the hayfield and take that stand right there on the fence."

ME: "Jeez."

Then, after everybody had chosen, my dad would turn to me and say, "Okay, you got the one in the backyard by the basketball goal."

"But Dad, I'm not gonna kill a deer by the basketball goal! Deer don't even like basketball."

Even so, I've never wasted my time hunting. You see the woods wake up. You hear a noise, it stops and it starts. Maybe it's a bobcat, or a hawk or a fox squirrel. An hour and a half later you suddenly see something flick, and you realize it's a deer's tail at the top of the hill. And then it's gone.

Today some of my happiest memories are of hunting and fishing with my dad. I know now that I was a pain in the ass to take, and that I cut down his chances of being successful. Yet he cared enough to take me with him. Whenever I did something good, he was the first one I wanted to show. I'd always think, "I want to go find my dad."

∗

Some time during this age-old ritual, if you get very lucky, you see a deer. Actually *shooting* one is like winning the lottery. I didn't get my first deer until I was a college freshman.

It happened on opening day of hunting season. I was in my stand, an hour or so after daylight, mulling over the big questions of life—like bacon and eggs, or more beer for breakfast. I looked down absentmindedly and saw a deer six feet away. I'd never even heard him coming. And he wasn't moving.

So I blasted him.

Larry Burns heard the shotgun report, came running over, and we stood around and admired the dead animal for half an hour. Then we got the truck, drove it into the woods to get the deer, and got the truck stuck in the mud. We had to trudge back to the house and ask my dad to bring *another* truck and a shovel to get ourselves unstuck.

Our troubles didn't dull our enthusiasm for the kill. Deer hunting is cathartic. I know guys who have hunted a hundred times between deer kills, and yet they keep coming back. Here's one secret reason why: The biggest thrill of deer hunting is *not* actually killing anything. No one *really* expects that. What the guys want to know is what you *saw*. After four hours up a tree, breakfast is just a bunch of guys stuffing their faces and saying, "Bill, did you see anything?"

"Nah, I didn't see anything."

"Tom, did you see anything?"

"Yeah, I saw two does about 9:00 A.M."

You had to list what it was and the time, what it did, and how long it stayed around. That was enough to get you back out the next weekend. If somebody saw a buck, that was enough to keep you coming back all year.

Our hunting reports were very much like sex stories. Once you get it, it doesn't really count until you tell everybody every detail. That's how you learned that there were different degrees of serious hunters.

For instance, Big George was one of the unluckiest hunters among my dad's friends. George was five foot six, weighed 310 pounds. Good shape for deer hunting, right? George loaded trucks down at the Pepsi plant. He was bald and very funny, and the first guy I ever knew who had a monster truck. He let us drive it and that made George a really good egg. But through the years it became clear that George was the only guy in camp who had never killed a deer. However, there were some "almosts."

"I saw a buck."

"Where were you, George?"

"Well, I was down there behind Skeet's house, down in that cornfield down there."

"What happened?"

"Well, I'd been sittin' there for about forty minutes, and I looked up, and saw a big buck jump the fence. He looked like a six-pointer, maybe seven even. He just stood there, eating right at the edge of the soybeans. So I picked up my gun, turned down the radio, lowered the window . . ."

"Wait a minute . . . you're *in the truck?*"

"Yeah, and I'd just turned the heat back on."

No wonder he'd never killed a deer: George drank coffee, smoked, and listened to country music with the truck running. None of those ingredients are listed on a bottle of Buck Lure. I know because I've bought all that stuff: Buck Lure, Doe In Heat Lure. You're supposed to put it on your clothes with the hope of attracting a deer. I think one was nothing but deer urine.

That's another female turn-on.

"Oh, if you could just wipe some of that doe urine on you, *that* would really get me hot."

✳

After you kill a deer, then what? Clean it. Eat it. If the buck is particularly impressive, visit the taxidermist. Gazing at the face of your adversary forever frozen, right above the fireplace or the marital bed (in the kitchen or guest powder room is bad taste), warms the hunter's heart. I've mounted and displayed my share of trophies, but my *favorite* deer-head story is about the one I gave away.

After college I worked at IBM. I first worked in dispatch, answering the phones and handing out service assignments. One of the guys, Ray Stubblefield, hailed from Florence, Alabama. Ray was a big deer hunter and I learned a lot about the sport from him. Every time he came to Atlanta, he would bring a stack of pictures of himself with these incredible trophy deer. We all believed that Stubblefield was the greatest deer hunter in history.

We were all wrong.

What we didn't know then was that while Stubblefield rode around all day as an IBM serviceman, he also kept a camera in his car. Any time he saw hunters with a nice kill in their truck at a gas station, at a country store, or at a meatpacking plant, Ray stopped and asked if they would take *his* picture with *their* deer. What kept us off the scent of this bighearted imposter was that he made sure he never wore his regulation IBM uniform—suit, white shirt, tie, wingtips—in any picture. Apparently he kept a camouflage jumpsuit in the car. I've always meant to check, but I believe all Florence, Alabama, males of hunting age had to keep at least one camouflage jumpsuit with them always. It was the law.

Ray's desire to impress didn't end with his IBM colleagues. He'd pose with these celebrity deer and then send the photos to regional magazines like *Georgia Outdoors* or *Alabama Outdoors,* for their camera corner. Soon Ray was a hero to hunters throughout the Southeast. Ray's freezer was empty, but he owed the film processing people his annual salary.

When Ray came to Atlanta for a few weeks that coincided with deer season, I invited him to come down to my dad's farm one weekend. I got lucky and shot a deer. It was a little spike. The horns were more like two half-pencils. In the middle of cleaning the deer and wondering what it would taste like, Ray asked me what I was going to do with the head.

I said, "I'm gonna throw it away." It certainly wasn't one I would mount.

Ray said, "May I have it?"

"What do you want it for?" I asked.

Ray had an idea, which he shared with me. It was so wonderful that I *had* to give him the head. Then he took it home and froze it.

Turns out Ray worked with another guy named Garrett—Garrett Quartier. Quartier was a very serious guy and much more straitlaced than Stubblefield or me. After Stubblefield went back to Alabama, Quartier came to Atlanta for two weeks for an IBM class. He asked

Stubblefield to look after his house and feed his cat. On Stubblefield's last night he took the deer head out of his freezer and put it in Garrett's master bathroom toilet, and shut the lid.

Try to picture what happened. Garrett Quartier came home, settled in, and eventually went to the bathroom. As he took a seat, he happened to glance down and there, between his legs, is a deer head looking up at him. Garrett Quartier swore that he had never been that scared in his entire life.

That's also when they discovered that Garrett Quartier had a heart murmur. His doctor prescribed medication and he avoided any further serious complications. It was Stubblefield's idea, but my deer head, so I'm taking half-credit for saving Garrett Quartier's life.

*

It's five o'clock in the morning and he's waking me up. But it's hard. It's summertime, I'm ten years old, and this is supposed to be vacation. The days of rest and relaxation. Then my eyes squint open. I can barely see his face, lined and ancient. But I'm happy. Very happy. Today my granddaddy and I are going fishing.

He creeps into the kitchen while I put on the clothes I selected the night before. Blue jeans, but not the good ones; instead the jeans I hoped would later that day bear the mud stains and the fish smell. It almost seemed like a rule. The more disgusting the clothes the better the day had been. If Mom made me undress on the porch before I even dared enter her clean house, I knew it had been a wonderful day indeed.

The shirt couldn't be white. Granddaddy said it spooked the fish, so I'm wearing my old blue football jersey. It is full of holes and has been placed on the forbidden schoolwear list. A dumb call in my opinion because this is one cool shirt. The numbers on it are white, but I'm banking on the fact that fish can't read.

I find my way into the kitchen. He has made me a cup of coffee. Lots of sugar and lots of cream. I can't imagine anyone drinking the stuff any other way. I bet none of my friends are drinking coffee this morning. I bet they won't drink coffee for another eight or ten years. I watch as he finishes loading up the cooler. There are no wasted movements. This is a task he has perfected over the years. You do something a million times, you learn to get it right.

The menu rarely changes. A thermos of ice water. Four Coca-Cola's in the little bottles. A few packs of peanut butter crackers and two *ham sandwiches. White bread. Mustard and mayonnaise.*

He tells me to get my coat. It's always cold before the sun comes up. Even in July. I grab my zip-up sweatshirt with the hood. I wish I had a jacket like his: a blue jean jacket with a red and black flannel lining. The jacket bears many miles, and they're not highway miles. I've never seen another one quite like it. He and the jacket seem to belong together. They fit each other.

Granddaddy unlocks the camper top and slides the cooler into the back along with the rest of the gear we loaded the night before. Everything has its place. The cooler goes in back of his tackle box, but in front of the trolling motor battery. I always insist on carrying the battery to prove I am a worthy fishing companion. Man, is it heavy! But I will never say so out loud even though I'm sure my labored stagger must give it away. I don't think I've ever picked up that battery without a warning not to spill acid on myself. Through all the years I've never seen one drop of anything come out of that battery, but I fear it nonetheless. Granddaddy's warning always makes it sound like the acid will burn a hole clear through my leg before I can even get my pants off. Very scary stuff.

He is a very methodical driver. I not sure of very many things in life, but I would be willing to bet everything I own, Ted Williams model baseball glove included, that he has never gotten a speeding ticket. Sometimes I have to glance down to make sure he's actually mashing the gas. I assume that he is because the black work shoe is resting on the pedal. Black work shoes with white socks. If he has another combination I've never seen it. Granddaddy is a man of few fashion surprises. I find the consistency to be comforting.

Our trips are never cluttered with chitchat. When he talks it is to brag about having the fastest radio in Georgia. He turns it on and off twice to back up his words. I'm confident that they don't hold contests to determine such things, but I still can't imagine anyone capable of proving him wrong. This is one fast radio. And it is always set to the same station. WSB AM, "The Voice of the South, with all the latest in news, weather, and sports." He always seems to be most concerned about the weather. I guess it's true what they say, people can always find something to worry about. I don't really care if it rains, I just want to catch a fish.

I can't remember riding with Granddaddy where he did not find at least one opportunity to pull the same corny joke on me. He points down the road and says, "There's your name on a sign. 'Old Stopper Head.' " Of course the sign really reads "Stop Ahead," but it never fails to make the two of us laugh. It's just one more reason I know the old man likes me.

We have a few regular fishing holes. Most of them are small ponds located on the property of different farmers he has met over the years. He always stops at the house to confirm that it is okay that we fish. I am required to go with him and to say "Thank you for letting us fish." We are always extra careful to lock gates and to never leave a mess.

Being the passenger, the opening and closing of the gates usually falls on me. I always hope that cows are not lingering too close to the gate. It's not that I'm afraid of cows, it's just that I don't like them to get too close. I've never heard of someone being killed by a cow, but they are big, and they have a funny way of looking at you—always with one eye. Cows never look you directly in the face. It's like they have a plan of escape, and they are just trying to work up the nerve to pull it off.

When we reach our fishing spot we unload the gear in the same fashion we loaded it: meticulously and painstakingly slow. But I'm always in a hurry. I worry that the fish will stop biting at any moment. Time is of the essence.

We always put the tackle boxes and the rods and reels into the boat last. Granddaddy's tackle box is roughly the size of a small barn. I'm sure it carries one of everything ever designed to entice a fish. Sometimes when the fish aren't biting I entertain myself just looking through it. I'm always asking what different things are, and he usually explains, and follows with a grand story of a fish that fell victim to its charm.

My tackle box, on the other hand, is about the size of a shoe box. I have painted my name and a picture of a bass jumping out of the water on top of it. It contains mostly the cherished discards from his box. There are a few lures I have bought myself—all replicas of the ones he holds in highest regard. Unfortunately, they never seem to catch nearly as many fish as his lures do.

My rod and reel are also hand-me-downs. They're old but in fine working order. His are the paintbrushes of a master. A Shakespeare Wonder Rod supporting an open-faced Mitchell reel. He has three of them. All exactly alike. I'm sure that if the manufacturers knew, they'd be flattered that he has picked them as his tools of choice.

I am always amazed at the ease and accuracy with which he casts. Granddaddy will always say something like, "Well if I hadn't of throwed right there I never would have caught this one." Then with the flick of his wrist he sends his lure sailing through the air and it comes to rest inches from a semisubmerged log that should have a sign painted on it that reads "Home of a monster bass." I try to emulate his technique, but I spend lots of my fishing time trying to pull my lure out of the limb in which it is firmly anchored. "Trolling for tree bass again?" I hear him say. This always fills me with a slight degree of panic. I don't want him to have to stop fishing to help me. Not that he ever seems to mind, but I am afraid that he'll one day grow weary of his fishing partner's ineptitude and choose someone with the ability to keep his lure in the water instead.

He always catches more fish than I do. Usually about fifteen to my one. How can he be so lucky every single time? When he hooks one he really seems to enjoy reeling it in. As he cranks he gives a play-by-play commentary complete with estimates about the fish's size, where he hit it, and guesses about what the scoundrel might do to avoid eventually joining us in the boat.

On the other hand, when I get lucky enough to hook one, I retrieve it with all the calmness of Barney Fife making an arrest. There is no savoring the moment. I reel so fast and pull so hard that I have been known to make a fish go airborne. You should see the look on a fish's face when he breaks the water, sails over the boat, and resubmerges on the other side. "He looks like a pretty good one" I hear my granddaddy chuckle. I ignore him, because this is no time for jokes. If I don't get this thing into the boat then I have no proof that I actually caught one. After all, who's going to believe a fisherman? It is understood, too, that if I actually do get him in the boat he is going home with us. Catch and release has no place in my ten-year-old vocabulary.

If I am fortunate enough to add one to the stringer, I must then continually check him out.

"Put those fish back in the water," I hear him say.

"I'm just looking at them" I reply. Even on a stringer with twenty or more fish I am always able to pick out mine. I know exactly what he looks like. He's usually the cutest one.

It is then as I'm staring at him that I am always filled with a little pity for the fish. Not because he started the day in a cool lake playing fish games with his friends and will end it wearing a cornmeal jacket in the bottom of a frying pan. I feel pity because he fell to me instead of the old man. What a stupid fish he *must be. Imagine the shame his family must feel as they tell the story to their friends and loved ones. "It wasn't even the old man! It was the goofy kid in the football jersey!" Their friends gasp that fish gasp and say, "Oh . . . We're so sorry."*

The fishing day always ends following a long period of no action. It has to be that way. Never has a fisherman left the water while the fish are biting. It's physically impossible because that is what fishing is really all about. This hope goes out with each cast: Maybe this will be the one that hooks the fish of a lifetime.

We conclude much the way we started, only in reverse order. We are careful to leave the place as we found it. Granddaddy says "That's how you get to come back." We pick up trash and lock gates. The cows aren't anywhere to be seen. God is looking out for me. We always stop back by the house and thank the folks for letting us fish on their place. Granddaddy always offers them our fish, while I silently pray that if they do take some, mine won't be in that number. Thankfully, that has never happened.

We return home to the ceremonial showing-off of the catch. Granddaddy is much more low key and humble in his approach than I am in mine. By that I mean that he doesn't leap from the truck, grab the stringer, and go running through the house screaming, "Look what I caught! Look what I caught!" Of course he is also spared the lecture from my mom about how hard it is to get the smell of dripping fish out of the living room rug.

Finally, I am required to help Granddaddy clean the fish, though it is a job I don't mind. The combination of scales and entrails is enough to make the football jersey truly disgusting. I wear the mess like a medal. It is a proud moment.

Job complete, we head back into the house. Already I am growing excited and planning our next trip, the trip that may net one of us that fish of a lifetime. Granddaddy knows what I'm thinking. He musses my hair and smiles. I hope I can go fishing with him forever.

Years later, standing in the river, watching my line bob up and down in the current, I often thought about those trips with Granddaddy. Compared to my fishing expeditions with Burns and Chastain, they were an island of tranquillity.

Fishing with the guys was about as tranquil as the day Atlantis sank under the ocean.

Once, the three of us spent the day catching

nothing. Finally, Chastain got a live one and reeled him in. But instead of letting him go or putting him on the stringer, we just left the fish hooked to the line and put him back in the water. Then we fished for another fifteen or twenty minutes. Still, no one got a bite. But we had planned ahead. We took the rod with the fish out of the water and passed it to the next guy. Then he slung the fish—still on the line but rested now—back into the river about fifty yards so *he* could have the thrill of catching something. After an hour of this, the fish wised up and as soon as he hit the water he started swimming for the boat as hard as he could. Eventually he just skied in on his side, not even fighting anymore.

Another time, we caught a bunch of fish and brought them back to the house in a bucket. I'm not sure why, but for some reason we forgot about them. We should have cleaned the fish because real sportsmen never keep anything they're not going to eat. But something more important came up—probably a car wreck we had to see, or maybe somebody's field was on fire—and we forgot our catch.

The next day we discovered our bucket of *really* dead fish. That was the first and only time we played fishball. One guy batted, another pitched, the third narrated.

"Here's the windup, the stretch and . . . *fish on the way*. Ohhh! He was looking for a catfish, threw him a bream."

When the batter connected it was really disgusting. There's nothing like the way a fish disintegrates when it meets a Louisville Slugger going the other way.

"Oh! He got all of that fish!"

The pitcher got covered with scales from head to foot. I think that's why fishball never really caught on. Plus, it's hard to turn a double play when the fin is between first and second, and the head's just tripled down the right field line. However, you do get a truer fish bounce on Astroturf than on grass.

We made important discoveries while fishing. For instance, you can pee off the side of a boat and still catch a fish. Whereas, if you pee out of your deer stand, your day is pretty much over. Also, with fishing you pretty much eliminate the possibility of dying every time out. You're not going to get shot. No hunter will mistake you for game. Even if you're a kid wearing a moose costume to school on Halloween, it's a good bet that carrying your lunch box where it can easily be seen will keep even the most aggressive sportsmen—like those waiting for a deer to wander near the elementary school—from firing spontaneously. But if it's safety you're after, I'd stick to fishing, where the worst injury is a fishhook in the ear.

Trout fishing involved a practice called "looping." It's not about tying lures but about getting the best position in the river. The idea is to always be upstream of everyone else. So if you saw one of your buddies going around you, you'd cut up through the woods and go around him. Not only did you then get first crack at the fish but you also totally screwed up the catch for anyone downstream. The problem is that fishing spaces you out. So it's pretty disheartening to see a guy upstream, loop him, and discover that you've been looped by *everybody*.

Should nature call when you're out in the wild, you have to use whatever accommodations are handy. Especially at night. On one fishing trip we all had a big argument with Buddy Hammond about how far away from the tent we should be to use the "restroom." It was a matter of honor. You were supposed to take your toilet paper and go out into the woods somewhere. We knew that if you could still touch a tent flap, you weren't far enough away. But not Buddy.

"Oh, for God's sake, Buddy! We gotta sleep here, you dumbass."

Other than that, Buddy was the Marlon Perkins of outdoor hygiene. I've always admired Buddy for that, and for sharing his wisdom. If you forgot your toilet tissue, he knew which leaves made the best substitutes, which had a nice texture, and which wouldn't just crinkle and disintegrate. He also knew which leaves were poisonous. The stories of how he acquired that knowledge would make your skin crawl.

Burns never listened to Buddy, or learned from him. Before I left the house, the last thing I always did was grab a roll of paper and stick it in my coverall pocket. Burns, for some reason, never grasped this concept. When we were deer hunting, we could put Burns on his stand before dawn and come back four hours later and he'd be wearing a shirt with only one sleeve.

We knew the answer even before we asked the question.

"Oh, man, I had to go bad."

"But that shirt cost twenty bucks! Toilet paper is eight cents, you idiot."

You know the cut-off sleeve look that Bruce Springsteen made popular? I wouldn't be surprised if he'd found a shirt Burns had worn hunting twice, at a garage sale.

❋

My father always used to fish with my grandfather, and both of them used to fish with me. Now that I'm a father I sometimes fish with my two young daughters. Just carrying on the tradition, I guess. Last month I learned you can get goldfish out of an aquarium using a Dustbuster. That's the most efficient fish-catching device I've ever seen. Next time we go to the lake, I'm taking a Sears ShopVac. Not only will we catch our limit, but we'll leave the outdoors just a little cleaner than we found it.

❋

Hunting and fishing are fine, but to really be a man you had to chew tobacco. I first tried it in the ninth grade. Everybody else on the baseball team did it so I figured I might as well. I adapted pretty well, although it's never been the most charming taste in the world.

For those of you not familiar with the wonderful world of chewing, here's a few facts you ought to know:

1. Chewing tobacco is not pipe tobacco. It's more like wet, sticky leaves. Okay, mulch.

2. A real chewer will open his pouch with

a screwdriver, stick his face in it, and just pull out the tobacco with his teeth. Most of us aren't that sophisticated, or willing to answer impertinent questions if someone sees us trying this in public.

3. Most people can only chew on one side of their mouth or the other. It's a lot like masturbation: There's not a lot of swapping off. You pick your side and you stick with it.

4. To get a chew going you pull out a handful and pretty much eat it. You put it all into your mouth and you work it around with your tongue and your teeth, until you get it into a little ball. Then you take the ball and stick it outside your teeth, but you leave a wedge of tobacco that goes between your teeth. You chew and suck on that, and spit out the juice until it gets down to nothing.

5. Chewing doesn't get you high, but if you get a good chew working, you may suddenly start hearing Hank Williams songs go through your head. Don't panic. Sing along.

Dip is a little different. It's fine-grained, more like cigarette tobacco. Walt Garrison said it so well: "A little pinch between your cheek and your gum." But when it comes to the quality of spit, dip spit's not very good. It almost looks like spit, whereas *chew* spit can ruin somebody's brand-new boots. We learned that pretty quick. Just for fun we'd wait until we saw somebody with new hunting boots or tennis shoes. Then we'd walk by, never say a word, and PFFT! land a gob on their leather uppers. Took the new right out of their footwear.

"You bastard! I paid eighty bucks for these!"

Chew spit will also take out the hurt and the poison of a beesting. And it's great for making an exclamation point at the end of a sentence.

"So what'd you do after you spit on his boots, Jeff?"

"I told him to kiss my butt." PFFT! "But only if he could catch me." PFFT!

There's a fine art to spitting, and we were its masters. If a guy wasn't listening while we talked to him, we could easily spit on his shirt without him even knowing it. You just had to make the spit as silent as possible. To do that, put your fingers up to your lips, like you're holding an invisible cigarette, spread them a bit, and PFFT. Spit on a guy's shirt is not a pretty sight, particularly in church.

When we played baseball we would take Bubble Yum chewing gum and loosely wrap a string around the chew to hold it. But you had to be careful if you ever slid into a base. You *did not* want to swallow the chew. You'd spend the rest of the day vomiting. Even swallowing only a little juice can make you turn green, and your buddies red with laughter.

My favorite use for chew was to make Larry Burns sick. Knowing the secret ways to gross out your friends to the point of hurling was powerful knowledge when growing up. Forcing a friend to dry heave could make you happy for a long time. Larry was immune to so many things, but once, when Burns, Chastain, and I were building a fence down at my dad's farm, Chastain and I discovered Larry's weak spot.

We took a break and I said, "Burns, would it make you sick if Chastain and I exchanged chews?"

"Don't do that!" he said. Right then I knew I had him. I immediately pulled out my chew. Chastain did the same. We traded and stuck them in our mouths. Larry ran off and dry heaved into the creek bed. Chastain and I gave each other high five after high five. By the way, Burns deserved it. Just to make someone sick he'd do things like walk through the cow pasture and pick up a big handful of cowshit and go, "Anybody wanna eat this?" and stick it right up to your face. You'd go, "Oh my God!" and try to control the vomit impulse.

Years later I learned that Burns's real kryptonite was snot. The best I ever got to him was one morning while deer hunting. We were walking through the pitch-black woods, and all I could think about was how Burns had lately done horrible things to me. I had a bad cold, and so I did one of the grossest things I'd ever done. We've all done it as little boys: Hold one side of your nose and blow out the other.

I followed Burns through the woods, slowly blowing my nose into my mustache. Snot and a mustache are a lethal combination. When we got to his deer stand Burns said, "Will you hold my gun while I climb the tree?" and I said, "Fine." It was dark. We couldn't see each other. Then I said, "But before you climb the tree, do me one favor and look at this." I turned my flashlight on my face. He fell to his knees at the bottom of his own deer stand, dry heaving. I didn't care if I saw a deer that morning. I had dropped him.

As with hunting, chewing tobacco has never been a big hit with women. The gals we dated knew we chewed, but we also knew better than to load up around them. I've never heard a woman say, "You know what I really like about Jeff? It's when he *chews that tobacco* and it makes his breath stinky and his teeth yellow. And we have little cups full of spit all over the house. That's such an endearing quality."

Instead, we'd hear, "I'm not kissing you, you've been chewing."

"How can you tell?"

"Well, you've got spit all over your shirt."

"That's not my spit. Burns got me."

"Oh, in that case, kiss me, you fool."

We never tried to get the girls to chew, either, unless for some reason we also wanted to make them puke. Besides, any woman who could get the hang of chewing wasn't on our "must date" list. In fact, any woman who chewed tobacco (a) didn't prefer men or (b) men didn't prefer her. Any day now, just to make my life miserable, I'll expect a picture of a gorgeous woman I could never get to first base with chewing tobacco.

Of course, these are just fond memories. It's been a while since I've chewed. It's not easy to do with a wife, kids, and job.

"You might be a Redneck if . . . PFFT! . . ."

Not much of a career in that.

*

Masculine habits and the sporting life all prepare a young man for joining the adult world and for that most human of pursuits, the biological mating imperative. When we succeed with the opposite sex we like to think it's something we've done on purpose, a move we've practiced, or an element of our personal style that turned the trick. But as any hunter knows, achievement is really more a matter of patience,

persistence, and luck. The last, more than anything else, was the rationale behind Big Jim's
reminder to always ride out a streak no matter
what the cost. I've always considered that sage
advice from a versatile hunter.

I once had a lucky streak that's never been
repeated. Even if I tried to mess things up, I
couldn't.

I'd spent a week hunting and was driving
back to Atlanta from the farm, down I-20, in a
beat-up green pickup truck. I had a mounted
deer head in the front seat beside me. I hadn't
showered for four days, so it was probably hard
to tell me from my passenger.

Suddenly three young women in a car pulled
alongside and motioned for me to roll down the
window. Of course, I did. For a moment no one
said anything. I looked horrible, they were
laughing, and I figured it was at me because I
was the only one in my car with a stupid smile.
Then the prettiest girl said, "What kind of guy
would ride around the interstate with a deer in
the car?"

I said, "What kind of girl would *talk* to a guy
who's riding down the interstate with a deer in
the car?"

She laughed. I said, "You should call me
later, we'll talk about it." Remember, we were
hollering and going seventy miles an hour. I

said, "Here's my phone number." I didn't even ask for hers. When I got home, she called. She said, "Come over. I want to talk about the deer."

I said, "Let me take a shower. Where do you live?" An hour later I was at her place. I had one drink. She said, "Excuse me a minute," disappeared into her bedroom, and came out in a bathrobe.

As I sat there in shock, I thought of all those times I'd prayed for the biggest deer to walk within range, or for my cast to hook the fish of a lifetime. This wasn't quite that, but it was close enough. I looked up at the apartment's cottage cheese acoustic ceiling, imagined I could see through it to the blue sky above, and thought, "God, I didn't even *try* for this. Thanks."

Clearly, men also delight in pursuits that please a woman.

With any luck it's sometimes even her idea.

It's Nice Work, If You Can Avoid It

Finally, the day your folks warned, promised, and usually threatened would come has arrived. For better or for worse, your whole life changes.

I'm not talking about holy matrimony. This is worse.

No more allowance.

Out of gas and oil for the old Plymouth Duster? Need cash for dates? Want shells for the .22 and tobacco to chew? Bowling ball need repair? Forced to pay your own bail on a drunk and disorderly warrant?

What's a twenty-one-year-old to do?

Time to get a job. Time to see if Vern down at the garage thinks your talent for hot-wiring luxury vehicles can be bent to fixing them as well. There's lots of good jobs available. Besides, things could be worse. Just remember that somewhere, someone else is doing something with hot tar for five dollars an hour.

Thanks to Big Jim, I have a strong work ethic. I've always wanted to pay my own way and support my family. I like the freedom money in my pocket affords. Yet the conventional wisdom is that when the subject is work, Rednecks want to change the subject. People think we're lazy. The truth is that we're salt-of-the-earth working men and working women, even if the salt gets a little soggy in the humidity.

Then to what may we assign the blame for our slothful reputation? Once again: our accents. It's understandable. When it takes someone three times as long to make an excuse about why he's late for work—for the fifteenth time—it just *sounds* shiftless. But is that really fair? I don't think so.

It's hard work to come up with a believable lie.

✳

By the way, I'll be a bit late coming in for this chapter. I slept in, but if anyone asks, I'm saying my pet goat got ahold of my alarm clock and ate it. I don't want to waste your time, so while you're waiting for me to shower, dress, have coffee and breakfast, read the paper, run a few errands, and maybe catch a matinee, I'll be happy to pass along some wisdom I've gathered about the art of lying to get out of work. I know I'm getting ahead of myself. I should probably talk about *working* before I get to the *lying*, but a good lie is like a good joke, and I can't resist a good joke. Both require forethought, timing, and a surprise ending.

Let's say you hit the snooze button fourteen times and you're running fifteen minutes late for the job. First, if you actually *show up* only fifteen minutes late, you're going to look like you kept hitting the snooze button. So relax. Sit, read the paper, drink a couple of cups of coffee.

I'm sorry. I can't go anywhere without my

day-of-the-week undershorts, and I can't find
Monday. (Musta been a great weekend.)

Now, for the lie. Don't use the standard, "I got stuck in traffic." They'll know you're lying. Think of something that is so bizarre that your boss will honestly feel sorry for you.

I don't recommend the dead relative lie for two reasons. First, it's hard to keep up with whom you've killed off and who's still living. Grandma can only pass away so often, although in some families like mine—remember, between Big Jim and Carole, they've been married nine times—there can be plenty of Grandmas to go around. But then up crops the second problem: guilt. If you're like me, saying, "Uncle Fred got hit by a train," will make you worry that Uncle Fred *will* get plowed by a locomotive. Then you'll be up on a murder rap for knowing way too much. So if you use a relative, don't kill them. A serious illness is just fine, and it could keep you out of prison.

I'll be out of the bathroom in a minute. I've
still got to brush my tooth.

You can always claim that you're sick, but be sure to name an illness about which no one would dare ask questions. Projectile vomiting is acceptable, but explosive diarrhea is my personal favorite. That should end all discussion on the matter. If pushed, mumble something about "bad sausage," then say, "Oh-oh, here it comes aga . . ."

If you decide to feign personal injury, I recommend wearing an Ace bandage. Stuff an old T-shirt under it to simulate swelling, and moan constantly for effect. Make sure it's a believable injury. Falling in a corn reaper is too much if you only plan on being out for a day or two. Plus, strapping your arm to your side so your empty shirt sleeve can flap in the breeze will eventually become a big pain in the ass, possibly tear a rotator cuff, and ruin your fly-fishing cast.

I swear, I think the dog ran off again with my car keys.

What you really need is a story that will not only excuse tardiness but encourage your boss to give you the *entire* day off. With pay. How about this: "The sewer backed up into my house, the furniture is floating, and I can't find the kids." Who would expect you to work while your couch is drifting away. It's just bizarre enough to possibly be true. That's all you're shooting for anyway: possibility. Once you create a reasonable doubt for yourself, you are home free. So to speak.

Should anyone give you the third degree on your return to work, don't hesitate to become indignant and stomp out of the room. Crying is also extremely effective. Especially if you are a man.

All right. Got my excuse, got my handkerchief, and am heading for the door. Wait . . . I think I forgot something . . .

❧

You can't love every job you have.

The summer I was sixteen, I applied for a job at the new Six Flags Over Georgia. I wanted to work the Great American Scream Machine, or even the Log Ride. Instead, after a test and interview, they said, "We've given your talents a lot of thought and we've decided that you'll be sewing names on hats."

Makes you want to go right out and buy some mouse ears, doesn't it? Oh gosh, was that a bad job. I had to wear black double-knit pants, a black-and-white smock, and black loafers. These were the kind of clothes that if you offered someone the shirt off your back, they wouldn't take it. Still, it was a better job than the kind for which you don't need a shirt at all. (Tar. Five dollars an hour. Don't forget.) However, since the primary reason for having an amusement park job when you're sixteen is to buy gas for your car so you're able to date, and, if you're smart and lucky, to meet those dates at the park, I knew right away I would be my own worst enemy. I just couldn't imagine girls leaving Six Flags with stars in their eyes, going, "Did you see the guy in the smock in the hat booth? Oh my God!"

Sewing names was embarrassing, but at $1.65 an hour the pay was good. Besides, there were even more humiliating jobs. One was working the Flying Jenny, which was just some damn mule walking around in a circle for the kids who were scared of everything else. The boredom factor must have been out of this world, unless, of course, you made friends with Jenny. Then, a little hay, a little conversation, and who knows what could happen?

Sewing was also difficult. The machine was a table with a long handle on a swivel underneath. We had to practice for a month before the park opened. They gave us big black pieces of cloth and pink thread—which did not help the insecurities that went with the sewing machine—and a chart with the one hundred "Most Common Names." John, David, and Mary might seem simpler than Brandon, Jordan, Emmett, and Brittany, but they were all tough to stitch.

When the park finally opened for Sneak-a-Peek Weekend, there I was with my clean smock and double-knit black pants. I had my hundred names down so cold that *you* could do them in your sleep. My first customer was a guy and his wife and their daughter. He bought a sailor hat for the little girl. I said, "Would you like her name on it, sir?"

"Yes."

"Her name is?"

He said, "Cajava."

I had not practiced Cajava. C-a-j-a-v-a: the first name I sewed on a hat. Cajava. Where is she now? I hope she still has the hat.

Oh, I hated that job. I *hated* that job. But I loved the money. My first paycheck was $24.32, after taxes. I took it, walked to my car, and thought, "How the hell am I gonna spend this much money in one week?" And the next week there would be twenty-four more big ones coming in. Whoo!!!

Years later I discovered that my wife, Gregg, had *also* worked at Six Flags Over Georgia that summer. (I don't recall meeting. Trust me, I would have remembered.) Her job was even more demeaning than mine. Gregg had to roll around the park on skates, with a broom and a dustpan, cleaning up. Most of the time it was just trash, but occasionally it was a Code Thirteen. Vomit.

Eventually, Gregg and her sister and her cousin (who also worked there) got jobs in the

Crystal Pistol, which was the song-and-dance review show. The only reason you went inside was to escape the stifling Georgia August heat. Gregg's ex-husband *sang* in the show, which I've always considered the only less-masculine job there than mine. I've only seen three pictures of the guy, and in every one he's got one hand on the piano and the other one lifted in the air. His mouth is open. Any time Gregg gives me grief about what I do, I just go, "Now here's a salute to those great American railroads! Let me get my hat!"

By the way, Twilley also worked at Six Flags. They put him in the candy shop. It was hardly a prestigious position but, of course, Twilley managed to have sex with a coworker. Seems he had to give her a ride home, and they wound up naked on her pool table.

I quit Six Flags before summer ended. Working at Six Flags was a lot like going to the state fair: You could see lots of body hair and always spot a family that made you feel very good about your own. Still, I'm sometimes nostalgic about my time there. Or maybe it's because somehow the words to the park-closing announcement are indelibly etched into my brain cells and I'm mistaking that for sentimentality.

"Ladies and gentlemen, the hour for closing has now arrived and we must say goodnight.

Our hosts and hostesses hope you've enjoyed your stay and will come back to visit us soon. The park will reopen tomorrow morning at 10 A.M., but for now a pleasant goodnight."

Slam!—went the door on the hat booth, and I was gone.

❧

Some jobs require you to work alone, but I've always been a people person. Besides, you don't get tips when you work by yourself.

After Six Flags, I took a job as a bellhop at the Sheraton Emory Hotel, right by Emory University and Emory Hospital. We were also across the street from the Centers for Disease Control, which always made me nervous. Part of my job was to change the letters on the sign out front—WELCOME LIONS CLUB—and I'd always hold my breath because I knew some strange things were going on at the CDC.

I learned fascinating bellhop tricks on the job that you might watch for the next time you check in. As I picked up someone's bag, I'd sneak a peek at their name tag to see where they came from. Then as I walked them to their room, I said, "And where did y'all come in from? Seattle? Oh God, I love Seattle. My brother lives in Seattle and he just says it's the best place in the whole world."

The bellhop's life was great preparation for a life of making a fool of myself onstage, though now it's for a lot more money. But back then, I knew that if I could get a hotel guest talking to me, I'd get tipped. Sometimes I could hear the hand in the pocket go from rolling change to grabbing actual folding money.

I also quit that job—surprised?—but soon returned to the hotel as a maintenance man. It wasn't such hard work, since the place was falling apart and there was no stopping it. The hotel also didn't have enough heat in the winter or near enough air-conditioning in the summer.

I worked for Craig Todd. He was funny and decent and he taught me the joyous art of screwing off at work. Once, just for fun, we cut the heads off three thousand books of hotel matches, and stuffed them in a copper tube that we'd crimped one end of in the workroom vise. Then we crimped the other end almost shut, got a coat hanger, made a launching pad, and trailed a fuse of match heads across the back parking lot. While Craig and I sat there arguing about whether or not our little rocket would work, we noticed guests curiously looking on, wondering if we were some sort of free entertainment. They're probably still complaining that there was no champagne buffet.

We lit the fuse and hid behind somebody's car. That thing took off and I swear it has not yet come down. Somewhere a projectile crashed through someone's roof and they're still wondering if was part of a secret government rocket, or if miniature extraterrestrials had invaded their home. In the South it could be either, you know.

As a public service, there's another hotel secret I feel I should reveal, if only to redeem myself for playing with match heads and probably causing three weeks of alien invader headlines in the *National Enquirer*.

In the summer guests would constantly call to complain that their air-conditioning wasn't strong enough. Frankly, there was nothing at all we could do about it. The central unit was old and the hotel owner wasn't going to put any more money into it. So Craig taught me a workaround. He said to always carry a small screwdriver with a pocket-clip on it. Then, when I got an air-conditioning complaint, to walk into the room and say, "Whoo, boy, this isn't right." Next, remove the thermostat cover, stick the screwdriver in, twist it back and forth, and pretend to adjust it. As I did that, I should put my hand in front of the vent, tweak, test, tweak, test. Then motion to the guest. "Come over here. Does that feel better? Tell me when it gets good." They'll put their hand up and finally go, "Right there, right there."

It always worked. I'd leave with a nice tip, they'd be smiling, and I hadn't done a damn thing except perfect the art of bullshitting.

✶

When my friend Jim Kumpe quit his job at Kroger's deli he recommended me for the position based on the fine work I'd done for the Sheraton Emory. He went to Europe and left me to slice ham and bologna. That job drew down $7.00 an hour and I thought I was rich.

Say what you want about slicing bologna, the grocery store is still a great, great place to meet women. The aisles were always well stocked and many young ladies who passed through regularly were either single or not happily married. Slice their bologna right and anything could happen. I was so shameless in my pursuit that more than once the managers pulled me into the office for a lecture about "fishing off Kroger's dock." And to think of all that time I wasted fishing with Burns and Chastain.

Kroger turned out to be about more than meeting women. That's where I first learned how to handle a microphone and discovered that I liked it. One day the boss asked if anyone was interested in doing the sales announcements for the store. I said, "Yeah, I'll do it!" I had to read them into a tape recorder. They'd play every fifteen or twenty minutes all day long, over the public address system.

Soon, the whole town could hear me saying, "Attention, Kroger shoppers. In our deli today we feature Virginia baked ham. Regularly three-eighty-nine a pound, this week only two-nineteen. Also, try some delicious mustard potato salad. Regularly a dollar-nine, this week only seventy-nine-cents a pint."

Slowly, I learned to work the grocery store crowd and make them excited about being out shopping. I was good at it. Soon, any time the store had a spot announcement, I was the guy. <click> "Clean up on aisle five. Broken glass on aisle five." <click>

These announcements made me a celebrity, especially to my family. They shopped at Kroger and they'd hang around just to hear me say things like, "Attention Kroger shoppers. Visit the meat counter and find out about our boneless ham shank special." My family would find me in the store and say, "Just heard you doing the thing about the ham. Nice work."

You know, it just doesn't get any better.

Not only did I work for a living, I also went to school at Georgia Tech. I won't go on about it except to say that after three years they asked me not to return. I wasn't a discipline problem. I'd committed no crimes. Burns and I hadn't flashed BAs anywhere on campus. I simply felt out of place and my grades reflected it. Though I'd done very well in high school, college was a tough adjustment. I'd gone from a small town and a small school where I was one of the two top dogs to being a face in the crowd. I wasn't involved in any campus social life. Nobody knew me. I didn't fit in. I didn't study because I took courses that didn't interest me. My major was industrial management. You can imagine me in a suit and tie, behind a desk, right? The only reason I went to Tech was that it was the closest school to home. I suppose I planned to prepare for a life doing what my dad had done. But I couldn't work up any enthusiasm for the allure of corporate life.

Those were my lost years. However, I've since been acknowledged as a Distinguished Alumnus by my alma mater.

Thank you very much.

✳

After I left Georgia Tech (and Kroger), I hung out a lot at my father's farm. I grew a full beard and my hair went past my shoulders. I drew and painted and worked lights for a friend's rock and roll band. In other words, I was going broke in a hurry. Through some back channels my dad finally had some friends call and tell me there were a few job openings at IBM, and maybe I ought to apply.

I decided to take the plunge. When I went down there, every guy waiting for an interview looked like a Harvard graduate. I looked like I'd just swept up the office. When it was my turn, the man in personnel said, "If we hired you, would you get rid of all of this hair?"

"Yeah, if you hire me," I said. "But I'm not getting rid of it for the interview."

He said, "Tell me good stuff about you." So I talked and talked and talked. Then he said, "Tell me something bad about you."

I said, "Man, I'm trying to sell you a product. I'm not going to tell you what's wrong with it." He laughed and I got the job. I was nineteen or twenty. I worked in the Atlanta office, in dispatch. My first assignment was to take calls from customers who had broken machines.

"IBM dispatch. May I have your area code and phone number please? What machine are you having a problem with? And the nature of your problem? All right, sir, I'll have a representative get it touch with you as soon as possible."

Like all other IBM employees, I had to conform to the dress code. I think even the janitors had to wear suits and ties. So I went right out and got a couple of $40 suits and some awful shirts. Then I went into my dad's attic and pulled out his old wingtips—we wear the same size—and polished them to look like new. Then I fit right in. Just like Joe Luckie.

Joe Luckie—isn't that the greatest name of all time?—worked right across the hall in parts. Joe came from New York. For his first two years Joe wore only two suits. He only *owned* two suits: one blue and one brown. He'd wear the blue one Monday, Wednesday, and Friday, the brown one Tuesday and Thursday. The following week he'd alternate it, just to mix it up. Finally, after a couple of years, his parents sent him a gray suit for Christmas.

IBM's office occupied the fourteenth floor of a high-rise in Atlanta's Colony Square. One morning before work, Joe and I bought coffee and doughnuts in the central shopping area downstairs. Afterward, we got on the elevator for the ride up to the office. We stopped on the sixth floor and a guy got on that neither of us had ever seen before. He was just another of the thousands who worked in the high-rise.

When the door closed the guy looked right at Joe and did a double take. Then he said, "Hey, you got a new suit!"

That's when Joe suddenly realized that everyone in the building knew he *only* had two suits. I tried to keep from falling down, laughing. Joe worked to contain his embarrassment.

Isn't it nice that there's always someone around to make you feel better about yourself?

The ideal job is one in which you like what you do. The next best thing is one in which you can have fun. The great thing about IBM was that even before I considered doing stand-up, I got to hone my comedic skills and have more fun than shooting fish in a barrel.

After I'd been at the company a while, they promoted me at dispatch. Now I worked in a "quad" with Dwight Stanton, Jesse Frank, and Cynthia Sloane. We no longer took customer calls. We assigned work to servicemen instead. We did really well, always scoring at the top of the performance charts and getting tons of work done. Even so, we were so terribly bored that the only way to avoid devolving right on the spot was to play practical jokes. For instance, each of the servicemen had his own radio number. They'd all call in every day with the same routine. For example:

"Hello, this is Lester Nobby, 509." Lester had a distinctive voice that reflected his religious and straightforward nature. He was always pleasant but always all business.

We quickly learned to imitate the servicemen. Then we would pretend to go to the bathroom, run around the corner, call our quad, and try to fool the other guys. One day Dwight Stanton announced that nature had called. He turned the corner and, sure enough, three seconds later the phone rang. Jesse and I looked at each other with the same thought: "Dwight's trying to get us."

Jesse picked up and heard, "This is Lester Nobby, 509." He motioned to me and I grabbed an extension.

Jesse said, "Lester, you ole sonofabitch, what the hell are you up to?"

Nobby was aghast. "What the . . . ?" he said.

"The hell you say, Lester," Jesse added.

Suddenly Dwight walked around the corner. Our mouths dropped open and we did the mature thing and hung up. Then Lester called back.

"What the heck's going on up there?" Lester demanded hotly.

"What are you talking about, Lester?" I said.

"Well, I just called up there and got cussed out."

"You didn't call here, Lester. We've been sitting here all day." (If you're reading this, Lester, sorry.)

Another stunt we pulled to relieve our boredom was to send guys on temporary assignments. That meant they had to take a different job or territory for a few days. My favorite victim was a guy named Clay Felton. Felton was a legend because he was only twenty-seven and three times divorced. He also played softball fanatically. This one weekend we knew he had a statewide-level game scheduled. So on the Thursday before the game we decided to send Felton on temporary assignment.

First we left him a message to call "Jerry Duncan" at headquarters.

"What the hell's that all about?" said Felton, when he checked in with me.

"I don't know," I said.

Since the servicemen always called in from phone booths, I offered to connect him to Duncan.

"Yeah, if you don't mind."

"Sure, no problem." I put him on hold and then said to my quadmates, "I've got Felton on the line. Cynthia, you're Jerry Duncan's secretary." Then, back to Felton, "Okay, hold on,

Clay. Talk to you later, buddy." Then Cynthia picked up the phone.

"Jerry Duncan's office."

"Yes, this is Clay Felton returning Jerry's call."

"He's on another line, could you hold one minute please?" A minute later, I came on as Duncan.

"Jerry Duncan."

"Yessir, this is Clay Felton, I had a message from you."

"Clay, glad you called me back. We've got a secret installation going on at NASA this weekend. We're pulling about twenty guys from throughout the country and you've been selected as one of those going."

"This weekend?"

"Yes, Clay, and I have to tell you: This is going to look extremely good on your resumé."

"When would I have to leave?" Felton asked, clearly unhappy.

"Well, we need you to leave right away, Clay. God, we've got over one hundred and fifty 420s to install."

"I've got to call my wife," said Felton, looking for any way out.

"Clay, we'd ask that you not call your wife, it's top secret."

"Okay, sir. Thank you," said Felton. Then

he hung up, defeated. We laughed for a good five minutes, then beeped Felton. When he called back I said, "Felton, listen, by the way: Do you recognize this voice? 'Jerry Duncan, headquarters.' "

All we heard on the other end was a scream and the words, "You sonsabitches!"

Yes, working for a big corporation was more fun than I'd expected. The servicemen never knew what hit them. I did one of my favorite tricks whenever a guy named Mike Lewis called in. He was way too upbeat.

"Hey, Jeff! This is Mike Lewis! What's going on!"

I'd go, "Hey, Mike, listen, you gotta call . . . ufacturing . . . and what . . . going . . . and they need . . . 3-8 . . . 0-2."

"Jeff, you're breaking up."

"Mi . . . go . . ."

"You're breaking up, I'll call you back." Then he'd hang up. Since he was in a phone booth, I'd think, "There's one quarter." Then he'd call back. I'd say, "IBM dispatch."

"Hey, Jeff! It's Mike! Man, God, that was weird! You were breaking up like crazy!"

"IBM dispatch."

"Yeah, Jeff, it's me, Mike!"

"Hello? IBM dispatch?"

"Jeff, it's me, Mike!"

"Hello? Hey, if you're there, call me back." There's two quarters. Then Mike would call back again.

"Hey, Jeff, it's me, Mike! Something wrong with the phones up there?"

"I don't know, Mike, we've been having problems with them all day long. It started . . . ," and I'd just cut the line dead. There's three quarters.

Now you know why it took so long to get IBM's machines fixed. The servicemen usually spent all day in a phone booth just trying to get their assignments. Do you think we were at all responsible for the big layoffs at Big Blue? Nah.

We didn't limit our practical jokes to the men in the field.

The main receptionist used to drive us bonkers because she was so stupid. She'd always disconnect us, or connect us to the wrong place, or cut our callers off altogether. (Come to think of it now, maybe she was just giving us a taste of our own medicine!) It got so we hated her and we made it our mission for a month just to mess with her.

Once we had Joe Luckie linger in the lobby

and watch her. Then Jesse called the receptionist and said, "This is Jim Johnson with the telephone company. We have a reported problem
with 555-6200."

The receptionist said, "Yes, I have been having problems with this line."

"What we're gonna do," said Jesse/Jim, "is
have a gentlemen working on that line for about
the next five minutes or so, so we'd ask that if it
does ring, *please* don't answer it because we're
sending a burst of power across the lines. If you
pick up, the electricity could severely injure the
phone repairman."

The phones were set up so that if no one answered after about three rings at the receptionist's station, the lines would roll over down the
hall to the secondary receptionists. We waited
about sixty seconds and called the main receptionist. Joe Luckie, our lookout, later said that
the woman just sat there staring at the phone as
it rang. No way she would answer it. Suddenly,
he said, her eyes got as big as saucers and she
jumped up from her desk and took off running
down the hall.

"DON'T ANSWER THE PHONE! DON'T
ANSWER THE PHONE!" she yelled. But the
call rolled over, someone answered it, and Hil-
lary screamed. "ARRRGGGGHHHHH!!!"

Next thing we knew the receptionist was in

the break room with a cold washcloth on her head, saying, "You killed the phone man! You killed the phone man!"

Another time, again posing as repairmen, we told her to put her entire phone console into the trash can because we were going to blow the dust out of the lines and we didn't want her to get dirt all over her desk. And she did it.

I worked in dispatch for a year, but I could tell there wasn't much room for career growth. Fortunately, the company held aptitude testing and I signed up on the chance that I might get a better position. When the results came back, they said, "You have an aptitude for sewing names on hats." Just kidding. They wanted me to become a serviceman and fix machines. I just had to go to the IBM school.

ARRRGGGHHH!

I guess I deserved it. The weird thing was that if I opted to go to school and didn't pass, I couldn't go back to dispatch. I'd lose my job and I'd *really* have to sew hats, or worse, work with tar. Though naturally pragmatic, as you know, I took the leap and went to school. I passed. My big reward was a transfer to Sarasota, Florida.

I was the youngest guy at that backwater office and got to handle every crappy assignment. If three calls came in—two blocks away, four blocks away, and 185 miles away, I got to take the long drive in my Volkswagen Beetle with no air-conditioning and no radio.

Of course, whenever I had to call dispatch, my old friends tried to mess around with me. I didn't mind. Even if I was the junior repairman, I was at least out on the road and my quadmates were still in the office.

Okay, there was a downside. Because it was a suboffice, I often went on calls to repair machines *about which I knew nothing*. In retrospect, this was also good comedy training. I had to walk into a strange place and pull it off. Sometimes I'd stand there, with my arm resting on a big metal something, and say, "So, where's the machine?"

They'd go, "You're leaning on it."

"Oh yeah," I said, acting like I knew what I was doing. "This baby here." I had to read manuals to learn how to take the *covers* off some machines. But I learned that if the customer liked me, I could buy a little time. It was just like making hotel guests like me for tips. Then I'd fix what I could and for the rest I'd scream for help. Mostly, on pure instinct, I did okay.

IBM was a good employer and I wanted to do well on the job, no matter how many practical jokes I orchestrated. My dad had helped me get on board and I wanted to make him proud. In fact, I pretty much wore my cheap suits into the ground doing so. Then one day I found a really good deal—$89—for a gray wool suit. (Maybe because I bought it in June?) I bought it because, based on my performance in dispatch, the company had invited me to one of those breakfast-with-the-president functions.

I decided I would introduce myself to the bigwigs and let them know exactly who Jeff Foxworthy was. And that's just what I did, very confidently. Afterward, as I stood in a corner, drinking my little good-morning orange juice, a guy I worked with came up and whispered in my ear: "Hey, Fox, check out your pants." Not only were they unzipped, they gapped open wide enough to fly a Frisbee through. I was mortified. Meet the president then zip your pants. I looked over at the higher-ups, standing by the podium. I knew what they were saying.

"Did you see that goofy Foxworthy kid with his pants unzipped?"

Hey, at least they remembered me. What more could an entertainer want?

Roommates and Their Habitats

Sooner or later, we all have a roommate. Parents and siblings don't count because they're just part of the deal—unless they come to live with you when you're an adult. Then, they'll call themselves house-guests. After a couple of days you want to call them anything you can get away with, including a taxi. With our spouses, we *supposedly* had a choice about being together, though I'm certain many of us don't remember it that way. Don't even get me started on in-laws.

Roommates are tough. You've got to pick someone you can beat up on because you never get along with everybody always. Even if you shared an apartment with the Pope, I guarantee that three weeks into it you'd be going, "Hey, you mind picking up the cape, man? And quit leaving the papal miter on the kitchen counter."

I've always looked for a roommate with a sense of humor, someone roughly like me, only different. I'm not so sure living with myself is any piece of cake. You definitely don't want someone wilder than you are. You want the same degree of wildness. If you're the wild one you'll feel like you're living with your Aunt Florence. If your roommate is the wild one, *you'll* feel like Aunt Florence while he's holding a naked Twister Bingo session in his bedroom—or worse, in the living room, where you can see it all. You both need to stagger in side by side. The *Odd Couple* approach never works.

An ideal roommate has a horny sister. Or *is* someone's horny sister. Or is one and has one. Or knows one. I'm not just kidding around here.

Paying the rent on time is also a good quality.

One person to absolutely avoid as a roommate is an ex-wife, no matter what sick circumstances drive you to again share the same living space. First, you don't want to be around when she's getting phone calls from other guys. Second, she doesn't want to be around while you're burning her clothes.

No matter how you fare during these days of swine and losers, I promise that you will soon miss the times when you were wild and free and living with someone you could just move out on at any time. Maybe for no other reason than that I'm a sentimental guy, about five years ago I got nostalgic for the apartment life. Then Gregg got pregnant. She ate all my food and threw up once a day. It was just like having a roommate all over again.

*

When I first left home, I got lucky and lived for a while with my dad. You can just imagine the fun we had.

Big Jim lived on Atlanta's north side. He drank, threw parties, smoked, and cussed. Yeah, Big Jim was pretty cool to have as a father. When I was still in high school I'd try to spend the weekends at his condo. I had a car and I'd drive to Big Jim's Friday evening with my girlfriend.

Jim would say, "Hey, you kids wanna spend the night?" Music to a teenager in heat. I'd say sure. Then my stepmother would call my girl-friend's mother and go, "Is it okay if the kids spend the night?"

Did I already say he was cool to have as a dad? Now you know why I moved in with him as soon as I could.

When I couldn't stay at the condo legiti-mately, because he was at the farm, I'd sneak over—again, with a girlfriend. But I didn't want Big Jim to know. I was so meticulous in covering my tracks that I'd even measure how high the window blinds were off the sill so I could put them back in exactly the right place.

"Okay, I think it was an inch and a half below the middle of the window."

"Are you sure," my girlfriend would say?

"Get dressed and then get me a ruler, okay?"

It would take me an hour to get the house right.

Ten years later, for reasons that still elude me, I confessed all this to Big Jim. "But I bet you never knew I went over to the condo."

"Of course I did," he said. "You went there every weekend when I was gone."

Kids. We think we're so smart. Parents know everything because they've usually done *everything* themselves. Then Big Jim continued, "I'd always come back and go, 'That little bastard's been here screwing.'"

"You should have told me you knew," I said, as I tried to keep my composure.

"Why?" he asked.

"You could have saved me a lot of time cleaning that I could have spent doing, uh . . . other things."

"That's why I didn't say anything. I even had to let the maid go because you did such a good job."

But if Big Jim did me a favor by letting me use the condo—though he was clearly well compensated—I took care of him, too. For instance, sometimes Big Jim would say, "Look, you and I are going out and having a few drinks tonight."

I'd say, "Daddy, I can't. I've got a date."

"Well, I know that," he'd say, "But if anybody asks, you and I are going out for a few drinks tonight. Okay?"

"Okay. Where did we go?"

Nothing like covering for your dad.

Once he called me, excited and upset, and said, "I've locked my keys in my car."

"Where are you?"

"I'm at the bar at the end of the street."

"At the end of *your* street?" Big Jim wasn't married to my mom at the time, but he *was* married. So I delivered his keys and found him drinking with his secretary.

"Dad," I said. "I'm eighteen years old, and even *I* know to get farther away from the house, for God's sake. If you're going to fool around, at least get out of the sight line of the kitchen!"

Big Jim took risks on his own, but he wasn't about to let me be an idiot. When I lived with him he had a rule that when I went out I should always call him if I was, say, too drunk to drive and didn't plan to come home that evening. I respected him and called when the situation arose. But once it got to be four in the morning, I was plastered, and I was scared to death to call. I decided I had to drive home, but my friend Eddie wouldn't let me. (He was right.) I said, "I ain't calling home at four in the morning and waking up Big Jim. I'll take my chances."

Eddie said, "I ain't letting you in the car. I'll call him." We went to Eddie's apartment. I lay down on the sofa and Eddie called my dad. I could only hear his end of the conversation.

"Mr. Foxworthy? This is Eddie Harlen? I'm fine, how are you? Oh, good, yeah, school's going all right. Yeah, yeah, I'm still going out with her. Anyway, I just called to say that Jeff's had one too many and he's gonna be sleeping on my couch tonight. Oh, I appreciate it. I surely will. Okay, bye." He hung up the phone and I was speechless. Finally, I said, "He didn't get mad?"

Eddie said, "Nope. In fact, he just came in the house five minutes ago himself."

After my dad moved to Tampa I shared an apartment with my sister, Jennifer. Poor Jennifer. The only thing worse than being a Redneck is having a Redneck brother.

We were pretty pathetic.

The needle on our record player was so worn out that we had to pile spare change on the arm to make it work at all. It started with a penny, then a penny and a dime, then a nickel, then all three. By the time we got to a dollar twenty five it was time to break down and get a new needle. But at least we'd saved enough money.

I also seemed to collect food. By the time I married Gregg, I had refrigerator items that had lived with me in eight different apartments. I just couldn't throw them out. We'd been through too much together. I've still got a jar of olives that's been with me since the beginning. I just don't think it's fair to move to the nice house with the subzero refrigerator and throw away stuff that's stuck with me as long as it took me to make something of myself. I figured the olives should live the good life, too.

Jennifer and I belonged to the Utility of the Month Club. You don't really want to be a member. That's when something different is shut off each month. This always seemed to happen when my dad came up to visit to check on how we were doing. I remember the phone being cut off and having to drive to the 7-Eleven to make calls. The next month it was the electricity. I made my sister go down to the department of water and power and tell them our aunt lived with us, and that she was on a dialysis machine, so they would they *please* turn it back on.

They did.

Eventually we got all the utilities running at the same time. That's when General Motors Acceptance Corporation tried to repossess my wheels. I worked at IBM and I had to have a two-tone Rally Sport Camaro. Big Jim had said that if I got enough for a down payment, he'd match it. I saved the money and after a series of "walk away" negotiations—Big Jim did the walking while I drove my friends past the car lot and pointed to the Camaro behind the fence and said, "There's my car!"—I got it. It had close to $1,000 worth of stereo equipment, including an equalizer and a power booster. Even at minimum volume it would make the windows shake.

But I was behind in the payments. One night the GMAC guy showed up at the door about 6:00 P.M.

He said, "Mr. Foxworthy, I'm from GMAC. I've come to get your car. You haven't made a payment in three months. Unless you can give me $500 right now, the car's going with me."

I said, "500 bucks? Who keeps that kind of cash on them?"

He said, "Can't you write me a check?"

"A check? Hell . . . *yeah*, I can write you a check! I thought you needed money." So I wrote him a bad check and hid the car in a friend's garage until I got caught up on my payments. I couldn't believe he took the check. I was tempted to pay the *whole* thing off right there. Maybe even say, "Tell you what, here's $500 extra. Go get your wife something nice."

I'm gonna be a congressman when I grow up.

Eventually my sister and I *did* break up, but not because we'd lost interest in each other. Nope. It was because of Bear.

Bear was a little white poodle—as you

know, one of my least favorite dogs—that Jennifer insisted on having in the apartment. Bear always crapped on the floor. Jennifer and I worked all the time, and often stayed out all night, so it wasn't really Bear's fault that no one was around to walk him. Thank goodness he only weighed four pounds. It was relatively simple to clean up after him. But it was nonetheless a nuisance.

One night I finally decided I'd had enough of Bear. I decided to make my sister pay for bringing him to live with us.

It was Halloween. While we were out "trick or treating," Bear had again relieved himself in the apartment. I came home first and could smell it but could not find it. I searched for half an hour, then gave up and plotted my revenge. I took a big Tootsie Roll out of my candy bag and as I watched TV and wondered where the dog had buried his treasure, I kneaded the Tootsie Roll into a familiar shape. (Remember, I'm good at this.) I put a little bend on it and a little taper on one end, and then I put it on the floor next to the couch.

I waited until Jennifer came in. She went straight to the refrigerator for a Coke. She lit a cigarette. When she walked into the living room, her nose crinkled at the smell and I said, "Oh God, Bear messed on the floor again!"

"I'm sorry," she said.

"Don't be sorry," I said. "Just help me *find* it. I can't even find it. I'm gettin' so SICK of this."

"Okay, okay," she said. "I'll help you look."

She got down on her hands and knees and started searching. I pretended to look around, too. Suddenly I said, "Here it is."

"I'll get a paper towel," she said.

"Don't bother," I replied. I double-checked to make sure it was *my* little creation, then I popped it into my mouth.

Jennifer dropped her Coke and ran to the bathroom. The sounds she made let me know that my mission had been accomplished.

Bear moved the next day. So did I.

Only in Georgia can you share an apartment with your sister and later get away with an explanation like, "Yeah, but we broke up for the sake of the dog. . . ."

*

There's a reason for clichés like, "You don't know what you've got until it's gone." After my sister and I split up, I moved to Florida and I couldn't find another place for four months. I had to sleep on the foldout couch of a guy I worked with at IBM. Ralph Hubbard was forty-eight, wore two hearing aids, and let me keep my clothes in a suitcase in the hall. He was actually a great guy, but we couldn't go on living like that. Then somebody told me that Stanley Cobb had a great place on the beach in Sarasota and wanted a roommate.

If I thought living with Hubbard was odd, Cobb beat it by a mile. He was a bullshit artist deluxe. Every month Stanley would say, "Just write a check to me for the rent and the utilities, and I'll pay for everything." Six months later I came home and found an eviction notice on the door. He hadn't paid the rent for nine months. That was a Friday night. The notice said that we had until Monday morning to be gone, or the marshals would throw us and everything we owned out on the street. I sat on the living room couch and tried to figure out what to do next. That's when Cobb called. I made things worse when I lost my temper and threatened to beat his ass. Now he wouldn't even come home. Then all these other people started calling, saying, "Hey, he owes me 800 bucks, that bastard."

Then it struck me. I said, "Really? Come on over! Stanley has a really nice TV, probably valued at close to eight hundred bucks. I'm going to be in the bathroom brushing my hair. The door's open."

All weekend long I let people come in and take his stuff.

It was my first and last rummage sale.

*

I figured my luck could only improve, and I was right.

My next roommate was named Dexter McDougal. Everybody called him Dex. I met Dex when I dated his sister, but he and I ended up hitting it off better than she and I. Pretty soon we moved in together. (Dex's sister even spent the night from time to time.)

I consider my place with Dex my first singles apartment. Singles apartments are the same all over the country, aren't they?

Let's walk through the place room by room and I'll show you the highlights of fine Southern, twentysomething living.

The apartment had two bedrooms, each with a bathroom. Also, a little hall, a kitchen, a dining room, and a living room.

In the living room we had the telephone wire spool for the coffee table. Saw it sitting off the side of a road, borrowed a pickup truck, and hauled it home. Some people shellac them, others like the natural pitted, tar-smeared look. We painted ours with the only colors we could find

in Dex's dad's garage: aqua and black. That
went really well with the green-gold shag carpet and the orange sofa. The spool top was always cluttered with the remains of a wild
Saturday night, usually from three months earlier.

We were lucky to have the sofa. We also
found it on the street. I remember cruising by,
seeing it balanced on the curb, and thinking,
"Heeyyyyy. If that baby's there after dark,
she'll be in my living room before midnight."
We also had a bean bag chair covered with duct
tape to keep the "beans" from falling out and
the material from simply disintegrating.

Our place had the same green-gold shag rug
that you find in apartments everywhere. I'm
certain that there's one manufacturer who car-
pets every apartment nationwide, and that it's
part of a government conspiracy, and the real
reason for our staggering national debt. This
carpet turned up naturally at the corners and
smelled like someone had soaked it in spilled
milk, Jack Daniel's, and cat pee. This was when
it was new. When one of Dex's friends parked
his motorcycle on our living room carpet, we
got an oil stain as a bonus. Within months,
we'd tramped down the rug by the front door
so much that we couldn't even rake it back up.
Every time we'd try, we'd kick up a rabbit.

Of course we had the cinder blocks and boards shelving. We finally painted them black to give them a nice look. The stereo was really just an old receiver I'd bought for eight bucks at a garage sale. All the panel lights were burned out so you could never tell which station you were listening to. Our TV was a plastic Ford Philco model. Ford has always been known for making a damn good television, right? The transmission broke in it a couple of times, but what the hell, this was in precable days—we had the aluminum foil antenna—and there wasn't much to watch anyway. I think it was a color set. Well, kinda color.

I had a deer head on the living room wall. He sported a baseball cap, sunglasses, and a cigarette. He looked like he'd been shot while walking in the parade at Mardi Gras. Something that nice you *have* to show off.

I don't think we owned anything framed. Everything was stuck to the walls with tape or thumb tacks. We had posters of different things like cars, women, and rock and roll singers. The important things in life. We also had a lava lamp in the living room, but it didn't work. The light would go on but it was otherwise impotent. The lava would just sit there and never go up.

Our bedrooms were your basic pigstyes. Dex's mattress sat on the floor, mine on a box spring without a frame. Clearly, I had the deluxe accommodations. Both were protected by huge piles of clothes, some dirty and some clean. It was always tough to tell the difference, although we did the laundry every month at Dex's parents' house.

My bedroom had milk crates for nightstands. Also, my collection of stolen road signs. Dex's bedroom had an ironing board that he used for bookshelves. One of my brother's friends said he made it with a girl on that ironing board during a party. We're still not sure if we believe that. Both rooms also featured the hippest in bedroom decor: blankets for curtains, old pizza boxes, and drinking glasses growing new forms of life.

A small hallway with a mystery stain on the carpet and a Budweiser mirror on the wall connected the bedrooms and there was a balcony off the back. We were on the top floor of a two-story building. Location is, of course, everything, as I'm sure the couple who lived below us soon realized. They were both in their eighties and retired. I'm sure they learned some stuff in their golden years. Occasionally we'd hear them holler things at Dex like, "Don't let him bring your sister over again!"

The balcony had a rusted-out hibachi grill, and an old towel in the corner that you wouldn't have touched even with a stick. If you did, you'd have had to register at the Centers for Disease Control. The towel had been rained on and was covered with spider webs. It was also as stiff as petrified wood. I'd always meant to string some yellow police barrier tape around it, but I never found the time. We also had a bike with no chain on the balcony and plants that we moved out there when the leaves finally fell off, leaving only sticks and dirt.

The dining room was empty except for another bicycle and some old bags of trash we never took out.

The kitchen was tiny. The drawers held two forks, two spoons, and a turkey baster. (You figure it out. I can't.) We used the stove to light cigarettes. The refrigerator had a couple of beers, some junk food, and my olives. We had a can of she-crab soup in the pantry, though I don't know why. Neither Dex nor I was ever hungry enough to eat it. When we did eat, we would leave the dishes in the sink until there were none left in the cabinet. Then Dex would talk his mother into coming over and washing them. Somehow he'd also get her to clean up the place.

Both our bathrooms made the local Shell station restrooms look immaculate. We even posted signs reading "For customer use only" but it didn't help. We had shower curtains no one could approach without a radiation suit. Plus, there was never enough toilet paper. Occasionally I'd steal a roll from IBM. (See, a lot of those Redneck jokes are firsthand.) Dex would let it run out then he'd use the cardboard rolls it came on or duckwalk to the kitchen and get a paper towel before he'd break down and buy a new package of TP. More likely, he'd steal it from some public restroom.

The saddest part of all this is that we actually brought women there!

You might think our living conditions were awful, but it's all relative, just like fame. We had a friend eating out of a hubcap, so we felt pretty good about ourselves. Still, it's no wonder why singles apartments are about as close as we all come to being homeless.

The only good thing about a singles apartment is that you never *really* had to get your roommate's mother to clean it up. At least not until the day you moved and tried to get the security deposit back. Then you'd argue with the landlord.

"No sir, the back door was missing when we moved in here. The pizzas were always on the ceiling."

As you get older, if you still live the apartment life, you find you have to tidy up occasionally. Or you have to at least try to make people think you do. We've all done that, been home on the weekend, had the phone ring: "Hey, we're in the neighborhood, thought we'd stop by and see y'all."

You always say, "Sure, come on, we'd love to have you." You hang up and do that flight of the bumblebee. Ninety miles an hour, fluff and stuff. You're sweating when they get there, and the first thing you always say is "Excuse the house, it's a mess. Y'all come on in." Why don't we just tell them the truth? "Y'all, this is the cleanest our place has been in six years! Just don't open the closet, you'll kill yourselves."

This refusal to play by the commonsense rules of hygiene is one reason why single people throw the best parties: They don't have to worry about their furniture getting messed up. Their friends can destroy everything in the place. They're out fifteen bucks, so what?

Single people *do* throw the best parties, don't you think? There's always a good chance somebody's coming out of their clothes before the night's out. Most of the time it's the woman who's dancing by herself way too early in the evening. "It's only 7:15 and Peggy's dancing by herself. That shirt's coming off tonight, I guarantee you."

Single people don't consider it a good party unless the cops have been there at least a dozen times. When they arrive it's the same scenario every time: 400 drunks trying to act like they're not drunk. One guy is the spokesman for the group. "It's the cops, turn the stereo down! Put your shirt on, Peggy! Y'all be cool, let me do the talking. Welcome back, Officer Mitchell!!! Don't shoot!"

Then to the crowd: "I told him don't shoot!"

Then back to the cops. "I'm glad you're back, I wanna report a crime. Larry puked in the aquarium. Stinks very much bad in here. Hey listen, if I lie down on the sidewalk will you draw my picture with that little chalk y'all have?"

No one ever went home from those parties. They just slept where they fell. When you'd get up the next day, it'd look like *Jonestown: The Morning After*. You'd try to wake up people you'd never met before. "Hey man-with-no-pants-and-a-fireman's-helmet-on, please get up, I've got to go to work. All right, lock the door when you leave. I just found a new sofa, and I don't want anything to happen to it."

I once went to a toga party from which I walked home naked. Thank goodness it was only two blocks from the apartment. I'm still trying to figure out where I had the key. If you know, please don't tell me.

Throwing parties, like everything in life, adheres to the principle of the Great Circle. I used to be the king of throwing a big blast. Then, the first time I realized I had gotten older was when I worked in Daytona Beach one year during spring break. I found myself at three in the morning standing on my hotel balcony in my boxer shorts, screaming, "Go to bed! Go . . . to . . . bed! People are trying to sleep!" Then I walked inside, threw myself back into bed, and realized I had become an old man.

Dex worked the three-to-eleven shift at the Sarasota Hospital, monitoring machines in the intensive care unit. He would often get bored and call home, and I would relay the baseball game to him over the phone.

"Here's the wind, the stretch. Low and outside, ball three."

Then Dex would say, "Ah crap, somebody just straightlined."

"Okay, I'll let you go."

"Nah, just one more pitch," he'd say. That

was pretty much Dex's attitude toward life. And death.

During the summer, Dex got an even better job. He worked in a mental institution and had to show up every morning in the smoking room to light the patients' cigarettes. For some reason, they wouldn't allow them to use their own matches.

Dex told me about one guy in the institution named Art. He said when he first met Art he had no idea why Art was in the mental institution. Dex would light Art's cigarette, then Art would sit there and say, "Hey, did you see that Cubs game last night? Man, that was something else. Cubs score three in the second, they come back, the Reds get four in the fifth." He said Art was as normal as anybody he'd ever met until his cigarette got down to the last couple of puffs. Then suddenly Art would start shaking like a dog passing a pinecone and would spew the most vile and common curse words. Then he'd reach in his pack, pull out a new cigarette and light it with the burned-down butt, take a drag off it and, as if nothing had happened, go, "So anyway, in the eighth, Sandburg comes back with a two-run homer . . ."

Dex and I were not only pigs about how we lived. The word sometimes described our personalities, too.

We called our apartment the Penile Palace, "where every night is Ladies Night. Thursday night is Titty Night. Bring one, get the other one in absolutely free!" I'm sure it was this enthusiasm for women, and not grievous errors in our upbringing, that led to Dex and me to stage monthly contests based on our conquests of women.

Isn't it great what you can get away with when you don't live at home?

We had a chart in the kitchen, right over the phone, and an honor system. We devised an intricate point system based solely on our womanizing. You could get bonus points if you did it in the bathtub. Even more points if the water got cold. We were extremely competitive, but invariably, at the end of every month we would always be within four or five points of each other.

Sometimes Dex would be so close that he'd say things like, "I know this girl at work. I could beat you this month. I could call up this girl and win."

But he never could because I had an unbeatable threat. All I had to do was say, "Dex, don't make me call your sister."

I think what scared him more than his sister being two quick points—unless I also went for a bonus—was that afterward he would have to hear all the details. That was part of the honor system. We had to identify the woman and describe exactly what had happened. If nothing else, it was an important lesson in telling the truth.

People ask me now if looking back I'm ashamed of this base and degrading behavior. Of course . . . not.

*

You have to trust your roommates. But sometimes they take advantage of you just for the heck of it.

I had to be at IBM each morning at eight o'clock, wearing my suit and tie, to fix machines. Dex got home from the hospital each night at eleven-fifteen. Every night he'd say, "C'mon, man, just go with me for one beer. One beer. I've been working all night, I just want to go have one beer and unwind."

I'd say, "Dex, I gotta get up in the morning."

But he would always talk me into it. He was either the king of peer pressure or I was an easy mark. Probably both. Then we'd go out and next thing we'd close down some joint at two-thirty in the morning. Every time he'd laugh and say, "I can't believe you fell for the one-beer line again!" I think he set a record by getting me to go out eleven nights in a row.

I got him back, though.

Every guy has a dream girl, his own little fantasy. From the time he got his first erection, Dex's dream was his older sister's best friend. Unfortunately, she never paid much attention to Dex, and one day she got married and moved away. But while Dex and I shared the apartment, she came down to visit Dex's sister for the weekend. At the same time, Dex's childhood best friend, Gary, stayed with us.

One night, when Dex had to work the graveyard shift, Gary, Dex's sister, her friend, and I went out dancing and later ended up back at our place. Sometime in the middle of the night I got up and stumbled into the kitchen for a glass of water. Then a noise made me stop in my tracks. I snuck a peek into the living room and saw Gary and Dex's sister's married girlfriend going at it.

Since they didn't have any idea I was just around the corner, I managed to hide myself and watch. Gary did quite a number. I think there were bonus points being awarded left and right. I saw things that I had never imagined could happen with a coffee table and a sofa. This was rugged.

The next morning the girls left and Gary and I went to pick up Dex and have breakfast. Dex wanted to drive so I sat in the front and Gary in the back. Then Dex said, "So what'd you guys do last night?"

"We went out and had a few drinks," I said.

Dex just grunted.

"You know what might be interesting?" I continued. "Ask Gary what *he* did last night."

Gary punched me around the side of the seat. Dex just kept driving. I couldn't let it go. "Remember your dream girl, your one-and-only, your true love forever?"

Dex thought about it for a minute. "Yeah," he said. "She's visiting my sister."

"Well Gary did her on the coffee table last night."

"NOOOOOO!!!!" Dex swerved the car into a ditch.

"Sure," I continued. "When I looked in the living room, I thought I was watching a naked rodeo."

"NOOOO!!!!"

I know it might seem like I did a cruel thing, but I had to. Gary was *never* going to mention it, and I had Dex in such a vulnerable position that I felt obligated to destroy him. It was the guy thing to do. Besides, Gary had too much history with Dex to break his heart that way.

Aren't men odd? You can ruin a man's dream, as long as you don't talk about it to his face.

Dex being Dex, he got over it.

✳

While we're on the subject of women here's a classic story I've been dying to tell for a couple chapters already. Now that we're all grown-up, I think this is finally the place.

I was with another friend of mine, Wally Pace, at the Monday Night Football Game, watching the Falcons play the Rams at Fulton County Stadium. We were drinking boilermakers at the food concourse with some of my co-workers from Kroger. We quickly got as drunk as coots, sang beer songs, and leered at the local scenery. Then a woman in a green dress walked by. Wally said, "Hey! Do you believe in love at first sight?" She turned around and kind of laughed, and said, "I don't know." Wally stood up, wobbled over to her, and *kissed* her!

When they finally quit kissing he said, "Do you think it's love or lust."

She laughed again and said, "I don't know."

He said, "Do you want to go in the parking lot and find out?"

She said, "Why not?"

And they took off, leaving us to stand there with boilermakers in our hands, and our mouths hanging wide open. I know we all had the same thought: "This does not happen to anybody."

Halfway through the fourth quarter we saw little drunk Wally at the bottom of the steps, trying to find our seats. He ran up. Eddie Harlen said, "You didn't do it." Wally made Eddie smell the perfume on his shirt and elsewhere, and said, "*Tell me* I didn't do it!"

According to Pace the story went something like this: "We walked out of the stadium and I'm thinking, Where am I gonna do this? At first we thought about doing it on the grass outside but figured no, we'll surely get caught. Then I saw a bus driver sitting in his bus with the door open. She walked in front of me and over her head I waved at him, and signaled: 'Me, her, boom-boom-boom, your bus?' and the driver waved us over.

"But then I realize it might be too kinky and the guy would want to watch. So I ended up leaning her against the ladder of a Winnebago and we did it right there in the parking lot. When we finished, I said, 'What are you doing the rest of the night?' and she said, 'I really have to get back. I just went to buy my boyfriend a beer.' "

Ladies and gentleman: Casanova Wally Pace.

✳

Single people have the best sex stories, even if they have girlfriends or boyfriends. I know one guy who told me he had scored just because he wanted to shoot some ducks. He had walked down to the lake with a young lady and when he suggested blasting a few water fowl she became horrified and said, "You're not going to shoot no ducks."

"Why not?"

"You're just not."

He thought about that for a minute. "Hmm. What's it worth to you for me not to shoot them?" he said to her.

Just like a guy, isn't it? She said, "I don't know." He said, "Let's go into my trailer and find out." Turns out it was worth quite a bit. Trailer park guys have all the luck. Later at dinner, he suddenly said, "Mmm. Ya know what? I feel like shooting some ducks."

"No, you aren't," his girlfriend said.

"Really, I want to."

"I said no."

They went outside to his car to argue. You know what? She somehow convinced him to be kind to animals after all.

Now you realize *why* we know that single people have the best sex stories. Because *they share them with everybody.* They slop on the intimate details. I didn't ask to hear this last story, but the guy couldn't help it. We all know these people. We see them in the break room at work. They always have a crowd gathered around. "So there I was, tied to the Black & Decker Workmate when she brings out the ShopVac that cleans both wet and dry. Next night we did it with motor oil smeared all over our bodies. I also love it when she comes into the bedroom with a saddle and a set of jumper cables."

Married people just can't compete with this. What are we going to come back with? "You know, last night Marge vacuumed in her good robe. When she bent down to get underneath the sofa, I saw her butt. I started to get excited until I realized I could watch Hoss on *Bonanza* anytime!"

Married sex doesn't quite hold up, does it?

*

One problem with roommates is that they're always borrowing your stuff. Clothes, food, women. Dex used to borrow my car. His was a piece of crap. He called it Bob, for Beast of Burden. You could hear Bob coming eight blocks away, ten minutes before Dex got home.

I had a Datsun 240Z. I'd wake up and there'd be a note that read, "Jeff. Took the car. If the police call, just report it stolen." I would never know how long he'd had it.

One night Dex loaned Bob to some friends and they called us at two in the morning and said, "Dex, your car has broken down in the middle of the road and we can't move it. What should we do?" We were too wasted to move. I took the phone away from him and said, "You do not understand: We cannot leave the house." They said, "Well, we're just going to leave the car in the middle of the road."

"Do what you have to do," I said. "If we get in my car to come over there, we will never get out of jail again."

We got Bob back the next day, but he wasn't long for the road. One night Bob broke down again on the soft shoulder. Dex said it needed water. I scampered down the hillside with empty beer bottles and found water in a ditch, in the dark. We kept filling up the beer bottles and pouring them into Bob. After about fifteen trips we decided to crank the engine. Bob went "pffflt" and died. About that time someone stopped by with a flashlight and shined it in Bob's radiator and we discovered it was full of tadpoles. We left Bob there and never went back to get him.

RIP, Bob.

*

One day, just like Bob's demise, the roommate experience is over. You move on. Maybe it's to a place of your own, or your own room back at the folks', or if you're lucky, you meet the significant other of your dreams. That's what happened to me. I met Gregg.

I was wild in my single days, but I think that's okay. I can't apologize for trying to milk everything there is out of life. I had to go through, not around, the experience of trying it all. But one day I realized that my wallet and my back and my heart couldn't take it anymore. I couldn't continue to do all the stuff my parents told me never to do—because it was fun—and remain employed and a viable member of society.

I didn't actually think that clearly at the time. I worked pretty much on pure instinct. Let's just say I knew that if I didn't sow the wild oats and flush the tadpoles out of my system, then I might one day break down and be left on the roadside after giving in to the temptation to try that stuff under inappropriate circumstances, like when I was married with children.

I knew it was time to grow up.

From This Day Forth...

The whole time I worked in Sarasota I nagged IBM to transfer me back to Atlanta. I missed my family, I missed the great state of Georgia, and for some reason I couldn't get a date if my life depended on it. They finally broke down and sent me home in

April 1984. The following month my buddies threw me a "Welcome Home" party. I spent much of the evening on the balcony, drinking beer, telling stories, and making people laugh. Finally, Rob Burkett, who also worked at IBM, said, "Have you ever thought about going on-stage at the comedy club? We go down there all the time."

I said, "No, I've never even *been* in a comedy club."

"Well, go with me next week and watch."

The next Tuesday I sat through the agony and the ecstasy of amateur night. Afterward I said, "Okay, I'll try that." Compared to shooting doves at the airport and jumping off a moving truck onto a hay bale at forty miles an hour, five minutes on a stage seemed unlikely to get me into much trouble or cause great pain.

At home I wrote some material about my family. One bit was about Big Jim's toenails, and how toenails change as you age. Another joke was: "When people celebrate a football win they tear down the goalposts and carry them over their heads. Life doesn't really work like that, does it. When you sleep with someone for the first time, do you tear off the headboard and run around the apartment complex? I have, however, spiked a couple of pair of panties."

Horrible stuff, but I did it for Rob and my

brother. They laughed loudly enough that I decided to take the next step. I'd risk my reputation as a funny guy in the IBM break room and repeat my routine in front of total strangers who didn't give a damn about me because all they wanted was more to drink and for the headliner to come out and make them laugh. There was only one problem. When we called the Punchline to get a spot on amateur night they told us it was temporarily canceled for the summer because for the next twelve weeks the club was hosting the prelims for the Great Southeastern Laugh Off.

"Wait a few months," they suggested. However, we were extremely fired up, so Rob got everybody he worked with to call the Punchline and ask, "Is Jeff Foxworthy going to be on next Tuesday?"

"I don't know, why?"

"If so we'd like to bring forty people." It was a total bluff. You'd think comedy clubs would have caught on by now. But by the time they got the fiftieth phone call the club owners had probably decided that they couldn't take the chance that it was a hoax; they had to think instead about paid admissions and big liquor sales. So the people at the Punchline said, "Yeah, he's gonna be on." No one went down except Rob and me, but I did get my spot—on last—in a contest that was really only for working comedians.

That night was the only time in my career I've needed a drink to perform. Four Seven & Sevens did the trick. I was still so nervous I could not look at anybody, so I stared at the floor instead. My first words before paying customers were: "I am a virgin comedian. This is my first time."

I won my night, eventually made it to the semifinals, and came in fifth overall. They only took four finalists and I'd missed it by half a point. My mistake? My set went too long.

That first time I was thrilled because I had actually gotten laughs. Without laughs there never would have been a second time, I promise you. However, figuring that my first five minutes had worked, I brimmed with confidence and wrote a new five minutes. Then I went on at another local club, Jerry Farber's. Rob went with me and this time brought people. I went totally down the toilet.

Even so, I knew I had found my calling.

❧

A new career would have been enough, but the night was still young. I didn't know it, but my future wife was in the audience that first night at the Punchline. We didn't know each other. I don't remember this, but she later told me she came up and said "Congratulations." Gregg thought the "virgin" routine was just part of my act and that I was a working comic from Florida. When she got to know me better, she also told me she thought I was a snob because all I did that night was say to her, "Oh, thanks," and turn away. The truth is that I was a nervous wreck. If I'd known better I would have paid more attention at the time. Anyone who reads women's magazines like I do (a man's got to take something up in the tree to pass the time) will know that they're full of articles insisting that what women want first and foremost in a man is a sense of humor. Take some advice from a guy who's never had any trouble making people laugh: This can't be true. Every woman in the world could say "sense of humor" until the cows come home, but you never see women throwing their panties onstage at a comedy club. Except in those rare circumstances, like when you have a top-ten-rated TV show or you're the last man on the planet, comics don't have groupies.

Fortunately, Gregg also told a friend she thought I was cute. Unfortunately, I only learned this after three years of marriage, during a fight about whose family was crazier, when she took it back.

We met again a few months later when the friend who'd taken her to the club the first time decided to go onstage on amateur night at the Punchline herself, and she talked Gregg into being her audience. At first Gregg said, "I don't know if I want to go," but her friend said, "Well, Jeff Foxworthy's going to be there." (Said it provocatively, you understand.) So Gregg said, "Okay, I'll go." God bless her for being willing to give me another chance.

After the show we were formally introduced. I remember trying to be cool because in the intervening months I had gained a little stature as one of the better amateur comics in Atlanta. (I was definitely funnier than the other two.) I recall exactly what she was wearing: tan pants and a little zigzag sweater over a white shirt. The sweater had no sleeves. I'd like to credit my romantic personality for remembering her outfit, but honestly, it's because I walked up and immediately spilled my drink down the front of her pants and sweater. After fumbling the kickoff, so to speak, I was ready to forfeit the game.

"Well, I guess this means you'll never go out with me," I said.

She said, "You haven't even asked."

Time to throw the long bomb.

"Okay, will you go out with me?"

"Yeah."

Touchdown!

Boy, was I smiling on the outside. Inside I knew I was a dog. Not two days earlier I had returned from a weekend with a woman at a cabin in the South Carolina mountains. But once I met Gregg I forgot all about anyone else. I disappeared on this woman and never called her back. I imagine, as just retribution, that she's never written me a letter saying she's my biggest fan. She probably thinks I'm the scum of the earth.

Gregg and I spent the rest of the evening standing at the bar, talking. I discovered that Gregg was an actress who had just played the lead in a movie called *Ocean Drive Weekend*. She also did local commercials. I thought she was big-time show business, which didn't make her less interesting at all. However, it's good that besides wanting to hitch my wagon to a star, Gregg had other great qualities. I've always liked brunettes. I've always liked small women. I like them with spit and fire. She had all three.

Finally the lights came up and it was time for everyone to go home. Gregg and I had already planned to go out later that week, but as I said good-bye, I did something that I'd never done before without at least a date under my belt. I kissed her goodnight. This was not a little peck. I kissed her very well, which, in my book, involves cutting and shampooing my mustache, exercising my lips for ten to twenty seconds to warm up, and, if I'm in a really sexy mood, applying a little lip gloss and peach slicker.

Gregg later told me she'd never kissed a guy so soon before, either. I said that was nice, and that I'd *never* kissed a guy *at all*, even if I'd known him for years, and I hoped it wouldn't jeopardize our getting to know each other better. Now that I think about it, our first kiss was like that moment in *Annie Hall* when Woody Allen smooches Diane Keaton to "get it out of the way" before they get all tense about it at the end of their date. I'm no short, neurotic, brilliantly funny, New York comedian who ponders the ineffability of love and death and questions the nature of existence, but otherwise I like to think that I'm a lot like Mr. Allen.

"If you think challah is what you do when a tractor runs over your foot . . . you might be a Redneck."

As I was saying, I'm surprised that Gregg and I kissed. Watching a couple make out in public is not a pretty sight. I always think, "Oh my. Geez. I'm trying to keep some nachos down. Would you guys knock it off?" Stranger still, we'd both recently ended unsatisfying relationships and didn't want to get involved so soon again.

That was a Tuesday.

"Don't want to rush into anything," we both said.

*

The Saturday we went out Gregg had, coincidentally, just moved in with one of her best girlfriends, in Marietta, Georgia. I drove down to pick her up. While I waited in the living room for Gregg to get ready, her roommate said, "You're gonna be smitten." She didn't even know me, but she seemed sure that it would happen.

I took Gregg to a party. Sixty people were crammed into a little house. We walked in, grabbed two beers, and went directly to a bench on the back porch where, beyond the loud music, we sat and talked for hours. We were oblivious to everyone and everything, although we did stop talking for a moment to watch a woman dancing by herself in the corner.

"Hey, it's only 8:30 and Peggy's dancing by herself," I said. "That shirt's coming off tonight, I guarantee it."

Gregg looked at me like I was some kind of cretin.

"Just part of the act. Just the act, I promise."

Then we got lost in each other.

Three hours later we realized it was three hours later. I know this sounds stupid, but honestly, all I remember is that at some point early in the conversation I looked at Gregg and thought, "I'm gonna marry this girl." She must have been thinking about forever, too, because that's when she said, "Honey, would you mind getting me another beer?"

It was all I could do to not blurt out, "Will you marry me?" right there.

On the way back to Gregg's I decided that I would be a perfect gentleman at the door because I didn't want to screw up my long-term possibilities. No way did I want her thinking, "Oh gee, we get to the door and he starts pawing me like a cougar." I wasn't going to do any leaning in on the leg. None of the poodle-on-the-living-room-floor stuff.

I hope I'm not confusing you with these Redneck mating terms. The first means that when you're kissing a woman, you lean in and make them aware of your package.

"What the hell is that?"

"Sorry. I've got a severe thigh cramp."

I don't know what the second term means, but it sounded intriguing. There are other moves. The accidental forearm across the breast is always a good one. Hand sliding down to the rear end is another.

"Oh, gosh, I didn't realize my hand was on your butt."

"Well get it off or you'll really have a severe thigh cramp."

The most serious move is kidnapping.

So far I haven't had to resort to that.

I kissed Gregg goodnight, then I backed away and said, "I'll call you." To my surprise, Gregg just grinned and said, "Get in the house."

"Alll-riiight, okay, going in the house now."

I believe she might have put the chain on the door. Good sign and exactly what I wanted, not that I had anything to do with it. Although my fortunes had brightened I certainly wasn't going to initiate anything, even if I had made it over the threshold. You've got to go through the little ritual. You can't just walk in the door and go straight to the bedroom and say, "Where do I hang my pants?"

I'm glad we stayed in the living room to talk. One of the first things Gregg told me was, "You've got to get out of your job at IBM. You've got too much stuff trying to come out of you."

I said, "If you only knew . . ." I was impressed that she had encouraged my need to entertain and be funny, on the first date. This made me even more crazy about her.

Then she did something funny. She walked toward the bedroom and said, "Enough chat. Come in here, I want to show you something."

Clown paintings. She had clown paintings!

I wish I could say that before I knew it I heard birds chirping and it was the next morning. But at the time I lived in my mother's basement. So I had to get up before our passion cooled and call Carole. How impressive is that? I said, "You know, Mom, it's really late. I'm across town. I think I'm just going to stay at Rob's house tonight." It was pretty embarrassing. I'd met the true love of my life and I had to say, "I need to call my mother." Fortunately, Gregg didn't react badly at all. She laughed. She'd just moved out of her dad's house. She knew exactly what I was going through.

🍢

The next morning I had to face Gregg's roommate. I had that good-morning hair and the previous night's disco clothes. I said, "Hi, how are you? You guys have any orange juice?" One look at her face and I knew what she was thinking, "What kind of slut have I moved in with? She's here for eight hours and . . ."

"By the way," I said. "You were right. I'm smut."

"I told you so," she said.

After that night Mr. Slow-and-Easy became like a tick. You could have burned my butt with three thousand hot match heads, and I still wouldn't have let go. We were inseparable. We went out every night. Saturday, Sunday, Monday, Tuesday, and Wednesday. On Thursday morning we finally decided, "Whoa, better slow down. Remember, neither of us wants to get involved. This is going really fast. Thursday night we will not see each other." That lasted until about nine that night, when I called Gregg and we talked for forty minutes on the phone. I said, "Let's meet for a drink somewhere," and we did. After that we were more or less living together. My routine became: go to work, get off, meet Gregg.

I had to keep telling my mom that I was staying at Rob Burkett's. I was an adult and could do what I wanted, but moms are sensitive that way. No one wants their kid to walk around with a large "Living in Sin" sign stamped on their forehead. Besides, my mom is a religious woman. It's a wonder she didn't get suspicious of me and Rob, since Carole thought Rob was really cute. I *guess* that's what she meant when she said, "Rob Burkett would be handsome in a barrel." Come to think of it, she probably could have handled the news that Rob and I were in love more easily.

Eventually, I told my mom I was moving out of the basement and in with Big Jim across town. I didn't go there much except to grab some clothes.

*

Once again, Gregg urged me to quit my job at IBM and try comedy full-time, and I finally took her advice. When I walked out the door at Big Blue on December 31, 1984, I had eleven minutes of material. I banked my career on that. Nobody knew me. Most of the time they didn't care. I was just a distraction while people got drinks and chatted before the headliner came on. Even so, I spent my entire day getting ready to work fifteen minutes a night.

About five weeks into this new arrangement Gregg realized I wasn't making any money. So she did the only thing she could do, besides dump me at the roadside like Bob the car. She quit acting and doing commercials and took a full-time job to support my dream. What can I say? All I could do was wonder what I'd done to deserve this woman. I still think that. Within twenty minutes on a night in June 1984, I'd not only discovered what I wanted to do with the rest of my life, but I'd also met the woman with whom I wanted to spend it. That's even better than bagging a deer, catching the biggest lake bass, and sleeping with every woman DeWayne Twilley has known—all at once. That's really saying something.

When a man is with the right woman, one day he must actually declare his love. Saying, "I really like you," "I'm crazy for you," or "You're more fun than the Home Ec. teacher" just won't cut it anymore. I'd bit my lip bloody for weeks, trying not to tell Gregg that I'd loved her from the first date. Finally, I couldn't contain myself. We were standing in a restaurant parking lot, three weeks after our first night together, and I said, "I've got to tell you something."

She said, "Don't."

I said, "No, I've got to."

"Don't."

"No, I've got to tell you this."

"*Please* don't."

"I love you."

"Oh my God."

The worst part is that she didn't say it back.

When you say you love a woman and she doesn't respond in kind, certain things go through your head like, "She's going to change her phone number in the morning." Suddenly I felt like a candidate for one of those talk shows where you have the tearful reunion five years later.

> HOST: *Remember you were going out. You had a great time. He said "I love you." You disappeared and moved to Nevada. Well, now he's rich, he's famous, and he's still single. Here he is again!*
>
> ME: *(looking very sharp, but wiping a small tear from my eye)* Hi.
>
> GREGG: *(impressed) I do love him. I just forgot to say it. He's rich? Yeah, I love him!*

That's her joke now: She married me for my money.

If you're looking for advice about saying "I love you" first or holding out, don't look here. Once you're in love, you just become stupid. Part of you thinks, "Don't say this yet. She hasn't given any indication that she's gonna say it back. Bide your time. It's going well. Ride it out." But that "in-love" part of your brain goes, "It's okay, just say it. Just damn well say it! Shout it from the rooftops!" That part always overrides everything else. I've only said it to a few women and I've always meant it, except for a couple of times when the woman in question was sitting on top of me. Naked.

*

Here we were falling for each other and it felt as glorious as screaming "Free Bird" at a Lynyrd Skynyrd concert. Although Gregg didn't say she loved me, I wasn't afraid that she'd suddenly leave me. I knew that because the first night she'd told me that she had promised herself never to get involved with another man unless he was smart, funny, and sexy. She *had* to have all three. Being an insecure, amateur-night comic, I waited until morning and asked: "All right, so how many out of the three do I get?" I don't have to tell you the answer, do I?

Maybe I do, but I won't. I was raised right.

*

Eventually, Gregg uttered the magic words. "Honey, would you mind picking up some barbeque on the way home?" She also confessed to being in love with me. Before long we began to talk about marriage. Well, I talked about it. We'd moved in together, I wanted to get married. She didn't. I hounded her for a little while, then decided to let it go. Suddenly she "kind of" wanted to get married. I pouted and said, "No. You broke my heart. You didn't want to get married when I wanted to get married, so now I don't want to get married." So we stopped talking about it altogether, but only for a while.

*

The summer after I met Gregg I again entered the Great Southeastern Laugh Off at the Punchline, and this time won it all. Part of the prize was $500 and a trip to New York to play at Catch-a-Rising-Star in Manhattan. Gregg and I went up together. I had no money. She had a credit card. We stayed at a place on 49th and Broadway. Great neighborhood. Looking out our bedroom window we could see a huge movie theater marquee across the street. I'll always remember what was playing: *Horny Sluts*.

Give my regards to Broadway.

Since we were in town and flush, we decided to get married. We'd talked about it enough and New York seemed like a cool place. No family or friends, no hassles. I called a comedian friend of mine, Rob Bartlett, who is a very funny guy and, at the time, was the *only* guy I knew in New York. I said, "We've decided to get married. I need a best man." We went to City Hall to get a marriage license. Then we started looking for a justice of the peace. We couldn't find one in the phone book, so I called churches. Finally one minister said he'd marry us and only charge $300.

"I don't have $300," I said. "Why is it so much?"

"Well, it's $200 for the chapel and $100 for me."

"Look, we don't need the chapel," I said. "We can do this in your office. Do it in the hall. Even out back."

"You know what?" he said. "I'm right across the street from the garden at Central Park. If you want, I'll walk across the street and do it for $100."

I said, "You've got a deal. Thursday at noon."

When the time came I wore a $35 suit. It had no lining. I think it was part of the prize for winning the Laugh Off. I've still got it for special occasions. Rob Bartlett showed up with his wife, who was about eight months pregnant, and a twenty-pound bag of rice he'd bought on the way. Then Reverend Leonard arrived.

We had our vows ready.

ME: *Hey, you know, man, I'm gonna try an' stop foolin' around with other wimmens now and everything. You know I love you.*

SHE: *What with the baby comin' and everything, I figured we might as well get married.*

ME: *She likes to party.*

SHE: *And so does he.*

ME: *(To her dad) It's okay, man, put that shotgun down. I'm pledgin everlastin' luuuvvv.*

Bet you believed it for just a second.

It was a fine day for a wedding. Just the four of us; oh, and the guy sweeping the park, around the fountain in the garden. We had to plead with him to move out of the way so we could get married. He stood to the side while the Reverend recited the standard ceremony. Afterwards the sweeper said, "Please, please don't throw that rice or I'll have to clean up again."

"But we've got to throw the rice," I said.

Bartlett gave him twenty bucks and he was happy. He's also in our four wedding pictures. That was part of the deal. There we are: me, Gregg, the Bartletts, Reverend Leonard, and Andre the park sweeper, who also somehow managed to get his arm around my new wife.

By the way, I hear you're not supposed to throw rice anymore at weddings. Bird seed is preferred. Apparently the birds eat the rice, then when they drink water the rice puffs up, and the birds explode. Really. Forget the wedding. I'd pay $100 to see that.

Afterward we took the Bartletts to the Tavern on the Green for lunch. Then Gregg tried to inject a little culture into my life and we went to see two plays. Between the first and the second we called our respective families from a phone booth to give them the big news.

It's better that way, believe me.

No matter what your love life is like before marriage, the vows change everything. This is probably not news to anyone except hermit crabs and certain movie stars who keep marrying and hoping for something to change. (Remember, insanity is doing the same thing over and over while expecting a different result.) But considering all the advice books sold on how to find a mate, please your mate, talk to your mate (and, for beginners, how to tell the difference between potential mates and common barnyard animals), it's not like everyone's doing such a great job here. We seem to need all the help we can get. So please, benefit from my experience, or my complete naiveté. Whichever works in a pinch.

FRIENDS

Even before you're hitched, your friends put out an all-points bulletin that you're missing in action. At first they wait to see if you're just having another of your renowned three-week relationships: court them, catch them, cash them in. But if it continues longer, then they can't avoid the Truth: you're no longer available to trade babe stories, pull all-nighters, and bar hop—unless you can do it in the living room, with the wife's permission, after she falls asleep. Even so, this doesn't help much because your friends will still resent your woman for taking you away from them. And she will be uptight because when you entertain the old gang, she has to listen to them tell stories about the crazy things you did when you were single.

Later, when you're lying in bed hoping to get lucky, she'll say, "Tell me you did not moon a bus full of nuns."

"I didn't know they were nuns."

"How could you not know?"

"I wasn't *looking* at them."

"It was still your ass on the window. You ought to be ashamed of yourself. Goodnight."

Fortunately, you don't have to shoulder all the blame. Whimper enough and your wife will turn back in your direction and say, "I know you couldn't have done it all by yourself, honey. It's those no-account friends. I love yew."

Such is the power of rationalization and, if you're really in the doghouse, tears.

The smart man reveals as little as possible about his past activities and convinces his friends to do likewise if they want to have any hope of seeing him again in their lifetimes. You can tell some cute little stories, but the trip to Mexico to see Pepe the Wonder Donkey is probably one to keep close to the vest.

Even more important, never talk about old girlfriends. I'm always stunned and amazed when I meet couples who tell each other in graphic detail everything that they've done sexually with other people before they met. I hear that sometimes this can be a stimulating marital aid, but even so, Gregg and I made a pact immediately: We didn't want to know any intimate details of previous relationships. I don't want to hear about it. My imagination's too vivid.

So as far as I know, neither Gregg nor I have been with anyone before being with each other.

INTIMATE RELATIONS

Marriage alters both the quantity and quality of your intimate relations. Anyone who says it doesn't is either single or lying. With married sex you never have to worry about dislocating your shoulder. With single sex, you always do it like there's a crowd watching and someone's keeping score. Initially, married sex is really not *that* much different from single sex, but the longer you do it the tougher it is to find ways to keep it interesting. Finally, you're just trying to find ways to stay awake. (I say that in jest, honey, because I want to *continue* to have sex.)

A big difference between married and single sex is that the former now seems to take place much more within the home, and specifically the bedroom. I don't know what women do, but when guys get together they will eventually talk about the weirdest places they've gotten lucky. That's always a fascinating conversation. Not always believable, but still compelling.

I know one guy who was quite proud of doing it on top of an off-balanced Maytag washing machine in the middle of the spin cycle. Apparently that was the key: in the middle of the spin cycle. Seems you get some type of vibrations there that you can't get anywhere else on the planet.

Another guy once told me he did it in a deer stand twenty-five feet off the ground.

"Didn't see any deer, didn't give a damn."

"What about the silence is golden hunting rule?"

"Lifted it."

What's truly amazing is that he was a sane, rational person who had a good job, made his mortgage payments, and knew exactly what to do if a deer wandered past while he was mating in a tree.

"Stop, reach for the shotgun, and fire. You should always keep the gun nearby, with one in the chamber. Deer don't come along that often. But if you've got a romantic bone in your body, you finish the act before you clean the deer."

My point is that when you're married you *have* to keep things interesting. I've sometimes thought, "Why didn't we try this five years ago?" But then I guess it just never occurred to me to bring a spatula to bed.

SIGNS ALONG THE WAY

To have any chance of sex materializing, all the proper signs and signals must happen. When you're single, a stop sign will suffice. If it's not a busy intersection, what the hey? When you're married, other important considerations arise:

1. Does she have to get up early for work?

2. Is any family member in the midst of a crisis, and could he or she call and force you to discuss it at an inconvenient time?

3. Are the dishes washed? Women can't do it with dirty dishes in the sink. I don't know why, but the smell of rotting food does not stimulate the sex glands. My advice: Learn to wash dishes. It's mindless, relaxing, they've got soap that won't chaff your hands, and if you don't tell on me I won't tell on you.

4. Body temperature is important. If it's too hot or too cold, you ain't doing it, buddy.

"You want to do it?"

"Oh, God, it's so hot, I couldn't possibly do it."

"You want to do it?"

"Oh, God, it's too cold." The trick is to lie and say, "Okay, we'll stay under the covers." After you get started you can whip them off.

"You oughta be warm by now! Yee-hah!"

5. Physical problems. Has the missus had any significant aches or pains in the last thirty minutes? If she's free and clear, make your move. The longer you wait the higher the odds against you. This is purely a gender thing. Guys could cut their knee off with a chain saw and before they go to the hospital if the wife said, "You want to do it?" they'd say, "Okay, we'll put a towel around it. Could somebody hold the ambulance?"

6. What she's wearing. Check what the little woman's wearing to bed. If it's something she can rake leaves in, you're out of luck. Or in for the kinkiest night of your life.

Oh, by the way, no shirt, no shoes, no problem.

If you've made it this far, sorry—there's still a way to go. Once you've mastered these basic issues, you simply get to move on to more complicated ones.

7. Cycles. According to medical science, guys get interested in sex roughly every ninety minutes. And we talk about it for the other eighty-seven. This even happens when we're asleep. Sometimes you wake up right in the middle of a dream about you and the latest *Playboy* Playmate and you want to do it. Unfortunately, not many women want their men rousing them from REM sleep expecting something he didn't make reservations for two days in advance. I don't understand that. I'd even accept, "Okay, but try not to wake me."

8. Sex and food. The adage that the way to a man's heart is through his stomach is generally true. If my wife wants her way with me she fixes me something I like to eat. But you've got to be careful not to overeat. Sex is not a good idea *after* eating. There's nothing worse than sleeping on a full stomach, especially hers. Big Jim told me that nothing kills passion quicker than a distended belly. Big Jim says you can do it if you've had too much to drink, you can do it you've had too little sleep. But you cannot do it on a full stomach, unless it's yours and then you want to be on top.

9. What's on TV? Be careful what you watch on TV as your foreplay. The story about the kid whose parents died and left him in an alley where he raised himself and survived by eating from a dumpster is not going to help. It can't be anything tearful. Stay away from *20/20* and *Nightline* and any infomercial featuring exercise equipment, chatty Aussies, or motivational demigods. You don't want your woman motivated to exercise and run away with Mel Gibson.

10. Watch the clock. Depending on how much sleep your partner has had during the week, you could still get the arched eyebrow at 12:10. Or it could already be too late at 9:40.

"I thought we were going to do it tonight."

"It's too late."

"It's 9:40! For God's sakes, *ER's* not on yet! We could do it and *still* watch *ER.*"

11. Real foreplay. The most important thing to remember about sex after marriage is that you have to warm up your woman. (The second most important thing is afterplay. Any intelligent man knows it greases the way for the next time.) With the spontaneity of single life gone, women became hard machines to start. Everybody's had a lawn mower they couldn't kick over. You add gas, check the oil, and pull the choke, and still nothing. It *should* run better. Maybe it would if you used it more than twice a month when the grass grows, and let it idle once a week in the winter. If *men* were lawnmowers they might *look* like crap but they'd start up on the first pull and run until the last drop of gas got sucked into the carburetor.

Tell you a little secret. Men always say they long for a woman who starts up like a

man, but I think most of us would get bored
if it was too easy. We might kick and scream
and insist we wouldn't, but it's true. A good
analogy is the thrill of fishing. If every time
you threw in your line you instantly caught a
fish and pulled it out, fishing wouldn't be
very much fun, would it? You've got to put
on the right bait, deliver the line smoothly,
retrieve it with finesse. Then when you get
one, you're proud. "Man, I must be pretty
cool. I got a fish."

Now, coincidentally, you know why
women *aren't* big fisherman. They toss out
their line and men *always* take the bait.
Doesn't matter what she looks like, a woman
can always get some guy interested. (Yes, I
know. A woman's reason for fishing is not
the same as a man's. Women actually have
to *like* the fish.) That, my friends, is why
women make a game out of sex. They know
they *can* get it anytime. They've *always*
known it. It's in some book they all get when
they're born, I'm sure.

Another reason men don't really want a
woman who is overly eager is that we're so
insecure that we're always thinking, "If I can
start her up so quick then what is she doing
while I'm at work?" Men like to think
they're the only ones with the keys to the

machine. Men have good reason to be insecure. Haven't you woken up in the morning
and done it before either of you have brushed
your teeth? Then you walk into the bathroom, look in the mirror, and think your hair
looks like frame 237 of the Zapruder film.
Plus, your breath is horrible, you've got gunk
in the corner of your eye, and a little trace of
drool down your chin. You think, "My God,
if my woman would do it with *this*, she will
do it with anybody."

And if she wanted to, you can't stop her.
Women have all the power. Men have none.
They're like Caesar's wife at the gladiator
show in the Coliseum. Do one thing wrong
and it's thumbs-down.

12. Be romantic. The old cliché is that
women give sex to get love and men give
love to get sex. So what else is new? Men
are not, by nature, romantic creatures. But I
think we discovered early on in the game that
if you don't learn how to be romantic, you're
not going to win very often. So we shamble
and ask, "What is romance?" Too bad we
don't like the answers: "Comb my hair nice?
Put down the remote control? What if I
spray-paint your name on the side of the
house? I don't give a damn about the neighbors. I want to tell the whole world how I
feel about you."

If only we could. In the end we're like circus bears. We need to be trained to do what we must to get the reward at the end of the act.

You know what? We gladly do it.

*

Since the night I first told Gregg I loved her, I've not gone a single day without saying it, and meaning it. Each day I also remind her that she's the prettiest girl in the whole world. One more thing: Because ours is the greatest love story known to man, in the twelve years since we met I have never, ever farted in front of my wife. Take me on a camping trip and I can clear out a pup tent pretty quick. But never in front of Gregg.

Maybe I'm not such a Redneck after all.

...Till Death Do Us Part

You know you're married when you're lying in bed with somebody and you suddenly think, "Uh oh, I've got to go home, my wife's waiting on me."

Never happened to me, of course.

I walked into my marriage with my eyes

open and have never regretted it. Never fooled around and never wanted to. But once or twice, I've had those moments where I suddenly realized I was married—as if I could ever forget—and wondered how I'd gotten there. The first time that happened, I made an important discovery that you can only make *after* you're married: The person you were dating who said "I wouldn't change anything about you" was *lying*.

It's not just a female trait.

But it's *mostly* a female trait.

No wonder marriage is a big decision: It's the choice between the freedom to live as you please or with someone else's relentless analysis of your shortcomings.

Have you ever heard women in the supermarket checkout line talk about what their men were like before they met them? It's almost as if they'd captured and tamed wild animals.

"First time I saw Tom, he was naked on the side of the road, eating roots and kudzu with his bare hands. I took him home, taught him how to wear a shirt and eat with a spoon, and later we got him a job. Still eats roots. If you don't watch him like a hawk, he'll pull his clothes off and go out in the backyard and start digging around the trees."

Among women, the things they've gotten

their husbands to do are a badge of honor. "Since he met me, Narvel takes a shower every Saturday, whether he needs it or not." This is usually the prelude to the conversation about the stuff their husbands *still* won't do. "Then I said, 'How about if we get naked in the satellite dish?' But I don't think he heard me over the football scores."

Women are shameless. Sometimes just for fun, and right out in public, they'll compete with other women they don't even know, over whose husband most embraced and abused the notion of bachelor living.

"Before we got married, Ed's refrigerator had a potato inside that was *alive.* I had to kill it."

"Oh yeah? I donated the mold on Randy's shower curtain to the CDC. They took one look at it under a microscope and found a cure for jock itch."

"Earl slept with the light on."

"What's so bad about that?"

"Every morning he couldn't figure out why the car wouldn't start."

When I see this happen, I have to laugh softly to myself. Any man would because we're all thinking the same thing: "Yeah? So what? *You slept with me.* What does that say about you?"

Most women are obsessed with clothes. I don't
mean their clothes. (This book would be twice
as long if I wrote about that subject.) When a
woman wants to change a man, she often be-
gins with his wardrobe. The whole time you're
dating she never says anything when you wear
hip waders to the covered dish Christmas dinner. She thinks it's cute. But women are
sneaky. Once you're sharing a bedroom and
closet, she will get rid of your clothes when
you're not looking. All of a sudden there's so
many bags of stuff marked "charity" that the
Salvation Army pulls up in an eighteen-
wheeler. I once came home from the road and
discovered that Gregg had done me "a favor"
and "cleaned out" my closet. I immediately
ripped through the boxes she'd piled in the hall.

"You can't get rid of this shirt!" I said.

"But it's out of style."

"Out of style? Are you kidding me? When I
watched *Bewitched* last night Darren had on
one just like it. That's not out of style!"

Men aren't stupid. We know it's out of style.
We're just waiting for it to come back.

What's even worse is that if your wife
spends any time going through your things,
your clothes start to smell like her perfume.

Then you can't wear anything because your friends will give you a hard time.

"You smell nice, Jeff. New fabric softener? Haw, haw."

This is one reason why it's always a good idea to keep your hunting clothes in the garage, ready for an emergency.

Heaven forbid that I would ever go into Gregg's closet and do *her* a favor. I wouldn't dare think about it because (a) I'm too lazy to do it, and (b) I just wouldn't dare.

I might *fool around* in her closet, though. I've cleaned out her underwear drawer occasionally and put everything back where I found it. (Never a problem. As you know, I graduated from Big Jim's College of Leaving It Like You Found It.) I also check to see what new accessories she's bought. I keep hoping to find something frilly and exciting, but it pretty much comes down to belts and shoes. I've got three belts and three pairs of shoes. She's got 700 belts. I'm still counting the shoes.

Women have too much choice. Any time we dress to go out with friends she says, "I can't wear that."

"Why not?"

"I wore it six months ago. The last time we saw these people."

"So? How are they going to know?" I can't tell you what *I* wore yesterday."

When women go out, they come home and talk about what other women wore. "Did you see the Jaclyn Smith skirt Darlene had on? I know I saw it last week on the Kmart closeout table." Never do you see two guys leaving the bowling alley at the end of the evening going, "Did you see the shirt Fred was wearing? Oh my God. And those pants, they had to be from last year. Come on Fred, show some fashion sense, for God's sake."

Women also try to get you to cut your hair a different way, and to care for it with their girly conditioners. Why they think it's a waste of perfectly good automotive products to use transmission fluid to keep a pompadour set is beyond me. Besides, it gives your hair an Elvis-like sheen.

Guys don't want to change a lot about women. Guys just like consistency. They want more food, less nagging, and more sex. As regularly as possible. Otherwise, men are pretty flexible. If a woman suddenly stopped her share of the housekeeping duties and the dishes piled up in the sink, a guy would think, "Oh, we've chosen a new lifestyle. Okay, I can do this. I've done this before when I lived with Boomer."

One thing we don't want is a lot of questions. For instance, "What are you thinking?" When two guys ride together in a truck, never does one turn to the other and go, "Chuck, whatcha thinking?" Ask a woman what she's thinking and it's either about your shortcomings or about food. You've got to feed them regularly to keep them out of a bad mood because that's when they start thinking about what's wrong with you. (Everything in a woman's universe is connected, Buddha buddy.) I don't know how often my wife and I have been on the road together and she's said, "If I don't eat soon, I'm going to get a headache." I've ridden a billion miles with guys and I have never heard a man say, "God, if I don't eat soon, I'm gonna be hell to live with. Scratch the hell out of the dashboard, I'll tell you that. I don't want to get pissy, but I need fries."

I don't know what women want. We married them, but that doesn't seem to be enough. I think they'd rather have great-looking shoes that are comfortable. Eyeliner that doesn't run. And jewelry. I hear you can never go wrong at the jewelry well.

My wife doesn't deny it, but I get the feeling that even if she had all that it still wouldn't be sufficient.

"I just want you to show me some attention," she always says.

"Sure thing, sugar dumpling," I always answer. "At halftime."

One satisfying aspect of marriage is attending your friends' weddings and trying not to fall on the floor laughing because they have no idea what married life will be like. Just because they'd lived together since they were brother and sister doesn't mean a thing. You'll also laugh at yourselves because you know that no matter how hard you try, there's no way to explain it to them.

Even so, weddings typically offer the best entertainment value for your community property dollar. I remember when my friend Jimmy got married. I was one of six groomsmen. We decided right before we arrived at the church that we were going to convince Jimmy that he had a cliff-hanger; in other words, something in his nose. Jimmy came out and stood near the altar. As each of us walked down the aisle to join him, we'd point discreetly to our noses. Jimmy spent his entire wedding picking at his nose. He would look over at us like, "Did I get it?" We'd look back and silently mouth, "Nah, you didn't get it." The whole thing is on video. I can get you a copy.

Once or twice I've wondered what it would be like to be a woman. I think I'd probably get kicked out of public places for playing with my breasts a lot. "Ma'am, you're going to have to stop fondling yourself in front of the other diners."

Seriously, I would love to sit around with women and talk to them *as* a woman and find out what they really want from men. Guys *are* totally clueless. But even if I discovered the secret, changed back to a man, and told my friends, they probably wouldn't believe me.

"Nah, Jeff. It couldn't be *that*. You musta heard it wrong."

⚥

Things change slowly, as Don Henley once sang on the Eagles' *Long Run* album, "if they ever change at all." So it is with couples. It's only when spouses accept that they can't really change each other that the mature marriage becomes possible. With the pressure gone to be someone else, each of you gets to relax and be who you are. There are risks, however. The shock of realizing who your husband or wife *really is* could make you feel as if you just fell into a mountain brook in the middle of winter. You'll instantly go numb and just want to get out as soon as possible. Or with nothing left to nag each other about, the energy that also *kept* the marriage together might evaporate and the whole thing could come apart like your intestines during a bad bout of Montezuma's revenge. Then it's adios amoebas.

By the way, if you ever break up with someone, destroy all the cards and letters they ever gave you. If you don't, no matter where they are hidden or how ancient—the sender could be dead twenty years—your next spouse will find them. "So, you carried Gloria's books to school, you never carried mine . . ."

But it's not all bad news.

Some couples understand the nature of marriage. They know that a relationship *requires* two people: One to run into the grocery store, and one to sit in the car, look at the time and say, "Oh for crying out loud! You said three items. Let's go!!"

See? Some couples can accept and understand what's really important to their partners. They learn how to compromise. For instance, when a friend of mine realized how much it bugged his wife when he left his underwear on the living room floor, he took it off in the kitchen instead.

That's what I call respect.

Arguing is a lot more fun when you're married.

Lots of things can start an argument. A question like, "Are you going to wear your hair like that?" is pretty much the start of a crappy evening for everyone.

A lot of fights begin with the phrase "What's wrong?!"

"Nothing!"

"You set the cat on fire! Don't tell me nothing!"

This is also why most fishing trips began with the phrase "I have had about enough of this shit."

When you're single and you argue, once you're through running each other into the ground there is nothing else to fight about. When you're married, once you get through trashing your partner you can bring a family member into it. No matter how bad you're losing, slamming a relative will turn everything around. You need never lose a fight again.

"Oh yeah? What about your uncle Clark? Last time I checked, nuns' habits were, well . . . for nuns."

If you're behind in the fight, don't hesitate to bring up an unemployed brother or sister with six kids. But remember, once you use these, your mom's prison record is fair game.

Lots of times fights happen on the way to

family functions. "Oh, jeez, your dad's going to be there. I don't know why we have to do this every year. Your aunt May's gonna be plastered and I bet Aunt June hasn't learned how to chew with her mouth shut yet. The woman's eighty-six years old for goodness sakes. We're going to have to draw straws to see who sits across from her. Last year I got her food all over my face!"

Bringing family into a fight increases the duration by at least eight days. God created the world in less time than it will take for you to kiss and make up. Plus, you're no longer arguing about the topic at hand, you have gone off down an entirely emotional road. This is toughest for the man, who is usually the logical one. (Hey, want to make something of it?) But it's no wonder that taking scatter shots at family hurts. These days most families are the product of divorces and remarriages. It always seems like every time you split the tree, the branch gets a little thinner. For some reason I get the feeling that the Foxworthy tree is suffering from dry rot.

The worst thing a woman can do to a man is nag him in front of his friends. I'm less afraid of slandering someone's family than I am of arguing in public. My wife can pin me to the floor with a butcher knife, but I just want her to wait until we get home. It's even more embarrassing being around a couple when they're fighting.

"Yeah, Tina, why don't you tell them about the time you pushed my mom down the basement stairs."

"They don't want to hear about that."

"Yeah, we would!"

Or say you're on a double date, and they're going at it in the backseat. You don't want to interfere, but after a while something happens that forces you to voice your opinion.

"Jerry, you should have asked me to stop the car before you made Dolores get out. At the least I could have slowed down. You just had to ask."

Too bad we get too old to hit people with a dirt clod when we get mad at them.

Here's something to always remember: When fighting with your wife, never get so mad that you walk out without your keys. I've got a theory that 98 percent of the homeless are people who walked out without their keys and couldn't convince the other party to let them back in.

If fighting persists, divorce, however previously unthinkable, might become an option. But I wonder at how effective a solution dissolution is. After all, isn't divorce when you pay a lawyer a lot of money to arrange it so you can move out and leave everything you own with someone you hate? On the other hand, we can also regard divorce as the legal alternative to murder. In most cases.

It's better just to learn how to avoid arguments. Lots of time women ask questions guys should not answer honestly. My wife always asks me, "Honey, please tell me if my butt starts getting fat."

Yeah, right. I don't care if she's knocking lamps off the table, I'm saying, "You got a really nice butt there, Tundra, I swear you do."

When in public, women should also avoid pointing out other women to their men and asking, "Honey, do you think she's pretty?" She will not get the answer she's looking for. When Gregg does that I always say, "Lord no! Oh, I hate blondes with big firm breasts. I feel lunch coming up. I'm sick as a dog here."

We know better. You'd think she'd know better.

Do women really want men to be honest with them on subjects like their hair, clothes, butt, and women on the street? I don't know. But loyalty is a valued quality. For instance, I've never strayed on my wife. No sense in it for lots of good reasons, from my respect and love for Gregg to not wanting to suffocate suddenly in my sleep.

✻

If you're single and dating someone new, you have no idea if the sex game can be won easily or at all. Marriage is more complicated and becomes increasingly so the longer you're together. However, as a married man, your one advantage is knowing that you've won the game before and you've always got a chance to win it again.

Once, I was on the road and I read in *USA Today* that the problem with most men sexually is that they do not spend enough time with their women. We're too wham-bam-thank-you-ma'am, the story said, and women need more than that. Then, unlike most articles that just bash men and leave us to pick up the pieces, this one offered suggestions. Most prominent was to try giving your woman a hot oil massage that lasts an hour. Sounded great until I got to the part that said the whole idea was *never* to touch her in an intimate place. I could go *right up* to the place but I couldn't touch it until the time was up. According to the story, after an hour with the hot oil any woman would be a quivering volcano of passion, ready to erupt.

The night after I got home I told Gregg to just relax. I put the kids to bed. Then, in the privacy of our bedroom, I set up the frying pan and the Coleman stove right by the bed, and warmed up the oil. I put on a romantic CD. I think it was *Mating Dance of the Timberwolf.*

"We're going camping," I said. "You lay back, listen to the music, Daddy's home." Then I did the massage exactly according to instructions. Toes, feet, calves, thighs . . . hey, I'm not going to draw you a picture. Let's just call it all the semimagic spots. I also watched the clock, trying to time things just right. I didn't want to go over the hour mark because the magazine story warned not to try it for longer without supervision. When the hour turned, I looked down hopefully at Gregg. She had her head back and her mouth open. A little drool ran from the corner of her mouth down her cheek. She was fast asleep.

Suddenly the "don't wake me up" rule was in effect.

Damn.

I decided just that once to try and override it. I shook her gently and said, "Hon? You want to . . . ?"

"Oh, I feel too good to do it," she mumbled, somehow knowing what I had in mind even though I hadn't actually mentioned that I was a quivering volcano of passion, ready to erupt. "I couldn't do it. Ohhh, thank you so much. Ohhh, I'll just go to sleep."

She knew I wanted to do it and she just left me hanging.

Maybe she was just concerned about getting oil all over the bed. I didn't care if it was 10-W-40. Besides, I knew it wouldn't go through the paint-covered plastic tarp that I had strategically placed over the mattress. But I had to bite my tongue and not press my no-longer-ulterior motives. So I just put my good deed in the "bank" and said, "Just wanted to make you happy. Didn't care if we did it." Of course, the idea with banking is to be certain to let her know there's something on deposit. All the next day I hinted, "Did you enjoy that hot oil massage? You looked like you enjoyed it. Yeah, I did it for like an hour. Yeah, I could have been doing other things. I don't know, I just love you so much I wanted to do something to make you feel good."

Inside, I couldn't help but wonder how she could say no, particularly when she felt so wonderful. I've never said no to my wife. Actually, there *was* the time I had kidney surgery and was on intravenous morphine. She said I passed on sex—but being semiconscious, it's her word against mine.

One surefire way to tell if a woman feels romantic is if she suddenly starts cleaning the house. I like it when my wife wears the high heels and the little apron. Years ago a woman who liked me sent flowers to get me in a romantic mood. They were nice, but I told her that if she really wanted to push my thrill button she should wash my car.

If a woman wants romance, what might help turn on her man is a visit to the trashy lingerie shop. Or she can just leave her Victoria's Secret catalog lying around. Now, that's never been a big deal with me. I prefer a woman in a T-shirt, white panties, and old Levi's that really fit. I don't need garter belts, corsets, and fishnet stockings. I don't even fit in most garter belts, corsets, and fishnet stockings. I have to think about these things, since I sometimes play dress up when Gregg is out for the afternoon. What man wouldn't? I've just never gotten the hang of all those buttons and snaps.

But that doesn't mean I don't like looking at the pictures in free, home-delivered catalogs of women in their underwear. God bless America. Think about it: We never saw anything like that when we were growing up and needed it. All we ever got was the Sears catalog full of high-waisted granny panties. You could measure first downs with those. "Bring that bra in here, Pete, we gotta take a measurement. First down!"

But that underwear they make now, it's so skimpy that Victoria doesn't have a whole lot of secrets left, does she? You give a couple of guys one of those catalogs and they can entertain themselves all weekend.

"Oh my God, Mike, look at this. That's gotta hurt like hell right there. Just that string going right up your butt like that. Seems like every time you bowled it'd just cut you right in two."

I'll be honest with you: I'd rather look at the catalog than go in their stores. If you're a man, you always feel like a pervert when you're in Victoria's Secret. You do! You feel like the girls behind the counter have the sex offender directory and are just trying to find your picture.

"Sally, look at the guy with the panties on his head. That is the *same* guy." It's gotten so that just because I'm not really a pervert doesn't mean I can't act like one. So every time I go in among the panties and the teddies and the push-up bras, I pick up a body stocking, sashay to the counter, and go, "Where are your dressing rooms." They have to let you try it on. It's the law. Got one on right now, in fact. Little tight in the shoulders, makes it hard to reach all the keys on this keyboard, but it's not really too bad.

There's one question I've never been able to answer: What do women do in the bathroom that takes so long? My wife can be in there six hours, easy. Okay, forty-five minutes, but that's still a long time when there's no shower or bath involved. I go in, shave, brush my teeth, use the facilities, and I'm done in five to seven minutes, tops. The same goes for women and their closets. A man walks into his closet, sees a shirt he likes, smells the pit. Hey, it's okay, and we're out of there. A woman must spin a cocoon.

I suppose one clue to this mystery is a woman's purse. For all her talk of cleanliness, there is nothing a guy has—garage, junk room, fishing box, lint collection—that is more disorganized than a woman's purse. A purse is a dumpster with a shoulder strap. They put garbage in it. They put used Kleenex in there. They put in half-sticks of gum. They put pens that don't write back into the purse. (Buddy Hammond's mom has *ants* in her purse. Wonder why?) The typical purse bottom is so full of spare change it always sets off the metal detectors at airports but not the theft sensors at department stores. Normally having that much metal on one's person would mean a customer *must* be stealing something, but these are women selling to women. They know better.

If my wife dropped her keys in her purse, finding them would make the search for the Holy Grail look like an Easter egg hunt. She thinks she's protected because she's got a can of mace in the purse. That's like protecting your home by keeping a gun somewhere in the attic.

Not a guy in the world has a wallet as disorganized as a woman's purse. Men don't have purses because we'd always lose them, even if they were the size of cars.

*

As we know, men like things that women don't, like stuffed dead animals on the walls. You never see deer heads in beauty parlors. A sport, to women, is shopping. It really gets them worked up. Here's how I know: "multiple orgasm" and "mall opening" begin with the same letters. Prove it to yourself. Go find a mall under construction and see if at lunchtime there aren't women shouting at the builders to quit eating and get back to work.

Men hate to shop. I guarantee it. Just stop any man you can find and say, "Would you rather spend the whole day shopping for clothes or having exploratory rectal surgery?" Most men would answer quickly: "Now if I had the surgery, how long would I be out of work?"

✻

Clearly there's a world of difference between women and men. Even words mean different things.

When a woman says, "I'm almost ready," a man interprets that to mean "by the year 2000." If you're reading this and that year is already behind us, that still doesn't mean she's ready yet.

Women are always late.

Last year I played for the president at the White House. Sure enough, I looked at my watch, realized we were not ready, and yelled, "Gregg, we're going to be late to meet the president."

"Oh, my hair's not flipping right."

"Nobody will care. Nobody will *know*."

"I'll know. Where's my other earring?"

"This is the White House! Why couldn't this be the one day you were ready twenty minutes early! It's not against the law to sit in the hotel room and watch TV for twenty minutes before we leave."

"Now that I have it on, I don't like this dress."

"Change it."

"Or these shoes." And that's when she starts the flamingo posing, with different shoes on each foot.

"These or these?"

"Let me see it again."

"These or these?"

"Again."

You never see a man with a hunting boot on one foot and a tennis shoe on the other asking which looks better.

"These or these?"

"Let's see that again, Bob."

Sometimes it seems like my whole life with Gregg has been spent running out the door. The problem is that helping my wife get ready also makes me late.

"You got my tie?"

"Yeah, it's in my purse."

"Where's my pants?"

"I don't know. C'mon, c'mon, c'mon."

We always arrive fifteen minutes after everyone else does. Or fifteen minutes after closing time. I was afraid that by the time we got to the White House there'd be a new administration.

Some women in my family will probably be late for their own funerals. The chapel will be full and for some reason the bodies won't be prepped well enough, and we'll all be waiting on them again.

Part of the problem for most women is that they don't know how to calculate driving times. However long it takes to drive somewhere at midnight, with no traffic, going fast, and green lights all the way, is the time they figure it takes to get to the same destination at noon. The fact that it's bumper-to-bumper traffic doesn't come into play. It's still twelve, right? Numbers *look* the same, why shouldn't the driving time be the same? It should always take nineteen minutes to get across town.

Even if a woman can do the math, her *sense* of time is still screwed up. Time is pretty much whatever works for them. Gregg can talk to her mother on the phone for an hour and a half. But if I say, "You've been on the phone for an hour and a half," she'll go, "It's only been half an hour and besides, you talked to your brother last night for forty-five minutes!" Well, I talked to my brother for eleven, but it's not going to help my argument to say so.

Of course, when we're in bed, she goes the other way.

"That was only five minutes."

"No, honey, that was a half an hour."

"No, I looked when we started. It was 11:07, it's 11:12 now and you're finished and smoking."

"No, it was 10:31 when we started."

I suppose in the end, none of this really matters. All I know is that now that I'm married, I always realize right in the middle of sex, "Wow, this is really nice. How could I have forgotten?" This perception is even more intense when you have kids and you have to make an appointment to be intimate. No longer can I think, "Well, if it's not so good tonight, it will be different tomorrow."

Now tomorrow is next week.

So I work really hard at being good in the sack. I want everything to last. But then one of us will move the wrong way and it's over.

"Oh my, I'm sorry, I'm so sorry."

You know it was great sex when you end up apologizing.

*

Men and women. Husbands and wives. We need each other. Without my wife I wouldn't know what clothes I want to wear or what movies I want to see. I wouldn't have anyone to ask "Where are my socks?" Without me, my wife would have a hard time opening a jar of pickles. She'd also have to buy a bug zapper. "Get it, oooh! It's gross! Smash it, but don't kill it."

With any luck we eventually reach an understanding with each other that allows us to coexist. I don't flush the toilet while she's taking a shower, and she doesn't use the blender while I'm watching *Bass Fishing with Uncle Bullsheets*.

We've lived happily ever after.

The Patter of Little Hooves

A few years ago I became a father. A couple years later the miracle happened again. Now Gregg and I have two young daughters. I thought I knew what I was getting into—at least the second time—but you can't prepare for being a father any more than you can practice loading the entire contents of a four-bedroom house into the trunk of a Buick LeSabre. Believe me, I've tried.

❧

Before Gregg and I got married, she said, "If you want kids, I'm not the person you should marry." I'd wanted kids my whole life. But I was so crazy about her, I was willing not to have kids to be with her.

One morning six years later, Gregg heard a strange ticking. Actually not so strange. We'd had a wild night and she was sleeping on my wristwatch. But later at breakfast she suddenly said, "I want kids." As you can imagine, I was surprised, but Gregg said she was sure, so we immediately began to try—and I do mean immediately. For months nothing happened. So we tried and tried and tried some more. To be perfectly honest, at times I felt I was trying harder than she, but we still kept at it. It's a good thing God made "trying" so much fun.

One Sunday night about ten o'clock, my brother called and said, "Guess what? We're pregnant." We were very happy for Jay, and, naturally, a bit jealous. So that night we tried again. The next morning, right in the middle of making coffee for breakfast, Gregg suddenly said, "You know what? I'm pregnant."

I said, "Get outta here. We only tried last night." (I kicked myself under the table for not having asked her about insanity in the family years ago.)

She said, "I'm telling you, I'm pregnant."

Just to show her that neither my years spent carefully observing the mating habits of farm animals, nor our taxpayer dollars spent on health education in the public schools had been wasted on me, I put down the newspaper, threw on sweatpants, and ran three blocks down the street to the store. I bought two EPT's and came back. She took the test . . . and she was pregnant. She took it again. Same answer. I called my brother. "You're not going to believe this. We're pregnant, too. Yeah, it's great. Oh, listen, while I've got you on the phone, do you know how to get in touch with the people from the *Guinness Book of World Records*?"

After the doctor confirmed the home-test results, we told everyone in the family the good news. When Big Jim found out I was going to be a dad, he just laughed and said, "It's payback time for all the shit you used to do." He was right.

✽

Kids are exactly like marriage and sex in the sense that you can hear other people talk about it, but until you actually do it you have no idea. (Death is the other mystery, but as of now no one's come back to fill us in.) Instead of boring you with the usual heap of platitudes and parental commonsense that you can frankly find in many other books, I'll just pass along the simple advice I give most couples when they're pregnant with their first child.

Sleep.

Let me expand on that. Sleep around the clock. Come home from work and take a nap. Take a nap at work during your lunch hour. Sleep at stoplights and business meetings. Anything will work. You're stockpiling because you're never going to sleep the same or as well for the rest of your life.

&

To be totally prepared for childbirth, Gregg and I did what all beginner parents do: We took a Lamaze course. I don't know who this Lamaze character is, but the class was chock-full of wonderful tips and stories. One of my favorite moments occurred when the teacher told the group this very important information.

"Now, after your wife's water breaks, do not have sex."

I raised my hand. "Is this really a problem?" I asked. "Are there really men so insensitive?"

The look on her face told me the scary truth: She wouldn't have mentioned this unless someone had actually done it.

"So just how far apart are the contractions there, sweet thang? Seems like a shame to waste this semiprivate room."

⚓

It never really struck me that we were having a baby, despite nine months of vomiting and Gregg's stomach the size of Guatemala. I only realized it when the doctor held up my oldest daughter for me to see. (By then she was already two years old and I suddenly understood why everyone had been trying to get my attention.) Seriously, I didn't know that when babies were born they were blue, and that they didn't kick and scream. When I saw her she wasn't moving. I went from that "it hasn't really sunk in" feeling to the "somebody hit you in the stomach with a baseball bat" panic that something was wrong with my kid. The nurses took her over to the table and started working on her, and in a minute I heard "Wahhh."

Only a year after my daughter was born did I tell Gregg what had happened and how I'd felt, and then I just started crying.

✻

Everywhere I go people keep asking me if we videotaped our daughters' births. No, we did not. Got some nice footage of the conception, but nothing on the delivery. I mean, why would anybody want to film that? Because it's such a beautiful moment? I was there. Having a baby looks like a wet Saint Bernard trying to come in through a cat door. Do you really think I need a film to remember this? I think any guy who films his wife giving birth ought to return the favor by letting his wife film his hemorrhoid surgery later.

"Look girls, here's Tony fully dilated. What a trooper he was."

✻

I learned a lot about babies pretty quickly. For instance, babies are nauseated by the smell of a clean shirt. You put on something freshly laundered and they're gonna spit up just like that. My wardrobe looked like we had condors living in our yard. If you play with babies too hard, they'll spew like a can of beer. I used to shake up my daughter, then hand her to people I didn't like. "Hold her just a minute, would ya?"

I also learned that you have *got* to change those diapers every day. You do! When it says "six to twelve" pounds on the side of the Pampers box, they're not lying. That is all those things will hold.

Changing a diaper is a lot like opening a birthday present from your grandmother. You never know what's inside, but you're pretty sure you're not going to like it. Changing a diaper after your kid eats a box of Crayolas will stop you dead in your tracks. Looks like a souvenir from Jamaica.

Babies have taught me a few things about moms, too. Moms will clean up anything. I read recently in *Scientific American* that a mother's spit duplicates the exact chemical composition of Formula 409. It can get rust off a car bumper.

*

I love being a parent. It's weird, it's hard, you sacrifice decades of your life raising someone who, I guarantee you, will one day tell you that you didn't do a damn thing right, and move out in a huff. Next thing you see the kid on *Oprah* blaming you for everything from her mustache to wanting to sleep with his sister (the one with the mustache). I'm getting a little tired of that. Just once I want to see somebody go, "You know what? My daddy was great, my momma was great, I'm just a jerk." Just one time.

People have always told me that I'd learn more from my kids than they'd learn from me. I now believe that. I've learned that as a parent, when you have sex your body emits a hormone that drifts down the hall into your child's room and makes them want a drink of water. If you're extremely lucky they will call this order in, because there are few surprises in life to match looking your wife directly in the eye and feeling somebody tickle the bottom of your foot. So now every night we just bathe the little girls and put them in their nightgowns and their cowbells.

Our youngest child has discovered the little silver handle on the back of the toilet. She's making more stuff disappear than David Copperfield. My wife's lost three combs. I lost my good sunglasses. We're pretty sure she flushed the remote control because every time we go to the bathroom the TV comes on.

Once when I came home from work I discovered that somebody had colored on the dining room wall. My oldest daughter told me the dog did it. I about went crazy. We've had that dog eight years and *now* he starts coloring on the wall.

Between the youngsters and the animals the house just goes to hell. The rule around our place is: If it ain't broke, it ain't ours. They've destroyed everything. My wife has this little statue. It used to be a ballerina, now it just looks like the victim of a tragic farming accident. We have a sofa, but if you sit on it in the wrong place you can't have kids.

Babies today come with technology. Anybody with a baby has a monitor, which for those of you without kids (and who swear after reading this that you will always be without kids), it's like a one-way walkie-talkie that allows you to listen in on them. You have to be real careful to put the right end of this thing in the right bedroom. We realized we'd made that mistake when we didn't hear our daughter cry for five months and her first words were, "Oh yeah baby, just like that, that's really good, that's good . . ."

Anybody with kids knows I'm lying now. When you're young and you've got a choice between sleep or sex, you take sex every time. When you start getting older and you've got a choice between sleep and sex, you take the sleep and just hope you have a dream about sex.

All parents think their kids are the smartest kids ever born. My mom thought my daughter was a genius because she would lie on the floor and talk to the ceiling fan. I said, "Mom, Uncle Harold does that and y'all call him an alcoholic."

It's not that I don't think my daughters are bright. Even if they *are* my kids. (Gregg's got strong genes.) It's just embarrassing to say so out loud because then I sound like every other parent. Who takes these parents seriously anymore? When's the last time you visited someone with little kids who said, "Hey, come in here and look at little Tommy. He is as dumb as a brick, boy. Turn on the light. He won't even know. Turn the light on. He'll just sit there all day long, cross-eyed and drooling."

I have a cousin who thinks her oldest child is going to be the next Einstein because this kid stands out in the yard and goes, "Air'pane. Air-'pane."

I finally took her aside and told her. "Listen. He's fourteen years old! It's time to reel it in. I don't want to break your heart, but he's got a job with deep fat frying in his future." I think I may have whispered too loud because a couple of my relatives suddenly said, "Wait a damn minute here."

One thing I *will* brag about is how cute my daughters are. Intelligence is ephemeral, but pictures don't lie. (If you believe that, please put this book on your nightstand next to the copy of *Eleanor Roosevelt: The Supermodel Years*.) I am glad my daughters are comely because frankly I worried about that. Can you think of anything worse than people who have ugly kids? Gregg and I call those unfortunate children "Hi babies" because when you meet a kid so ugly that you can't say anything nice to its parents you say, "Hi, baby."

Parents with "Hi babies" are also always the first ones to whip out their snapshots and shove them in your face. This annoys me so much that when I worked at IBM I got this baby picture that was actually a composite of the ugliest features of forty questionable looking infants. The result was fairly horrible. Whenever guys would start pulling out pictures of their kids, I would dead-serious take out my composite snapshot and go, "That's my son." I just wanted to watch their faces. This "baby" had crossed-eyes, huge ears that didn't match, one eyebrow, one tooth that was directly in the middle, and huge nostrils. People were afraid to say, "That is not your kid," because it might have been. So they'd try to say something nice, and go, "What a cute outfit."

＊

When our oldest child learned to walk we finally had to babyproof the house. You've all heard of this, right? You have to put latches on your drawers and cabinets so your children can't hurt themselves. We don't want them taking knives out of the silverware drawer and playing Ed Ames on the *Tonight Show* anniversary reel.

I remember when I was a kid, my parents had a 900-pound television on top of a TV tray. The Eiffel Tower standing on its point was safer. But my dad's theory was "Let him pull it on his head a few times, he'll learn." He had a similar attitude about sticking metal objects in electrical outlets. "Oh, you want to put a penny in the light socket? Sure. Try that out. Oh, hurt like hell, didn't it? Don't do that no more."

＊

Raising kids is the hardest job in the world. It's a lot like that military commercial: "We do more before 9 A.M. than most people do all day." That's our household. Now we look back and realize why we suddenly stopped seeing our friends who'd had kids. We thought we'd done something wrong. The truth was, they'd moved on. They had a responsibility that could not be ignored or even postponed. You can change jobs and spouses and houses, but you can't change your kids.

I read in the newspaper about someone who got in trouble for trying to lose his kids in a mall. Obviously he didn't know that the law only allows you to do that with your wife.

Now that we're parents we are on the other end of the equation. We used to have single friends, but not anymore. We miss them, but we understand that single people don't want to sit around and hear our conversations about birthday parties, car pools, and the preschool staff. My single guy friends are interested in *dating* the cute kindergarten teacher. The dads I know just want her to watch their kids so they can take a nap. Single people want to talk about things other than tinkle and poo-poo and pee-pee. We college-educated parents would also like that, but you'd be amazed at how "doody" has become a sizable part of our vocabulary.

As our kids grow, they've also adopted *our* terminology. Gregg and I have a code phrase for having to go to the bathroom. "I'm going to

go check the mildew on the shower curtain."
Recently our four-year-old walked into our
bedroom and said, "Mom, I think I'm gonna go
check the mildew."

Gregg said, "Where did she get that from?"

I just looked at her and said, "Where do you
think?"

Gregg did a double take then said, "Oh she's
so smart." Just like a parent.

*

Sometimes when I help around the house
Gregg really appreciates it. Not only will she
shower me with praise but she'll tell her girlfriends.

"Oh, he fed the girls dinner and he's bathing
them now."

"He bathes the girls?!"

"Oh yeah, he bathes them every night."

Unfortunately, those friends then tell their
husbands.

"Robert, do you know that Jeff bathes their
kids every night?"

Soon I'm getting angry calls giving me a
hard time for making the guys' lives miserable.

"Thanks a lot, you sonofabitch. I got railed
on for a week because you bathe your kids."

*

All my oldest daughter wants to do from the moment she gets up is play. I wish she'd learn to tell time already so she wouldn't wake me up so early to play with her. But that said, all I really want for her is to enjoy this time of life since it's the *only* time she'll get to play so freely. What would be nice is if life worked the other way around. When we retire we should all get to sit on the floor and play, and not just in senior homes.

As a dad, I'm a pretty good playmate considering that I get tired after about twenty minutes of fooling around with Legos or my daughter's Pocket Puppies. I don't mean to complain. Playing with those is actually easier than trying to keep up with a kid's imagination. Plus, my scenarios are always a little more gross than Gregg's.

"Oh, Winnie the Pooh ate too much honey. Bluh, he vomited all over Tigger!"

Gregg will roll her eyes, but my daughter loves it.

She is an interesting child. She likes accident stories.

When I put her to bed at night I normally say, "We're going to read a couple of stories." Her eyes light up and she says, "Then we'll tell accidents?"

"Okay."

"Dad, tell me a frog accident."

Then I have to make up a bad accident that happens to a frog. "Frog went out to play; he was jumping, chasing a butterfly, and he bumped his head against the tree."

"No, Daddy, it's got to be a better accident than that."

Then I have to come up with something involving stitches or a cast or dismemberment. Frog parts winding up in a French restaurant is always good, although there should be a happy ending, if possible, like "and he tasted very much like chicken." I've now struck a deal with her that she's got to tell me one accident story for every one I tell her. She's getting pretty good at it.

"Okay, Daddy, the bird was flying in the air and he ran into a giraffe, and his beak poked the giraffe in the eye and the giraffe had to go to the hospital. They put a patch on it and they thought he was going to be blind. But after a few weeks the rhinoceros doctor took the patch off and the giraffe could see, and his mother was so happy."

Just to keep this from being a totally bizarre and sick experience that is guaranteed to make her need therapy, Gregg and I use the stories to teach her important lessons like not going into the street.

"Dad, tell me a rabbit accident."

"There was a rabbit named Donny. One day he wanted to go play with his friend across the street, but Donny didn't always mind his mother and daddy and he didn't stop, look, and listen. Donny hopped into the street and just then a big truck ran over him and crushed his legs. The bones were sticking out."

Just trying to get my point across.

We have a doctor friend who visited recently and she loved the accident stories so much that she actually wrote a kids' book. My daughter described the accidents and our friend Jane wrote them down and did illustrations.

"Okay, there were two cows and one's name was Yakky and the other one's name was Shoe-new. Shoe-new was not a nice cow and would stab Yakky in the stomach with his horn. One day Yakky died and Shoe-new was so mean, he died too." We always try to include a moral to the story. For instance, "Never stab your friends in the stomach with your horns."

We now have a book full of accident stories that the insurance companies would love to get their hands on. We're saving this for when she grows up. It will also come in handy as a discipline tool should she turn out to be a difficult teen.

"You'd better straighten up, young lady, because we've got all we need *right here in this book* to send you away to a girls' school for the rest of your life!"

*

A kid's job is to drive his parents crazy.

I like to think of my childhood as a job well done.

My mom was always "having a nervous breakdown." Sometimes she'd say we were giving her a brain tumor. Seems like she's had one since we were four. We think the tumor is mobile. Sometimes it's on the left side of the head, sometimes it's on the back. I just thank God that in thirty-three years it's never become fatal.

Too bad Carole was never much good at discipline. She couldn't hurt you when she whipped you. She would *think* she hurt you, but we never really felt it. That's when I first learned how to act.

"Oh God, Mother, stop. Oh, oh, I'm just about to pass out."

"You are not."

"Then I will surely bleed from these welts."

It was all I could do not to laugh. Whether she used her hand, a belt, or a switch, she didn't have it in her heart to spank hard. I remember one time she whipped me and my sister, Jenny. Afterward we started up the stairs and broke into laughter. My dad heard it and told us to come back down. Nobody laughed the next time up the stairs. Big Jim could wear out your ass. He was like a gunslinger. He could do that Magic Dad thing, where he'd hold his hands at his side, reach, unbuckle his belt, pull it off and have it doubled over in one hand in less than two seconds.

Nowadays you can't spank your children in front of other people, which is why my wife and I stay home all the time. Seriously, I guess they have to implement these rules for the people who go overboard. We have to be concerned. But I certainly don't think a swat scarred me. Look at how normal I am! Most of us grew up with corporal punishment. Now it's a time-out. You go sit in your room with the door closed. Tough life. That's what I *wanted* to do.

"Oh darn, I've got to go sit in my room for five minutes. Maybe I better check out these toys. They look lonely."

Don't get me wrong. I'd rather not whack the kid on the bottom. Only once. Lightly. As if a gentle breeze were wafting by. When I have to, I feel bad about it. Our parents were right: It hurts them more than it hurt us. My fingers *always* sting for a few minutes.

Kids think nothing of manipulating their parents. It's just another line in their job description. When I put my daughter to bed I tell her we're going to read two books. As we start on the second she will say, "You know, Daddy, I love you soooooo much. Can we read *three* books tonight?"

"All right, three books."

Three hours later I've got on my heavy coat and I'm just coming back from the public library.

If there are two parents present, the kid will play them off each other. They figure out which parent they're most in trouble with and then they cozy up to the other. Of course, as a parent you've got to take advantage of that love whether it's real or not.

"Damn right your mother's crazy. It's you and me, honey."

When a child wants something their most effective tool is whining. I don't know a parent who would not take a million dollars for their four-year-old after a trip down the cereal aisle at the supermarket. It's like running the gauntlet: shooting the rapids and squealing like a pig. What's worse is that by four they already know all the cereal brands—especially the sugared varieties—as well as the jingle tunes. If only they'd one day pay that much attention to their homework.

Kids whine when they don't get something they want.

"Can I have a Popsicle?"

"No, it's before dinner."

"Wahhh . . ."

You get so sick so quick that you give in. You're not supposed to, but they wear you down. It's like basic training.

I think adults should employ this technique more often. Why give it up just because you've left childhood behind?

"You know, John, I only like you as a friend."

"Wahhh . . . I don't want you to like me as a friend, I want you to sleep with me one time . . ."

"But . . ."

"Wahhh."

"Okay. All right. Once! One time I'll sleep with you."

*

All new parents eventually realize that they are just like their own parents, only, they hope, different. All those things that we swore when we were thirteen years old that we were never going to say to our children, just blurt from our mouths. Then we look in the mirror and think, "Oh my God, I just said 'Because I said so.' I can't believe I said that."

But I also found that as soon as I had kids, I appreciated my own parents a lot more. I started calling my mom and dad regularly. Suddenly I understood the sacrifices they had made. Not only financially, but timewise. Just between wiping my butt and my nose and changing my clothes, they spent a lot of man/woman hours getting me grown.

*

The number one parent complaint in the world is "I never have any time for myself." Why is this? Simple. All our lives we've been given bad information. Since we were five years old, we've been told, "Don't act like a baby. Don't act like a kid." I think if you *would* act like a kid you could have a lot of time to yourself. Say you're introduced to somebody you've never met before. Act like a kid. Put your finger in your nose. You never have to worry about this person calling you, writing to you, or wanting to spend time with you again. Go to somebody's house and jump on the bed. He'll never invite you back. Tell your boss you can't work and that you're scared because there's a monster in the break room. You're going to have plenty of time for yourself until your unemployment runs out.

❋

Before we were married, Gregg and I used to sit around in the morning and read the paper over breakfast. Before we had kids, I loved it when Gregg could come back to bed in the morning after feeding the pets, and it was playtime. Now I love it when my wife gets up with the baby and lets me sleep.

Kids change everything. Now when we drive down the street and Gregg sees a billboard with a woman wearing a bikini, she will say, "Honey, I used to look like that before I had kids."

So I will say, "That's *why* you had kids, honey."

Women are never happy with their bodies afterward. Men should probably have kids because we don't care about how we look the same way women do. Stretch marks on our butts? We never *look* at our butts. There's not a guy in the world who looks at his posterior—or will admit it. I just assume it's there because my pants haven't fallen down.

I learned something about men's butts when my wife sent my brother and me to the Atlanta Braves Fantasy Camp for Christmas, where guys get to live out their major league dream and play with the real players. It cost $3,500, and you have to be at least thirty to go. Most of the guys were doctors and lawyers. Most were also between fifty and sixty years old. At the end of the week one of the Braves asked me "Did you learn anything?"

I said, "Yes, I did. I have learned there is nothing uglier than an old man's ass." Looks like somebody hung a bean bag chair over a clothesline. I suppose this is inevitable. Unlike our wives', our butts don't get fat. The bottom half just disappears. It's like an alien ass. I've never seen an alien ass, but I'm assuming that's what one would look like. You can't look at one and not shudder, I know that for a fact. When I walked through that locker room, every BA I'd ever flashed came back to haunt me. The only thing worse that I've ever seen was my grand-mother naked. Purely by accident. I will re-member that vision until the day I die. Weeks later I'd still get full-body shivers. Nothing was in the right place. She looked like a bloodhound in a shower cap. I thought about it for a while and I decided it was God getting even with me for all the times in my life I tried to see women naked.

"Hey, Jeff, you want to see naked women? Huh? Here's your grandma!"

The hardest part of Fantasy Camp was accepting how out of shape we were. Guys could still hit. Some could still throw a little bit. But nobody could run any more. You hit it to the wall and it'd be a bang-bang play at first. When I was seventeen my fantasy involved two red-heads and a gallon of Cool Whip. When I first arrived at camp, my fantasy was to hit a triple. After four days my fantasy was to put my socks on by myself. Everybody was so sore. After two days the hotel sounded like a brothel. I'd walk down the hall and hear guys in their rooms going, "Ooo. OOO. OOOOO."

"Hey, you got a girl in there?"

"No, I'm just taking my shirt off. Now I'm brushing my teeth."

❧

Onstage I talk about my vasectomy. This is not something I just invented to be funny, although sometimes I wish it were.

Before I got the procedure, I had to get counseling. The doctors think it's a good idea. They want to make sure you know what you're doing. Somehow, I don't think dropping your pants for some guy with a razor is an impulse decision.

I didn't really want to do it. Like all guys I thought, "What if I want to have another family? You might call that a tradition with the Foxworthys. Or what if Gregg got hit by a bus tomorrow? Then I'd need to marry a gorgeous twenty-year-old and start all over again. Or I might get really adventurous and become one of those weird guys who have whole families in different towns and manage to split their time between both by telling their wives they are traveling for business.

"Gonna be on the road for half our married life, if it's okay with you, dear."

Of course, the idea of my vasectomy didn't bother Gregg a bit. After two difficult pregnancies, she was all for it. She was properly sympathetic about what I was about to endure, but not about my other fears because the doctors had assured me that in most cases the procedure was reversible. Yeah right. All I need is to be forty-nine and have Gregg suddenly say, "I need another baby," and not be able to answer the call.

Now that it's a done deal, a friend told me that the only way to handle the dark wellspring of this mortifying trauma that still haunts me is to share my experience.

"Talk about it," she said, "One day you'll get over it." So I use it in my act. It's painful, but not as painful as listening to other men tell me stories that make me want to live in a deer stand for the rest of my life.

Here it is. You lie on a cold, stainless steel table. You're not wearing pants. Right where you can see it—whose sick idea is that?—is a tray with a razor, a hook, a soldering iron, and two large syringes. My brother-in-law, Richard, told me that when he got his cords cut, they used the soldering iron and discovered it wasn't grounded.

The words "torture implements" and "no pants" don't even belong in the same sentence. When I asked a friend about his vasectomy, he only got as far as the word "razor" before I felt a sudden pain in my package. I looked down and realized I had crossed and squeezed my legs together tighter than a torqued bolt. You could hold a million dollars in front of a guy and say, "I'll give you all the money if you can just sit with both feet on the floor and listen to how it's done," and you'd never lose a penny. It's just not possible. Even after the operation is complete and you've healed, reached retirement age, and started collecting Social Security, you're never over the terror.

The anesthetic is local, though it seemed long distance to me. I got a shot in both sides of my scrotum to numb it. (The memory is so painful that it took me ten minutes just to type out the preceding sentence.) Meanwhile, I tried to make small talk with a doctor who reminded me of Buddy Hammond making his mom a change purse, while he kept talking about country music.

"Hey, you know who I really like?"

"Somebody with a high voice, I assume."

I didn't really feel the first shot. The second hit a nerve. That hurt so much that when I got home I couldn't even use the remote control. Then my equipment went into hiding. I had to stick my finger up my butt and holler "Snake!" just to pee.

The operation is also embarrassing. For some reason, there's a nurse in the room. I kept hoping she wouldn't look at me. There is better-looking plumbing in the newborn room at the hospital.

The preop instructions say you have to bring a jockstrap with you. When you're done, they pack the front full of gauze. I looked like Tom Jones in concert. Walking from the doctor's office to the car, I got invited to three proms.

"Leave me alone, my wife's waiting on me."

While recovering I actually wanted to call

people and get them to look at my bruises of many colors. No body part has ever been these colors before: yellow, green, mauve, taupe, black, purple. But don't try to get any sympathy from your buddies. They always say, "Oh, it doesn't really hurt." They're lying. But pretty soon you're telling the same lie. The reason is that if you were dumb enough to fall for the whole deal, you want to get somebody else to fall for it.

The good thing was that when the pain *really* went away I felt like a sixteen-year-old. For the first time in my sexual life I didn't have to worry about getting somebody pregnant. When my wife said, "The baby's taking a nap," I said, "Hey, the baby's taking a nap! Perhaps you and I should take a nap."

"Get away from me with that thing."

Damn. Got a new one and can't even use it.

⚲

Of course, there's a good reason to endure such embarrassment and pain. The alternatives are worse. I'm not talking about unwanted children. You always want them. But other preventive methods make spontaneity fly out the window. IUD's are a hassle. The pill causes some women to vomit pea soup, like Linda

Blair in *The Exorcist*. I've got no problem with women hurling, but I hate it when the bed levitates halfway to the ceiling.

Contraceptive foam is the pits. That stuff is almost as effective as the pill yet it contains no ingredient that actually prevents pregnancy. The way it works is this: When you're finished making love and you go to pee, it burns so bloody awfully that you feel like the star client at your local VD clinic. I felt as if I were engulfed in flames. Suddenly I didn't want to have sex for another six months. When you only do it twice a year, the chance of conception is very low.

Six weeks after the vasectomy operation you're supposed to take in a sample to the doctor. Then wait four months and take another. They give you two little cups to use. Someone knowing what you're *really* doing in the bathroom takes all the thrill away. It's humiliating, taking the cup into the doctor's office and announcing to a full waiting room, "Hey, here's my sperm sample." I suppose it could have been worse. I might have had to do it in a little room at the doctor's. How much time is appropriate to spend summoning the sample? If you're back in forty seconds, they'll talk about you. If you're gone an hour, they'll talk about you. Maybe I should have stayed an hour and then when I came out, said, "Sorry, the first four weren't perfect, so I threw them away."

❧

I don't feel that terrible about not having more kids. I used to want a son, bad, but it might be tough being my son. I'd relive all my sports fantasies and make his life miserable. I'd want him to be a football star and I'm afraid that at halftime, when all the other dads go to get hot chocolate, I'd be saying, "Sorry, fellas, I've got to stay. Eugene's got a baton solo tonight."

I worry about my daughters, too. I spent the first half of my life trying to get into girls' knickers and I'm going to spend the rest of my life trying to keep other guys out of theirs.

Hey, cut it out. This is no laughing matter.

When Cousins Marry

I believe in the family. I've always told stories about my relations and even used them as the inspiration for a Redneck joke or two . . . hundred. Without their example to draw on I might still be doing stand-up over

Kroger's intercom and checking stock in the backroom between "sets."

I'm feeling kind of grateful and spiritual now, so I'd like to share with you what family means to me.

Your family is a pack of idiots whom you have to love. We exist on earth to love each other, and our family is the test. Family is different from friends. You can pick your friends. It's easy to love your friends, *because* you pick them. But with family, God just sorts through the whole pile of souls and says, "This one will hate this one—okay, they're brothers. This one will drive everyone crazy—she'll be the aunt." You just get stuck with these people, and most of them are nuts. You let family get away with behavior you wouldn't put up with from your closest friends, let alone strangers. You love your family and hate them, fight with and fight for them. But in the end they're all you've got.

There are no secrets in my family. It's not that we don't try to keep them, it's just that my kin are the biggest bunch of blabbermouths in the world. To say, "Don't tell anybody I told you this," is to waste your breath. You might as well rent the Goodyear blimp and advertise.

"Don't tell anybody I told you this, but the girl Cousin Jerry's dating is four months' pregnant." Before the sun has set, some relative from Alaska will call and say, "We hear Jerry's dating a girl with a hunchback and three six-year-olds."

In my family they don't even try to get it right.

❦

The family reunion is your annual reminder about how weird your relations really are. Uncle Leonard has a bumper sticker on his bowling ball and is still upset that *Gunsmoke* was canceled. Aunt Ida is the state's only female Elvis impersonator. Cousin Joanie's talent in the local beauty pageant was making noises with her armpit. Her brother, Bradley, can eat a McDonald's double cheeseburger in one bite. And what about Grandma, who starts every day by asking, "Anyone seen my teeth?" The notion that these people swim in the same gene pool as you is enough to make you quit dating your second cousin and stop calling your van the "Love Machine."

On the other hand, some people look forward to family reunions, especially those who hope they will get to go after the parole board finally meets.

My maternal grandmother's family, the Sheats, always holds their reunions at a campground on the south side of Atlanta. When I was a kid, everyone wore their Sunday best. The adults sang church songs while the kids played football. We'd always tear something, but the beating was still worth not having to sing.

My grandfather Camp's family was also big on reunions, but that was because they all lived to be over a hundred years old. By then these folks didn't have much to look forward to *but* the reunion and that time of day when the prunes kicked in. Fortunately they were funny people, though considering their advanced age and their digestive systems, they had to be very careful how hard they laughed.

The Foxworthy clan didn't get together very often for reunions because our gatherings always ended in fights. Once we had all the relatives come down to Big Jim's farm for the weekend. For a while things went well. Then we decided to go to a hayfield for a family softball game. This game included a couple of cousins, Ben and Richard, that Big Jim had never much liked. In the middle of the third inning my brother, Jay, slid into second base and Cousin Ben tagged him too hard, I guess. Big Jim was up next. When he got to second base, he threw a big hairy forearm at Ben. Next thing, everyone was brawling in the middle of the baseball diamond. Somehow I'm certain that God looked down on that spectacle and thought, "Why did I give these people the ability to reproduce?"

It would take four or five years just for hurt feelings to heal enough so that everyone could talk again. Suddenly the attitude would be, "Come on, come on, live and let live. Let bygones be bygones. They're family!" Then we'd have another reunion and there'd be another fight.

Occasionally the Foxworthy side and the Sheats/Camp side would meet, mostly at weddings. Unfortunately, the spirit of love was usually confined to the lucky couple, since Carole's family didn't much care for Big Jim, for obvious reasons. However, Big Jim and my grandfather James Camp still fished together all the time. They'd leave at five in the morning, after my granddaddy had already worked a full shift. My dad said he learned how to drive when he was tired on those trips. My granddaddy's method was to pick something really far down the road, like a telephone pole, and then just sleep until he got to it. I remember riding to the farm with Big Jim and desperately trying to make small talk because I knew that otherwise he'd fall asleep. He hit a deer once. We were going about eighty. The impact woke him up, the car spun a 360 but managed to stay on the road. Unfortunately, the collision destroyed all the meat and we were really disappointed. I mean, what's a car bumper worth when you're talking about dinner for twelve?

There were some interesting people in Big Jim's mother's family, the Abstances. The one I remember most was Uncle Joe, a preacher. At one reunion, when I was in high school, I had already started to do imitations, like of the Reverend Billy Graham. At the gathering my brother kept saying, "Hey, do Billy Graham!"

It went something like this: "Well *you* know, people ask me, 'Billy, is premarital sex bad?' and I would say, 'Pray about it—no, wait, I tell you, premarital sex does not *have* to be bad. It all depends on who . . . you . . .' "

That's when Uncle Joe threw a glass of tea in my face. I stopped the imitation right then and there—until Uncle Joe left, and then I did it some more.

*

One of my favorite family members was Uncle Sid. He could always make me laugh. Uncle Sid was funny not only in life but also in death. He passed away at the ripe old age of ninety-two. When I went to pay my final respects, I found Uncle Sid lying in his coffin, decked out in his best blue suit. He had a button on his lapel that read, "Who farted?"

A funeral is really a family reunion minus one.

I may have a family of crazies, but there's also a select handful who don't include themselves in the seriously afflicted group. We intentionally do stupid stuff with a wink to each other. We're just kidding. The rest of them *really* need help.

For instance, my brother and I have a tradition. All our lives we have told each other what we're getting the other for Christmas the minute we buy it. My brother will come home from the mall and call me, and say, "You want to know what I'm getting you for Christmas?"

"Yeah."

"I got you a sweatshirt."

"Yeah? What kind?"

"Florida State."

"Oh, cool. What color?"

"Maroon. What'd you get me?"

"Oh, blah blah blah."

Then, when the family gets together to open the Christmas presents, my brother will hand me mine and go, "Here's your gift, Jeff, from me." Then he'll pause and say, "If you could have anything in the whole world, what would it be?"

I'll say, "God, anything in the whole world? You know what I'd really love? I'd love a sweatshirt."

"What kind of sweatshirt?"

"A Florida State sweatshirt."

"What color?"

"Maroon."

This is usually when someone in the family finally remembers what we do and says, "Dammit, you boys are doing it again."

❦

The family's covered dish Christmas party was always potluck. Everyone made something at home that they were especially proud of and brought it in a casserole dish. After some of the reactions these concoctions got as they were passed around the dinner table, I've wondered why the cooks remain so fond of their creations. My mother can't go anywhere without making a congealed salad. It's as if a bowl of Jell-O hit a can of Del Monte Fruit Cocktail at eighty miles an hour, then sat out on the roadside for a week. Adults will eat this stuff, but the kids just spend all their time picking out the fruit. One of my aunts cooks the green beans covered with "something." You scrape off the "something," save it to grease your car, and eat the beans.

＊

I always looked forward to seeing my uncle Jimmy at the party. He was a real character.

About fifteen years ago he was shopping in one of those warehouse outlet suit stores and found the ugliest suit of all time. It was double knit, with huge lapels and giant bell bottoms, and all in bright red with black-and-white checks.

The suit was on sale, of course, and Jimmy, sensing a bargain, bought it. Jimmy's a big man; probably six four, 250 pounds. For somebody that large to wear something that awful just made the sight of him walking down the street even more horrible. Still, one of the major attractions each year at the Christmas party was to see if Uncle Jimmy would wear his suit.

About four or five years ago the party was at Uncle Jimmy's house. When we arrived, he answered the door. He wore the suit jacket, but not the pants. I bummed out on the spot. All I could say was, "Jimmy, what happened to the pants?"

"I had to stop wearing them," he said.

"Are they damaged?"

"Nope."

"Then why?"

"They went out of style."

I've got a bet with my brother that the jacket won't go out of style before the pants come back in.

✳

The most fun I've ever had at a covered dish Christmas dinner was when I followed my aunt Dolores around and watched her work her special magic with an item called "fake vomit." This gag played best if associated with a recipe someone always bragged about. It wasn't the fake vomit that was particularly funny. In fact, it was disgusting in a latex sort of way. The best moments were Aunt Dolores' wonderful sound effects and profuse apologies. I laughed so hard I was afraid I'd soil my undergarments. Every time I heard her proclaim, "It must have been that long car ride, that's all I can think of," I would snort like a pig and have to run out of the room. What amazed me even more than Aunt Dolores' thespian talents was that the trick worked year after year after year. I guess people just don't file vomit in the long term memory column.

✿

The holidays are a time for giving and sharing; it's a time when love is in the air. Literally.

As a joke, my brother used to hang a pair of panty hose over his fireplace before Christmas. He said that all he wanted was for Santa to fill them. What they say about Santa checking the list twice must be true because every Christmas morning, although Jay's kids' stockings overflowed, his poor panty hose hung sadly empty and grew increasingly threadbare.

One year I decided to make his dream come true. I put on sunglasses and a fake beard and went in search of an inflatable love doll. Of course, they don't sell those things at Wal-Mart. I had to go to an adult bookstore downtown. If you've never been in an X-rated store, don't go. You'll only confuse yourself. I was there almost three hours saying things like, "What does that do?" "You're kidding me!" "Who owns that?" "Do you have their phone number?"

Finally, I made it to the inflatable doll section. I wanted to buy a standard, uncomplicated doll suitable for a night of romance that could also substitute as a passenger in my truck so I could use the car pool lane during rush hour. I'm not sure what a complicated doll is. Perhaps one that is subject to wild mood shifts and using a French accent for no reason at all. (That also describes a few ex-girlfriends.) Finding what I wanted was difficult. Love dolls come in many different models. The top of the line, according to the side of the box, could do things I'd only seen in a book on animal husbandry. I figured the "vibro-motion" was a feature Jay could live without, so I settled on Lovable Louise. She was at the bottom of the price scale. To call Louise a "doll" took a huge leap of imagination.

On Christmas Eve, with the help of an old bicycle pump, Louise came to life. My sister-in-law was in on the plan and cleverly left the front door key hidden under the mat. In the wee morning hours, long after Santa had come and gone, I snuck into the house and filled the dangling panty hose with Louise's pliant legs and bottom. I also ate some cookies and drank what remained of a glass of milk on a nearby tray. Then I let myself out, went home, and giggled for a couple of hours.

The next morning my brother called to say that Santa had been to his house and left a present that had made *him* very happy but had left the dog confused. He would bark, start to walk away, then come back and bark some more. I suggested he purchase an inflatable Lassie to set Rover straight. We also agreed that Louise should remain in her panty hose so the rest of the family could admire her when they came over for the traditional Christmas dinner. It seemed like a great idea, except that we forgot that Grandma and Grandpa would be there.

My grandmother noticed Louise the moment she walked in the door. "What the hell is that?" she asked. My brother quickly explained.

"It's a doll."

"Who would play with something like that?" Granny snapped. I had several candidates in mind, but I kept my mouth shut. "Where are her clothes?" Granny continued. I hadn't seen any in the box, but I kept this information to myself.

"Boy, that turkey sure smells nice, Gran," Jay said, trying to steer her into the dining room. But Granny was relentless.

"Why doesn't she have any teeth?"

Again, I could have answered, but why would I? It was Christmas and no one wanted to ride in the back of the ambulance saying, "Hang on Granny, Hang on!"

My grandfather, a delightful old man with

poor eyesight, sidled up to me and said, "Hey, who's the naked gal by the fireplace?" I told him she was Jay's friend. A few minutes later I noticed Grandpa by the mantel, talking to Louise. Not just talking, but actually flirting. Sadly, he thought he was doing well. It was then that we realized this might be Grandpa's last Christmas at home.

The big dinner went well. We made the usual small talk about who had died, who was dying, and who should be killed, when suddenly Louise made a noise that sounded a lot like my father in the bathroom in the morning. Then she lurched from the panty hose, flew around the room twice, and fell in a heap in front of the sofa. The cat screamed, I passed cranberry sauce through my nose, and Grandpa ran across the room, fell to his knees, and began administering mouth to mouth resuscitation. My brother wet his pants and Granny threw down her napkin, stomped out of the room, and sat in the car. It was indeed a Christmas to treasure and remember.

Later in my brother's garage, we conducted a thorough examination to decide the cause of Louise's collapse. We discovered that Louise had suffered from a hot ember to the back of her right thigh. Fortunately, thanks to a wonder drug called duct tape we restored her to perfect health. Louise went on to star in several bachelor party movies. I think Grandpa still calls her whenever he can get out of the house.

✤

Thanksgiving is also a magical day. One reason is that in my family we get to try out the same food we'll eat a month later at the covered dish Christmas party. Another is that we get a pretty good idea of how much antacid we should stock up on.

Thanksgiving is the way in which families spread hundreds of miles apart can be united. We share an afternoon and a bountiful meal, and soon enough hours have passed to remind us why we moved so far apart from each other in the first place. Then we all pile into our minivans and head back to our respective castles. The drive home is a wonderful opportunity to reflect with our spouses about who looked fat and how out of control their children were. We should stop to think about how wrong it is to judge others, but we don't, especially when we realize how quickly this conversation makes the drive fly by.

Being grateful on Thanksgiving isn't limited

to only that year's blessings. It's okay to give thanks for how lucky you are on Thanksgiving itself. For example, you can give thanks:

• For healthy, new babies and new in-laws (some prayers are more sincere than others).

• That you didn't have to sit across the table from Uncle Lou again, a man who loves to talk, yet doesn't like to wear his false teeth.

• That your home football team didn't play on Turkey Day, so you don't have to feel bad about sleeping through the second half.

• That your grandmother told the story about the time she went to church in two different colored shoes only fourteen times.

• That your cousin Mark didn't ask you for a job again this year.

• That Uncle Bob washed his kids instead of his car for a change.

• That Aunt Dorothy brought cake instead of that crappy dressing of which she's so proud.

• That Uncle Tom finally got his hearing aid repaired.

• That Uncle Tom's hearing aid batteries went dead just when you called him a no count *%$#*.

• That your cousin's new wife didn't wear a bra.

• That Grandpa hit your brother's car instead of yours.

• That to Uncle Frank, whom you see only at this time of year, you still don't have to say anything more than "Can you move your car so I can get out."

• That your mom finally got the dishwasher repaired and has stopped using the dog in its place.

• That your dad's video camera broke early in the day, so you didn't have do that stupid "smile and wave" all afternoon.

• That this year dinner was at your brother's house instead of Aunt Jessie's, which always smells like a combination of mildew and cold cream.

• That Cousin Doug for once couldn't make it. His habit of staring and licking his lips makes everyone uncomfortable.

• That on the first Thanksgiving the Pilgrims chose turkey instead of Spam.

• That today's dinner was not too slow crossing the highway yesterday.

Amen.

✳

This is a true story. A couple of years ago I did something I'd always wanted to do. I cashed in all my frequent-flier miles and took everybody in my family to Hawaii. Thirteen people. I thought it would be the vacation of a lifetime. It ended up being *The Clampetts Go to Maui.*

If you can actually gather my family all in one place at the same time, I guarantee you there's an empty Kmart somewhere. They showed up at the airport with coolers and grocery bags for luggage. The skycap asked my cousin Fred, "Which one's yours, the Samsonite?"

"No, we got the Igloo with the duct tape on it and the five Piggly Wiggly bags right there."

At the ticket counter I asked my mother, "Mom, would you like to sit next to the window?"

She said, "Oh, I better not, I just had my hair fixed."

The movie they showed was *Homeward Bound: The Incredible Journey.* Five minutes after it began my brother turned to me and said, "You know that ain't them dogs' real voices." Then my sister got mad: "Well thanks for spoiling it for everybody else!"

In Maui we stayed right on the beach. From our hotel room balconies we could see whales migrating. They came right up out of the water. That first morning my brother was more excited about this natural wonder than I'd ever seen him excited about anything.

"Boy, I wish I had a gun with a scope on it," he said. "Anyone know how much it costs to mount a whale? I'd have to get a bigger trailer, I tell you that."

You could tell which rooms were ours from the underwear hanging off the railings. Our hotel also became the site of the only peeing-for-distance contest ever held in Maui. I am ashamed to say my aunt Rose won in the second round. I don't believe the hotel minded, though. They now include a little write-up about the contest in their advertising brochure.

I started to wonder whether I should have taken my family so far from home when my uncle Doug kept asking, "When we gonna convert our money to Hawaiian money?"

Later we went to a luau. After we finished the pig, they asked for volunteers to do the hula. Doug raised his hand. Halfway through the dance we all realized Doug wasn't wearing any skivvies underneath his hula skirt. When we asked him about it later, he said, "Well, when I went to put that skirt on I noticed I had a hole in my drawers and I didn't want to embarrass myself."

Got to give him credit for thinking it out, though.

I love my family anyway. They're good people. They just don't get out much, mainly because of that no shirt–no shoes rule. They loved that hotel, though. They stole everything they could. They swiped the ashtrays while we were *checking in*. Didn't even dump the sand out of them. One morning I had to dry myself off with toilet paper after my shower because my cousin had stuffed all the towels in a Piggly Wiggly bag. When the maid made the mistake of taking her lunch break and leaving her cart out in the hall, the family was on that like a pack of dogs on a three-legged cat. Picked it clean. Later I asked my brother, "What are you going to do with 180 shower caps?"

"Christmas presents," he said. Then his wife got mad: "Well thanks for spoiling it for everybody else!"

On the way back from Hawaii the family spent a few days with Gregg and me in Los Angeles. I took them to the La Brea tar pits to see the prehistoric fossils. My brother said, "Man, just don't seem like dinosaurs would come this close to downtown, does it?" I'm not making this up, I swear. It's just my bloodline.

As I said good-bye to everyone at the airport, I started thinking that my family must be the biggest bunch of goobers in the whole world. By the time we'd been together only a week I'd already had fantasies about being adopted. Maybe I had a normal family that was desperately trying to find me. I imagined that they were financially secure, morally sound, and lived to love and support each other. Then I realized there is no such thing as a sane, functional family.

The more I thought about it the more I understood that families are like chameleons. They can put on a good face and fool the outside world. However, put them all in the same house for a long weekend and they fall apart like a papier mâché bathtub. It's because everyone in the family knows everyone else's weaknesses and will gladly exploit them for the sake of an argument or for a good laugh. Addictions, unemployment, and undesirable physical features are all fair game where loved ones are concerned. If someone doesn't cry, throw a punch, or leave, it can't really be considered a family get-together can it? Each outing with loved ones should produce another level of emotional scarring for at least someone present. This in turn helps to feed the economy through the purchase of therapy sessions, self-help books, and alcohol. I think if families were well adjusted the economy would go into a tailspin.

✳

Suddenly I had an epiphany that made me realize why my family was nothing at all for me to worry about.

I remembered my first trip to the state fair. If you've ever been, this will work for you, too. In less than five minutes you could be saying, "You know what? We're all right. We're dang near royalty."

A state fair is the only place where you can see people who were born, raised, married, and had families without ever leaving their own property. You see people to whom you know walking upright is a fairly new idea. You see people who make you feel guilty for ever thinking you had a weight problem. You see people Kmart would ask to leave. You see people so ugly that you have to get somebody else to verify it.

"Come here, y'all gotta see this man! Get outta line, it's worth it! Over by the cotton candy. Don't look, don't look. Is that the hairiest back you've ever seen. Looks like Bigfoot in a tank top. Oh God, it's a woman! Oh, and she's got kids. Somebody slept with that woman!! Oh no, it's Aunt Betty!"

✳

I think it's only right that if I reveal secrets about my family I have to share a few intimate details about Gregg's. After all, our daughters are the product of our genes, and to be forewarned is to be forearmed.

Gregg's mother, Jane, God bless her, is the adrenaline poster girl. No matter what, she's always got a pot of coffee brewing at her house. She drinks coffee and smokes cigarettes day and night. If Jane goes to bed at 11:00 P.M., she'll be back up at 11:35. She'll have a cup of coffee, couple of smokes, and go back to bed until one, when she'll get up and do it all again. I finally said, "Jane, has it ever occurred to you that perhaps all this caffeine may be interfering with your sleep?" Deadly serious, she said, "No, hon. Coffee has never messed up my sleep. I get up every hour or two and have a cup."

Any time that Jane stayed at our house I could sleepwalk in the middle of the night and be sure I also had a conversation with Jane. She was always down in the kitchen with her coffee and her smokes.

Her husband, Elliott, doesn't drink anymore. He probably hasn't tossed back a stiff one in over a decade. That's saying a lot. He used to own a bar in New Orleans. Elliott's got some fabulous stories. It's a city of characters and everyone who came into the bar had a name. There was the Mannequin, who always dressed impeccably. He named another guy Crime, because he never paid. He called two young women who hung out at the bar the Tar Babies, because if you ever touched them you couldn't get rid of them.

Elliott's funniest story is from the time when he used to drink. Apparently he was out one night and didn't quite make it home. The next morning about 7:00 A.M., he called Jane and said, "Jane, you gotta come get me. I don't know where my car is."

Naturally, she was awake and had already cleaned the kitchen. Jane said, "Elliott, where are you."

"I'm at the big building."

"Elliott, we live in New Orleans," she said. "There's lots of big buildings."

"You know, Jane, the *big building*." But he wasn't making any sense and Jane got pissed.

"Elliott, put down the damn phone and go ask somebody where you are!"

He set down the phone and a minute later came back. "I'm at the Gulf & Western building, Jane."

"Elliott," she said, "you're across the damn street!"

Elliott later told me he called it "the big

building" because when they stood on their balcony and looked out the window, there was this big building obstructing the view.

*

The odd thing about my family is that we're all so different. Big Jim and Carole were married for fourteen years. Big Jim smokes, drinks, and is a womanizer; Carole doesn't smoke, doesn't drink, and goes to church five times a week. (I've always wondered what they had in common.) My brother is totally gregarious. He wants to try every food and everything in the world once. I'm that way, too. My sister prefers to stay at home.

When my folks divorced, it was probably hardest on Jennifer. She's always heard a drummer that Jay and I didn't hear. When she turned twelve, she got a phone for Christmas. We didn't really see her again until she got married. We called her bedroom "the vault" because she always locked the door. We'd play in the yard and she'd sit in her window smoking cigarettes, with the fan blowing the smoke out, talking on the phone with her friends. My mother never knew that my sister smoked cigarettes until the day she cleaned out my sister's closet and found seventeen shoe boxes full of empty cigarette packs. I still don't get it. Why did she keep the packs? And what was wrong with my mother's sense of smell?

As you know, divorce is a way of life in my family. In fact, my brother, Jay, is probably the first Foxworthy since Columbus landed to have stayed married to his first wife. This has caused us some concern. It's not that we don't love Rhonda, but we had a streak going. On more than one occasion I've called Jay and said, "Hey, I saw your wife downtown drinking with another guy yesterday."

My brother and I, and even my sister, have often said that we wouldn't be surprised if someday the doorbell rang and there stood a young woman who said, "Hi, I'm your sister."

What would surprise me is if it didn't happen at least four or five times.

Perhaps you have finally decided that all the clichés about Southern families are true. You know the ones: We all marry our sisters and look for UFOs. Well, they're not true. I'm just dating my sister and I couldn't swear it *wasn't* a weather balloon.

I think we did have some cousins marry on both sides of the family. Well, I'm *sure* on my mother's side. But they weren't first cousins because that would be sick. I think they were first cousins once removed. Most states have laws against intrafamily marriage, anyway. Unfortunately, having to pass a law to prevent something that to many seems entirely natural doesn't make us Rednecks look too good.

❦

Once, a fan asked me to try and describe being Southern. I know he didn't mean Redneck, but the answer was still easy. I said it was a night at Stone Mountain.

Stone Mountain, just outside Atlanta, is the world's largest rock. They call it a mountain, but it's a single piece of granite. On one side there's a pasture in a clearing and every night from spring until fall it's the biggest tourist attraction in Georgia. Families gather at sundown with picnic baskets to watch the laser show on the side of the rock. They play music and the beams flash and draw pictures and the characters dance. The theme is always patriotic. The lasers will trace pine trees and make a picture of Ray Charles, and he'll sing *Georgia*. They'll also throw in *God Bless America* and *Proud to Be an American*. People just sit there with their kids and their coolers of beer and sandwiches, and stare like these were visions from heaven.

Carved into the other side of Stone Mountain are the Three Horsemen of the Confederacy. It's the world's largest carving—bigger than Mount Rushmore. During the laser show the thing goes jet-black and then the laser outlines it in perfect detail. The horses are dead still. Then Elvis starts singing *Dixie*. One of the horse's nostrils flares and he shakes his head, and the horses start walking. Soon, *Dixie* blends into *The Battle Hymn of the Republic*, and the horses start running. That's when you see the hair on the necks of grown men in CAT hats and flannel shirts stand up. They drop their chicken and dissolve into sobbing messes.

"You okay, Daddy?"

"No no no, I'm not okay."

By the way, for singing the song, Elvis gets all the chicken that hits the ground.

Another great thing about Stone Mountain is the game ranch, where you can walk through and pet different animals. They stock the place with magnificent white-tailed deer; native to the East Coast, they sport huge antler racks. Every three years or so some guy can't stand it anymore and shoots one through the fence. That's real hunting. He always gets caught try-ing to drag it out.

"Where'd you get him?"

"He was right next to the candy dispenser. Just gave him a graham cracker and boom! I popped him."

A Redneck for sure. No "might be" about it.

If I didn't know better, I'd say he was part of my family.

Redneck or Not... Here I Come

People always ask me "How do you come up with these Redneck jokes?" By now you realize it's not like I had to do a lot of research. It's pretty much a case of "Welcome to my life."

But for those of you who *still* don't get it, I

thought it would be fun (and instructive) to share some of the real stories behind a few of my favorite Redneck lines. Think of it as a peek inside Granddaddy's shed. Maybe you'll finally discover what those plastic bags of rabbits' tails are really for.

*

"If you know how many bales of hay your car will hold . . ."

Ten. I had a Camaro. I could put three in the trunk, six in the backseat, and one in the passenger seat. The reason I know is because Big Jim decided he could make some extra money by selling farm hay. On my days off from school he would send me to the farm to get the hay which he'd sell at two bucks a pop. For instance, the people down the road needed ten bales for their horse. Like the pizza man, I delivered. I'd drive four hours just to make twenty dollars, of which I had to spend sixteen for gas.

"If you see no need to stop at rest stops because you have an empty milk jug in the car . . ."

That's how we dealt with bathroom stops on the way to the fair. It takes too much time to pull off the highway and pee. You lose two valuable minutes and guys don't want to waste that kind of time on a road trip. You can pee in a milk jug instead. Just hope you also brought the cap with you. Even mom would do it if it was cold.

"If Thanksgiving dinner was ruined because you ran out of ketchup . . ."

Honestly, this isn't that funny to me because we have ketchup on the table during Thanksgiving dinner. We do! Sometimes people come over for dinner and observe our liberal use of ketchup and get grossed out. If there's ever a ketchup ban, my family will die. I put ketchup on everything. I used to put it on scrambled eggs. When I did it as a kid my dad would look at my plate and go, "Oh, for God's sake, looks like a damn Korean war over there." I also put ketchup on grits. And turkey. Tried it on ice cream once just because somebody said, "You'd probably put ketchup on ice cream." I'll tell you the truth, it's not that bad. Ketchup is also good with potato chips. We call it the poor man's dip. It makes a fine spaghetti sauce, too.

"If you've ever hit a bump on the highway and lost half your worldly possessions . . . "
Big Jim again. When we had the farm, Big

Jim always made us load up the truck with junk from the farm and take it to the dump. Thing was, we always came back from the dump with more than we took. In the middle of throwing things away, Big Jim would say, "Oh, man, somebody threw away a good toilet down here." So stuff would be going out one side of the truck and in the other side. It was a good old Chevy truck, too. We knocked the passenger door off three different times. I'd be trying to back the truck through the woods into the dump and my brother would hold the door open, look out, and say, "Come back! Come back!" Then I'd hit a tree he wasn't watching and the door would pop right off.

After we unloaded and reloaded at the dump we took our new possessions back to the farm and put them in the place where the old junk had been. A year or so later Daddy would go, "God dang, we've gotta clean out behind the barn." Then we'd pick up that stuff and go off to the dump again for a new load.

Whenever we did this we weren't really big on the tie-down theory. We'd just throw the junk in the truck bed and take off. So many times cruising down I-285, the interstate in Atlanta, we'd have to pull over to the side of the road so Big Jim and I could run out to the center lane to pick up a sofa that had bounced off the back of the truck. It was embarrassing to a fourteen-year-old. Cars sped by at eighty miles an hour and we were out there trying to pull a sofa off the highway. The sofa wouldn't even be worth twenty bucks, yet we risked life and limb to save it.

Once my friend Steve and I were hauling two mattresses and box springs we'd gotten at Goodwill back to Big Jim's farm to use on the homemade bunk beds at the farm. At some point during the drive he threw a cigarette out the window. I turned to Steve and I said, "That didn't go in the back of the truck, did it?"

"No, no."

About five miles later I looked in the rearview mirror and saw the back of the truck engulfed in flames. I pulled off the road, jumped in the truck bed, and started hauling the mattress onto the shoulder. My first thought was to pee on them, but if you've ever tried to put out a mattress fire then you know it's damn near impossible. Mattresses are like the trick birthday candles that you can never blow out. So Steve got the cooler out of the cab and began pouring perfectly good cold beer over the fire. I said, "That's good beer, man! Don't be wasting our good beer."

When we showed up at Big Jim's we had one box spring and half a mattress. He wasn't real happy about that. It was an investment of eleven dollars down the drain.

"If you've ever shot rats at the dump for entertainment . . ."

My granddaddy used to take a magnetic flashlight, stick it to the side of a .22 rifle, and shoot rats at the dump at night. It's great and cheap entertainment since .22 shells are probably two cents apiece. That's a hundred shots for two bucks.

If you hit them just right they usually roll. Sometimes when the flashlight beam hits them they'll just sit still and you can pick them off easy. But that isn't really a sport, so it's best to have a friend holler at the rat while you're aiming.

"If you refused to watch the Academy Awards when Smokey and the Bandit was snubbed for Best Picture . . ."

The last time Big Jim went to the movies was to see *Smokey and the Bandit*. I think he felt like it would never get any better than that. It had it all: a cute woman, car wrecks, fights. You don't need anything else. Plus, he loved Jackie Gleason. My dad could quote his lines. In fact, he'll still walk into an old Hickory House restaurant and go, "Gimme a diablo sandwich and a large Dr Pepper, and make it snappy 'cause I'm in a damn hurry." Thanks, Dad.

"If you've ever stolen a bulldozer . . ."

One of my stepbrother's friends stole a bull-dozer and got pulled over while driving down I-75 in Atlanta. I know what you're thinking. I don't know where he was headed, but he wasn't getting there very fast. It's hard to blend into traffic. I don't care if you tuck in behind a van, it's hard to look nonchalant when you're sitting in a bulldozer on the interstate.

"If you've ever been too drunk to fish . . ."

That was me. When I worked at Kroger a couple of coworkers and I drove all night one time to go fishing. It didn't dawn on us that perhaps we might need sleep. Or that we shouldn't drink. When we got there in the morning we didn't even have hangovers; we were still so drunk. But how drunk do you have to be not to fish? I kept having little black-outs—two or three seconds max—and I dropped my hundred-dollar rod and reel straight to the bottom of the lake. Those things don't float.

"If 'Foxy Lady' is airbrushed on the front license plate of your car . . ."

Saw it in Panama City, Florida. Swear to God.

"If you've ever driven a Camaro into the top of a tree . . ."

This happened down near where my uncle lives at Lake Jodico. Somebody got drunk, drove off the road, and the car got airborne and landed in the tree next to the house. You know and I know that somebody took his friends back down there to see it, too.

"Come here, you ain't gonna believe this shit."

"If the Salvation Army ever declines your mattress . . ."

When Gregg and I got together she did something that all women do when they're getting ready to move in with a man. They go through your stuff and see if anything you own is anything they want in the new place. Don't count on it. Nothing that the guy has is ever going to make it onto the permanent list. You've got to fight like hell for just one or two items.

"Well, you know, I really like that table."

"Okay, we'll use my dresser and we'll use my bed. And, oh God, what is *this?* I can't imagine." I ended up taking a bunch of stuff to the Salvation Army, including my mattress. When we took it off the truck they took one look at it and said, "No. No thank you." They were right. Lord knows who all had slept on it. It had so many stains on it. It was really nasty.

It really makes you feel good about yourself when homeless people cannot use the stuff that you've been living on.

"If your dad walks you to school because you're both in the same grade . . ."

This was inspired by a guy who was in the fourth grade with me. His name was Eddie. The rest of us weighed fifty pounds, he drove a car. He used to mesmerize us in the bathroom by showing us his pubic hair.

"If you've ever brought a siphon hose to show and tell . . ."

Big Jim taught me to siphon gas out of a truck when I was still in elementary school. You always end up with a bad taste in your mouth. If there's some other way to do it, please tell me. One time Burns siphoned too much gas and got a mouthful. He spit it all out, but he burped the rest of the weekend and smelled like an Amoco station. On the positive side, there probably weren't many kids in the fifth grade who knew how to do that.

"If the flood history of your area can be seen on the living room walls . . ."

I was watching CNN when I heard these people who lived on a flood plain talking about how they had been wiped out in a flood—but it wasn't as bad as how they'd been wiped out the year before. And the way they were wiped out two years before was *really* bad. That's when I yelled at the TV: "Here's an idea: Why don't you move?!"

"If you've ever shot a deer from inside your house . . ."

Ask my Uncle William. It was the best deer he ever got. William shot him from the bathroom window, and I'm pretty sure Uncle William was somehow indisposed at the time. Of course, now he tells it as like, "I shot it right out behind the house." Well, the *deer* was out behind the house.

The truth is that he was sitting in the bathroom reading the latest issue of *Hound Dog Weekly* when he spotted the deer through the window. So without pulling his pants up, he did a little duckwalk to the gun rack, grabbed his loaded 30–30, came back, cracked the window, and shot the deer. I'm assuming he cleaned up before he went out to gut it.

We found this out because Aunt Rose told

on him. Apparently the reverb of the gunshot echoing off the shower tiles scared the crap out of everyone in the house. Dishes broke.

"If you've ever financed your tattoo ..."

When I worked a job in Lexington, Kentucky, I saw a tattoo parlor with a sign painted on the window: "Financing Available." My first thought was "How do you repossess one of these when somebody doesn't pay?" Meanwhile, somewhere a guy is pointing to his arm, saying, "Three more payments, this sumbitch is *mine*."

"If the receptionist is responsible for checking the rat traps at your place of business ..."

I was scheduled to do an early-morning radio show in Oklahoma. When I got there at 6:30 A.M. I had to wait in the lobby for someone to let me in. Just to kill the time I looked under the credenza, and there was a rat trap with a dead rat under the bar. When someone finally showed up, I said, "You've got a dead rat under there." The woman said, deadly serious, "That's the receptionist's job. She checks them every day." She just left it there. When I finished the interview, I stopped in the lobby and asked the receptionist if she'd gotten the rat. She said, "Yeah. He was a nice one!"

"Stacey? Could you check the rat traps and get me a cup of coffee?"

"If you've ever peed in an ice machine . . ."

When the gang stops at a gas station and everyone has to relieve himself, it's hard to find places to go. Usually, one guy is already peeing in the toilet, another is peeing in the sink, and if you've gotta go, man, you've gotta go. And peeing in the ice machine by the gas station office is creative. Most Rednecks will risk going to jail if it means they can get their buddies to laugh. This is even funnier if you are a woman.

"If you run down the bowling alley and slide into the pins . . ."

There's actually a competition like that every year in Illinois. These guys wear silk shirts, get a running start, and the idea is to hit the pins with their bodies. To get a strike they have to turn sideways as they collide with the pins. Afterward, most of the contestants have huge blue welts on their foreheads where they hit the pins wrong trying to pick up a spare. No one wears helmets. This is one of those things you see on television and think, "Thank you, God. There but for fortune go I."

Could be worse, though. As I mentioned earlier, just after Gregg and I moved to Los Angeles, I spotted an ad in the newspaper for a national farting contest. If you're a comedian, that's an attention grabber right there. My first thought was that it had to be a bunch of fraternity guys. Then I read the list of who would compete: "Three-Time Nebraska Champion, Bill 'Bo-Bo' Browner." I told Gregg I had to go. I had too many questions. Were these guys like other entertainers. Did they have groupies? Were women hanging around backstage going, "When we first started coming to see you, we wouldn't even gag or anything. But now, you make my brother vomit."

"Oh thank you, little lady."

Would I see fat guys eating beans right out of the can?

"Please, no lighted cigarettes in the auditorium."

One of the few regrets I have in life is not finding a way to attend this contest.

"If your hobby is stealing road signs . . ."

I stole many. There's an art to it. They're not just wood. They've got bolts. To do the job correctly, you've got to carry the right size wrench and a big screwdriver. You hold the bolt on one side and crank it on the other. But you've got to do it at night. You drop one guy off and then you drive away, and you let the guy work. If you're the job man, you shinny up a pole and you crank. If a car comes by you drop down and lie flat on the side of the road, and wait until the car goes away. It can take a long time. On a busy street you may only get one or two wrench turns at a time. On a country road it's a better deal. The hardest to swipe are interstate signs. One thing to remember, you don't steal road signs just for the sake of stealing. It has to be something you want. for instance, if you find a sign that says "DANGEROUS CURVES AHEAD" and the pictured curve in any way resembles a breast, it will be something you need. Dex got us one of those.

One time Buddy Hammond and I decided to steal the road sign with our street name on it. We weren't really good thieves because we were stealing it at four o'clock in the afternoon. I sat on Buddy's shoulders and worked the bolt while cars kept driving by. As we were leaving, Buddy thought he saw a cop car cruise by, so after we had the sign in the house for a few minutes, we went back and put the sign up again. It was a lot more difficult than taking it down.

I don't list this on my résumé, but for a year or two, while going down to the farm, I may have ranked in the top five nationally in the sport of hitting road signs with beer bottles at high speeds. I was great at it. I could hit them with anything. I got so good I could hit mile-marker signs with a pony Miller bottle, without even leaning out of the car. People always want to throw the bottle *at* the sign. That's wrong. The trick is to gauge how fast the car is going, and then you throw it straight out. All you want to do is get height and distance from the car.

When you hit a sign, the glass shatters on the grass just off the shoulder. Don't feel too bad about that because if you've got to pull over, you've probably got a flat tire anyway. So what's the big deal?

Eventually hitting the signs got boring. Buddy Hammond was pretty damn good at driving and throwing one over the top of the car and hitting a road sign. I got bored hitting signs on my side of the road, as well. So I'd sit on the passenger window sill while we were going seventy and throw them over the top of the car, across the other lane, and hit signs on the other side of the road. What could possibly go wrong? All I had to do was sneeze and I would have been dead.

Never got caught at that, either.

"If you've ever painted your car with house paint . . ."
Danny Chastain had an old station wagon that he called the Eggmobile. It looked like pure crap so one day we decided to paint it. We weren't kids with a lot of money, so we went to the drugstore and bought spray paint. We figured we'd spray it black in Burns' side yard. About halfway through the job, the wind started blowing. It was fall and soon leaves were stuck all over the body. Every time we pulled a leaf off, it left a pockmark, and soon the car went from being the Eggmobile to being the Acnemobile.

"If the primary color of your car is Bondo . . ."
That was my Datsun 280-Z. I had to have the car because it was so fast. In fact, that car inspired several Redneck lines. Another was *"If you have to get a tetanus shot to drive your car . . ."* The car was originally from Michigan and it was so rusted that you could pretty much put your foot through it. Another was *"If your car uses more oil than gas . . ."* This car burned oil but also burned rubber going into fourth gear.

Anyway, as I got money, I had the body re-done. It was Bondo color for a year before I finally got it all painted.

"If your dog can smoke cigarettes . . ."

Somebody who worked with my dad at IBM had a basset hound named Boozer who would drink beer out of his bowl. Then he would sit there with a cigarette in his mouth.

The Redneck Aptitude Test

You've learned how Redneck jokes are created. Now let's see what you remember. Give yourself a point for each right answer. On second thought, just give yourself a point for trying to answer. No use making this too difficult. High score gets a lifetime supply of Doe-in-Heat.

Part One: Just Pick One

1. What does a divorcée call herself?
   a. Lonely
   b. In recovery
   c. Hot to Trot

2. What's the best way to move the wedding party from the church to the reception?
   a. Car pool

b. Limousines

c. Announce there's a keg at the reception

3. What should I say to the bride in the receiving line?

a. Congratulations

b. Enjoyed the ceremony

c. I like your mustache (and your baby is real cute)

4. At what point should a host ask a guest to leave?

a. After coffee

b. When you go to bed

c. When you go to work

5. It is all right to make an off-color toast at:

a. A family reunion

b. A wedding

c. A funeral

6. Does proper etiquette allow a woman to wear shorts in the city?

a. Yes, if it matches her tube top

b. Yes, but both legs should be cut the same length

c. Who goes to the city?

7. What should you do if you can't remember someone's name?

a. Ignore them

b. Call him Hoss
c. Pretend to be blind
d. Look at his belt buckle

8. What should you do when the national anthem is played?
a. Stand up
b. Take off your John Deere hat
c. Turn off the TV and go to bed
d. Put down your beer

9. If the person next to you on the airplane is a chatterbox, you should . . .
a. Pretend you're asleep
b. Tell them you're a Jehovah's Witness
c. Pass gas

10. Why should one check suitcases and other items instead of taking them on planes?
a. It's rude to other passengers who need the leg room your cooler takes
b. Crowded aislcs are a hassle for flight attendants
c. It's hard to put a goat in the overhead compartment

11. When you desire service at your table, you should . . .
a. Whistle
b. Beat your beer bottle on the ashtray
c. Throw a biscuit at the waiter

12. How should one introduce a speaker?
   a. Stand up and check your fly
   b. Beat your beer bottle with a spoon
   c. Holler "Y'all shut up. We got somebody that wants to talk!"
   d. All of the above, in that order

13. How do you write a proper letter of resignation?
   a. "Adios, butt-heads"
   b. Spit on the desk and work it around with your finger
   c. Dear Sirs: I love the bowling business but can no longer handle the pressures of league night

14. If a bug crawls out of your lettuce while dining at a friend's house you . . .
   a. Scream
   b. Eat it discreetly, using your salad fork
   c. Mask it with your coffee cup
   d: Pocket it for a future fishing trip

15. If you encounter a fish bone, you should . . .
   a. Spit it into your napkin
   b. Save it to pick your teeth with later
   c. Open your mouth, stick out your tongue and announce, "Look, see-food"

16. How do you use chopsticks?
   a. Ask the waiter

    b. Sharpen them with your knife and stab food
    c. I don't know, and it don't matter if you're from the South

17. When looking for a new home, the prime considerations are . . .
    a. Convenience of schools and shopping
    b. Property values in the community
    c. Whether or not your old lady can swing the payments on her Dunkin' Donuts salary

18. A Redneck should not name his son Theodore because . . .
    a. No stock car drivers are named Theodore
    b. It's too long to write on a shirt pocket
    c. It would require a huge bladder to write his name in the snow

19. When disposing of beer cans while fishing, you should . . .
    a. Use a handy recycling bag
    b. Crush them against your forehead and skim them across the surface
    c. Fill them with water so they sink to the bottom

20. How far is too far on a first date?
    a. Halfway

b. All the way
c. Chattanooga

Part Two: Roadkill and Other Edibles

If you have more than five of these in your icebox . . . you've got a serious problem.

1. Piña colada mix
2. Dip
3. One shelf devoted to beer
4. Leftover SPAM
5. Rotten watermelon, with seeds
6. Frozen burritos, thawed more than a week
7. Cool Whip
8. Pigs' feet or tongue
9. Pot of macaroni (including spoon—bonus points)
10. Open can of dog food (No tinfoil cover—bonus points)
11. Cigarettes (by the carton—bonus points)
12. Suppositories in the butter dish
13. Collection of Taco Bell taco sauce packets
14. Half a burger (more than five days old—bonus points)
15. Spilled Kool-Aid
16. Yoo-Hoos
17. Batteries

18. Deviled ham
19. Half a Big Gulp
20. Deer sausage
21. Used cooking grease
23. Empty pizza box
24. Pickled eggs
25. Baking soda (extra boxes—one bonus point each)

Part Three: Redneck Cinema

Which of these classic Redneck movies have you seen?

1. Smokey and the Bandit
2. Walking Tall
3. Deliverance
4. Gator
5. Cannonball Run I and II
6. White Lightning
7. The Longest Yard
8. Ernest (any)
9. Mad Max
10. Halloween
11. Katie: Portrait of a Centerfold
12. Jan Michael Vincent film (any)

Part Four: The Rube Tube

If you haven't watched more than three of these shows, you are definitely not Redneck material.

1. Any fishing show
2. The Andy Griffith Show
3. The Beverly Hillbillies
4. Green Acres
5. Mr. Ed
6. Adam 12
7. F-Troop
8. Mutual of Omaha's Wild Kingdom
9. WWF (rasslin')
10. The People's Court
11. Cops (to help locate your relatives)
12. Charlie's Angels
13. Club Dance
14. Brewster McCloud
15. Baywatch

Part Five: Redneck Wear

How many of these items are in your wardrobe, good buddy?

1. Any convenience store cap
2. Jeans with hems walked off
3. Orange vest
4. Camouflage underwear
5. Snakeskin boots
6. Hulk-a-Mania T-shirt
7. Acid-washed tuxedo
8. A Harley vest
9. Shirts without sleeves

10. Sleeves without shirts
11. Shirt with race-car picture
12. Tie-dyed nightgown
13. Jaclyn Smith negligee
14. Panties big enough to slow a dragster
15. Hank Williams Junior sweatshirt

Part Six: Redneck Home and Garden

A true Redneck will have ten or more of these in his front yard.

1. A major appliance
2. A motor hanging from a tree
3. An oil pan still full
4. A pair of men's underwear
5. Chickens (live)
6. Half a motorcycle
7. More than twelve tires
8. A deer carcass
9. Corrugated metal
10. A car door
11. Coffee can flower pots
12. A buried pet
13. Crime scene tape
14. Pile of gravel
15. Fish skulls (not alive)
16. Dogs on chains
17. Past-due bills
18. One hunting boot

19. The front door
20. TV dinner trays
21. Pink plastic flamingos with the heads shot off

Part Seven: Redneck Decor

These items are on my walls. What about yours?

1. Deer head (extra points if deer wears sunglasses, cap, or beads)
2. Beer mirrors
3. Dried food
4. Velvet painting of Elvis
5. License plates
6. Poster of Dale Earnhart
7. Picture of your wife on the toilet
8. Fish (any variety)
9. Gun rack
10. Flags
11. Motley Crüe poster
12. Hooters calendar
13. Autographed picture of Rick Flair
14. Spit

How'd you do? Don't worry if you didn't pass. You can keep repeating the second grade until you get it right *and* you and your kid can walk to school together. As for the rest of you, now you know why I say that being Redneck does not depend on where you reside. It's more a glorious absence of sophistication. Whether temporary or permanent, Redneck is simply a state of mind where some people live and others just come for a long visit. I think there's a little bit of Redneck in us all.

Now pass the pickled eggs and deer sausage. I've got *Smokey and the Bandit* on the VCR, my CAT cap on my head, a six-pack in the cooler, and I'm settling in for the afternoon.

The Road to Stardom Ain't Necessarily Paved

It's easy for a Redneck to become famous among his own. Just hit a highway sign with a beer can out a car window at fifty miles an hour. Have a favorite T-shirt declared offensive in thirteen states. Shoot a deer from inside your home. Know the most ways to sneak liquor into high school sporting events. Eat a double-bacon cheeseburger in one bite. Send a photocopy of your bare butt along with your Christmas cards.

Do any one and they'll tell your story at deer hunts, dove shoots, and keggers clear to the county line.

But sometimes a Redneck becomes well known by people beyond family, friends, creditors, and the local law enforcement community. When this happens, he must quickly learn that widespread recognition involves greater rewards, larger responsibilities, and the possibility of being arrested by mistake. Sometimes the price of stardom for these special few is simply learning to write. Scratching an "X" just won't cut it when fans ask for an autograph. In any case, life will never again be as simple as just having to quickly reassemble a transmission in the bathtub before company arrives.

It would be nice if there were a manual explaining how to be a celebrity. Unfortunately, it's pretty much a learn-as-you-go proposition.

*

One evening when I was washing dishes and watching the TV, I realized that I might be more well known than even I suspected. I saw a com-